By E.J. Rekab

PHOENIX CREST
PUBLISHING

Copyright © 2023 E.J. Rekab

All rights reserved

The characters and events portrayed in this book are fictitious. Any similarity to real persons, living or dead, is coincidental and not intended by the author.

No part of this book may be reproduced, or stored in a retrieval system, or transmitted in any form or by any means, electronic, mechanical, photocopying, recording, or otherwise, without express written permission of the publisher.

E-BOOK ISBN: 978-1-7369272-8-1
PAPERBACK ISBN: 978-1-7369272-9-8

Cover Design by Moonpress | www.moonpress.co
Map Artwork by Melissa Nash

ROSE RED

The Sythea Chronicles Book One

By E.J. Rekab

MAP OF SYTHEA

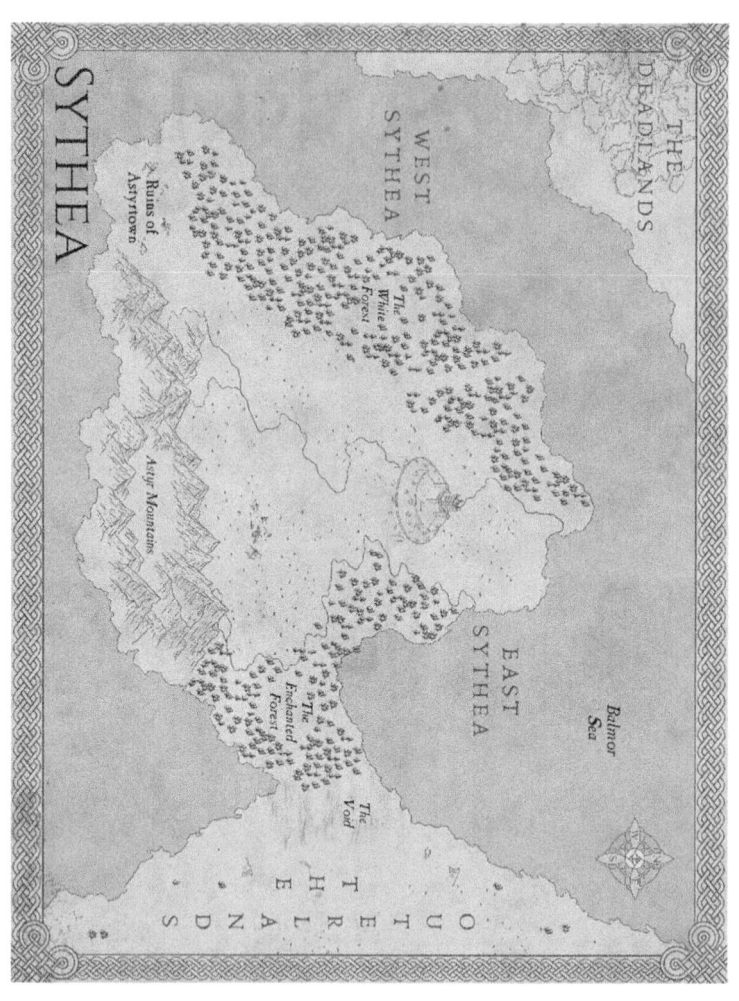

PRONUNCIATION GUIDE

Aegan	EE-gun
Emrys	EM-ris
Feyleen	Fay-LEEN
Gaoth	GOW-aht
Korvyn	COR-vin
Lysia	LISS-ee-uh
Rhea	REE-uh
Rhegus	RAY-gus
Sorcha	SOR-kuh
Sythea	SITH-ee-uh
Talamh	TAH-lum
Teine	TIN-uh

AUTHOR'S NOTE

Content Warning: This book contains scenarios that might be triggering for some, such as self-harm, suicide and the contemplation of suicide, and one non-con scene. Please be advised before continuing.

For my mother, whose strength and courage will continue to inspire me every day.

THE WHITE WOODS

1

Rose

THE LAST WORDS THE HUNTER SPOKE WERE OF his king.

"He will eventually find you," the faerie spat. His face had reddened from hanging upside down, dangling from a tree.

"Your king will *never* find out about this," I snarled.

"Don't—"

He never got a chance to finish begging for his life—if he'd ever had begging in mind at all. I found most fae too indignant. Besides, it was quite hard to speak with a slit throat.

I slashed, cutting deep, my blade sliding through flesh like a spoon through cream. It was razor sharp; it was my father's, and I took great pride in its careful maintenance. I used it to hunt those who would hunt me. And now, I watched one of those hunters die, choking on his own blood. I did not do this for pleasure, but necessity. This was the only way my grandmother and I managed to avoid detection and *survive* all these years.

After the faerie stilled for good, I cut him down. His body fell to the forest floor at my feet, nothing more than a bloody heap now.

The faerie had been caught leg first in one of my traps. Thanks to my parents, and a bit of handed down magic, I'd gotten very good at setting them. And very good at slitting the throat of any fae with the misfortune of stumbling into one.

This fae could have passed for my age, his face drawn into a mask of surprise at being caught, even while unconscious. He was undoubtedly sent out to scout the lands to track down my kind, and more would follow. They'd been getting too close, wandering into the woods skirting our cabin in greater numbers. My family relocated to the White Woods for peace years ago, fleeing Astyrtown when the fae invaded. But now it was only my grandmother and me; my parents were slain a mere two years prior.

Crouching beside the body, I did what my parents and grandmother taught me to do: cover my tracks. A simple spell and the body was camouflaged, swallowed by the forest floor, grass and weeds covering him like a carpet and dragging him downward. Reclaimed by Mother Earth, never to be seen again.

"As dust you began, and to dust you shall return," I muttered to the corpse.

His hand, curved into a claw, was the last thing to disappear, and then he was fully gone. A fly in a Venus trap. The earth would digest.

Satisfied, I began the trek back to my cabin. I wished the journey were longer. It was barely more than a two-hour walk, which meant our enemies had ventured much too close for comfort. And they would continue to push forward until they found us, which meant our worst fear was coming true. My grandmother and I would make the proper arrangements and leave as soon as we were able. We were no longer safe.

When I arrived home, it was nearing dusk. I pushed back the hood of my red cloak and surveyed the grounds. Our cabin was a quaint home, made of carefully-fitted, interlocking logs, the front yard decorated with patches of colorful flowers and vegetables. Gray smoke curled up from the chimney. I ascended the porch steps, brushed past a softly tinkling wind chime and my father's favorite, rustic rocking chair, and shook the remnants of moss off my cloak. It was from another camouflage spell I often used on myself, one that allowed the earth to conceal me while I hunted.

After I was satisfied my cloak was spotless enough for Gran's liking—she was obsessed with keeping a clean house—I entered through the front door and shed my soiled boots. My grandmother stepped out of the kitchen when she heard my entry, quick to notice the blood on my cheek.

"How close were they this time, Rose?" Her gray brows quirked in question, the lines of her face etched with concern.

"Much too close," I replied. "I believe they'll be here within a week's time at the rate they're going."

Gran pushed back her wiry hair, jet black sprinkled with white. My grandmother had hair like my father's. My mother and I, on the other hand, shared the same auburn-colored waves and emerald green eyes.

My grandmother had been baking; flour streaked her chin and apron, and the smell of something delectable tickled my nostrils. Normally, after a long day of hunting, I would be famished. But that day, I couldn't bring myself to work up an appetite.

A tear in Gran's eye caught the light, glimmering as it paved a trail down her cheek. "I cannot leave, Rose. This house is the last thing I have of your parents. The last thing either of us have."

"I have Papa's sword," I pointed out. "We can pack whatever trinkets we can carry. But if we stay, we are as good as dead. One faerie, I can handle, if I keep my wits about me. But they'll send more and more until they overpower us completely. You know that."

Gran sat at the kitchen table my father had crafted with his bare hands, made of white pine from the surrounding woods. An array of protective charms hung from the ceiling, dangling over her head. She placed her elbows on the table and rested her head on her hands, an action my mother would've scolded me for if she were still alive. But she was not. Gran looked thoughtful as she stared out the window.

"I wish things could be different," she said wistfully. "Once, long ago, there was a semblance of peace between our species. I wish that was still so, with every ounce of my being."

"It's hard to imagine peace ever being possible."

"Of course, you feel that way. Such a shame that the only world you have ever known is one of violence. All I want for you, Rose, is to one day live a life not so onerous. To experience true peace, just once."

It certainly sounded far-fetched to me, and I said nothing in reply. Why get my hopes up for something that would never be?

My gaze followed my grandmother's out the window. It was late summer, nearing Autumn. The weather was warm, the days still long and sunny, and the trees were fully green. Normally, such travel conditions would be ideal, but good weather also meant more hunters out and about, which meant more potential dangers at every turn. My grandmother did not move nearly as fast as she used to, and especially not when we would be carrying a number of supplies on our backs and in our hand wagon. This journey would be treacherous.

"We will flee south, following the forest line back toward the Astyr Mountains," I said. "Papa had said that after the fae invaded Astyrtown, they razed it and left it in shambles, moving their conquering farther north. Maybe all the fae are gone and it is safe to go back now."

"Why must they hate us so?" Gran lamented instead of responding to my plan, her gaze still drawn outside. "Simply for existing as we are?"

I wished I knew the answer, all I knew was that as long as I'd been alive, my kind had been rounded up by the fae for imprisonment or slaughter, presented to the high king for bounty and for him to decide our ultimate fate. Death or slavery, those were our options. And the king was especially fascinated by witches like my grandmother and me.

While all witches were human, not all *humans* were *witches*. The humans who possessed no magic—called *nomas*—were mostly labeled as witch sympathizers and killed outright. It had been ages since I'd seen one alive. Witches, on the other hand, were *taken*, and rumors of the sadism the king inflicted upon them made me shudder.

"We are Doyles," Gran continued. "We are descended from one of the most powerful covens, and this is what we are reduced to: hiding in the woods, fleeing from the fae, our kind all but gone. Our ancestors would be rolling in their graves."

I could not argue with her, because she was correct. But what else were we to do? Stay and die, or flee and live to fight another day? The choice seemed obvious. Although, sometimes I wished we had another course of action.

"If only we still had the grimoire," I said.

My grandmother's head shot up at that. "Do not *say* such things, Rose," she snapped. "That grimoire was dangerous."

"But it was a family grimoire—"

"An *ancient* family grimoire," Gran corrected.

"But still, I never understood why I was forbidden from ever going near it as a child, why it was kept in a box and buried under six feet of dirt in the woods behind our home. Or why it got left behind in the ruins of Astyrtown. Surely the book had spells that could help—"

"No!" Gran slammed her hand on the table. I had very rarely seen her lose her temper and I instantly bit my tongue. At my troubled look, Gran's expression softened. "We were only meant to protect that book from falling into the wrong hands, not use it ourselves. And we failed. When the fae invaded, everything just happened so fast, and... well, you know. You were there to witness. Even being a child at the time, I'm sure those events were hard to forget."

I inhaled a sharp breath and waited for her to continue. Finally, she did.

"The grimoire contains the most dangerous spells known to witch-kind. With the dark arts, anything goes, and a single use of any one of its spells is enough to plant the seeds of corruption in even the strongest of witches. It can send even the purest of souls down a frightening path, one from which recovery is exceedingly difficult, if not impossible. Once you taste the darkness, it is hard to un-taste it."

I couldn't help the shudder those words sent through me. Instead of continuing the conversation, I redirected, sensing that Gran was finished discussing this, anyway. "I will help you with supper," I offered, but my grandmother waved a hand.

"It is already done. I suppose we may as well eat, even though my appetite is swiftly going away."

We soundlessly served ourselves a helping and sat at the table across from each other. My grandmother had made fresh bread, and we ate a warm loaf accompanied with apple jam and cured meat, taking small, half-hearted bites. We ate in heavy silence, and I barely tasted the food as I thought about the fact that tomorrow, we would spend the day packing and scouting safe routes. Then the day after that, we would be on our way, leaving the only things we'd known for so many years behind.

ROSE RED

Eventually, my grandmother's voice cut into my thoughts again. "We will get through this," she said. "I am sorry for my outburst, my doubts, but... I know if we stay together, we Doyle women can do anything."

She reached across the table to grasp my hand and I squeezed her fingers back, doing my best to offer a reassuring smile, though I was sure it wavered.

After supper, my grandmother cleared the table and I gathered some firewood from our stack outside, carefully arranging the logs in the fireplace. I sat cross-legged on the floor and Gran sat in her favorite chair adjacent to the fire.

"Teine," she muttered, and a flame shot from her fingertips, arching like a golden rainbow and landing in the fireplace, instantly igniting the logs.

Many witches only mastered one element in their lifetime, though a decent number of the more powerful covens mastered two. It was very rare for a witch to master three and almost unheard of for one to master all four. I was a master of fire and earth, with fire being my specialty, just like Gran. We took great pride in that.

"Sorcha," I whispered, directing the spark on my fingertips toward the lantern on the table behind me, providing some extra light in the room.

Gran smiled. She leaned back in her chair and sighed deeply as though feeling an ache in every bone of her body. It was hard to imagine that this would likely be the last time we would sit before the fireplace like this. The flames crackled, wispy smoke curled around my face, and Gran's voice broke the silence.

"I know you believe in sprites," she said, and I turned my head to face her. "All witches believe in them, even though not all witches have *seen* them. You haven't. But I have. Did I ever tell you that?"

"No." I leaned forward, listening intently, and pulled my knees up toward my chin.

"It was my husband—your grandfather—after he was captured and killed. A fortnight after he failed to return home, I received a visit. That's what sprites are for, Rose. Our loved ones who cannot move on from this plane until they have given us whatever message is in their hearts. And Arnie told me that Astyrtown would soon be invaded. He told me we'd be forced to move to the woods. I'd thought it a dream at the time, but... it was truly him."

I had been too young to remember much about my grandfather, other than the fact that he used to bring me chocolate and smelled like woodsmoke from reading by firelight most nights. Maybe that was why Gran thought of him now: the fireplace. Maybe it just served as another reminder of all we'd lost.

"Why are you telling me this?" I asked, blinking back unexpected tears.

My grandmother's kind blue eyes crinkled at the corners as she responded. "Because, my beautiful, bright girl, should I pass before you—as I pray to the goddess that I do—rest assured that I will find a way to visit you. I will find a way to tell you whatever the living cannot see. My joints may be aching, my bones may be crumbling, my muscles weakening, but I will always do everything in my power to keep you safe. Sprite or not."

With a watery smile, I scooted over toward her and rested my head against her knobby knee. I felt her fingers comb through my hair, the same thing my mother used to do. "I love you, Gran," I whispered.

And together, as we watched the fire wear down to embers, I became fixated on a singular, driving thought.

I had never hated anything in my life more than I hated the fae.

ROSE RED

MY SLEEP THAT NIGHT WAS RESTLESS, AND I WOKE feeling far from refreshed. But every second was precious; I needed an early start.

Gran would stay in the cabin and pack our hand wagon while I scouted to ensure our chosen escape route was safe and gather some provisions for our journey. Mostly herbs, cloves, even some mushrooms for warding off negative energy, maybe some berries for extra sustenance if the chipmunks hadn't already cleaned out the bushes.

By the time I made it out of my room, my grandmother was already in the kitchen cooking some eggs.

"I'll be back soon," I said, heading toward the door to pull on my boots.

"Not so fast. You must eat first."

"There's no time."

Gran turned her head from the pan to face me. "I will not have my granddaughter scout on an empty stomach. Taking an extra ten minutes to eat won't set you back that much. Now, sit." She snapped her fingers and gestured toward an empty chair, adopting a tone that told me she was in no mood for arguments. Her hands shook a bit as she served up the eggs with some leftover bread.

"You'll be careful out there today, won't you?" she asked as she sat beside me at the table.

"Of course. I always am."

"I know you are."

She smiled tightly and patted my back before turning toward her plate to eat.

Once we were finished—and I'd eaten enough for my grandmother's approval—she bid me good-bye with a kiss on the cheek. I set out into the woods with my father's sword sheathed on my back and a satchel slung across my shoulder for gathering. I flipped my cloak's hood up over my head and emerged into the patch of trees just as the sun peeked over their canopies.

For a while, I busied myself gathering wild rosemary and thyme that sprouted in thick throngs along the well-trodden path near our cabin, a footpath that narrowed until it disappeared completely. I knew it would be tough getting our wagon out of there. It had been many years since we'd settled here, and the forest had had plenty of time to reclaim the original trail.

Overhead, birds chirped calmly, a pleasant tune, and something scurried into a thicket of brambles nearby. It was something small, certainly not fae, but I was on my guard nonetheless. I moved as quietly as I could, choosing each footfall carefully. I may have been rather observant for a human, and stealthy, but even with my magic, I'd be no match for a faerie if caught off guard. As much as I was loathe to admit it, fae were strong, with better senses of sight and hearing. My biggest advantage was my cunning and the element of surprise, which was exactly why I had to stay sharp and focused.

"Goddess, be with me," I whispered, praying for strength, for courage, and for a clear path to freedom.

So far, there was no sign of anymore scouts. No footprints, no shifter tracks, nothing to cause alarm. Not yet. For now, my blade remained sheathed.

But that wasn't true for long.

I had only been walking for about twenty minutes when I heard another noise, this one not so benign. It was the distinct snapping of a branch that could only be caused by bigger game... Or fae. A tremor of fear coursed through my limbs as I looked left, then right, unsheathing my sword all the while in the most careful of movements. Another branch snapped behind me, to my left, in front of me, and this time there was no doubt. Either I was surrounded, or I was being circled by a large creature on the prowl.

ROSE RED

My pulse pounded in my ears and my hands gripped the hilt of my sword tighter as realization sank in, creating a cold tingling sensation that skittered down my spine.

I had become prey to a circling predator; I was being hunted.

A flurry of motions caught my eye, a quick flash of dark fur skirting the trees to my right. I gasped and whirled in that direction with my sword held at the ready. A distinct sound floated toward me, one that made the fine hair on my neck rise.

Snarling.

Just before I was attacked from behind.

I dived to the side seconds before the creature could maul me. It pounced face first into the brush mere feet in front of me, sending grass and little stones flying up into the air. It was a wolf; the biggest one I'd ever seen. Certainly a shifter.

Which meant the fae were here.

It shook its head as though to clear it, muscles rippling beneath fur, and whirled around. Its fierce eyes locked on my face, lips curling back on its snout, revealing large, pointed teeth.

I adjusted my grip on the hilt of my sword. My palms were sweaty. I'd dealt with shifter fae before, but this one was far larger and more intimidating than the others. Furthermore, I'd already lost the element of surprise, and I had no traps set in the immediate area. I never dreamed they'd be this close to home this soon.

I remained frozen to the spot, staring down the wolf and bracing myself for inevitable attack, though I refused to make the first move.

It seemed the creature was assessing me the same way I was assessing him. He took several steps to the left, moving in an arc and forcing me to take countering steps and mimic his movements to keep him in front of me.

"What are you waiting for, shifter?" I challenged. "I haven't got all day. I've got places to be."

The shifter tilted his head, amber eyes widening a tiny bit. Maybe he expected me to be more frightened than I was. What he didn't know was that I was, in fact, terrified, but I had grown accustomed to hiding the emotion well. It was what one did when they needed to survive.

"Come at me, already!" I yelled, eager to get this over with.

The creature's eyes narrowed. He snarled, pawed the ground, and attacked again.

He was fast, but I was nimble, too. I side stepped and swiped with my sword, opening a cut on the wolf's side midair. The wolf's reach was astoundingly long, and his claws slashed my arm at the same time, tearing my cloak and drawing blood. I cried out in surprise.

The creature was not done with me yet. But I still had another trick up my sleeve.

"I am tired of killing things," I said, trying to buy myself a moment to catch my breath. I held my hands up as though surrendering. The beast briefly paused to listen, seeming quite taken aback by my brazenness of speaking to it in the first place. "Truthfully, I am just *tired*. But letting you go to alert the king to our whereabouts is not something I can allow."

The wolf barked toward the sky as though laughing at the mere notion that I had any say over whether it lived or died. It sank on its haunches, preparing to pounce again. Before it could, I summoned the earth to help me.

"Talamh," I whispered, picturing in my mind exactly how I wanted the earth to react, and the earth responded in kind.

Dirt from the forest floor flew up into the air, spiraling like a maelstrom, and sailed directly into the wolf's eyes. He howled in pain and shock.

ROSE RED

I took the opportunity to plunge my sword into the wolf's side. He howled louder and fell over, chest spasming until his breathing became shallow, barely existent. Grunting, I removed my sword and plunged into the wolf again, right where I knew vital organs to be. He whimpered and stilled, chest rising with breath no more.

Relief flooded through me; I had won.

I reclaimed my sword, yanking it free, and wiped the bloody blade on the grass before sheathing it quickly. The wolf lay motionless on its side, paws splayed out on the grass. I took no real pleasure in its death, but one less faerie in the world was not a bad thing, either. One less hunter meant one less threat.

Hunter. The word bounced around in my head like a warning bell. There could easily be more hunters now.

"Gran," I whispered in horror, my relief short-lived.

If a shifter had ventured this close, others may have already found the cabin, which meant one awful, terrifying thing.

My grandmother was in grave danger.

2

Emrys

I STOOD IN A DARK TUNNEL, UNABLE TO SEE much more than my own hands stretched out in front of my face. But I did not need to see. This was a path I had walked many times.

I had to bend slightly to navigate the tunnel as its sloped ceiling lowered. My boots skimmed over a rough surface. It was stifling in here, stuffy. I was eager to get out.

The tunnel curved up ahead, making a sharp left. And then, there it was. A pinpoint of light at the very end.

"I'll make it this time," I said. I *would.*

But I always said that. Every single bloody time.

I broke into a sprint. I could no longer shift into my wolf form here. My two faerie legs would have to do. I pumped my arms, breathed deeply. I raced toward the light that gradually grew in size as I neared it. Voices floated toward me from the brightening light, so many of them. Some of them so familiar.

The entrance to the Otherworld.

I was almost there. I was so close.

"Wait!" I shouted.

For the first time, I was met with a reply.

"Emrys." A voice echoed down the tunnel from the light. I didn't know who. My mother? Father? Maybe both at once. Whoever it was, it was the sweetest sound I had heard in a long time. Too long.

"It's me!" It was rare I was able to decipher any of their voices. Perhaps the curse had finally worn off. Perhaps my grueling journey would soon be over for good. The light was so close it was blinding me now. I had to shield my eyes as I ran.

"I can make it," I muttered for my own benefit. I wanted to believe it. Then, louder, "I can make it!"

"*Emrys. Do not fear. Bind the blood,*" the voice from the light said.

I had not the slightest notion what that meant, but I would ask them. In person. Speak to them for the first time in 300 years.

Just as I was about to dive through the entrance and sail into the light, the entrance closed all at once. I flew through the air and collided with a solid tunnel wall. Pain rampaged through my jolted body. I fell to the floor. A defeated heap.

"No," I groaned. "No. Not again."

I felt the burning grip of life grasp my ankles. It yanked, dragging me back painfully across the rough tunnel floor. I was scraped. Battered. Forced back to the land of the living against my will.

The awful pull of my curse.

As a shifter, my nose was a sensitive instrument. My father always smelled like leather and linen. My mother like heather and honey. This time, I could smell them. I'd been so close...

But I was never meant to enter the Otherworld.

No physical injuries could match the pain of a soul being forced back into its body when it didn't want to be there. A bevy of colors flied through my vision, making me want to retch. Then it was over once more.

When I opened my eyes, I was lying on the forest floor once again.

"Fuck." The only word I could ever think to say when I returned.

The witch had good aim with her sword. Quite the little warrior she was. But it made no difference. Getting stabbed in the gut never tickled, no matter the circumstances.

Not that anyone could possibly be under the misconception that getting stabbed was a joyful experience. Though when one was maimed on a far more frequent occurrence than the average creature, one got used to the sting of the blade. I wasn't entirely immune, however. I still felt pain. I could bleed. I could, for all intents and purposes, die.

The problem was that I could not *stay* dead.

Even if my heart ceased beating, it would start back up again as though massaged to life by an invisible hand. My wounds would heal. Each jagged edge of flesh would stitch itself together until whole. Then I'd breathe once more. Just as I had for the past 300 plus years.

When I slipped from consciousness, I awoke in the never-ending tunnel. The bridge between the living world and what my people called the *Otherworld*. The place we all were meant to go when we passed from this life.

Each time I would see the light at the end of the tunnel. I was so ready to embrace the notion that more happiness waited for me there than it ever did on the side of the living. But I could never exit the tunnel. Could never enter the Otherworld before I was yanked back to the cruel realities of the harsh living world.

And life was a right bastard.

Now, I looked down. My neck was as stiff as my limbs. I watched the wound on my gut heal. The skin fused back together like a mouth closing, leaving only a smudge of red beneath my now-torn shirt.

"Gods," I muttered.

ROSE RED

It seemed to burn more this time. Often, the process of healing was worse than the wound itself. Another intended side effect of my curse, it would seem. Also, I would need a new shirt. How irritating. The king must've gotten tired of constantly having to send his tailor my way.

I was back in my regular fae form. My body always shifted back at some point after I died. Once a faerie was dead, their magic could no longer sustain itself. But now that I was healed, I could transform once again.

I crouched onto all fours and felt my spine shift and my back lengthen and rise. My joints popped to face in opposing directions. This process never tickled, either. My skin prickled as fur poked through flesh. The grass was soft under my paws, dirt tickling the pads. I could travel faster in my wolf form. Four legs were always better than two. When traveling without a prisoner in custody, that was usually the form I took on.

The witch that just stabbed me did not know I had been tracking her for the past half hour before I'd even pounced. But this witch was curious. She was frightened but refused to acknowledge the emotion. She didn't look devoid of life the way the other witches had looked by the time I'd taken them in. Like they had already abandoned all hope.

No, this one had fight.

Her green eyes were fierce and full of vigor, her hand steady and sure. She had a tuft of auburn hair waving wildly about her lightly freckled face, matching the fire apparent in her soul. It was rare I got bested in battle. Though I had not been trying very hard. I wanted to see how far she would go, and this witch was bold. Clever. What she lacked in brawn she made up for with clear wit.

I found myself liking that more than I should. Finally, a worthy opponent.

While shifters like myself lacked the ability to enchant or conjure or create glamours, we made up for it in other ways. All fae had excellent vision. Shifters also possessed a keen sense of smell on par with a bloodhound and a keen sense of hearing that surpassed any hawk. Both were very useful tools when hunting. Right now, for example, I smelled the distinct perfume of a witch on the air. A younger witch. The same one whose sword punctured my organs. She must have had a homestead somewhere nearby. And I would find her again soon, now that I had her scent lingering in my snout.

In fact, I looked forward to finding her again.

It had been some time since I'd brought in a bounty. The king thought I was going soft. Perhaps I was. My heart simply was not in the hunt the way it used to be. Admittedly, my heart had not been in anything for a long time.

Numb. I was always *numb*.

I even passed up the opportunity to bring in the last two witches, a double bounty which Callum and Talyn gratefully took in my place. Received a handsome bonus for it, too.

But the king also knew how to snap me to action: by holding the one thing I wanted most over my head. And now, I knew I needed to claim a bounty to appease him. This bounty was *mine*, and she would very much regret stabbing me and leaving me to die.

Soon, I would have her in my custody. I would take her to my king.

I sniffed the air once more. Caught her scent.

I've got you, I thought with a smirk, preparing for the final chase.

And then, I ran.

3

Rose

I SPRINTED AS FAST AS MY LEGS AND BURNING lungs would allow me, not pausing until I'd reached the cabin. I whirled around, immediately sensing that I was not alone, and yet there was no sign of life outside, the forest eerily still and silent.

With a deep breath, I passed the small wagon grandmother was supposed to be loading and ascended the three porch steps. My heart skipped when I found the front door slightly ajar.

"It's only ajar because Gran is going back and forth carrying things for the wagon," I whispered for my own benefit, trying to convince myself that all was fine. That we could still leave in peace.

My hopes were soon dashed. When I entered the cabin, I could feel something was terribly wrong. My grandmother was humming a tune, seeming much too cheerful for what should've been an emotional time, considering all we were supposed to be leaving behind. It was a tune I was unfamiliar with, certainly nothing we'd ever sang together, and gooseflesh prickled on my arms.

"Gran?"

She spun, placing her hand flat over her heart. "Oh, my girl, you startled me. You're back so soon!"

"Did you hear anything around the cabin? I was attacked. They are coming. We must go now, there is no time for the wagon."

"What are you talking about, dear heart? I heard nothing."

I reeled back, blinking rapidly. "You've never called me *dear heart* before."

"I haven't?" She tilted her head to the side. "Well, perhaps I should. It's a nice thing to call someone, isn't it?"

I took a hesitant step forward. "Gran, your pupils are very wide." My eyes narrowed in suspicion as I studied her face.

"The better to see with, dear heart." Then she threw her head back and barked a truly chilling laugh. Not my grandmother's laugh. That's how I knew it in my bones: she'd been enchanted. A fae enchantment.

My stomach twisted in a knot. Few fae possessed enchantment powers, and every single one, to my knowledge, was in the employ of the king. Which meant the king's hunters had officially found us. Our plan to leave was too late.

I heard the distinct scraping sound of metal and realized that Gran had lifted a butcher knife from the wooden block on the kitchen counter. She weighted it in her hand and raised it menacingly, slicing the air a couple of times before speaking in a voice that was far deeper and more menacing than her own.

"The king awaits, dear heart. We must go to him now, and I suggest you come quietly, or I shall be forced to cut out your tongue."

Tears sprang to my eyes, terrified to realize that the person speaking to me wasn't the same kind, caring woman I'd known my whole life. I felt robbed, violated, disgusted, and I wasn't even the one possessed.

"Gran," I tried. She slashed at the air again. I held my hands up, refusing to draw my sword on my own flesh and blood. "You are enchanted. Please, don't do this. Drop your knife. We can still leave here together. You just have to fight your enchantment."

"Nonsense, dear heart. We must go to the king now." But I noticed the knife wavering in her grip, a slight twitching of her eyes, a flaring of her nostrils. My grandmother was trying to fight, and I needed to reach her.

"Do you remember when we used to gather around the fire out back? The two of us, and Mother and Papa. We'd drink Mother's cider and sing our favorite song. Do you remember the song?"

My grandmother took another step forward, knife still raised, but this time, her shoulders twitched. I was getting through.

"Well, I remember the song. And I still sing it when I want to bring myself back to those happy times. You know I've never been much of a singer—not like Mother—but I will try to sing it now." I sniffled, suddenly fighting back raw emotion in my throat that caused a slight rasp to my voice as I sang.

> *"She walks above the dampened soil,*
> *Runs naked 'mongst the trees.*
> *Her raven hair flows past her waist,*
> *Skirting 'top her knees."*

My grandmother hesitated, the knife lowering a bit. I continued singing.

> *"She sings a song to Mother Earth,*
> *And dances in her forest.*
> *The moonlight streams through canopies,*
> *And highlights gifts so dearest."*

Gran's lips parted and a single tear welled up in the corner of her eye.

*"She bathes in streams and wades in rivers,
Knowing she is blessed.
And when her eyes grow weary,
'top the moss her head shall rest."*

I finished singing and Gran lowered the knife to her side, trembling all over as the pooling tear paved a trail down her cheek. "Oh, Rose," she cried.

I moved forward to hug her but she took a step back, shaking her head. "No, you mustn't get any closer. I don't know how long I will be in control, for the enchantment is strong. The cabin is surrounded. There are at least three of them, and they are waiting for you. You must use your wits and your magic to do whatever it takes to escape. The king cannot have you."

"Then we will fight together," I said. "We will leave here together. Right now."

"No. It is too late for me, Rose. You must save yourself. I will only slow you down."

My voice grew desperate. "Please, Gran. Come with me."

"I cannot. I have grown feeble in my old age, Rose. Even if I somehow fought the enchantment for good, I would only slow you down, and you must move the fastest you have ever moved to get away. But do not weep for me. I have lived my life, and I have been blessed. And I have loved you so."

"Please…"

"Promise me something, Rose. Promise me that if you ever see an opportunity to embrace peace, to embrace love, you will take it."

"Gran…"

ROSE RED

"Love is so special, Granddaughter. It is because I love you that I must protect you from myself. Now, *run*." With that, my grandmother lifted her knife, sharp edge pointed inward.

And dragged it across her own throat.

"Don't!" I screamed, but it was too late.

Blood oozed from the deep line on her throat, trailing down her chest like red rain, and she crumpled to the ground. I sank to my knees beside her. She looked up at me once more, gurgling, and then her eyes slid shut and her chest stilled.

Dead. My grandmother was *dead*.

"No," I managed to squeak out, placing my hand atop her chest and sobbing, hanging my head over her now-lifeless body.

The kind, brave, no-nonsense woman I'd known my whole life was gone. Just like that. Suddenly, I found myself angry with her. I gripped the frail bones of her hand, the very same hand she'd used to stroke my hair last night. The same hand she used to bake bread and make fire. Now nothing more than a glove of skin and bone.

"Why, Gran? We could've escaped together. You could've fought the enchantment."

Tears trailed down my cheeks, dripping onto my grandmother's face. The worst part was that I did not have proper time to mourn or curse the world. I only had time to react as I heard footsteps on the porch outside. My head snapped up.

They were coming. No matter how angry or devastated I felt, I *had* to escape; I could not let my grandmother down.

Thinking quickly, I bent to draw on the ground in the only ink immediately available: my grandmother's blood. Bile rose in my throat, but I swallowed it down, fighting the strong urge to retch. As I drew, I whispered the words of my people, a spell passed down through generations of witches.

My fingers shook and hot tears continued to stream down my cheeks, but I refused to stop until this was finished. Until I had accomplished my grandmother's wish and successfully escaped. Then, I could mourn properly. But not now.

The front door's handle turned, clicked. They were here.

With the spell finally finished, I leaped to my feet and ran toward the kitchen window.

"Good-bye, Gran," I whispered in a trembling voice as I turned to look upon her still form once more.

Shouts erupted behind me just as I climbed out and jumped from the window. The fae walked right into my trap. Sparks shot up, trapping them inside a tall ring made of fire and likely charring the kitchen in the process. The flame would not burn those inside the ring, but it would hold them long enough for me to make my escape. Over the chaos, as I fled, I could just barely make out what they were saying.

"I cannot break free!" one faerie shouted to his partner.

"Nor can I! What witchcraft is this?" the partner asked.

"And did you see? Half of our bounty is dead."

"Not by our hand."

"Try explaining that to the king! And try explaining the lost wages to our pockets."

Their voices faded as my feet crunched over the grass behind the cabin, my satchel bouncing around my hip, my father's sword unsheathed and gripped in my hand. I had been so distracted by the chaos I'd left behind, my thoughts drifting to my grandmother's bloody death, that I'd allowed my concentration to slip. I was caught off guard by a third faerie who tackled me, charging inhumanly fast. Of course, the two in my kitchen weren't the only two after me, and now I was pinned to the ground beneath a snarling fae. He had a dimpled chin, wide, rounded eyes, and a neck thick as a tree trunk. His long, unbrushed hair tickled my face as he hissed down at me. My sword—knocked away in the skirmish—lay several feet away in the dirt.

"Found you, witch. And what a fine bounty you will bring."

I spat upward into his face defiantly. I may have been caught without my sword, without any means to set a trap or cast a spell as my hands were pinned, but I would never be caught without my dignity. The fae's lips curled back from his teeth, his nostrils flaring.

"You'll pay for that. No filthy witch spits on me and lives to tell about it."

His cold fingers wrapped around my throat and began to squeeze.

"No!" I attempted to scream, but my breath was crushed from my windpipe along with my words. My vision quickly began to dim. My thoughts became singular.

I'm sorry, Gran.

But just before I could lose consciousness, the fae was ripped off of me. He flew through the air, hitting a nearby tree with enough force to rattle its trunk before slumping to the ground. A fourth fae stepped forward, this one both tall and admittedly handsome, though there was something almost predatory in his expression—in my view, that was a common trait of all fae. His cheekbones were sharp, his wavy hair dark and his irises a stunning shade that fell somewhere between honey and gold, with a crescent shaped scar around his right eye. He wore heavy boots, a leather vest, and bracers on his wrists, a large dagger holstered near his hip. Undoubtedly a hunter.

"W-Why did you just kill him?" I asked, sputtering and confused by this turn of events as I attempted to reclaim my lost breath. I lifted my upper body on my elbows.

"I only stunned him," he replied. "When he wakes, he'll be furious. He's an independent bounty hunter operating outside of the king's direct employ, which means he needs the coin much more than I."

I sat up quickly and attempted to push myself to my feet as the stranger approached. "Why would you stun him?"

"Perhaps it is because I am tired of seeing my kind come after your kind, and I wish for peace."

In a move so fast he nearly blurred, a movement that would outmaneuver any human much less one still recovering from nearly being strangled, he lurched forward and slapped cuffs around my wrists. His mouth curled up at the corner.

"Or perhaps it is because I want this bounty for myself."

4

Rose

"NO," I CRIED, IMMEDIATELY TESTING THE integrity of my shackles and desperately trying to summon my magic.

I quickly realized that these cuffs were not only heavily reinforced—and far too tight—but also enchanted. I could not use my magic while wearing them, nor could I reach for my sword, which still sat several feet away on the grass.

But my feet were free; I could run. And I did.

I'd made it barely twenty feet away when a snarl erupted behind me and a flash of dark gray fur leaped in front of me, knocking me down and pinning me to the ground. Suddenly, I had a wolf with fierce golden eyes glaring down into my face, baring its teeth. Its massive paw on my chest reminded me that it only had to press down with its claws to kill me in an instant, that it could crush my ribcage right now if it so chose. And up close, its sharp fangs looked perfect for tearing out a throat.

The fae shifted back, still straddling me. His gaze snapped back to meet mine, eyes flashing a deeper shade of gold. "Nice try, little witch," he said, clucking his tongue.

Wait a second... he was a *wolf?* My eyes widened in recognition as my brain finally caught up with this turn of events.

"You're the shifter I stabbed. But how? I stabbed you in a vital place, I'm sure of it."

The corner of his mouth twitched upward again. "Well, perhaps you should practice your swordplay more. As you can see, I am very much alive."

He was toying with me, and I hated him all the more for it. His eyes narrowed as I tried to use my cuffed hands to hit him wherever I could, only to find both wrists pinned over my head the next instant in one of his large hands. His face hovered closer to mine as a result, and I could see every fleck of amber in his golden eyes as they scanned my face, every slight twitch of his strong jaw.

"Now, I want you to get all thoughts of running out of your head. As you've seen, I am a wolf shifter. You will never be faster on two legs than I am on four. I'll give you this attempt for free, because it was to be expected. But try to flee again and you will not like what happens next. Do we understand each other?"

Unable to do anything but play along—for now—I gave a stiff nod. Yet the faerie did not move, still bending over me, still grasping my wrists in his hand. His eyes bounced around as they scanned my face, drifting over my nose, my lips, the curve of my throat. His gaze drifted downward toward where my chest rose and fell with heaving breaths.

"Your heart is racing," he murmured, transfixed as he continued to stare. "Calm yourself. It's very... distracting."

My brows rose. "Y-you can feel my heartbeat?"

"I can *hear* it. Just as I can smell the fear on you right now. Though I must say, you put on a very good show to hide that fear."

At his words, my pulse quickened further, and I knew he heard it too. Stars, this faerie was built to hunt. He could hear heartbeats, smell fear, run extremely fast, and he was obviously *very* hard to kill if he could simply walk away after being stabbed the way I stabbed him. Suddenly, I felt

ROSE RED

hopeless, and I bit my lip hard to keep from crying out in despair and frustration. I would not give him the satisfaction.

He leaned closer still, until his face was mere inches from mine and I could feel his breath fanning across my cheeks. His fingers twitched around my wrists and his voice was low as he spoke. "Do not give me cause to hurt you, and I won't."

Finally, he released my hands and climbed off of me before walking back to retrieve my fallen sword. His fingers curled around the hilt and plucked it from the ground. He whistled and shook his head as he eyed the dried blood on its blade.

"Seems you've been rather naughty," he said, lightly dragging a finger along the sword's pointed edge. I said nothing, and he continued speaking, his attention fixated on my blade as though admiring it. "This sword is a brilliant work of craftsmanship. Sharp too, you maintain it well. I noticed the same earlier."

"That sword is *mine.*" I said it through clenched teeth. Seeing it fall into the hands of a faerie triggered a visceral reaction in me.

"Looks like it's *mine* now. As are you, little Red." The shifter circled me while still clutching my father's sword, assessing me as though I were the prized mare to be sold at auction.

"Do not talk to me like I'm a little girl. I am twenty years old." I'd just turned twenty barely two weeks ago. Gran and I had baked a small honey cake together, though that seemed a lifetime ago now.

Some birthday month I was having.

"Still little," the shifter said, sizing up my relatively short stature. I stood barely three inches above five feet. This fae was well over six, and he towered over me. But I refused to cower, pointing my chin up instead.

"Perhaps I am small, but I'm as tough as they come. Why don't you remove these cuffs and find out just how tough?" Maybe I promised the shifter I wouldn't flee, but that didn't mean I would go quietly, nor did it mean I wouldn't attempt to run again if the opportunity presented itself. I knew I needed to do whatever it took to derail this journey.

"It's adorable how you think you can best me, Red." The faerie threw back his head and barked a laugh toward the sky, which frustrated me further. I felt the tips of my ears heat to scarlet. I did not like being underestimated.

"Afraid of a fair fight?" I snapped. "You fae are all the same, especially the scouts and bounty hunters. You think you are invincible, but at the end of the day, you bleed too. Ask me just how many of your kind I've killed."

With that, the shifter's head snapped down, and his expression instantly darkened, eyes narrowing. "Careful. Your confessions only raise my bounty and strengthen the severity of your punishment."

I huffed at that, still indignant and refusing to give this monster what he wanted: my submission. "I will die no matter what the king chooses for me. Once my freedom is taken, my soul will die. What does it matter what happens to my physical body?"

"If you saw the things that I've seen in the kingdom dungeons, you'd be singing a different tune." He sauntered closer, bending down until his eyes were level with mine, gold flecked with amber. "You should be terrified right now."

"And you should be ashamed. For proliferating the slaughter of an entire species."

His nostrils flared at that, accompanying a twitch in his jaw—the slightest ticks indicating a displeased reaction to my words. But he betrayed no other emotion, simply straightening up and speaking in a low voice. "Regardless, it appears as though you are coming with me."

He tugged the chain attached to my enchanted cuffs, and together, we began to move through the forest toward the king's castle.

And toward my certain doom.

AHEAD OF ME, THE FAERIE LOOSENED THE LACES of his left bracer and fiddled with something on his wrist, though I couldn't make out what from behind his wide shoulders.

I sniffled as we continued walking, unable to control my emotions as I thought more about my grandmother's awful final moments, about how she died protecting me. My throat seized up and my eyes burned, but somehow, I was able to hold the tears in. I refused to cry in front of this monster of a fae. In fact, I wanted nothing more than to slit *his* throat.

The aforementioned monster stopped abruptly, spun, and waved his now bare wrist in my direction, making three small circles in the air. I frowned. Was he attempting to perform some kind of magic?

He advanced on me once again. I recoiled as his fingers brushed my hair aside and his bare wrist pushed against the nape of my neck in another movement so quick, I barely had a chance to react. I yelped as I immediately felt a stinging, burning sensation at the touch. I bucked away and the fae released me, stepping back and relacing his bracer around his wrist.

"What did you just do to me?" I demanded, reaching my bound hands up to curve my fingers around the back of my neck and examine the now-tender area.

"Nothing that concerns you."

"When you touch me, it concerns me. Especially when the touch *burns*."

"It doesn't burn that badly."

My mouth tightened at his words, which were spoken as though he had personally experienced whatever he'd just done. "Did you mark me, fae?"

"Again, that is none of your concern."

"You will *never* touch me again."

"I promise that will be the last time I touch you unless you do something that forces my hand." He raised his hand in the air, curled his fingers into a fist, then released, as though attempting to remind me what his hand was capable of. As he lowered his arm, he lifted a brow at my expression. "Why are you glaring at me like that?"

"Aside from the obvious—taking me captive and burning me—you also killed my grandmother," I spat, forcing as much venom as I could into my tone. It wasn't hard; all I had to do was think of Gran choking on her own blood in her final moments.

His expression was impassive as he replied, "I did no such thing."

"Maybe not directly, but she killed herself to break the fae enchantment and protect me, so you may as well have."

The shifter tilted his head, dark brow twitching at my words. "She was enchanted?"

"Yes."

"Hm." He nodded at that. "Well, I never set foot in your cabin. I am a shifter, so I don't even have enchantment powers. Though I know quite a few who do."

I frowned. "You didn't enchant her?"

"No. I did not. I was waiting for you to come back out of your cabin. But as I said, I never set foot inside. I never made contact with your grandmother."

My breath hissed between my teeth as I let out a stiff exhale. If it wasn't him, then it must have been the other one he fought off for the bounty, or the ones who I trapped in the kitchen. The kitchen now destroyed by the fire ring

I'd created, where my grandmother took her own life and drew her last breath.

The kitchen inside the cabin I would never see again... The grandmother I would never see again...

As before, I was in danger of letting my emotions get the better of me. Now, desperate to talk about anything else to take my mind off my grandmother's last moments, I changed the subject.

"How far is this castle, exactly?" I asked as nonchalantly as I could muster, already tired of being dragged along like a wayward horse.

Whenever I slowed or faltered in my step, the faerie tugged my chain to throw me off balance. I felt even more like the prized mare being led to auction. Or in my case, certain death.

The fae kept his eyes on the overgrown path ahead as he replied, "As long as it takes, witch."

"Stop calling me *witch.*"

"Whatever you say, Red."

"My name isn't *Red* or *witch,*" I snapped. "It is *Rose.*"

"Demanding little thing, aren't you?" He chuckled at that, tossing me a glance over his shoulder. "Rose, hm? Such a fitting name, really. A small, delicate, crimson thing covered in thorns. Your parents were quite clever in their naming."

"Don't ever mention my family, shifter."

At the venom in my tone, he smirked. "I can see I've struck a nerve. But, very well. I won't mention them again. In the spirit of sharing, perhaps I should tell you... My name is not *shifter.* It is Emrys. And the castle is roughly six days' walk, maybe a week. Half that time when I can run in my wolf form. But I cannot do that with a bounty in tow, now can I?"

I fell silent at that, and through that silence, just above the distant calling of birds, I heard the distinct sounds of a babbling brook up ahead, at once reminding me of how parched I was. Despite my thirst, however, I had other plans in mind. The shifter was right; he would always be faster than me in wolf form, so thoughts of running were fruitless unless I was armed.

I required my sword, and I would do whatever it took to get it. This faerie was tough to kill, but with a weapon, maybe I *could* incapacitate him enough to get away like the last time. If only I had my blade...

"I need water," I said, stopping abruptly. "Or else I will drop soon. After everything that's happened, I am already getting dizzy."

The faerie turned and examined me for a long moment before acknowledging my request with a single nod of his head. "Very well. I could use a refill as well." He held up a corked leather pouch that hung on a thin strap around his shoulder—he wore a cross-body satchel as well—and steered us through a part in the trees up ahead, following a narrow path toward the brook.

Once at the water line, I dropped to my knees and cupped my hands as best I could in their cuffs, dragging delicious, crystal-clear water to my lips. All the while, I watched Emrys from the corner of my eye. He dropped my chain lead to bend forward and refill his pouch, and I realized this was my one chance.

With him preoccupied and facing the water, I jumped to my feet and attempted to unsheathe my sword from his back. But my grip faltered, clumsy as my hands were in their immoveable bonds, and the next instant I was pinned to the creek bank, my hair pressed to the moistened soil. Then the shifter's large hand curved around my throat.

And squeezed.

5

Rose

"I THOUGHT I TOLD YOU NOT TO ATTEMPT TO escape again," Emrys snarled.

"You told me not to run, you didn't say a thing about trying to retrieve my sword."

"Well, aren't you a clever little witch." To my surprise, Emrys grinned, though the expression quickly faded back to anger. "But try that again, and you'll be dead long before you reach the castle. I could so easily strangle you right now. Or transform into a wolf and tear that pretty throat right out. Is that what you want?" His fingers twitched against the delicate skin of my neck.

"Go ahead, kill me," I challenged defiantly, glaring up at him. "My guess is that the king won't like that one bit. We witches are supposed to be his play things, after all. His to decide our fates. I think he will be very displeased if you take away his choice. Bounties are meant to be taken alive."

His fingers tightened just enough to begin to make breathing a little more difficult. "Perhaps I'll break the rules for you."

"What are you waiting for then? Do it."

I held his gaze, green on gold, and my captor let out a huff that sounded a cross between amusement and annoyance. After several more long, tense moments, he reluctantly released my throat, drawing his hand back, and I inhaled a deep breath. I was right.

He stood and stepped back, dusting himself off as he spoke again. "Just remember, I may be obligated to keep you alive, but the king says nothing about how many fingers you should arrive with. Unless you'd like to feel the sting of my blade. Would you?" He patted the dagger on his hip and lifted a brow.

"No."

"Then learn to play nice, witch."

Instinctively, I balled my hands into fists, wrists flexing against the impossible, too-tight cuffs. They were starting to rub my skin raw. I climbed back to my feet slowly, shaking dirt off my cloak.

"Exactly how many of my kind have you handed over to the king to do with as he pleases?" I asked.

"Dozens," Emrys admitted without hesitation. "Yet none even as remotely and insufferably chatty and obstinate as you are."

"And you freely admit to this. You're an even bigger monster than I thought."

His head darted around so his gaze met mine again, expression fierce. *"I'm* the monster? Your kind slaughtered..." He trailed off, cleared his throat, and amended his words. "I've seen your kind do terrible things. Like killing unarmed, sleeping victims. Perhaps the least dignified form of murder there is. You alone admitted to killing many of my kind in the woods."

"Only because they were hunting my kind, and I couldn't risk them finding my cabin. It's laughable how you think you have any moral high ground."

"I am not paid to slaughter. I don't *kill* unless I have no choice. I simply deliver my bounty, collect my coin, and carry on."

"That's even worse. You don't have the stomach for killing anything by your own hand, but you are perfectly fine handing over living beings for torture by another."

He shrugged, his tone flippant. "Not my problem."

"You are weak and pathetic," I spat, forcing as much authoritarian malice as I could into my voice. But Emrys didn't seem ruffled anymore, once again expertly masking his emotions.

"Does that make you feel better?" he asked, cocking a brow.

"You *disgust* me."

"And I don't much care what you think of me. Now, are you done?"

"No."

"Well, too bad. *Move.* Call me what you wish as we walk, but we need to stay on schedule for the king. He doesn't like to be kept waiting."

As we continued our journey, Emrys made it a point to tie the chain attached to my cuffs around his wrist. He gave it a tug for good measure. "This chain may appear thin and light, but allow me to demonstrate." He took the dagger from his hip holster and sliced the chain with ease, snapping it in half. But my jaw slackened as I watched the chain immediately fuse itself back together, like two tiny snakes reaching for each other and then melding into one. He was making one thing very clear: I wouldn't be getting away anytime soon. My magic had been neutralized, the chain was unbreakable, and his natural strength—and speed—was greater than mine to a significant degree. I would not be able to run.

We walked for a while in near palpable silence, until a sudden noise made us both stop in our tracks: the strangled cry of an animal in pain coming from up ahead. Emrys seemed keen on discovering its source, and I had no choice but to follow where he led.

Soon, the source of the noise became apparent. Turned out, it was a sizeable rabbit with its foot caught in some brambles. I wondered how it managed to get itself so twisted up, but we were in luck; one of my grandmother's specialties was rabbit stew, and it was rare a rabbit got itself caught like this without a man-made trap present.

But what Emrys did next was the last thing I'd expected; he kneeled next to the rabbit, tugging me forward with him, and pointed off to the side. "Stand right over there where I can keep an eye on you. Don't move."

To my surprise, rather than snapping the rabbit's neck, Emrys worked carefully to unwind the bramble until the creature was loose, then held it steady, feeling down the rabbit's hind legs as it attempted to kick to freedom.

"The leg isn't broken. He should mend."

Emrys opened his hands, releasing his catch. The rabbit paused as though confused by how it got off so easy, before hopping away and disappearing into the brush.

"Why would you do that?" I asked, utterly baffled. "That could've been dinner!"

"Quit whining." Emrys stood and shook the dirt off his knees.

I frowned. Surely, he didn't have enough food in his satchel for the both of us. "But—"

"But *nothing,*" he snapped. "You will eat when I say you eat. Besides, there are plenty of fruit trees between here and the castle, plus clans of low fae who will fetch whatever the high fae ask of them."

I shook my head. "So, they are slaves to the high fae just like us witches. Good to know."

"They will do as their superiors ask," Emrys clarified. "It's just the order of things."

"And you'd rather send a low faerie to collect your goods than kill a rabbit yourself."

"As I said, I don't like killing things unless it's absolutely necessary."

"How very noble of a bounty hunter." I snorted at the irony, and Emrys's ever-present smirk faded into a scowl. Was he *sulking?*

Maybe there was more to this faerie. Maybe there was even a level of kindness—no matter how silly or small—that I could appeal to, if I treaded cautiously enough.

"Come." He barked the order while tugging my chain sharply and making me stumble forward.

"I am not a *dog.*" But the protest was met with silence followed by another sharp tug.

I looked up toward the sky, silently begging the goddess to help me. Because far too soon, we would be on castle grounds.

And my fate would be sealed.

WE WALKED FOR WHAT FELT LIKE AGES WITH little break. I was no stranger to long walks. Sometimes I would venture quite far from the cabin to hunt and scout the far perimeters of the forest. The difference was, I would pause for breaks as needed. It seemed fae did not believe in—or needed—breaks quite the same way humans did.

I had to complain more than once to sit for a moment, to rest my aching feet and grab a drink, or to relieve myself in the bushes, which was no easy feat given my cuffs. Emrys would stand with his back to me holding my lead tight while I did my best to maneuver around the chains.

As exhausted as I was, I found myself wishing for a horse right about then. I may have been used to traveling on foot, but never for this long and this fast with little break. Horses were expensive and conspicuous, so we'd never owned one at the cabin. But you would think someone in direct employ of the king could afford a horse or two, or that the king would supply one on occasion for longer journeys. My exhaustion loosened my tongue. I must have mumbled about horses under my breath without realizing, because Emrys chuckled.

"Why would I need a horse when I can shift into a wolf and run *faster* than any horse?"

I opened my mouth to reply, but he cut me off before I could.

"And before you can ask, no. You cannot ride me. I'm afraid we must continue on foot."

"As if I would ever touch you much less ride you, shifter."

Emrys smirked; it seemed he found my objections amusing.

Soon, the sun hung much lower in the sky, and it was finally the time where even the fae needed a break. We set up camp shortly thereafter and Emrys got a fire going quickly—not as fast as *I'd* have been with access to my magic, but still fast. Emrys sat upon an old log beside the fire and reached into his pack, pulling out some dried meat, an apple, a chunk of bread, and what looked like a hunk of cheese wrapped in paper. He began to eat, and it was only then I realized how hungry I was. My stomach grumbled so loudly that Emrys looked up.

"When's the last time you ate?" he asked.

I shrugged. "Not since early in the morning. I was out scouting and gathering herbs when you attacked, and here I am now. You released the rabbit that would've made for good stew."

"Still angry about that, are we?"

"A bit. Living in the woods while trying to hide from capture doesn't afford us the luxury of turning down any food that presents itself. Not like with you spoiled fae."

His mouth curved at that. Definitely amused. "You think me spoiled?"

"You all certainly possess privileges I don't. At least you are not constantly looking over your shoulder and scavenging to make ends meet. You get to go back to your cushy room on castle grounds after this is over, no doubt, while being very well compensated for your disgusting job."

"Is that what you think?" His responding chuckle was almost mirthful.

"Tell me, since you find this so amusing. Is this a game for you?"

"Perhaps." He examined me for a long moment before unholstering his blade from his hip, slicing his apple in half, and tossing it to me along with half of his bread and cheese, too, wrapped in the paper. "Eat," he instructed. "I'll need you to keep your strength up for the journey. I don't much feel like strapping you to my back."

I didn't argue, but only because I was famished. The bread was bland and stale, but the cheese was creamy and flavorful, and the apple juicy and sweet. I finished quickly and wiped my mouth with the back of my hand. When I did, I realized Emrys was staring at me intently.

"What?" I asked.

He shook his head and averted his gaze. "Nothing," he replied.

We fell into uncomfortable silence, listening only to the hum of crickets and the faint hooting of owls. Desperate to remind myself of better times, I found myself singing without even realizing I'd started, first barely a whisper, then louder than I'd intended once I became overcome with emotion. It was the same song I'd sung to my grandmother just before she sliced her own throat, the one my parents and I used to sing around the fire when times were good.

*"She walks above the dampened soil,
Runs naked 'mongst the trees.
Her raven hair flows past her waist,
Skirting 'top her knees."*

    The fire crackled as I sang, staring into its dancing flames and watching the embers rise. Soon, I was weeping as I thought about my parents, about my grandmother, all dead now. My entire family was gone, and I was utterly alone in the world. The realization sank like a stone in my gut.
    My voice broke on the final chorus. When I looked up, I realized Emrys was once again staring, his expression thoughtful, almost pained. Angry with myself, I swiped away my tears, hoping he hadn't seen my weakness.
    "What song was that?" he asked, and I shrugged.
    "I never knew the name."
    "Hm," was all he said in response.
    "Do you know any good songs?"
    "Oh, plenty. But I'm no bard. I don't much like to sing."
    "Any stories then?" I asked.
    I didn't know why I was making conversation with the faerie who wished to turn me over to a sadistic king for coin. Maybe because there was simply nothing better to do. Or maybe because, as my mother always said, you attract more bees with flowers than barbs. Maybe I could learn something useful in conversation. Something that could *help* me in some way.
    Emrys stared off into the distance for a moment, quiet before he softly replied, "The only stories I tell now are tragedies." His words were barely audible above the crackling of the fire, but there was a twinge to his voice I recognized: the pain of loss. A pain I knew all too well.
    Before we went to sleep, Emrys wrapped the enchanted chain around a nearby tree and locked it. The chain had

enough lead that I could lie down, and I was close enough to the fire to stay warm, but not close enough to reach anything of importance, like my sword. Or Emrys.

"Is this really necessary?" I asked, lifting my shackled hands now bound to the tree.

He raised a brow at that, and I sighed my relent. Of course, if he left me unbound I'd sneak off as soon as he fell asleep—if I didn't slit his throat first—so he was right. As much as it pained me to admit.

When he saw the last vestige of fight clear from my expression, he reached inside his satchel and pulled out a small, thin blanket. He held it out toward me, and I blinked in confusion. "To use as a blanket or pillow, your choice," he clarified before tossing the fabric to me.

I caught the blanket, fighting the instinct to thank him. Manners had been ingrained in me from a young age, but it was fairly absurd to be grateful to one's captor. Although my treatment could have been worse than it was.

Emrys settled at the opposite side of the fire. He stared at me across the flames as I bunched the rough material of the blanket into a pillow for my head. My captor's eyes rivaled the color of the flames now, and he lifted his chin as he spoke to me.

"We need rest for our journey. Get some sleep. And don't get any ideas. Remember, your cuffs are quite unbreakable, as is the chain," he reminded me.

After a while, he was sleeping peacefully. And from this angle, with his arms crossed over his chest, his legs bent to the side, and his head resting on his satchel... He almost looked innocent, with the sharp lines of his face softly lit by the dwindling fire nearby.

"Teine," I whispered, hoping the shifter was deep enough in sleep to not hear my attempts at conjuring magic.

But not so much as a single spark presented on my fingertips. I tried again and again, with every earth and fire spell I knew, and the result was always the same—nothing at all, as though my powers had never existed in the first place. I didn't have anything sharp to attempt to sever my bonds with either, and even if I did, Emrys had already demonstrated how the chain fused itself back together. Which meant I was—as suspected—still horribly, miserably stuck.

"Goddess, help me," I pleaded with my head tilted toward the star-lit sky. "Show me a way out of this. Guide me." For a while, I prayed silently, imploring anyone who was listening to *please be merciful.*

My prayers soon dwindled into incoherent mumbling. After the day's emotional events, I was the most exhausted I had ever been. Any remaining fight leaked out of me like a stricken whisky barrel, and my heavy eyelids were impossible to ignore any longer.

Just as I was about to drift off to sleep, the shifter stirred, his limbs twitching at the other side of the fire. His hands curved into fists, and suddenly he thrashed about in his sleep.

And then... Emrys opened his mouth and screamed.

6

Rose

HE LET OUT ANOTHER STRANGLED CRY. "NO," he whimpered in his sleep, his voice almost child-like. "Don't hurt them. Don't do this, don't *fucking do this!"*

"Shifter," I called over the fire in an attempt to wake him.

"No," he moaned. "I'll do anything you want. Just leave us be."

"Emrys!" I shouted, louder, in case he was more likely to respond to his given name even in sleep. I was too far away to touch him, so I could not shake him to rouse him, but I needed to do something. His nightmare sounded awful, so awful that it was bound to give *me* nightmares. And I would like to get a little sleep tonight so I could awake with a sharp enough mind to contemplate more ways to escape.

"Please... You're hurting them! Why are you doing this?"

I felt along the ground beside me until my fingers bumped small pebbles. That would do. It was difficult to aim with my hands shackled, but I did my best, raising my fists and hurling the tiny rocks at Emrys's face. The first one hit the ground beside his arm, the second one bounced off his chest, and the third sailed directly onto his nose. With that, Emrys's eyes flew open and he sat straight up, his blade instantly in his hand and ready to stab any would-be attacker. He turned his head toward me before lowering his knife and reaching up to rub his nose. I couldn't quite tell, but there appeared to be a small scratch and a dot of blood.

"Were you throwing rocks at me?"

"Yes. But only to wake you up because you were having a bad nightmare. You were talking in your sleep and thrashing about like a fish caught on a bank."

He frowned. "Oh."

"What was the nightmare about?"

"I can't remember." But the reply was too quick; I knew he remembered, he just did not want to share, which was fine with me.

"If you could keep your nightmares to yourself, that would be lovely. Because if I get no sleep tonight, I'll be in no shape for a long journey tomorrow, and you might have to strap me to your back, after all."

Emrys rolled his eyes, turned over, and went back to sleep. For the moment, he was silent, and I soon lost my own battle with sleep. Creeping exhaustion dragged me back into its depths. I drifted off, lulled by the nighttime sounds of the forest around us.

***

THE NEXT MORNING, I WAS VERY RUDELY AWOKEN by Emrys, who clapped his hands right in front of my face. The sound instantly made me sit upright with my hair poking this way and that like a bird's nest.

"Time to go," he said, staring at me expectantly. He was already packed, his bag slung across his body, the fire doused.

Still bleary with sleep, I blinked up at the sky. The sun was not quite fully up, bathing the forest in that early dawn glow that made everything appear gilded.

After he unfastened the chain from around the tree trunk, he tossed another apple at me, which I caught between my cuffed hands. It seemed he enjoyed testing my reflexes. "Breakfast on the move," he said.

He bent and hooked a hand around the crook of my elbow to pull me to my feet. "Do not *touch me*, shifter," I hissed, shaking him off. "I can stand by myself."

"Not quickly enough," he fired back, but he released me nonetheless.

As we walked, I chewed my apple before tossing the core aside, which would be reclaimed by the earth, maybe sprout an apple tree or two. I shuddered to think that by the time the new trees grew big enough to produce fruit, I would most likely be long dead.

Ahead of me, Emrys kept a lead on my chain, though he didn't tug too hard today.

The sun was fully up now. A bird swooped low across the canopy overhead, and as my gaze followed its path, I stumbled just as Emrys abruptly stopped walking. I collided with his broad chest the same way one might with a tree trunk; he was *solid*. He gripped my upper arms tight, lips curving into a smirk. "Watch your step, witch."

I broke his grip and backed away, clearing my throat to speak. "I was just distracted by the goldcrest. I figure there might be a nest with eggs nearby." Living in the woods, we had learned a lot about birds and their migratory patterns. Even if the bird itself was too small, their eggs still made for good enough eating, if you could find a full nest.

Emrys squinted up at the bird I'd just been tracking, now perching on a branch overhead. "That's a robin."

"It is definitely a goldcrest. Do you not see the strip of yellow atop its head?"

He chuckled and shook his head. "Never thought I'd live to see the day a witch corrected me on bird identification."

The bird flew away as though equally perturbed by our conversation. My scowl returned, and we fell back into silence as we continued walking.

The pines of the White Forest spread out farther, making way for towering weeping willows and silver birches, their branches swaying ahead in the gentle breeze. Soon, we crossed into a most peculiar patch of woods, and I couldn't quite put my finger on *why* it was peculiar, other than pure instinct. Almost like this area had more to hide than the rest of the woods. "Every forest has their secrets," my mother would say. "It's when you hear the trees themselves whispering that you have to worry."

And that's exactly what I heard now, little whisperings amongst the trees just above the swaying of leaves, like tiny voices traveling from treetop to treetop. I spotted the small, colorful houses built upon the tree trunks, hiding under dangling willow branches and carved into the knots of the silver birches, and I instinctively knew where we were even before Emrys voiced my suspicions aloud.

"We've entered a low fae area," he said. "They can find us extra food."

"Ah, yes, your other slaves. I almost forgot." I rolled my eyes. High fae really *were* spoiled creatures who viewed all other beings as beneath them.

Ignoring me, Emrys approached the nearest tree. Up close, I could see all the details of the little houses built up into the tree—their walls made of sculpted bark and their thatched roofs made of mushroom caps and woven leaves. Tiny, winged faeries flittered in and out, whispering to each other. They were wide-eyed, plump for their size, and almost cute. Of course, I knew of the low fae, but I had never seen one this close before. These faeries were notoriously elusive.

"My friends." Emrys addressed the tiny beings as if he knew each one personally. I scoffed; who ordered their friend to fetch them dinner at will? "Do you know of any bird nests in the area?"

The low fae exchanged glances and cupped their tiny hands over their tiny mouths, whispering to each other some more in their high-pitched voices. After several minutes of this, they turned to face Emrys once again and nodded, pointing out into the forest.

"You've seen some? That way?" Emrys clarified.

More nods, their little heads bobbing.

"Excellent. Please fetch us some eggs. From whichever nests are closest."

I could swear I heard the low fae groan a little, as though this was a great imposition, but they did as they were commanded. I was surprised Emrys even used the word *please,* considering how low fae servitude seemed to be compulsory.

Five low fae flapped their wings and flew out from under the willow, their movements so quick they almost blurred.

"It won't take them long," Emrys said. He watched them fly off with his arms folded casually over his chest and his legs crossed at his booted ankles, leaning against the trunk of the nearest birch while careful to avoid any faerie structures. "Low fae are quick. We'll be back on our way to the castle in no time."

"Please tell them not to rush on my account," I murmured, not at all eager for what awaited me at the castle.

Unfortunately, Emrys was right. A few minutes later, the five seeker fae each returned with two yellow eggs. One by one, they dropped their bounty into Emrys's outstretched palm—a total of ten—and he carefully wrapped them up in cloth before placing them into his satchel for safe keeping until supper.

The creatures looked worn. While Emrys did thank them for their service, I could not help but take pity on them. Having no choice but to obey every whim of the high fae must have been exhausting.

Now, they rested against their little houses, panting as they recovered their breath from their errand, leaning against their tiny doors and wiping beads of sweat off their brows. I felt compelled to show my gratitude, as well, and I slowly edged closer to the tree and bent forward.

"What are you doing?" Emrys asked suspiciously, but I ignored him to speak directly to the low fae.

"Thank you."

The faeries stared up at me, their wide eyes unblinking. They tilted their heads as though trying to understand what I was saying.

"We appreciate your labor very much," I added for clarity's sake as I reached my hand out, attempting to show them I meant no harm. But no sooner did my finger get within inches of the tree than one of the faeries leaped forward, bared surprisingly sharp teeth, and chomped down on my finger, drawing blood.

"Hey, that hurt!" I yanked my hand back and stuffed my finger in my mouth to stave the flow of blood. "They bit me."

"Yeah, they tend to do that. Feisty little buggers that aren't very fond of witches, either," Emrys said from behind me. He dissolved into a fit of laughter, tossing his head back.

"I can see that now." I should have known better. Nothing with fae blood could be trusted, even the ones that looked tiny and innocent.

"You berated me for showing mercy to a rabbit. Yet here you are getting bitten by low fae." He wiped tears of laughter away from his cheeks and sobered up. "Alright, time to carry on. Let's move."

I did move, because as always, I had no choice in the matter. Besides, I wasn't keen on hovering near the cranky low fae any longer.

The walking felt endless, incessant, with each step bringing me closer to the castle. Two more nights of setting up camp and eating whatever scraps Emrys felt like giving me came and went. Two more nights of trying every spell in my arsenal overnight, hoping that one of them, against all odds, would work. Two more days of Emrys leading me by my chain and throwing snarky comments my way, subtly mocking me as he yanked me toward my demise.

Emrys allowed me to stop for breaks every so often, offering me a handful of berries or a sip of water from his pouch. I was surprised a fae would share his water with a witch, but again, he likely knew that water—and food for that matter—was a constant need for humans like me. If I went too long without, I would never make it to the castle alive, and the king would never have me in his clutches.

My skin prickled at the prospect, and for a moment, I felt in danger of throwing up the berries I had eaten earlier. Thankfully, I managed to swallow back the lump in my throat.

It was now the fourth day since I'd been taken from my cabin, the fourth day since my grandmother's death. Emrys silently led me ahead. All the while, I found my eyes drifting to his back, looking angrily upon *my* sword and *my* sheath that should've been on *my* body.

Our surroundings began to change once again. The trees still surrounded us on all sides, though not quite as dense, and the ground grew spongier, wetter, covered in thick moss, almost like a swamp. My boots splashed through mud that rose up to near ankle height, marring the bottom of my cloak and making walking more difficult. Ahead of me, Emrys seemed tense, his hand hovering over the dagger strapped to his hip. I began to wonder if there might be quick sand or floods in these parts, or maybe some swamp creatures I hadn't yet encountered, as this was officially farther than I had ventured *ever*.

"Why are you taking us through swamp?" I asked. "Surely, there is a better route."

"Not that I owe you an explanation, but this is the most direct route," Emrys replied. "I usually take the long way around. But not today. Reports of rogues and pilferers on that path. Don't want to take a chance."

My attention was drawn to my right, just beyond a rather sad patch of scraggly willows that almost appeared to be melting into the swamp floor. Something skirted my line of vision. I turned my head towards it and frowned, wondering what I was looking at as my feet splashed through the muck behind the shifter.

But then, Emrys froze in his tracks, and so did I. Because I had the sudden, uncanny sense that the forest had come alive, that we were being watched.

That we were not alone.

7

Rose

EMRYS CLENCHED HIS DAGGER IN HIS FIST, head darting around to survey his surroundings as he braced for an attack.

To our right, where I'd just seen the movement, a floating patch of stark white mist began to creep forward across the mud, rising up like a thick fog as it wove between the dying willows. For some peculiar reason, I found myself drawn to it like a wayward moth to a lantern.

The mist brought with it a strange barrage of noises, faint yet distinct sounds of moaning coming from within, as though it was hiding nameless creatures crying out in simultaneous pain. My head tilted in question, and I took several uneasy steps toward the floating wall of mist, which lengthened and stretched until it was about the size and height of my cabin back home, beckoning me to enter. Now, a flurry of whispers sounded from within; this mist had its secrets, too, and I could almost swear it called me by name. Transfixed, I reached out toward it...

And a hand promptly grabbed my wrist, snatching it away from the mist. Emrys glared at me as though I'd just done something entirely stupid. Maybe I had.

"What on earth are you doing, Red?" he demanded.

"Don't you hear it calling to you?" I asked.

"The mist?"

"Yes."

"No, I don't hear anything calling to me." Emrys shook his head. "What do you even mean by that?"

"I heard whispering," I explained. "Coming from inside the mist."

His brows quirked, grip adjusting on the handle of his dagger. "And your first instinct was to *touch* it? Why are you so keen on touching things? First the low fae and now this?"

I frowned. "It was... a compulsion. I can't explain it." He was right, I had been acting like a fool. I didn't know what came over me. "What is it?" I asked, still unable to look away from the strange fog.

"It is a Void pocket—a piece of the main Void that has broken off and floated away. That happens on occasion. Though I've never seen a pocket this far west."

My mouth dropped open a little. "Really? A piece of *the* Void? In West Sythea?"

"Looks like it."

"I've never seen a pocket before," I said. "The main Void borders the Outerlands. Why would a piece of it float all the way over here?"

"Not sure, but best we give it a wide berth. The Void hides ugly things."

From what I had always heard, the main Void hid many deadly things as well. It was a giant area of thick, white fog that created an impassible barrier between the Outerlands and the mainland of East Sythea, said to have been created as a consequence of clashing magic between faeries and witches during their decades-long war.

Now, it was almost like the floating Void pocket heard Emrys's words and took issue with them. The sentient cloud seemed determined to prove to the faerie that it was an even bigger threat than he realized, because it lurched forward. Misty fingers reached out to touch Emrys on the back, calling to mind a child poking their sibling to annoy them, only more sinister in nature. Emrys jumped at the cold touch—a reaction I never thought I'd see from him—and sprang backward, whirling around. The Void pocket had come to life; it churned and bulged, and then a great shriek erupted from within, echoing across the swamp.

"What is that noise?" I whispered, head darting around. And why had Gran or my parents never warned me about the potential for floating Void pockets? Unless even they had not known about them, having not ventured far from the cabin for years, like me.

"I don't know."

As Emrys answered, his gaze remained fixed on the Void pocket. But then he curled his hands into fists at his sides, one of which still clenched his dagger. He made a face that pinched his features, as though concentrating on something. He made the face again and again, and each time, his expression morphed into one of surprise.

"Were you just trying to shift into your wolf form?" I asked.

He answered without taking his eyes off the Void pocket. "Indeed, I was."

"Then why are you *not shifting?*"

"Excellent question. If you happen to know the answer, please do be so kind as to share."

"Wait, does that mean... are you unable?" My eyes widened.

"My powers do seem to be quite blocked at the moment. Peculiar." Emrys licked his lips and frowned. He tried to shift again before giving up altogether with a frustrated shrug. "It's like this piece of Void is preventing me from using my power."

"What?" My gaze darted back and forth between the Void pocket and Emrys. The mist continued to pulsate like a beating heart, bulging and contracting, and as we stepped back, it drifted forward. I suspected if we ran, it would chase us, too. It was an unsettling thought, to say the least. "Have you never noticed that happening before?" I asked.

"I've never been in the presence of one this long before. And never one that seems to *think* and follow like this one."

Strange. Why was this Void pocket different?

Slowly, Emrys holstered his dagger in favor of drawing his sword—*my* sword. I would much prefer he used his own dagger and give my sword back to me, but that seemed unlikely.

"Get behind me," Emrys said, still staring ahead at the pocket—and whatever was making the noise inside. Was he actually trying to protect me? Although a dead bounty meant no coin. Regardless, I was too transfixed to move.

"Do you see that?" Something appeared in the fog, at first just a shapeless blob, little more than shadow until it began to take on a more identifiable form. Loud moans were followed by an awful screeching, and the fine hairs on my arms stood on end.

A creature stepped out of the Void pocket, its feet sloshing in the mud. It was, in a word, *horrifying* to behold.

The thing could almost be human or faerie, as it walked on two legs, only it was neither. At least, not anymore. Its skin was grayed and pocked with open sores and marred with strips of hanging flesh, its eyes two horrible black, empty sockets. Its nose was gone and its cheeks were sunken, hollow, one side exposing chipped, decaying teeth. It smelled like rotted earth and shrieked an ungodly sound, making my ears ring. At the end of its hands were long claws that looked sharp enough to disembowel anything in its path.

"A wight!" Emrys yelled.

"Goddess, be with us," I whispered. I had never seen a wight in the flesh before, though we'd all heard the stories. Suddenly terrified, I shouted to Emrys, "My sword, give it to me now!"

Admittedly, I was no expert swordsman. My father's sword provided the death blow when I already had the element of surprise behind me, but I was desperate to be armed and hated feeling vulnerable.

My pleas went ignored, and Emrys clashed with the wight. This close, I could now tell the creature had once been fae, judging by the points at the tops of what was left of its ears. The wight swung at Emrys with its clawed hands, and Emrys slashed back at the creature. But when you were fighting something with no sense of reason or self-preservation—something that was technically already dead and could no longer feel pain—sword swipes barely even slowed it down.

As Emrys continued to clash with the creature, I heard the Void pocket whispering again, wispy tendrils of fog beckoning me forward. I could not stop myself from walking toward it, ignoring the wet slosh of the muck beneath my feet. I stepped around Emrys, who was otherwise preoccupied and grunting with determination and exertion.

Against my better sense, I dove right into the still-churning patch of fog.

Once inside, cool mist pricked my skin like icy fingernails. The sounds of the forest I'd just come from ceased all at once. I could no longer hear Emrys or the wight, no cutting swords or slashing claws or grunts of a skirmish.

"Come find us," a voice said.

I whirled around, not knowing which direction it came from. A rush of cool wind whipped my hair about my face, and then I was wholly disoriented, spinning this way and that, unsure where I had entered and where I could now exit. Maybe this pocket was somehow connected to the larger Void as a whole, because what was once a small-cabin-sized patch of fog felt much larger now, almost cavernous, its scale mind-boggling.

"Hello?" I called out. My voice echoed, bouncing back to me as though the endless mist somehow possessed walls. As I moved forward, my foot bumped something. It skittered across the ground.

Speaking of the ground, it was no longer spongy like the swampy forest I came from, but rocky like an entirely different terrain. I looked down to see a skull sitting near my feet, its hollow sockets staring up at me. It still had bits of cartilage around its nose and ears which clearly indicated the remains were fae. I gasped and staggered back, nearly tripping over another whole skeleton laid out behind me, propped up into a sitting position against a small boulder. Its jaw was hinged open, like its last action before death had been screaming. The bones were everywhere, the ground absolutely littered with them.

I didn't have a moment to contemplate what I was seeing before the ground began to rumble under my feet, making the bones vibrate and jump. A mighty roar sounded through the fog, so stunningly loud that I had to cover my ears to keep them from ringing. A sudden burst of heat licked the back of my head as though a massive fire raged nearby.

Slowly, I began to turn my head to look over my shoulder, trembling in fear of what creature I was about to behold...

But I never got to see it. I was unceremoniously spat back into the swamp, ankle deep in mud once more. The Void pocket vanished, leaving no signs of any strange, lingering fog. Still disoriented, I faltered in my step and fell back into the mud, splashing dirty water onto my face. My head darted left and right in confusion.

"What was that?" Emrys stepped beside me, peering down at me incredulously. He had a dark smudge on his cheek, and I wasn't sure if it was swamp muck or wight blood. "How did you do that?"

I blinked up at him and slowly climbed to my feet, shoving mud off of my now thoroughly soiled cloak. Behind Emrys laid the lifeless wight, but now with its head separated from its body. Its unblinking, glazed-over eyes stared up at the canopy overhead.

"I have no idea," I replied, tearing my gaze from the dead—or, dead-*er*—wight. "The Void pocket spoke to me."

"It *spoke* to you?" Emrys's voice was laced with disbelief.

After seeing the wight, the piles of bones, and hearing the massive beast that lurked within, I now understood why everyone feared the Void so. It was why no one had set foot in the Outerlands for decades.

"It felt cavernous in there, far bigger than it should," I continued. "And I heard a creature, something massive. I didn't have a chance to see it before I was thrown back out, right here." I paused for a moment to attempt to wrap my mind around what had just transpired. "What did you see?"

"I saw you dive right into the pocket. Next thing I knew, you were back and the Void pocket was gone." Emrys scratched his strong chin in thought. "I've never seen anyone enter a pocket before."

"I've certainly never experienced that before. I feel…" I couldn't put it into words. I felt strange and tingly and unable to understand what the voice I heard inside the Void meant, if I had heard it at all. *"Come find us,"* it had said. Come find *who?*

But now when I looked back to Emrys, his eyes had narrowed with distrust and darkened with accusation.

"The cuffs you wear are enchanted, but perhaps you are too powerful for them. Perhaps you summoned magic I was unaware you possessed." Without warning, Emrys advanced on me, and I found my own sword pointed to my throat as he stared me down. It made me furious to have my own weapon—my father's weapon—used against me. "Tell me, did you summon that Void pocket? Was it a clever ruse, an attempt to escape?"

"No," I replied evenly, speaking the truth.

I didn't even know Void pockets *existed* much less how to summon one. But Emrys didn't seem convinced. He lowered the sword and, moving faster than a human ever could, clasped me by the throat, pinning me to a nearby willow. My back scraped the rough bark.

"Are you lying to me, witch?"

I glared up at him defiantly. This was the second time he'd had me by the throat, and as before, he squeezed just enough to begin to cut off my air without fully strangling me, just enough to let me know he meant business, that he had the power to snap my neck like a twig if he so chose. It was why my parents taught me how to lay fae traps in the woods. When paired up one-on-one, with no weapons, no magic, and no element of surprise, a faerie would always win against a human with relative ease. Right now, I was fully aware that I was at Emrys's mercy, and I did not like it one bit. Though I also refused to show him weakness.

"You still won't kill me. So, what exactly are you trying to do?" I croaked out.

"Trying to get you to admit to the truth." He lifted the tip of the sword to my ear, pinching the lobe as his fingers flexed on my throat. "Perhaps I should start by cutting off an ear." The sword moved from my ear, dragging down over the side of my neck, pausing in the small valley between my breasts. Emrys's golden eyes followed the motion of the sword as though transfixed. "Or perhaps I should aim lower."

"Go ahead. I do not fear torture." It was a lie. Of course, I feared torture, but he did not need to know that.

The point of the blade poked the flesh over my heart, not quite hard enough to draw blood. "Your erratic pulse says otherwise."

Why did I always forget that annoying shifter super-hearing? "Afraid or not, I am telling the truth. I have no idea how to summon a Void pocket. Us running into one was pure coincidence, nothing more."

Even as I said it, I was aware that the coincidence was a very odd one, indeed, almost as though the pocket had sought us out of its own free will. Why would it do such a thing?

Thankfully, Emrys must have been satisfied enough with my answer, because he released me. Again, I drew a deep breath and lifted my cuffed hands to rub my tender throat. Emrys sheathed his sword—*my* sword. Catching me off guard, he yanked me forward and shoved my shoulders, forcing me into a sitting position on a stump next to a living tree. With nimble fingers, he fastened the enchanted chain around the base of the willow beside the stump and did a quick test of its integrity before backing up a few steps.

"What are you doing?" I asked.

"I'm scouting ahead to ensure the area is clear. And you are going to stay here while I do. Can't chance you diving into another pocket now, can I?"

"What? No, you cannot just leave me chained in a swamp!"

"Relax. I'll be back in no time, Red. Just sit tight."

With that, he clomped away through the mud and disappeared into the swamp, past the trees. And I was left alone with nothing but my thoughts and racing heart.

I HAD NO IDEA HOW LONG I SAT THERE attempting to break free of my cuffs. It felt like an eternity had passed with my boots sticking in the mud, my brow sweating as I attempted spell after spell to break the chains.

"*Talamh,*" I commanded the earth, picturing a leafy vine darting out from a tree to reach around my cuffs and snap the links joining them.

But the earth did not respond.

"*Teine,*" I tried, picturing my fire heating my flesh until the cuffs turned to molten metal and fell away from my wrists, sizzling as they hit the water of the swamp.

But my fire did not respond.

"Stars," I muttered after trying each spell again and again, each time in vain. I was already becoming tired from the exertion of attempting magic while wearing magic-prohibiting cuffs.

Nearby, something splashed through the muck, and I froze, holding my breath. But nothing approached me— maybe just an animal, likely more spooked of me than I was of it.

Thinking quickly, I peered down into the mud around my boots and dug my toe in to find anything I could use to break my chains. My boot hit something solid.

Bending forward on the stump, I dug my hand into the mud and emerged with a sizeable rock, enough to do the job. I stood, turned, and placed a small length of the chain upon the tree stump. There was enough give to it that I was able to raise my hands nearly above my head.

With the rock wedged between my hands, I grunted and struck down upon the chain, cleaving it in two. But I did not make it even three feet when the chain attached to the tree shot out, once again fusing with the broken half of the chain that dangled from my cuffs. I was yanked backward by the force, falling flat on my back in the muck, still helplessly attached to the tree. My wrists throbbed from the too-tight cuffs constricting even further around them. I fought the urge to cry.

The grim truth was that I would not be going anywhere anytime soon. The only one who could free me from these chains right now was Emrys, and he was nowhere to be seen.

Now, I was sitting on the stump again, idly picking at my nails and singing under my breath, listening to the ambient sounds of the forest. My backside started going numb.

When would Emrys be back? Or would I be stuck here forever, tied to this tree, doomed to succumb to the elements and starve to death, my body left to be picked apart by wild animals?

Overhead, it started to rain. At first it was just a gentle mist, but it quickly became steadier, soaking me through, and I shivered. Not knowing what else to do, I lifted my knees to my chest, placing the heels of my feet atop the wide trunk in front of me. I rested my head on my knees.

And waited for my captor to return.

8

Emrys

I HATED ADMITTING HOW MUCH THE WITCH WAS getting under my skin.

A part of me resisted the urge to immediately return and check on her. I knew she couldn't break the chain. Not for long enough to escape, anyway. No, it wasn't the chance of her escape that troubled me, which meant it must've been *her* I was worried about. The thought of something finding her defenseless.

The king was right. I *was* growing soft.

"Foolish," I muttered, shaking my head.

Regardless, I needed to scout for more pockets. Couldn't trust the witch to not make another escape attempt through them. How had she managed to step inside one and emerge unscathed? I'd get to the truth eventually.

For a while, I trekked through the mud. My boots sunk deep, making sucking sounds with each step. Branches hung in my face, spiders skittering about. I brushed away the obstacles and carried on. So far, there were no signs of disturbances. No strange mists. I hated the swamp. Now I remembered why I usually avoided it.

Luckily, a couple of low fae flittered nearby. They hovered ahead, prepared to fly away. I held up a hand to stop them.

"Wait," I shouted.

The little faeries buzzed in the air as I approached. Their wings beat hard as they waited for me to speak. Mostly because they didn't have a choice. Low fae were built to serve.

"Would you please scout the area? Check for any signs of danger. Large creatures, Void pockets. Anything of interest. Then report back to me."

The faeries nodded and darted off in a flurry of movement. I perched on a large rock seated above the mud and observed as low fae buzzed away and returned every twenty minutes or so. Speeding past me in all directions. They moved so quickly they were all but mere streaks of light across my vision.

I pulled out my dagger and a spare apple as I waited. Nope. The dagger was still tainted with wight blood. It would need cleaning before touching food again. I bit directly into the apple instead.

Shit. I should've given the witch more food before I left. She was probably hungry. I looked up as I felt moisture then. It was raining, too. A cold rain. She was probably shivering, and...

And why did I care, exactly?

By the time I'd finished my apple and tossed its core into the mud, the rain had slowed and the faeries had returned. They hovered in front of my rock.

"Any threats?" I asked.

They shook their heads. One by one, wide little doe eyes blinked.

"Thank you. You may go."

They buzzed away, darting past the clearing. Gone.

Relief flooded through me. No more obstacles. No more dangers. Should be smooth sailing to the castle.

I really should not have said that.

No sooner had I walked twenty steps past my rock than the ground gave beneath me. My boots were swallowed to the ankles before, but now they were swallowed to the calves. I was sinking. Fast.

"Of course, you jinxed yourself. Bloody idiot," I muttered to no one in particular. Did that more than I cared to admit.

I also did not care for my current predicament. I was caught in a bog and the bog would not let go.

Not good at all.

The mud yanked me down until my knees were covered. Then my thighs. The more I struggled, the more it seemed determined to consume me whole. Right now, the earth was a creature and I was its squirming prey. I wasn't used to being prey. I loathed the feeling.

Mud to my hips now. My chest. My shoulders.

It was all happening so fast, the dragging. Down and down. My arms were pinned to my sides now, only my head sticking out. The rest of me was caught beneath the surface.

"This is a pickle," I said aloud.

Just before my head was swallowed and I could no longer breathe.

Mud covered my eyes. It filled my mouth, my ears. All senses dampened.

This was proving to be my least favorite way to die. What little breath I had left was slowly crushed from my lungs.

Once the last of my air left me, I choked until the world went black. I awoke in the threshold to the Otherworld. That familiar tunnel.

Determined, I ran. Made the sharp turn. Kept running. My feet thudded on the dark, rocky floor. My arms swung. I was so close to the entrance, that telltale light. So very close…

As always, right as I dove through the air, the entrance sealed itself. I collided with solid wall. The burning hand of life wrapped around my ankle and dragged me back kicking and clawing the ground.

Only this time, I awoke still stuck in my mud prison. Still unable to move, unable to breathe.

With no air, I died again.

Gods, was I going to be trapped like this forever? Doomed to die, get ripped from the Otherworld, and die immediately again? An endless loop of misery.

Torture. That was the intent of the curse, and I had never felt it more than now.

I ran hard through the tunnel. Turned the corner. Dove toward the light.

And hit a solid wall again. Pain, so much pain. Dragged back to life again. More pain.

Awoke in the pit again. Choked on dirt.

Died again.

I knew I needed to focus. I needed to use what wits I had to get out of this fucked situation.

Unless... Unless I could make it to the light first. Unless I could properly die. I was *so close.*

But that was the nature of my curse. Dangle the very thing I wanted most just beyond my reach, forever taunting me with what I could never have.

This time as I turned the corner and approached the light, a voice floated toward me.

"You must go back, Emrys," it said. *"Bind the blood."*

"What do you mean?" I shouted, refusing to stop. Refusing to slow until I reached whichever member of my family spoke to me. Mother? Father? Merys? Merium? It didn't matter who. I knew it was one of them and their message felt important.

"Bind the blood."

"I don't understand." I'd have to move even faster to make it. The light was just twenty feet away. Now ten.

"Trust your gut." The voice was weaker this time. My family was drifting away again.

Not if I could bloody well help it.

I dove for the entrance, fingers stretched toward the light. Once more, the light disappeared at the last second. My hands met with solid wall, barely breaking the impact against my face.

My forehead slammed the wall next. Winded, skull aching, I pressed my palms to the solid surface. Willed it to open. To bare its entrance.

Instead, the familiar, crushing grip of life grabbed my ankle. Yanked me back.

I awoke still entombed in mud.

But I wouldn't be for long. I had the soul of a wolf and a bog prison would not contain me. I refused to let it be so.

With every ounce of concentration I possessed, I transformed into a wolf. Quite painfully. The process was usually painful, now even more so considering the pressure being forced onto my body from all angles. I could not even open my mouth to cry out, or I would swallow more dirt.

My limbs stretched. My knees bent backward, forcing the mud to move to accommodate my growth. The transformation process provided just enough give within the mud for me to shift. My paws reached out, touched something solid.

A large piece of rock.

Using it for leverage, I placed a paw upon it and propelled myself up. Mercifully, I breeched the surface. With low grunts, I pulled, heaving my body upward. My chest emerged. Then my hindquarters. Finally, my tail.

Exhausted, I flopped to the ground on my side and inhaled swampy air. My body shifted back, thoroughly spent. That was an experience I wasn't keen to have again.

"Fuck this swamp," I murmured.

ROSE RED

Drawing another breath of sweet—stagnant, yet sweet—air, I forced myself to stand. Brushed off as much mud as I could.

"Bind the blood."

With my family's words still echoing in my head, I began to make my way back through the swamp.

Back toward the witch.

9

Rose

SOMEONE WAS APPROACHING, AND I STOOD UP, prepared to go down fighting as much as I could. But it was just Emrys coming back through the trees, soiled from head to foot. He'd been gone for hours.

"You came back," I said, letting out a long, drawn-out sigh.

"I did."

"What took you so long?"

"That is a long story," he said.

"And why are you covered in mud?"

"Another long story."

I never dreamed I'd be relieved to see a shifter—a bounty hunter and my captor, no less. But I wouldn't starve to death here, forever chained to this tree, so that was at least something. Emrys unlocked the chain so I was just down to my cuffs again. My heart still thudded in my ears.

"The good news is that there appear to be no more Void pockets or wights anywhere nearby. The path should be clear," Emrys said. "The bad news: the bogs are in rare form today. Watch your step."

As soon as the words left his mouth, he frowned and looked all around, spinning one way then the other.

"What is it?" I asked on a whisper, reading his body language.

"Heartbeats. I hear intruders. Smell them too. We are not alone." His mouth tightened, face turning upward in exasperation as he muttered to himself. "Those little shits. I asked that low fae clan to identify any threats in the area and they lied."

"Seems witches aren't the only ones the low fae aren't fond of," I mumbled.

A scowl was my answer, though Emrys was too preoccupied listening for whatever headed our way to throw back a snide retort.

A branch snapped nearby, and then another, accompanied by wet splashing sounds. Emrys stepped beside me, instantly back on the defensive as the distinct sound of voices drifted forth. Not the moaning of wights or the rolling of a strange fog, but actual *voices*.

I stood tall, muscles coiling as four faces came into view, stepping from behind the trees. The one leading the pack grinned wide and flashed several gold-capped teeth, a dagger already drawn in his hand. It glinted in the small bit of sunlight that managed to poke through the dense canopies above, looking extra sharp from my perspective. The fae sucked on his tooth, running his tongue across it, and spoke in a heavily-accented voice.

"Now, what do we have here?"

For some reason, I found myself inching closer to Emrys. Maybe because these fae were wildcards and Emrys was the current lesser of two evils. Not that the thought was any comfort.

"Do you know any of them?" I whispered, and Emrys shook his head slowly.

"They're likely rogues. Pilferers who live outside the castle village walls and thieve for a living."

He must have said it loud enough for the other fae to hear, even though they were still a good distance away, because the one in front replied, "Rogues or not, you are on our land, and you need to pay the toll. No being crosses through our land without paying the toll."

"This isn't your land. This land belongs to the king," Emrys scoffed, and the rogue faeries blocking our path laughed heartily, hands on their bellies.

"You hear that, lads? This isn't our land," the faerie mocked us to his fellow thieves. Emrys's mouth twisted, unamused.

They did not seem to care who Emrys was or who he worked for. These fae had *brute* written all over them, and my guess was that they regularly attacked any who passed nearby to strip them of all riches. And now, we were their only target.

"Well, let's get on with it, then. What do you want?" Emrys demanded, his tone biting.

The thieves were rather big fae, some of them as tall as Emrys and even burlier, all with long, matted, unkempt hair.

Now, the clear leader of the group took another step forward, fully emerging from the trees into our small, shrouded clearing. Once fully visible, I could see that he sported an impressive set of gray, leathery wings that swayed as he walked. He had to be careful to tuck them at his sides so they didn't catch on the neighboring foliage. At least I didn't have to worry about him attempting to fly in this swamp; there wasn't enough room.

The winged faerie made a point of cracking his neck and popping his knuckles. "You are a bounty hunter for the king. You must have coin on you," he said.

"We want all of it," another one piped in, speaking from beside the leader.

"You can have my coin, if that's what it takes to let us pass," Emrys offered.

The coin probably didn't matter to him right now, since he'd likely be making much more when he handed me off to the king. He reached into his satchel and produced a small pouch, tossing it to the leader. The winged faerie caught the pouch and reached inside it, holding up five gold coins.

"This is a start, but it isn't enough," he said, placing the coins back into the pouch before pocketing the whole thing.

"What else do you want?" Emrys asked, exasperated.

"We've decided we want the lass."

Emrys stepped between me and the would-be attackers, blocking me from their view and instinctively shielding me from them. "You cannot have her. She is mine; my bounty. Now, take your coin and go."

"No. She belongs to us now."

Emrys lifted his chin and shoulders, puffing out his chest as he clutched his blade. "Then you will have to go through me to get her."

"You do realize that there are four of us and one of you."

"Two," I said, finally finding my voice as I poked my head around from behind Emrys. "You will have to fight two of us. If you dare believe I'll go quietly with you then you have another thing coming."

"Oh, do you hear that, lads? The little lass thinks she has stones." The leader thumped the shoulders of the two thieves at his sides, as though the notion of any woman putting up a good fight was utterly absurd, and I felt my cheeks grow hot at the insult. He sobered up after a moment and turned his attention back to Emrys. "Now, will you hand her over willingly? Or face our wrath?"

Emrys snarled, not one bit amused. "You are thieves on the king's land. How dare you."

The thief clucked his tongue. "Watch your mouth, bounty hunter. She's ours now, whether you like it or not."

"Lay a hand on her, and you will not live to see another sunrise." Emrys's lips curled back from his teeth, and the group of thieves looked at each other and laughed again.

"Why don't you just surrender now and spare us all the trouble?"

"Let me out of these cuffs, Emrys," I whispered behind him, once again wanting to at least be armed. "Remove them and hand me my sword. I can take two, you can take two. I can also cast a spell to confound with my earth magic. Together, we can beat them."

Emrys stiffened. I knew he'd heard me, but he stubbornly made no move to heed my words, either. Instead, he continued speaking to the thieves.

"I am giving you one more chance to walk away with your coin, and then I will not be so nice. So, which is it?"

The thieves raised their blades, and their answer was clear. My body stiffened, muscles coiling, prepared to fight.

With a shrill cry, the four fae advanced through the swamp, stomping and splashing, and at once, Emrys holstered his weapon and shifted into his wolf form, teeth curling back from his fangs as he snarled and ground his paws in the mud.

The thieves whistled and skidded to a halt. "We've got ourselves a shifter, boys! This just got a whole lot more fun."

The whole ordeal happened so quickly. Emrys dove for the leader's right wing and bit down hard, causing an awful tearing noise, and the lead faerie screamed in pain. At the same time, two fae advanced on me and I was shoved hard. I stumbled, feeling wholly exposed and vulnerable without my sword and without my magic that I could use as a weapon. One of the thieves grabbed me by the hair, but I whirled and kicked, hard, and my boot hit him square in the balls. That was something both human and fae males had in common—the weakness between their legs.

In response, he slapped me across the face so hard, my head turned and I saw stars. The headache upon impact was instant and blinding. I was given no reprieve, however, as the second thief grabbed me from behind, breathing into my ear.

"What are you going to do now, lass," he rasped, his breath stale, at which point I slammed my head backwards, making contact with his nose.

I heard a crunching noise, and the fae cursed, but he did not release me, instead squeezing so tight I feared my ribs would crack. One on one like this, caught in his clutches, I was no match for his strength.

I looked back across the swamp, desperate. Sometime during my own skirmish, Emrys had managed to tear the throat out of the other non-winged fae, and now he was once again facing off with the winged one, whose right wing was torn and bloody. The leader looked positively enraged, but at least now we were down to three thieves instead of four.

The one holding me barked an order to the one I had kicked in the balls. "Go take care of that wolf. I've got the lass. Oh, we will have fun with this one later. Show her who's in charge."

Despite making me want to retch, his words also gave me some relief. At least now I only had one thief to worry about, and I knew just what to do. If fae males had the same weakness between their legs as human males, then it also stood to reason that fae, especially fae like these, could've had something else in common with human men: underestimating women. My grandmother, my mother, even my own father had once reminded me of the dangers the females of our species often faced, even while we were tucked away in the woods, and their words had stuck with me. I would take advantage of this knowledge now.

I spoke in the weakest voice I could muster. "N-no, please, release me. I cannot breathe. I-I think I am going to..." I made my voice trail off. At once, I faked a swoon and went limp in the faerie's arms, allowing my knees to slump and my head to loll to the side.

I could only hope the fae holding me was too ignorant and distracted to listen for my heartbeat, which would undoubtedly give away the fact that my pulse was still racing and I was not, in fact, unconscious.

Mercifully, the fae chuckled and murmured, "Typical," before releasing me altogether, allowing my body to unceremoniously drop to the swamp floor.

I had to force myself to act against every instinct of breaking my fall, to keep myself from wincing as I landed wherever my body decided to drop. Pain jolted through me on impact, but I did not react.

"I'll be back for you soon," the faerie muttered down to me before moving off to help the other two fight Emrys.

He splashed off across the swamp and I opened my eyes. All of them had their backs to me now, and this was likely my only chance. I thanked my lucky stars and gave silent praise to the goddess, because glinting just feet away from me in the muck of the swamp was my sword.

Slowly so at to not alert the distracted fae to my conscious state, I crawled across the swamp toward the sword until I finally had the hilt in my hands. It was still half in its sheath, which must have fallen from Emrys's back when he'd shifted to wolf form.

Once again using the slowest of motions, I climbed to my feet and took careful steps forward. I could see now that Emrys had another thief by the throat. Another one dead. But it wasn't enough, and the winged leader impaled him from behind. Emrys howled and released the throat of the fae beneath him. It was too late for him, but now it may have been too late for Emrys, as well, who shifted back to his regular form.

We were down to two thieves, and the one that had been holding me earlier still had his back to me. I charged and stabbed him with my sword just beside his spine.

This was why I always kept my blade so sharp, smoothing its edges upon a rough stone block most nights; it made cutting so much easier, and now I felt my blade slide right into vital organs. The faerie had been too distracted by the skirmish ahead to hear me approach. He yelled in surprise, rage, and pain, then slumped over on the swamp floor. Dead—or soon to be—I hoped.

As I trudged forward through the mud, I realized it was just down to the winged leader. But when I approached, the faerie stepped behind Emrys, holding a blade to his throat.

I could have fled. I could've left him to die, and with only one fae to dispatch and my sword at the ready, maybe I could have escaped. But as much as every single muscle in my body wanted me to flee, if Emrys died, how would I get out of these cuffs? They were witch-magic proof and unbreakable, which likely meant that only a faerie could remove them.

Curse him and his enchanted cuffs.

The thief looked at me expectantly, gold teeth flashing as he sneered and shoved the dagger hard against Emrys's throat from behind. Blood beaded up and a thin line trailed downward, down Emrys's collarbone.

"You don't want to do that," I said.

"Or you'll do what?" he challenged, torn strips of flesh flapping on his injured wings as he shifted his weight behind Emrys.

Meanwhile, Emrys was trying to mouth something at me, something that the thief couldn't see with Emrys's back facing him. And it took me a moment before I realized what he was trying to say.

"Run me through."

I quirked a brow, convinced there was no way I'd interpreted that correctly. But Emrys nodded and repeated what he was mouthing. There was no mistaking it this time.

"Run me through."

Without further hesitation, I did just that, leaping forward and sliding my blade clean through his abdomen—doing my best to miss any vital organs this time since I needed him alive to release me from my cuffs—and stabbing the final thief behind him in the process.

They both gasped, Emrys in pain and the winged faerie in surprise. I yanked my sword free, and the thief slumped to the ground, his limp wings folding over him like a blanket.

Emrys dropped to his knees and winced. His eyes met mine before he fell to his side in the mud.

And slipped from consciousness.

10

Emrys

WHEN I WAS SMALL, MY MOTHER TOLD ME stories. Fables, really.

She would speak of sirens and kraken in the Balmor sea. Of giants with castles in the sky. Of a hidden land where time stood still, of fearsome dragons breathing fire. But there was one story that always stood out the most. One I asked her to tell me again and again.

"There lies in the Enchanted Forest a pool between two rock faces with three crystal waterfalls at one end, falling in three even streams. It is a healing pool, but it comes with a price. You may heal someone you love, but only if you, yourself, offer a great sacrifice. A sacrifice of something that means just as much to you as the person or creature you are trying to save."

"How do you find the pool?" I'd asked, leaning forward in intrigue. I'd always appreciated my mother's way of telling stories. She was so animated in her speech, illustrating each sentence with her hands, her expression. She responded to my question with a smile that lit her eyes. Ruffled my hair affectionately.

"My dear Emrys. You don't find the healing pool; the healing pool finds you. When you set foot inside the Enchanted Forest, and you arrive with something you desperately wish to save, something dying… the forest will know, and the pool will show itself. If you are proven worthy, that which you love can be saved. You must then offer your sacrifice in exchange, whatever the pool demands of you, for the pool will know what's in your heart. You will have quite the decision to make."

"What if you run before it can ask for your sacrifice?"

"Then the healing will promptly be reversed, and your loved one will die all over again. You must stay to make your sacrifice. Never run before the pool has spoken."

I had always accepted the fable as fact. When my family was murdered, I dreamed of taking them all there. Of healing them and paying any price. Even if it meant trading places with them. But according to the tale, the healing pool could only work for someone who was at death's door, not *fully* dead. My family was gone. There was no saving them.

Just as there was no way I could reach them now.

Like last time, I heard the voice. I still didn't know which family member spoke. But whoever it was, they were desperate to convey this message.

"Bind the blood," they said. *"It will save you."*

As always, I was dragged back through that cursed tunnel. The hot grip of life refused to let me go. Yanked me away from the light, back to the mortal realm. My wounds stubbornly healed under the curse's magic. The sensation was like tearing in reverse, if the wound were also set aflame at the same time.

My soul was tired of this. Tired of being dragged and shoved. Kicked around. Stuffed back into a body that didn't want it. But here we were, with no end in sight.

Gasping, I breathed the swamp air once more. Musty, damp.

"Back again," I muttered.

And I opened my eyes.

ROSE RED

WHEN I AWOKE AGAIN, ROSE WAS STILL THERE. Color me surprised. She sat on a nearby tree stump. Her chin rested on her fist. Her boot poked at the mud. Why wasn't she long gone?

"You killed the thief with the knife at my throat." I slowly sat up, my tone laced with disbelief. Rose started when she realized I was awake.

"Yes, I did," she replied. Her chin-holding hand lowered to her lap. "He deserved it. They all did. They would've killed us both without batting an eye. They would've slept peacefully tonight with our blood on their hands."

I was quite sure my face sported a mask of pure shock. I winced as my skin finished fusing itself back together. Whole again. "Why are you still here? You were free from my lead. You could have run away. Could've given yourself freedom. But you did not. Why?"

"I don't know how to free myself from these enchanted cuffs." She held up her bound hands. "I needed you alive for that."

"You're a resourceful witch. You could've figured out a way around them. Given enough time." A strange scent tickled my nostrils. I stared down at my fusing wounds. They were covered in some sort of green, pungent smelling muck. It seemed Rose had applied some sort of poultice while I was unconscious. "You tried to heal me." I couldn't help the incredulity that seeped into my tone.

"Yes, silly me. I should've let you die," Rose hissed. Her heartbeat quickened as she grew more frustrated.

"That would've been the smart thing to do," I agreed.

"I am through with your games." She stood. Raised her sword and held it out toward my throat. I did not flinch, but blinked slowly. Undisturbed. Somehow, I knew this witch had no designs on killing me—nor I on her. Even if she did, it made no matter. Her pulse sped even faster, all but making my own teeth rattle with its ferocity.

"You are right," she continued. "I could've fled. I could've left your wounds untended. The wounds were quite bad and I wasn't even sure the poultice would work, but by some miracle, it did. I don't know how you're still alive, but you are because of *me*. So, you will release me from my bonds at once and send me on my way."

I lifted a brow. "Well, you *did* impale me with your sword *before* attempting to heal me."

"You asked me to. Besides, I am certain I missed the vital organs this time. Though the thief who stabbed you before me... his mark was a bit worse than mine."

That explained the pain in my back. Instinctively, I reached up behind me, feeling just left of my spine. Sure enough, my fingers came away sticky. Another poultice. The witch had been thorough. I lowered my hand and spoke again.

"Assistance or no assistance, it wouldn't have mattered. Nothing any of them did would have killed me." Gods, I hated even speaking about this.

Rose's brows furrowed in confusion. "What do you mean?"

My responding sigh was deep. I often felt burdened by the heavy weight of the truth. *My* truth. "No matter what, I will always heal. Just as I am healing now."

"You mean, because of my poultice?"

"No." I shook my head. "Poultices can assist with healing. But have you ever seen them heal what should be a mortal wound completely and within mere minutes?"

"I do not understand."

It seemed a demonstration was in order. Without another word, I stood. I lifted the bottom of my shirt, exposing my torso to Rose's gaze. I shoved aside the poultice, rubbed my fingers through the dried blood. Just like always, my skin was fused back together. Some might call it a miracle of the gods.

But I knew it to be a curse.

Rose leaned forward, examining my wound more closely. "How?" she asked, flummoxed. Her eyes widened as she peered back up at me.

"When you first encountered my wolf form near your cabin, you thought you'd hit vital organs. You were right. You did not miss that time, Red. Your aim was true."

"If I didn't miss, then…"

I tipped my chin down. "Yes. My body mended itself despite the mortal wound. No matter what I do, my body will always mend itself. I will always continue living. Just as I have for the past 300 years."

Rose gaped at that. "You are 300 years old?"

"Yes. Actually, three hundred and ten. If we're being exact."

"I knew the fae had a longer lifespan than humans by a significant amount. Yet hearing a being say they are 300 years old when they look no more than the equivalent of twenty-some human years… that is still hard to conceive."

I shrugged. "It is far from an ancient age for my kind. But it is a long enough life for someone who's wanted to die for the majority of it."

"And you really cannot die?"

"No. I cannot."

She huffed. Shook her head in disbelief. "How is this possible?"

My distrust of witches ran deep, but this one had not left me to die when she could have fled. That must have meant something. A niggling feeling crept through my chest: gratitude. It was odd, feeling grateful toward a witch.

"My family was killed over 300 years ago," I finally said. "The murderers were human witches, like you. I was quite young at the time. Their slaying was my fault. I led the witches right to our doorstep unknowingly, and they slaughtered everyone in cold blood. Except for me."

Recounting the tale stung. Even to this day. The witch waited for me to continue.

"They spared me just so they could curse me. I was left with the bodies of my sister, my brother. My mother and father. Left to cry over them and beg forgiveness. And left with this as a reminder." I pointed to the crescent shaped scar around my right eye, still feeling its pain as vividly as the day I'd been cursed.

Rose went paler than normal. Perhaps my words were like a punch to the gut for her. "Witches did that to you?"

"Yes." Her green eyes pooled with sadness at the revelation. "Seems both our kinds have monster in us, Red."

"I... do not know what to say."

"Say nothing, just listen. This might be the only time I get to tell my story to a witch." I emitted a humorless chuckle. My shoulders jerked. "No matter how many times I tried to join my family in death, I never could. No blade nor arrow nor poison nor flame could bring me relief. I could jump from the highest cliff, shatter all of my bones, and wake up with my body mended the next day."

Rose still listened intently. "How did you manage?"

My mouth pulled into a tight line. "Two friends of my father's offered temporary shelter. A few months later, the king offered to turn the tides for good and brought me into his employ. He'd been fond of my father, a long-time client. He told me that once I'd collected enough human bounties for him, he'd release me from my curse so that I could finally rejoin my family. He claimed he knew how to reverse it."

"And he's been dangling that promise over your head this whole time to get you to do his bidding."

The thought was troubling. She wasn't wrong. As grateful as I was to King Armynd for all he had done for me,

I also resented him sometimes. Because the one thing I wanted most was the very thing Armynd hesitated to give me. A hesitation that had lasted far too many years.

Rose narrowed her eyes and tilted her head as though attempting to read my expression. Searching for any crack in my hardened exterior. Any sign that I was being dishonest. "I always heard the fae are master manipulators," she said. "But..."

"But what?"

"I see nothing but the truth in your eyes."

"Because I *am* telling the truth. And fae do not lie. We may omit the truth on occasion. But any direct statement we make, rest assured it is not a lie."

"Well then that... is awful." Her tone was sincere, with none of the biting sarcasm I had grown accustomed to. "That's what you were shouting about in your sleep. Your family. You were seeing them in their final moments, weren't you?"

I nodded, a singular jerk of my head. Gods, I still ached for my family down to my very bones.

"I have nightmares too, sometimes." She cleared her throat, shook her head. I could see the gears of her mind churning. "But... why did the witches come after your family? Why did they choose to kill in cold blood?"

"Retaliation. Our kind have been at war for centuries. At this point, it's rather unclear who took the first shot. But I suppose it doesn't matter now. What's done is done."

"Your kind took my family," she whispered.

"And your kind took mine."

She rubbed her cuffed hands over her forehead. "Stars, how has it come to this?"

"Perhaps the truth is just far more complicated than either of us know," I continued. "I do not always agree with my king's actions. But without him, I can never be free of my curse."

"How are you so sure he knows how to reverse it? What if he doesn't really know how, and he has just been dangling that over your head to keep you obedient?"

"He's got the witch who cursed me held captive."

Her brows shot up. "Is the witch not human? How is she—"

"He," I corrected.

"How is *he* even still alive?"

"Magic, I assume."

Her eyes grew wide as saucers at that. "Did the witch grant himself immortality? Is that possible?"

"You're the witch. You should know."

"My powers are elemental. Whatever that is... it is magic I have never touched. Likely blood magic. Dark magic."

"Good to know." I frowned. "But the immortal witch is locked away in a place unknown to all save the king. Which is mighty convenient."

"You don't believe your king?"

"I do. He only speaks truth. I just question how long he plans to make me wait for what I want considering he has never offered a solid date. It could still be hundreds of years, for all I know."

Her lips pursed, the clear indications of a fresh idea spreading across her features. "Even if all that is true, maybe you don't need the king."

My gaze snapped to hers in question. "How so?"

"I figure a human witch put this curse on you, correct?"

"Yes."

She nibbled her lip thoughtfully. "And you have a human witch currently in your captivity, do you not?"

I frowned. "I do."

"So... If you can remember how she—or he—cursed you, I can figure out a way to reverse it myself. No more waiting for the king."

I rubbed my chin in thought. "Why would you help me?"
"Because I won't help you unless you free me. Unless you assure me that I won't be chased anymore."
I glanced to her bonds, then looked back up at her. Her pulse had slowed again. "What assurance do I have that once I remove the bonds, you won't place a hex on me and run?"
"Do you not trust my word?"
"I have never trusted the word of a witch."
She sighed. "I do not place hexes. I wouldn't even know how."
"I don't believe you."
"Then how can I convince you?"
"Perhaps I can simply convince you not to flee first."
She lifted a brow. "And how would you do that?"
"By telling you the grim truth. I am marked, Red." I pulled down my bracer to show her a tattoo in the shape of an eye, etched on the inside of my wrist. She gasped as the eye blinked on my skin. It moved just like a real eye would, blinking and rolling about. I quickly pulled the bracer back into place, laced the strings. "The king marks all who work for him. We must return with bounty every so often. If we do not, there's no stone he won't turn to find us. To find you."
"To find *me?* But..." Her mouth fell open as realization crept through her. "Do you mean the king is watching us through your tattoo right now?"
"Not exactly. He cannot see us nor hear us through the tattoo. But the eye is always tracking my location, and always will no matter where I go within Sythea. And when I have a bounty in my custody, I am required to report through the mark." I demonstrated with my thumb hovering above the bracer.
"And how does the king know when you do that?"
"If you were to look at the king's bare chest, it is covered in marks nearly identical to mine. They are the original

tattoos. Each one has a counterpart, and he can sense our every movement that way. He can lock into the essence of our bounty to sniff them out too."

She reeled back, nearly collapsing on the tree stump again. "I've never even heard of such magic. He knows who I am and where I am now?"

I scratched my jaw. The witch wasn't going to like this, at all. "Basically, yes. Because of me, he knows you exist. He can track you. He'll stop at nothing until he has you in his grasp."

"That still does not make sense. If I do not have the same mark as you, then... how?"

"You do now."

"I... what?"

"When I touched the back of your neck. You said you felt a burning sensation. You demanded to know what I did. I'm telling you now."

At once, she leaped back up. Her cuffed hands moved up, fingers reaching around the back of her neck to feel for a tattoo. "You... you *branded* me, shifter?" She looked positively offended, violated. I couldn't blame her.

"Yes. Bounty hunters must mark all their bounties. And now, the king will not rest until you are in his possession. Escape will not be possible for you."

She shuddered at that, shoulders trembling. "Then what do you suggest we do?"

"Well, there is one way. The king, for all his faults, is also deeply entrenched in tradition. Tradition had been so important to the queen, his late wife. He continues to honor the rules of old just as she had. One of the rules being that a person cannot testify against nor be forced to turn over for arrest... their spouse."

Her eyes widened as my words began to process. "So, you're suggesting that we..."

"I am suggesting, Red..." I trailed off, licked my lips. Thinking about the words I'd heard at the threshold of the Otherworld. The message my family was so desperate to get to me.

"Bind the blood. It will save you."

I knew what it meant now. I spoke the words out loud.

"I am saying that we get married."

11

Emrys

IT WASN'T EXACTLY A PROPOSAL I HAD INTENDED to make anytime soon. But here we were.

Rose's head jerked so hard, I half-expected to hear a crunch of bones in her neck.

"Have you gone raving mad? Did you just say that we have to get *married?*"

"It is the only way."

"I find that hard to believe."

"It *is,* Red. In fact, it is only logical for us both. Agree to marry me, and I will free you from your bonds. Marry me, and you will come to no harm. Because as my wife, I can convince the king to spare you. But in exchange, you must figure out how to free me from my curse so that... So that I may finally join my family." I bit the inside of my cheek hard. An old habit to keep my emotions safely bottled.

"Won't the king have us both killed for mixing our bloodlines?"

"The king will honor our union."

"But how do you—"

"Because I know him," he cut me off, "and I can usually predict his actions quite well."

"Even if he accepts the marriage, once I break your curse and you die, he will come for my head then."

"As soon as you break my curse, I will arrange for your journey with those I trust. I will wait until I have received word of your arrival in the Outerlands before ending my miserable existence."

The witch almost laughed until she realized I was serious. "The Outerlands? You've definitely gone raving mad."

"Surely, life in the Outerlands must be better than death or imprisonment. Wouldn't you agree?"

"But, the Void..." She trailed off, swallowing hard. I could see her mind working, attempting to piece my words together like a puzzle.

"I know those who are confident they can navigate a safe passage through the Void," I said. That much was true. What I did not tell Rose was, to my knowledge, they had not yet *tested* their theory. But I trusted them with my life, just as I trusted their judgment. They would help me if I asked them, too. Aegan and Lysia were nothing if not dependable.

"Truly?"

"Yes."

Now, there was a different spark in Rose's eyes. The faint spark of hope. Though it quickly faded.

"Why do we even have to go through the trouble of marrying and going back to the castle for the king's blessing? Why can't we just stay in the woods and break the curse here?"

"Because I suspect such a thing will take quite some time for you to figure out. Likely weeks, if not months. You've already admitted to having no inherent knowledge of this form of magic, which means you will need to learn. As I said before, the high king is an impatient fae. He will send scouts for me if I'm not back soon."

After a long moment of contemplation, she spoke again. "And what if I say no to this proposal?"

"Then we continue to the castle with you in chains."

She huffed and shook her head. "So, what you're saying is I don't have a choice."

"These are the terms, little witch. But you don't have to say *yes* just yet. I will give you until we reach the inn."

"An inn? Why would we go to an inn?"

I smirked at that, because the answer was quite simple. I could not believe our luck. It was a place I often visited when I sought bounty in the White Woods, since it was somewhat on the way to the castle. A place owned by the very two fae I trusted and respected above all. Two fae who had exactly what we needed. All of it.

"Believe it or not," I replied, "because it's the only place I know where a faerie and a witch can be married."

ROSE WAS NOT A BAD TRAVEL COMPANION WHEN she didn't desire to kill me outright. Well, perhaps she still did. But she was wise enough to not act on her impulses. The protection and chance at freedom I offered her was a greater temptation than my maiming.

We briefly stopped near a creek so Rose could drink and I could wash the mud—and blood—from my face and hands.

"The cuffs," Rose said after we'd left the creek.

"What about them?"

"Take them off."

"And why would I do that? You have not agreed to the terms yet."

A noise from up ahead gave me pause.

Heartbeats. Accompanied by a familiar scent. Horses grazed nearby and two voices spoke. I placed my finger to my lips and grabbed Rose by the crook of her elbow, dragging her backward to conceal both of us behind some bushes. She had opened her mouth to protest, but snapped it shut when she heard the voices too.

"Would you quit your whining, Talyn?" one of them said. Gruff. Dripping conceit.

Ah, yes, I knew the voice. Those scents. More like a stench. I didn't much like them, either.

"We lost our bounty, and that is your fault. Why must you be so quick with the enchantments?" his travel companion said.

"The idea was to lure out the other witch, not scare her away. And what has gotten into you?"

"Sorry, Callum. I hate questioning you, but..."

"But nothing. Bite your tongue. We've still quite a journey back to the castle and your whining will drive me out of my mind."

The voices faded; their horses' hooves clomped away. We remained crouched while I sniffed the air, listened for any stray noises. They were gone for now, likely on the way to the same inn we were headed toward. On horseback, they would arrive before us. I'd have to stay alert. I should have sniffed them out long before this, but I'd been distracted by my company.

Beside me, the witch was white as a sheet. I gripped her around the elbow and pulled her upright. When she didn't protest my touch, I knew something was wrong. "You look as though you've seen a sprite," I said.

"These were the same two voices I had heard in my cabin. The ones responsible for my grandmother's death, no matter how indirectly." Her face paled further and suddenly she was trembling beneath my grip.

This could be precisely the opportunity I needed to convince her to agree to my terms. I had no idea why I was pushing the idea of marriage so heavily. Sure, it made sense for both of us. But I imagined I should have been more resistant to the idea than I was. My family's words from the Otherworld stuck with me, telling me to bind the blood. This had to be what they meant. If my parents were sending me a message from beyond, I would be an utter fool not to take heed.

"There are two of them and one of me, Red," I said. "Callum and Talyn are quite powerful. Should they find you and choose to claim you as their bounty, I may have no choice but to hand you over. But agree to marry me, and you are guaranteed protection."

Rose spoke through gritted teeth, even as she still trembled. "Mainly, for what they did to my grandmother, I would like to strangle them and heat my hands with my flame until their heads were burned clear off their bodies."

"That's quite a colorful picture you paint. I'm afraid I cannot allow it, but I *can* stop *them* from hurting *you*. So, what do you say?" At her continued hesitation, I decided to try another approach. "Of course, if you're still that opposed to the idea of marriage, I *could* just hand you over to Callum and Talyn *now*. They're eager to make up for their lost bounty, after all. It's also the quickest way for you to be rid of me and forget about the whole marriage proposal."

She gasped, her eyes rounding. "You would hand me over to those two brutes?"

"If that's what you want. In fact, I shall call them back right now."

When I cupped my hands around my mouth as though preparing to call out, Rose grabbed my arm. Her cuffed hands shook. "Please, no. Don't do that. Don't give me to them."

I lowered my hands. "So, I *am* the lesser of two evils then, hm?" I was relieved. I'd been hoping the witch wouldn't test me. The last thing I wanted to do was involve Callum and Talyn. But as I looked at Rose and noted the look of sheer panic in her eyes, I felt something... rather odd.

The distinct pang of guilt for making her so terrified. Odd, indeed.

"Fine," she huffed. "I'll marry you, shifter."

"A wise decision. This is the best course of action for both of us."

"We'll see about that." She sighed loudly. Shoulders slumped in defeat. "I must be raving mad to agree to this."

"Actually, it may be the smartest choice you've made yet. I am glad you finally saw reason." It was still quite humorous to me how she thought she *had* a choice in the matter. Any sane person would choose marriage over torture. Although to some, marriage itself might have been torture. With marriage to me being the worst kind.

Rose blew out a breath that made hair fly about her face. She held up her cuffed hands again. "Now, let me out of my bonds."

"Again, I ask you, why would I do that?"

"Because of our pact. Because we are about to be married?"

"So?"

"So? How do you expect anyone to believe that we are about to be married if I'm in cuffs? What if we run into someone you know between here and the inn? What would they think?"

"Perhaps that we have a very unique way of expressing our feelings?"

"Yes, because nothing says romance like a pair of cuffs."

"For some, it might." She scoffed at my words and I couldn't help but chuckle. I understood full well what she meant. I just found it so unreasonably fun to toy with her a little. The way her pink lips curved into a slight part, her cheeks reddening. It made me wonder what other parts of her grew red when she was frustrated. "But you are right. A fae hunter carting around a witch in cuffs screams *bounty*, not wife. So, I'll oblige, if you promise to be good. Remember, if you try to run the deal is off the table. I will easily catch up to you on my four legs versus your two. Then we will continue to the castle with you in chains, as my prisoner. And should you use your magic on me, the king *will* find you through your mark. It will only be a matter of time, and he will then take *extra* pleasure in punishing you. Are you hearing me?"

She scowled, but relented. "I hear you."

I removed her cuffs and frowned when I saw the raw, blistered skin around her wrists. I held her forearms and lifted to examine the marks, cocking a brow. "I made these cuffs too tight."

"Yes."

"Why didn't you say anything?"

"I was your prisoner. I wasn't expecting that you'd care."

"From here on out, you *will* tell me when you're in pain. As a wife would tell her husband. Understand?" I waited for her to acknowledge me. My brows furrowed as I stared down at the stark red lines that stood out against her delicate, pale skin. My fingers twitched around her forearms, reluctant to let go. Why did the sight of the marks bother me? "You'll have to try to keep your wrists covered so the cuff marks aren't as obvious."

"I figured as much." She pulled her arms free of my grip and walked ahead.

I shoved the cuffs back in my satchel and caught up with her in two long strides. She eyed the sheath on my back as she rubbed the red marks on her wrists, then extended her hand toward me palm up. An expectant gesture.

"My sword?"

I raised a brow. The witch was really pushing her luck. "Not a chance."

"But it's *mine.*"

"Not at the moment, it isn't."

She stopped walking abruptly and her mouth twisted. A crease formed between her brows as it always seemed to do when she was angry. Which was quite often. "I could just take it," she said.

I halted too. Turned on my heel. Gazed down at her. "I would love to see you try. Might I remind you that the last time you *did* try, you ended up on your back in the mud with my hand wrapped around your throat. Not that I would mind being in that position again." I smirked.

She tipped her chin up to look me dead in the eyes. Her small hands clenched into fists. Her tenacity, while troublesome, was also admirable. This witch never let fear best her. "I was cuffed then and I am not now," she pointed out. To demonstrate her power, she lifted her hand and produced a sizeable fireball. Ready to hurl it in my direction.

The flicker of the flames reflected in her emerald eyes. I felt my lips curl at the edges. Oh, I did quite like her fire—in more than one sense. I approached and stopped so close I could feel the heat of the flame licking my flesh. "No need for violence, Red. I do intend to return your sword eventually, but not yet. We are about to enter a fae establishment and if my witch betrothed wants to make a good first impression, it's best she arrive unarmed. Without sword *or* flame. So, why don't you do us both a favor and extinguish that fire?" I held her gaze without blinking, challenging.

Rose gave in after what seemed a prolonged staring contest. My siblings and I used to have those when I was a child. I never once lost.

"Fine. But you *will* give it back after we are married." She lowered her hand and doused her fire. Grumbling all the while.

Then, we continued onward.

OUR WEDDING DAY APPROACHED. IT TOOK another sleep and a full day of walking before Rose and I neared our destination. Perhaps just another hour's walk.

It was officially the day I would leave my bachelorhood behind. Not that my single life was ever much to write home about. Admittedly, I had spent most of it in misery.

We'd been able to find more fruit without the assistance of the low fae. Some eggs, too, to replace the ones that got smashed during our skirmish with the thieves. They'd made quite the mess inside my satchel.

I was mostly optimistic about our union occurring without incident, whereas Rose remained skeptical. "As a general rule of thumb, my family and I, along with any wayward humans we happened to run into, avoided towns, taverns, inns... Basically we avoided gathering at all to remain further inconspicuous. All human towns had long ago been rooted out, and either taken over by fae or burned to the ground entirely," she said. Her unsure gaze darted about. She was jumpy, on edge.

"Well, try to relax. You look stiff as a board, and your heart is beating far too fast." Her back was rigid beneath her cloak. The speed and ferocity of her heartbeat practically screamed in my shifter ears. "You are with me. No one will harm you if you stay by my side."

"And you won't harm me, either?"

"What do you mean? I agreed to the terms. I could've already handed you over to Callum and Talyn if I so chose, and I did not. This marriage benefits us both. We marry so I can keep you safe and out of the dungeons. You figure out how to break my curse in the meantime. After, we go our separate ways."

"And how do I know this isn't all a trick? That you won't have me tossed in the dungeons the second I break your curse?"

I stopped moving once again and swiveled my head around to look at her. "Do you really distrust my word that much?"

"We are natural born enemies, shifter. You captured me in *chains*. Of course, I have my doubts." She laughed mirthlessly, shaking her head.

"Is something funny?" I asked, genuinely curious.

"Long ago, my ancestors once believed the silly rumor that fae can't lie."

"We don't," I said, speaking the truth. As I always did. "I haven't lied to you about anything yet. Lying makes us fae rather... uncomfortable."

"The low fae lied about threats in the area before the thieves came," she pointed out.

"Every faerie has rules they must abide. Low fae must serve, though they are also more readily capable of lying. Not that they are free of the *consequences* if caught in a lie. High fae, on the other hand, are top of the hierarchy. But we are compelled to always tell the truth. It is called balance, Red."

"Fine. Maybe I accept that the high fae don't tell outright lies, but your kind has gotten very good at omitting the truth and bending those around them to their will whenever possible. This is why I have such a hard time trusting you now."

"As if your kind are known for their honesty, witch?" My tone was more biting than I had intended. Although, humans *were* a treacherous bunch themselves and lying came second nature to them. I could think of countless human indiscretions off the top of my head.

She opened her mouth to protest, but snapped it shut. "I suppose that's fair."

"I don't know how to convince you that I intend to honor our word. Really, we have no choice but to trust each other to get what we want."

"Alright, shifter," she replied simply. "Although I suppose since we are about to be married, we should at least start calling each other by our given names more."

"Agreed," I said. "You start calling me Emrys, and I shall stop calling you *witch.* Although, *Red* stays. I like it."

Rose scowled at that, but didn't protest.

"Let's continue on then, shall we?" I resumed leading the way. Rose followed without objection. She skirted closer to me as we moved, occasionally bumping my arm.

We emerged from the woods onto a narrow dirt trail. It led to an inn for fae travelers on their way to and from the castle village.

"I suppose there is no turning back now," Rose mumbled.

The path turned several times more before revealing the structure to us. The inn was two stories, quaint. There was a tavern on the first floor and rooms for sleeping upstairs. In addition, there was a small stable out back where horses could rest and eat hay. As we passed, I spotted four horses. The innkeepers never kept more than two horses, which meant they had other patrons.

Callum and Talyn. It had to be them. Yes, I could smell their scent lingering upon the air, though not too near at the moment. The witch was already a bundle of nerves, so I kept that knowledge to myself for now.

The witch. No, I had to stop calling her that. She was, technically, my betrothed.

Bind the blood.

"Stay close to me," I told Rose. "And put your hood up to hide your human features. Just to be safe, in case anyone from the kingdom happens to be here."

She nodded and complied with my request, flipping her hood up. I held the door to the tavern open, gesturing for her to enter.

The tavern was warmed by a single fireplace and lit by flickering candlelight. Heavy wooden tables were scattered about. The walls were decorated with dark sconces and mounted animal antlers. Deer, mostly. At the far end of the room sat a small bar. No one stood behind it. The tavern was quiet.

Callum and Talyn must be in their rooms or out somewhere. Perhaps hunting. Sometimes, the guests at the inn paid for their stay in food rather than coin. Callum and Talyn likely had some aggression to expel after their lost bounties.

But we had only moved a few steps inside when I froze at a noise coming from the bar. We weren't alone, after all. A figure stood behind the other side of the room, looking our way. I recognized that scent, too.

A familiar voice called out.

"What on the gods' green earth are you doing here?"

12

Rose

I SPUN AT THE SOUND OF THE VOICE COMING from behind the bar. We were not alone, after all, as there was a single man—no, a faerie—staring right at us, his hand curved around a mug as though poised to throw it. I hesitated, casting a glance to Emrys. But Emrys surprised me when his face split into a wide grin.

"Hello, old crone," he said.

The faerie set down his mug and his face lit up. "Emrys, my boy! I thought that was you."

He stepped from behind the bar and pulled Emrys into a warm hug, the two clapping each other's backs. It was strange, hearing this fae call Emrys a *boy* when he didn't appear much older than Emrys, though fae did age far slower than humans as a whole. The only thing that gave away the stranger's age was a slight silvering of the hair around his temples, and maybe an added weariness in his brown eyes.

Emrys pulled back from the friendly embrace, grasping the older faerie's shoulder. "I am sorry I missed you the last time I passed this way."

"That's fine." He gave Emrys's attire a quick scan. "Why are your clothes covered in mud?"

"That's a long story."

"And what brings you here today? Just a visit?"

"I have come to ask a very large favor, Aegan."

The older fae's smile wavered a little. "Of course. Your father was a great friend of mine, and so are you by extension. I am happy to help his kin any way I can. Just as I have always been."

"I am glad to hear it." Emrys reached back for my hand, and I accepted. Though I hadn't expected him to pull me forward with such vigor, and I stumbled against his side with a yelp as he tugged me. "First, I would like to introduce you to my betrothed. Darling, why don't you lower your hood?"

I did as was requested of me despite cringing inwardly—both at revealing my features to this fae and Emrys's use of such a pet name. When I pushed back my hood, Aegan all but gasped out loud, his jaw hanging open. "You wish to marry a *human*, Emrys?" His gaze darted back and forth between us as though awaiting the punch line of a very peculiar joke.

Emrys nodded slowly. "I do. I wish to marry her. And I request for *you* to be the one to marry us. Will that be a problem?"

"Surely you jest?"

"I do not."

"Well." Aegan released the word on a puff of breath and spoke to Emrys as though I was not there. "She is quite fetching. But... a *human,* Emrys?"

"My name is Rose," I said, tired of being talked *about* rather than spoken *to.* "And it's a pleasure to meet you."

I tried to make the words sound as genuine as possible, though of course, I couldn't say meeting any fae was a *pleasure,* not when I didn't know their true intentions. But I extended my hand, wanting to make a good impression on Emrys's old friend nonetheless. The older faerie accepted after an extended pause, his gaze scanning my fingers as though they concealed some nameless weapon. But even as our hands shook, he still could not mask the baffled expression on his face.

"Quite interesting to meet you," he returned before withdrawing his hand—notably wiping his palms on his shirt after releasing me—and turning his attention back to Emrys. "Goodness, but you do know how to shock an old crone."

"One of my many talents," Emrys replied, his mouth tugging up at the corners. "So, will you do it?"

"As I said, I will do anything for my old friend's kin. But first, I must know... Why?"

Emrys cleared his throat, and, to make a point, placed an arm around my shoulder and drew me closer to his side. I stiffened at first, but forced myself to relax against him as he replied, "As hard as it may be to believe, we saw past our differences and realized that we have both experienced loss and... have more in common than we had thought."

It wasn't exactly a lie—fae did have a knack for dancing around the truth when it suited them—but was it enough to convince Aegan? The older fae held a look of skepticism.

"I... love him," I added for good measure, trying not to choke on the words as Emrys cleared his throat uncomfortably beside me.

I did my best to keep a smile plastered to my face. As a human, I may have been more readily capable of lying outright than a faerie, but I had never been a very *good* liar. My grandmother always said my blush gave me away, and I felt my cheeks grow hot even now.

"A human and faerie marriage has not occurred in decades, to my knowledge, and I never thought I would live to see the day it happened again. Especially not from the likes of you, Emrys. Not after what happened," Aegan said, his expression darkening. He likely remembered Emrys's loss all too well.

I felt Emrys's arm tighten around me at Aegan's words, his muscles tensing. "Well, Rose... she is not like the others. I have found that some of her kind are... tolerable."

Tolerable. I nearly snorted at his choice of words, because he didn't seem to be selling his point too well. But to his credit, Aegan didn't question further.

"Well, this might take some getting used to, but if this is your choice, then so be it." Aegan waved a hand, gesturing us forward. "Come, then. I've got no patrons to tend to at the moment, as the only other two are currently hunting, so now is a perfect time. I'm afraid I cannot provide a fancy ceremony, especially not on such short notice, so you will have to make do with getting married behind the stables."

"That is perfectly fine by us. Thank you, Aegan," Emrys said, and the older fae nodded and drew his mouth into a tight smile, one still laced with a slight bewilderment.

"Won't the king have something to say about this?" Aegan asked as he gathered up a few items in his arms before beckoning us to follow once more.

"Oh, I'm sure he will have plenty to say," Emrys replied. "But he will be forced to accept this union once it's legal. You know how strictly he adheres to tradition."

"Indeed, I do." Aegan shrugged. "Well, I suppose there is no time like the present."

"We are to wed right now?" My gaze darted to Emrys in question. "I had always heard that fae weddings involve quests and... and that I would have maiden attendants and a whole seven-day ceremony."

"Typically, yes. That is how it works," Emrys replied. "But seeing as we have time for none of that, we must improvise. Aegan and Lysia specialize in abbreviated ceremonies for those who wish to wed quickly. An abbreviated ceremony is no less legal. It just cuts out some long-standing traditions for the sake of brevity, which many of the more superstitious folk believe will doom a marriage from the start. But even if our marriage is doomed, well..." Emrys trailed off, realizing Aegan was still listening. Though I knew what he was going to say. Even if our marriage was doomed, it did not matter, because it was not meant to be forever. We were meant to go our separate ways sooner than later.

As Aegan led us toward the tavern door, I was suddenly sweating from my palms and my knees shook. My grandmother had wanted me to find peace—it was her dying wish—and maybe this was the only way I could begin to do so. I was tired of fighting. But that didn't change the fact I was still about to marry a fae. My mortal enemy. No matter how short our union was intended to be, that was still a bitter potion to swallow.

"Wait!" I shouted, and the two fae paused and turned to look at me, eyebrows raised. "It's just... I appreciate you doing this for us, Aegan, especially on such short notice. But we are tired and dirty from our long journey. And famished, as well. Might we pay for a room to freshen up before our ceremony? I would... I would like to remember it fondly, and I would like to be presentable." This was not entirely a lie. Truthfully, I was dying for a bath and my stomach was rumbling with hunger. We could still be married before nightfall; I just needed a few moments first.

Emrys and Aegan exchanged a look. "I suppose I could stand to freshen up as well," Emrys said with a laugh, tipping his chin down toward his own soiled clothes. He reached into his pocket and placed several coins into Aegan's palm. It seemed Emrys had much more than he'd given the thieves.

"King's bounty hunter still pays well, I see." Aegan pocketed the coins. "Very well." He went behind the bar and rummaged around before producing a large metal key. "First door upstairs on the right. I'll send you food shortly. The room was just turned and there should be a basin of water to draw a bath. Lysia will be back soon; she's out gathering herbs for supper." He gestured toward a small door behind the bar that I imagined hid a quaint kitchen.

"Thank you," I said again as Emrys and I headed upstairs to the room—our *shared* room. Oh, my. How was I to change and draw a bath with this faerie standing in the room with me?

"I am just accompanying you upstairs," Emrys said, reading my discomfort. "Aegan will find a spot for me to freshen up downstairs. He wouldn't want us to live in scandal prior to our wedding now, would he?" He winked slyly. The small gesture caught me off guard.

"I suppose not."

"I'll have Lysia send you up a fresh cloak and dress to wear during the ceremony. And have your current attire laundered, once she arrives back. Enjoy your bath, Red." He slid the key in the lock, opened the door, and pushed it wide. A bubble of panic gurgled in my stomach then.

"Wait," I said, and he stopped, turning. "It's just... You are sure these fae won't harm me in any way?"

I wasn't sure when I had decided to start trusting that Emrys would stay true to his word, or why I looked to him for reassurance now. Likely because I had no other choice.

"I would trust them with my life, Red. I promise you that you're safe with them. It is your choice to believe me or not, but I can only give you my word."

I drew a deep breath, let it out, and nodded. "Alright."

Something flashed in his golden eyes as though he held something else on the tip of his tongue, but he said nothing more other than, "I will see you soon." Without further discussion, he pulled the door closed and left me alone.

I turned to take in the quaint room. It had a single bed, chair, and a wooden table with a lantern and two candles upon it. There was also a small tub in the corner of the room at the opposite side of the table. As Aegan promised, there was a bucket of water, in addition to a bar of soap and three folded rags waiting inside the tub.

I stripped off my soiled cloak and allowed my dress to pool around my feet before pouring the bucket of water into the tub. It was quite cold, but I could fix that. I placed my pointer finger into the water and gently swirled it around in a circle, first right, and then left.

"Teine," I whispered, and at once, drawing from the power of my flames, the water heated up to a nice, comfortable warmth. "Much better."

I climbed in and almost moaned at the feel of the warm water soothing my aching limbs. I dragged the soap over my body and created a good lather. It felt divine. I tried to revel in the moment rather than worry about the near future and the fact that I was about to marry a fae, my people's sworn enemy.

"Knock, knock!" a cheerful voice said, and my eyes widened at the intrusion.

A plump, jovial looking, short faerie with rounded, rosy cheeks and flowing blonde hair decorated with wildflowers appeared in the room. She chuckled as I hunched over in the tub to cover myself, careful to also hide the red marks on my wrists from the cuffs.

"No need to be shy, it is just us ladies. You must be Rose. My name is Lysia, and I am the lady of the inn."

"Pleasure to meet you," I said, brows creasing further. I drew my knees to my chest. Being naked around your own kind was one thing, but feeling vulnerable and exposed like this around fae was entirely different.

"I have a fresh dress and cloak for you. They should fit. Also, some freshly picked flowers to decorate your hair, and some bread and grapes to fuel you."

"Thank you, that is very kind of you. Can you leave it on the bed, please?"

Lysia set a tray and folded cloth upon the bed as requested, but she didn't leave the room. Instead, she walked forward and knelt right next to the tub, and I flushed under her scrutiny. Her face seemed kind enough for a faerie, but a bit shrewder than Aegan. She noted the steam rising from the tub, her gaze following the white wisps.

"That water should've been cool," she observed. "But right now, it is pleasantly warm. So, you are not just human, but a witch, I suspect?"

I wasn't sure what to say to that, but it seemed Lysia did not expect an answer, as she continued speaking.

"Surely you know of Emrys's history with witches."

"I know everything," I replied. "About his family. And about his... current profession."

"Then you should know why I have no choice but to question this union. That boy has been through a lot, and Aegan and I love him like our own. He is a good lad."

It seemed their definition of *good* didn't align with mine, because he *was* responsible for a lot of deaths. It did not matter if he wasn't the one to slip the noose around their necks, he still readily delivered them to their fates. But then again, my kind was also responsible for many deaths, as was I. A solid dozen fae had been caught in our traps throughout the years, fae that had met their untimely ends at the point of Papa's sword.

"Why do you wish to marry him, knowing what you know about him?" Lysia asked, idly trailing her fingers along the lip of the tub. "Perhaps there is an ulterior motive?"

I flushed further. "There are no ulterior motives," I replied, unsure how steady my voice sounded.

Lysia narrowed her violet eyes and tilted her head, examining me close. I held her gaze, refusing to give her cause to distrust me. After a moment, she sighed. "Well, you are quite stunning, really. And you seem... I am unsure, but there is a sincerity about you. I suppose I can understand what Emrys sees in you. Maybe not your kind in general, but you in particular."

I once again had to bite back a snide retort about the terrible things *their* kind had done. After all, they were being quite hospitable to me at the moment.

"Now, dear, finish washing, and then eat up and dress quickly. You won't want to keep your husband-to-be waiting."

With that, she stood and exited the room, leaving me to finish getting ready. After shrugging off the strange encounter and finishing my soak, I climbed out of the tub and dried myself off. I pulled on the lacy white dress and beautiful, shimmery cream cloak Lysia had supplied. I placed the white flowers in a crown around my thick auburn hair and ate the bread, which was fresh, and the grapes, which were sweet. Both served to soothe the grumble in my stomach until supper, though nothing could soothe my nerves.

When I went back downstairs, the tavern was still empty of other patrons. Lysia greeted me.

"Beautiful. I knew the dress would fit."

"Thank you," I said. "Truly."

"You are quite welcome. Now, let's go. They wait for you behind the stables." She gestured me forward. "I will lead you."

The blood began to drain from my face as we moved toward the stables out back, and soon I was fighting a wave of dizziness. Lysia must have noticed, because she patted my hand and assured me that I would be alright. But, would I? Marrying my mortal enemy for a tenuous truce?

We arrived at the stables far too soon and circled around the back. I blinked rapidly, taken aback to see a white arch covered in flowers. Apparently, they had enough time to at least set *something* up to make the ceremony just a little special.

I trembled as I realized that this was it, the moment of truth. I approached Emrys, who waited for me in front of the arch. He had cleaned up quite nice, as well, looking much more polished than before. His dark hair was neatly combed and his attire—no longer torn or bloody—appeared pressed and clean. I adjusted my fresh cloak around my shoulders. Aegan stood next to Emrys in front of the arch, and Lysia trailed behind me to witness the ceremony.

When I reached Emrys, he grasped my small hands in his larger ones. His skin was warm against mine, and suddenly, I felt as though without his support, my nerves may just make me fall on my face right there behind the stables. I had to remind myself why I was doing this: for self-preservation and to honor a deal. This would not last forever.

Emrys leaned forward. "You look... quite acceptable, Red," he murmured.

From the way Emrys's gold eyes skimmed my body up and down, he had deemed me more than *acceptable*, he just didn't want to say as much. So, I returned with enthusiasm to match his. "You look quite acceptable, yourself," I muttered.

Up close, he smelled like honey with a slight twinge of lavender and pine. My hands trembled in his as the ceremony began. This was not how I envisioned getting married, though frankly I'd never envisioned myself getting married at all. It never seemed to be an option for me.

Aegan said some words in a language I did not understand—I believed it to be old fae—and had us repeat some words back. Then it was time for the vows.

"I, Rose Doyle..." I began.

Emrys did the same when I'd finished. "I, Emrys Abrynth..."

Things happened in a blur. Aegan used a silver dagger to open shallow cuts on our palms before pressing our palms together, our fingers wrapping around each other's hands. Emrys cupped his other hand around our joined ones, and I did the same. The older fae said something about being bound by blood, though my heart thudded in my ears too loudly for me to hear all the details.

My cut palm started to warm and tingle, the warmth moving up my wrist, my arm, moving inward toward my chest. What was happening?

And then, all too soon, Aegan was saying that we could kiss. I looked to Emrys, heart in my throat, trying to hide my panic. How had I forgotten about this part of a wedding ceremony? Emrys offered me a surprisingly warm smile, causing the crescent-shaped scar around his brow to flex. He leaned forward ever so slowly, gaze locked on mine, and my breath hitched in my chest.

Emrys must have noticed my reaction. He lifted his free hand to clasp my chin between thumb and forefinger, holding my face steady.

"Breathe, Red," he whispered, his mouth drifting toward mine.

And then he kissed me.

13

Rose

AT FIRST, HE BRUSHED HIS LIPS AGAINST MINE in the lightest of touches, barely a shadow of a kiss. For some strange reason, I was left wanting more.

But I didn't have to wait very long.

A low growl sounded in the back of Emrys's throat, a distinct sound of possession. His free hand trailed down, grasped my upper arm tight, and pulled me close, deepening the kiss. I felt dizzy as his mouth claimed mine, his taste sweet. It was a strange thing, kissing one's enemy—and it was an even stranger thing to find yourself *liking* it on some level.

I was yanked from my strange, brief reverie as Lysia clapped. Emrys broke the kiss, pulling back to look down at me while I was left flushing with shame.

Faeries killed my family, and now I was kissing one. What would my mother and father say? What would Gran say, or any one of my ancestors that came before me?

You and the shifter have an agreement, I reminded myself. *And this is all part of it.*

Emrys didn't take his eyes off me as Lysia spoke, his eyes dark with... desire, confusion, guilt? If so, his level of internal conflict matched mine.

"Congratulations to you both," Lysia said. "Now, let's get you a proper wedding supper."

After the cuts on our hands were cleaned with soft cloths, we left the stables and went back inside where our hosts directed us to a thick, square table to receive our supper.

Lysia and Aegan proved to be exceedingly kind, but while we waited to be served, I began to grow nervous as more travelers shuffled into the tavern. Not many, less than half a dozen, but enough to be of concern should any of them recognize me as a witch and decide to claim me for a bounty. Though Emrys and I were legally married, the king had not yet given us his blessing, which meant I was guaranteed no protection just yet. Other than Emrys's own.

Emrys must have felt the same way, because he walked over to Aegan and said, "Thank you for everything, my friend. But I believe my bride and I should like to retire to our room for the night. Perhaps Lysia could send supper up for us?"

"She'd be happy to," Aegan said.

After accepting one more clap on the back from his friend, Emrys led me upstairs to our room. My knees trembled as I wondered what was expected of me tonight. What would our first night as a married couple be like?

Emrys's eyes followed my every move as I anxiously paced the room, wringing my hands.

"Well, my bride," Emrys said. "We have a little privacy, at last. A room of our own." His tongue slipped out to moisten his lips, and I swallowed hard.

Thankfully, Lysia interrupted us with swift knocks on the door moments later, and she entered to present us with supper. It turned out to be hearty stew and sweet red wine.

Emrys and I sat at the room's small table and I took my first bite. It reminded of Gran's rabbit stew that I could never quite replicate. Pain clenched my abdomen at the mere thought of my grandmother, a pang that I tried to force down because thinking about it right now would lead to nothing good. The grief would consume me, swallow me whole with ease if I let it. Instead, I tried to focus on the flavors in my mouth, and there were so many of them, all delectable. I must have made an audible noise of pleasure because I looked up to find Emrys staring at me.

"What?" I asked.

His eyes were alight with humor. "I've just never seen anyone enjoy food quite the way you do."

I sat up straighter and grabbed my goblet to take a sip of wine, which was also flavorful and cool on my tongue. "I imagine it's because you fae don't want for anything these days, and you don't have to scavenge the way we humans do in order to survive. You take food for granted, whereas I savor it."

Emrys's mouth tightened as he sipped his own wine. Maybe he'd never thought of that. "It wasn't always that way for my kind. Definitely not for me."

I thought about what he had revealed to me about his family and found it too awful to mention. Instead, I changed the subject. "This stew is delicious."

"I'm sure Lysia will be glad to hear it."

After we finished eating, an air of expectation hung in the room heavy, making the silence around us pregnant with an anxiety I felt compelled to address.

"What do we do now? Our first night as," I gulped, "a married couple."

I sat upon the edge of the bed, and Emrys sat next to me, his thigh touching mine. I stiffened, muscles tensing, pulse jumping. He leaned down and whispered in my ear, "You know, a marriage technically isn't legal until it's consummated. But it's your choice."

My cheeks flushed scarlet, my ears on fire. I had never been with a man. Aside from the wedding kiss with Emrys, I had only kissed a boy one other time before my parents moved us to the forest. Isolation in the woods did not create many opportunities for romance. And now... No, I could not do this. Could I?

Emrys pulled back and immediately frowned, his expression softening as he read the sheer panic on my face. "Relax, Red. I don't intend to force myself on you."

"But the marriage isn't legal if we don't."

"Technically. But it's not like the king is in our room watching us right now."

"What about the eye tattoos? Can he not see us through those?"

Emrys laughed at that. "No, the king does not keep track of the sex lives of his court through their marks."

"I need more wine," I choked out, and Emrys stood at once.

"Then I shall get you some more wine, my darling wife."

Emrys briefly left and returned with a fresh bottle of wine from downstairs a few minutes later. He poured more for both of us, and I gratefully tipped the cup into my mouth, downing the whole thing in one gulp. When I finished, I found Emrys watching with amusement.

"Is that good?" he asked.

"Delicious."

I grabbed a plump strawberry from the small pile Lysia had also provided for dessert, and took a bite, finding it, too, sweet and delicious. Once again, I felt Emrys watching me eat even as he chewed his own food thoughtfully, and I flushed under his gaze.

"Emrys, I... I don't think I'm ready to... consummate," I managed to choke out after I swallowed my last bite, despite the wine making my head a little fuzzy.

"That's fine," Emrys replied. "That can wait."

The way he said it made him sound fairly confident it was going to happen at some point. I almost pointed that out, but snapped my mouth shut instead and grabbed another strawberry.

"So," Emrys said. "Since we are wed now, I suppose we should at least learn a little more about each other. Things that lovers should know... should the king question our union."

"Alright." I bobbed my head in a nod. "What would you like to know?"

"Perhaps we will start with something simple. Like a favorite flower."

"Favorite flower?" I blinked, thinking about that for a moment. I did not need to think long. "Buttercups. They bloomed around our cabin in the spring in such vibrant, yellow patches. Yellow like the sun. I suppose I will likely never see those patches again."

Something inside of me broke at that, at the realization that everyone I had ever loved was dead, that I would never see home again, that I was about to be dragged into the beating heart of my enemy's civilization with no real guarantee that I would survive other than Emrys's word, who also happened to be my sworn enemy and former captor. This time, I could not help the tears that fell. I was able to control my tears in front of Emrys before but now they demanded to be released, and I was powerless to stop them. All at once I felt as though my chest had been hollowed out then filled with stones, my breath coming out in short spurts.

The next instant, I felt myself being lifted, and I was too gone with grief to protest. Emrys sat us both on the edge of the bed, drawing me into his lap and holding me, stroking my hair.

"Feel what you must, Red," he whispered. "Grief never gets easier. But it does get simpler."

My cheek was pressed against the soft material of his shirt, my tears soaking through it, accepting the comfort he offered. Emrys whispered more words to me in a fae tongue that I did not understand, nor was I coherent enough to ask.

He rocked me like a child, continuing to stroke my hair, and finally, I was able to reign my emotions back in. My grief was soon replaced by sheepishness and shame that I had allowed myself to break down like this.

"Why are you comforting me?" I asked, lifting my head and noting that I was still very much seated on his lap.

He quirked a brow as though the question was rather silly. "Well, you *are* my wife now. It's only natural that I care about your well-being, is it not? If my wife is beside herself with grief, it is my husbandly duty to comfort her."

I swiped the tear trails from my cheeks and rubbed my face. "I suppose so." I found my gaze sliding upward, over the gentle curve of his throat, up into his face, noticing how vibrant his eyes looked in the flickering candlelight. His arms were still around me, and his thumbs began to stroke my arm in soothing circles, his mouth parting slightly. I shivered, my gaze drifting toward his lips...

Oh, what was I doing? Did this faerie not have me in shackles just a couple of days prior, prepared to hand me over to his king for slaughter? I shook my head to clear it.

"I am tired, Emrys." Stretching my feet to the floor, I slid off of his lap, and Emrys released me, allowing me to stand.

"Yes. We do need rest for our journey," he agreed, and both of us looked to the one bed in the room at the same time. Emrys frowned as he stared at the bed as though the inanimate object might perform a trick at any moment. "I can sleep on the floor. If you'd prefer."

I considered it for a minute, then shook my head. "You just said our marriage technically isn't legal if we don't consummate. Should anyone manage to burst in while we sleep—Lysia could have another key for all we know—wouldn't it raise suspicion if we slept separately on our wedding night?"

Emrys nodded. "I suppose it would."

"I think we can at least trust that neither of us will slit the other's throat in the night, considering our agreement, so at least there's that." Plus, that kiss at the wedding... I found myself flushing even thinking about it. "You *won't* slit my throat, will you?"

"I have no plans to do as much. And you?"

"I need a path through the Void eventually, a means to get to safety, and I require protection in the meantime. So, no."

"Well, alright. We will share the bed. Which is good because I had no intention of sleeping on the floor."

"Then why—" I cut myself off mid-sentence. "You already knew I would say yes?"

He grinned. "Had a hunch."

"Such a gentleman," I grumbled.

"Not a man." His eyes narrowed. But then he blinked, maybe feeling as tired as I did. He pointed his chin toward the bed. "We should get a good night's sleep. We'll need to set out early tomorrow."

I got into bed and Emrys climbed in beside me, sliding under the covers. I felt his warmth against my side; this bed wasn't very big. I drew my body tight as a bow string.

"Again, you must relax, Red," he murmured, low voice soft behind me, though he may as well be talking directly into my ear. "We may have no choice but to touch considering the size of the bed, but I promise I won't intentionally lay any hands on you." He hesitated as though he might add the word *yet,* but thankfully he did not.

I tried to breathe, to relax, but I still found myself stiff. Emrys was the first to drift off, and I could hear him murmuring in his sleep. I wondered if he was experiencing the same nightmare of his family being killed. Former captor or not, I still could not help but feel sorry for him having to witness such a horrific scene as a young child.

Slowly, I turned over to face Emrys. He was lying on his back, one arm crooked beneath his head, another folded above the sheets over his chest. While asleep, he looked peaceful. And now, I found myself curious, having never been this close to a faerie in my life. My eyes drifted to the points of his ears. They looked soft, not sharp. For some strange reason, I found myself compelled to reach out and gently touch the tip of the ear closest to me, purely for curiosity's sake.

The second I made contact, barely a gossamer of a touch, Emrys's eyes flew open and his hand shot out to snatch my wrist in an iron grip. I gasped, surprised that tiny touch had woken him up.

Emrys blinked in confusion for a moment before registering whose hand he held. His voice was husky as he spoke. "A little tip, Red. Fae ears are very sensitive, so best to never touch them unless you have other plans for the fae that involve torture or fucking. Do you have either of those planned for me?"

"No," I replied too quickly. "Neither."

"Then perhaps tread more cautiously."

I nodded and attempted to snatch my hand back, my face flushed with pure mortification, but Emrys still held me tight, refusing to let go. Stars, what had I been doing? "I'm sorry," I said. "I didn't mean to wake you. I should have kept my hands to myself."

"Just say the word if you want this marriage properly consummated."

Suddenly, he yanked the wrist he was holding, placing my hand, palm down, against a hardened bulge that I quickly realized was all Emrys. My eyes widened even further, my flush deepening. He really was not joking about their ears being sensitive, and I could feel the evidence right under my hand.

"Do you understand now?" he said.

"I... no. I mean, yes, but that's not what I... I didn't know about the ears." I found myself sputtering, yanking my hand back when he finally released me.

"Well, now you do." He sucked a long, deep breath through his teeth. "Gods, Red, are you trying to kill me? Because if you'd prefer to break our agreement and go back to the shackles, that can be arranged."

"No."

"Then go to sleep. And stop touching things you know nothing about. Unless you don't care about the consequences that will follow."

"I'll be good," I said, feeling as though my flames might burst through my face unprompted.

Emrys grumbled and shook his head, letting out another long, drawn-out breath as he attempted—I assumed—to calm himself down. I did the same, turning away from him again and vowing not to move until I finally heard Emrys's steady breathing indicating he'd fallen back asleep.

Thank goddess.

For a while, I listened to his breathing, but I was restless, especially after what just happened. We didn't have any more water in the room, and I was parched. I hoped it was late enough that the tavern would be empty and I could slip through undetected. Earlier, Lysia had mentioned there being extra water available at the bar.

Holding my breath so as to not wake Emrys, I carefully slid out from under the sheets. I looked to the sleeping fae, my now husband, and he did not stir. Quietly, I slipped outside the door and eased it shut behind me so that it only made a gentle click. I tip-toed down the stairs barefoot, the stone steps cold beneath my feet. Everything was dark with the sconces all snuffed out for the night.

"*Sorcha,*" I whispered, sparking a small light upon my fingertips to lead the way.

I poked my head around the wall at the base of the steps. The tavern was empty, and I sighed in relief. It should be safe.

I crossed the cold stone floor toward the bar, found the water Lysia had promised, and scooped a little out with one of the clean cups behind the bar. I took a sip and closed my eyes, letting the water cool the back of my parched throat.

A noise from behind made me freeze, and I lowered my cup and spun around. Two fae stood behind me in the darkness, blocking my exit, one taller with blonde hair and one shorter with dark hair. Where had they come from?

"Well, well, well," the taller fae said to the other, eyes drinking in my body. "Looks like it is our lucky day."

14

Rose

THE TWO FAE LEERED AT ME IN A WAY THAT made my blood boil, and now the other one spoke, the shorter one with the dark hair. "Our lucky day, indeed."

"I smell a human whore." My eyes widened because I recognized their voices. The enchanter fae that I'd trapped in my magic at the cabin, the ones who Emrys and I had heard in the woods on horseback. They didn't know I was the same person that fled the cabin, however, because they never got a good look at me, nor I at them.

"She will get us great bounty with the king."

"Touch me and lose your limbs just before I put a hex on you, shriveling your balls." I knew no such spell, not even a single hex, but these brutes didn't need to know that. I only wished I had my sword on me. I wanted to murder them for enchanting my grandmother, for causing her to kill herself to protect me. They were responsible.

To demonstrate my power, I summoned the fire in my hand once again and tossed it at the wall behind the fae, lighting two of the sconces with fresh flames. To my dismay, the fae did not flinch.

"And a witch. We really *are* in luck, Callum! Our bounty just went way up," said the dark-haired one.

"I will not being going anywhere with brutish bastards like you," I fired back.

"And the little witch bitch has quite the mouth on her!" the blonde one—Callum—added. He was all muscle and thick limbs and sharp angles, his voice gruff, whereas his companion was shorter and lankier, his features a bit softer, his voice not quite as menacing. Though they still scared me equally right now in this dark tavern.

My muscles tensed, but before I had a chance to fight, a feral snarl sounded behind me.

"You dare insult my wife?"

Emrys stepped from behind me, emerging from the shadows. The sconces I'd just relit flickered, highlighting every curve of his jutting cheekbones.

"Emrys," Callum said, eyes widening in recognition. "What are you doing here?"

Emrys put his arm around my shoulders protectively, drawing me close as he spoke. "You are interrupting my wedding night, Callum. And I don't much appreciate it."

The fae Callum barked a laugh, thinking this a joke. But his face darkened as he realized that Emrys wasn't joining in his laughter. "You cannot be serious. You've married *a witch?*"

"Her name is *Rose.* She is my *wife.* And you would be wise to treat her accordingly." Emrys's arm tightened around me, molding me against his side. "Apologize to her right now, or I'll tear out your tongue and feed it to you."

"You... *what?* Now you're threatening me?" The faerie shook his head, perplexed. "She has bewitched you."

"No."

"We do not *bewitch*," I interjected, feeling outright offended by the accusation. It was a common misconception about witches that the fae loved to circulate, as though we just went about casually casting spells that bent the masses to our will. "You fae are the ones who enchant people into doing things against their better judgment. Witches do no such thing."

Callum ignored me as though I hadn't even spoken. He just kept addressing Emrys, making me even angrier. "I find that hard to believe. I should think you would be out looking for bounty, not a bride."

"This was unexpected," Emrys replied. "And you still haven't apologized."

"Nor will I." Callum's square jaw twitched. "I never understood the king's fondness for you, given your sheer idiocy."

"I've never cared a lick about your approval, Callum." Emrys kept his best neutral expression, though his jaw clenched, and his iron grip did not move from around my shoulders. "And I think you'd best be on your way now. You too, Talyn. You've never been anything more than Callum's lap dog, anyway."

The fae named Talyn growled at that and took a menacing step forward. Emrys raised his chin, daring him to attack. Callum placed his arm in front of Talyn's chest, holding him back. "It is not worth it, Talyn. Let's go, and leave the traitor to his witch."

"Watch your words." Emrys's tone was laced with poison, but the two fae sneered.

"I very much look forward to your hundred cuts," Callum said.

Emrys's nostrils flared, but he said nothing.

The pair walked away, cursing to each other before disappearing out the tavern door. Once they were gone, Emrys let out a long, deep sigh, slowly unclenching his jaw. "The only reason they aren't two blood stains on the floor right now is because I don't want to implicate Aegan and Lysia. They are responsible for whatever happens inside their establishment."

I changed the subject. "What are the hundred cuts?"

"No matter," Emrys replied quickly. "Are you alright?"

"Fine."

"Good. Now get back to bed."

It was an order, and I'd had my fill of being ordered around by him. I ducked out from under Emrys's arm and turned to face him. "I am going back to our room, but I won't be staying there for long." I strode back toward the stairs with a purpose, my face red and my body trembling with rage. Emrys grabbed my arm.

"What are you planning to do?" he asked.

"I am going to retrieve my sword so I can kill those two bastards," I replied through clenched teeth.

Emrys shook his head. "No, you aren't. They are part of the high king's court with me, and we want the king to accept our union. You killing members of his court will not do us any favors."

"I do not care. Let go of me." But Emrys's grip tightened around my wrist in response, making me wince as he pressed down where my flesh was still raw from the cuffs. My chin darted up and I looked him in the eye. "Remember, they were the ones who came into my cabin and enchanted my grandmother. I *know* it was them."

"You say that, yet I did not encounter them in the woods that day. Nor did I smell them. Although, I *was* quite preoccupied with *your* scent at the time."

"I set a witch's trap in the kitchen." At Emrys's puzzled look, I felt the need to explain. "Witches' traps are specific to each witch, harnessing their specific elemental inclination. Since my strongest power is fire, I trapped them inside a ring of flame. The trap likely held them for long enough that we didn't cross paths, but obviously they found a way out."

Emrys sighed, his grip slackening. "I am sorry. About your grandmother. And Callum and Talyn are no friends of mine," he said.

"You did not need to rescue me, you know. I could have handled them."

"By *handle them* you mean use magic? Not a good idea for a human witch to use defensive magic in a fae establishment. Besides, the pair of them are strong. They could make you turn your fire on yourself with a simple sentence. I have seen them do similar."

That was true. I had seen firsthand how strong their enchantments were, if my grandmother was any example. I shuddered.

"Also," Emrys continued, "even if you were capable of killing them, I could not allow it. For the reasons I have already stated. More importantly, I cannot have you just wandering around anywhere you like and getting yourself into trouble. What were you thinking just now? Sneaking out of the room like that in the middle of the night?"

My eyes narrowed. "Am I your wife or still your prisoner? I didn't realize needing a glass of water was a crime."

"It isn't, but you should've woken me. There are plenty who would not hesitate to... To do awful things to you. Which is an even bigger risk in the lawless land outside the castle walls. You *are* my wife now. Believe it or not, I do not wish to see you come to harm. Not anymore."

I sniffled and lifted my head. "Not before I've had a chance to break your curse, you mean."

Emrys did not answer at first, though his mouth curved down, a slight twitching at the edges. He finally said, "Come back to bed. Right now. We have a long journey to the castle tomorrow."

He brushed past me but paused at the base of the stairs, waiting for me to follow. After a moment's hesitation, I did, complying with his request because, truth be told, I was quite exhausted.

As we lay down in the single bed once again, I turned away from him, shifting toward the edge of the mattress as far as I could get in the small confines. In the darkness, I felt his eyes upon me, watching me until I finally drifted off to sleep.

15

Emrys

IT WAS A PECULIAR THING, WAKING UP NEXT TO a witch. And even more peculiar that I felt a smile ghost my lips at the sight of her. This was nothing I'd ever have imagined as a boy, trembling in fear of their kind. Nor in later years, delivering them to the king for bounty. Why did this witch affect me so?

She was far different than I had expected. Brave, no doubt. Stubborn as an ox. Resourceful. There was also a softness that she tried to hide. But it was there. Often bubbling to the surface when she least expected it to.

The morning sun was just barely peeking above the horizon. It streamed through the window and cast a perfect beam across her hair. Made it seem aflame where it lay splayed out upon the pillow. Her small form breathed evenly. The breaths of someone still slumbering soundly. She slept on her side, her fist curved under her chin. Her delicate features a mask of peacefulness that likely wouldn't last while she was awake.

So, I decided not to wake her. Not just yet.

Quiet as a field mouse, I slid out of bed and dressed. Lysia would have breakfast sent up soon. After, Rose and I must leave immediately to stay on schedule. I planned to help Aegan and Lysia gather provisions. But when I got downstairs, I found Aegan already waiting for me in the tavern.

"How did you find your accommodations?" Aegan asked. He leaned in conspiratorially. "And your bride?"

I had expected such a line of questioning. I chose my words carefully. "I found them both to be... quite... satisfactory."

Aegan nudged me with his elbow, teeth flashing in a grin. "I'll bet you did."

I could only provide an awkward smile in return. Mercifully, Aegan changed the subject.

"Lysia is preparing breakfast," he said, just as I'd expected. "But I am glad I found you first. We've got something to give you."

I had no idea what that could be. But I was quickly clued in when Aegan led me outside to the stables and placed his hand on the muzzle of a stallion in the first stall. "This is your wedding present. His name is Stardust."

Aegan stroked the muzzle of the stallion fondly. He was black with elongated, white spots that could've resembled shooting stars. His name seemed apt.

"I cannot accept," I said, shaking my head. "It is far too much."

"Honestly, the horse likely only has a couple more good years of service left. We have someone coming in next week to bring us two new, younger horses."

"Two new horses? Business must be good."

"We do alright," Aegan replied. "But please, take the horse. Let it make your journey to the castle easier with your new bride. Then let him live out his remaining days being spoiled in the kingdom stables."

"Very well. I cannot thank you and Lysia enough for your hospitality."

"I've said it once and I will say it again." Aegan clapped a hand on my shoulder. "Anything for you, my boy."

"If you truly mean that, Aegan, then... I may have to ask you the biggest favor of all. Sometime soon."

"Name it."

I lowered my voice to a near whisper. "You once said that you and Lysia knew a way through the Void. To the Outerlands."

Aegan's eyes widened in surprise. "Lysia has a theory. A very good one. Though it is untested, Emrys."

"How much do you trust Lysia's hunch?"

Aegan did not hesitate in his response. "I have the utmost faith in my wife. And if she believes something to be true, then I believe *her*. But why do you ask this?"

My voice dropped lower still. "Because I may ask you to secure safe passage for someone through the Void."

His thick brows shot up nearly to his hairline. "Truly?"

"Yes."

"Rose?"

"Yes."

"But why?"

"I believe it best I do not answer that, Aegan. But... you are certain you can help Rose? That she can get safely through to the Outerlands?"

"Without you? My boy, what are you planning?"

"Please do not ask me that, Aegan. Just assure me that your Void plan is solid. That Rose will not come to harm." My voice must have sounded more desperate than I realized. Because Aegan regarded me with a knowing yet slightly bemused expression.

"My goodness, you are already feeling very protective over your wife, aren't you?"

"Perhaps." I frowned. "Is that the blood bond?" Never had I expected to feel like this over a witch. Like I wanted to tear the throat out of anyone who even looked at her the wrong way.

"The blood bond will cause pain when you separate and allows you to empathize with your spouse more effectively.

It may enhance feelings of protectiveness. That's just natural. But..."

"But what?"

"Aside from the pain of separation and empathy, the blood bond cannot enhance anything that wasn't there to begin with. Which means on some level, you must've already felt protective over her."

"Huh." I bobbed my head, contemplating his words. Troubling. "It seems I still have much to learn about the bond, as well. Will it affect Rose the same way?"

Aegan shrugged. "Human and fae marriages have not been seen in decades. But my understanding is that your human wife will be affected on a lesser scale. Where you feel physical pain upon separation, she will feel a strong compulsion to return to you."

I had known a little about the pain of separation, but I also knew there were ways to lessen its effects. However, the rest of it was turning out to be more complicated than I had imagined. Suddenly, I feared the soundness of my decision making.

"Why did I not know much of this?" I asked aloud.

"Because you never inquired, I imagine. You lost your parents too young for them to give you the full marriage talk." Aegan clamped a hand on my shoulder. "But rest assured, if Lysia and I decide to go through with traversing the Void, we will guarantee Rose's safety."

"I would compensate you both handsomely for your troubles."

Aegan chewed his lower lip, his gaze drifting. "May we think about it? You know we would do anything for you. But I must run this by Lysia, as well, before we can make any decisions."

"Of course." I smiled tightly, confident they would come through for me. They always had. "I will send word. I would love to visit longer, but Rose and I must be leaving shortly. We still have yet to receive the king's blessing."

"I do wish I could be a fly on the wall when you tell the king this news." Aegan smiled once again. "And we figured you would dash off. Which is why Lysia is packing your breakfast for the road."

Rose met us outside, as did Lysia with breakfast wrapped in cloth. She placed the bundle snuggly in my satchel. Rose thanked them for their hospitality and they bid us a warm farewell. When I led Stardust out of the stables, Rose's mouth formed a little "O" in question.

"I thought you said you didn't use horses?" She stroked the animal's muzzle gently. Stardust let out a puff of breath through flapping lips. He seemed already taken with her. Perhaps I was, as well.

"Not typically. But who am I to turn down a wedding gift? That would be rude."

"A wedding gift? From Aegan and Lysia?"

"Yes."

"I should go back to thank them."

"I already thanked them on your behalf. Come, Red, we need to get going. Unless you'd prefer to continue on foot."

"No, I suppose this is much easier," Rose said. At once, I grasped her waist to lift her onto the horse. She stiffened, her fingers curving around my wrists to halt my motions.

"What are you doing?"

"Am I not allowed to assist my bride in mounting a horse?"

"I am perfectly capable—"

But even as she said the words, I was already lifting her up. She was rather light and I lifted her with ease onto the saddle. Though her features pulled into a mask of annoyance, she said nothing. Instead, she swung her leg around to mount the horse properly. Even as I climbed onto the horse behind her, she did not protest nor demand the reins. I imagined it was quite hard for her to bite her tongue. Much like a bird trying to fight its impulse to fly.

It had been some time since I'd ridden. Though I was raised on horses, and riding was a skill one did not forget. Rose settled in between my legs. Her back and ass pressed against my chest and groin, respectively. It made me twitch in a way I'd dare not say out loud. If she felt the evidence of my inconvenient arousal, she said nothing. I cleared my throat and snapped the reins.

"On we go," I said.

Stardust had barely taken two steps when Rose squirmed again. She adjusted her position in front of me. Perhaps attempting to make herself more comfortable. The result was making *me...* uncomfortable. I placed a hand upon her thigh to still her movements. Squeezed just above her knee.

"You might want to stop squirming, Red," I murmured. My lips hovered above the tuft of red hair that concealed her ear. "Unless you *want* me to drag you off this horse and consummate our marriage on the spot."

She stilled immediately. Though once again I could hear her pulse racing as she leaned close. I drew a deep breath as we set out on the final leg of our journey. And with Rose nestled between my legs as she was, I imagined it would be a long one. The gods had indeed sent this witch to kill me; I was sure of it.

I flicked the reins harder and Stardust took off at a gallop.

Closing the final distance between us and the kingdom.

THE KINGDOM

16

Rose

THREE MORE DAYS PASSED. EMRYS AND I SPENT our days on horseback, our nights curled up on opposite sides of a fire exchanging tidbits about our likes and dislikes, should the king question our relationship. My legs were increasingly sore and stiff—I was not used to riding, especially not for such extended periods of time.

On the last night, Emrys sat on the ground leaning against a tree trunk, his elbow propped on his knee as he idly munched on a plum.

"Your favorite food?" he asked. "Other than rabbit stew, of course."

I only had to think for a second. "Chocolate. My grandfather used to bring me some as a young child. It was a rare treat—he'd have to barter in town for weeks to get some—but I remember loving it so much. I haven't tasted its sweetness in many years."

"Chocolate? Well, you're in luck, then. The king usually serves some at his banquets."

Of course, he did. Somehow, that left a bitter taste in my mouth.

Emrys chewed his last bite thoughtfully before tossing his plum pit aside. I wasn't hungry. My jitters made it nearly impossible to eat the closer we got to the castle. I rubbed my palms near the fire. It was already unseasonably chilly, which meant we'd be in for a long, rough winter.

Emrys must have seen me shudder, because he asked, "Are you cold?"

"I'm fine."

Soundlessly, he stood and wrapped his own cloak around my shoulders. I frowned as he returned to his spot to sit.

"Why did you do that?" I asked.

He shrugged. "My wife was cold. I gave her my cloak."

I pulled the rough material tighter around my neck—it smelled like him. "But why are you keeping the husband charade going when no one else is around to see?"

"Charade?" He rubbed his chin. "I *am* your husband now, am I not?"

"Yes, I suppose, but—"

"Would you prefer worse treatment?"

"No, that's not what I meant." I squeezed my eyes shut and sighed. "I'm just saying that you don't have to pretend when no one is around."

"Red." I blinked and met his gaze. His golden eyes flashed in the flickering flames. "Who said I'm pretending?"

With that, he stood again and crouched nearer to the fire to stoke the dwindling flames with a thick branch as Stardust, who was tied to a nearby tree, huffed loudly.

"What do you mean?" I asked.

"What I mean is that, witch or no, you'll likely be the only wife I ever have. I intend to do it the right way in the limited time we are allotted." He dropped the stoking branch and caught my gaze across the fire. "You do realize that once a fae marries, it is for life. Divorce isn't an option like with you humans."

"Then why did you agree—"

"Because I will honor our vows until death. A death that is swiftly coming for me."

"What happens if a faerie divorces?"

His mouth curved into a slight smirk, the scar around his eye flexing. "As I said, not an option."

"Why not?"

"Our marriages are bound by blood."

I paused, thinking about how we cut our hands and pressed them together during the wedding ceremony. My hand had started to warm and tingle, the feeling rushing to my head, my heart. "What exactly does the bond mean?"

"It means that if we physically stray too far from each other, we will feel the pull back toward each other. You are human, so what you will feel is a compulsion to return to me. A faerie spouse, however, will feel physical pain."

Stars. I wished I had known that before. Being married to a faerie was one thing, but being blood bound? I did not like it one bit. "How is that supposed to work for us?"

Another shrug. "I am used to pain."

"And what about my compulsion to return? That's not ideal when my plan is to leave."

"There are ways to dampen those feelings. For both of us. When we know we must separate, we bring a vial of each other's blood along. Now, do you have any other questions?"

"Yes. Millions." I sighed. "But I am tired. I'll ask later."

Emrys laid on the opposite side of the fire again, his hands braced under his head, his long body stretched out on the ground. I dozed off, curled up in a second cloak.

The next morning, a sense of dread crept through my belly. It was the first official day of Autumn, and we were nearly to the castle, according to my husband.

My husband.

Oh, what a strange thing to say.

My blood-bound fae husband was about to present me to his king who would much rather I die or live in enslavement than wed one of his own. I was the most nervous I had ever been; my life quite literally hung in the balance.

I sat in front of Emrys again, wedged between his legs on the back of a horse, as I had been for the past several days. At some point, as the horse slowed, he pulled the reins into one hand and his arm gently curved around my hip, his free hand resting idly on my thigh as though he'd done so without thinking. I could feel the warmth from his skin soak through the fabric of my dress, and I did my best to ignore the unexpected tingle that simple action sent through me.

Ahead, the woods opened up into rolling hills, which quickly became larger, rockier. Not mountains, but the terrain was uneven enough to slow down the journey. Stardust trudged beneath us, but he seemed less happy about our path and let out annoyed huffs every so often to make it known.

And then, there it was. The kingdom loomed large in front of us, and my nerves grew even worse.

We passed by some homes grouped together around the outside of the castle town, mostly farms with pens containing goats and sheep that bleated softly. We continued past them until we reached a towering stone wall, easily five stories high.

"The city walls," Emrys clarified.

The walls stretched around the entire perimeter of the town, with tall guard towers spread out at even distances and massive, thick gates.

Just as we arrived, Emrys halted Stardust and leaned forward to speak into my ear. "We're wed, so you have nothing to fear as long as I'm by your side," Emrys said. "But best to not stir up a crowd before the king has had his chance to give us his blessing. Keep your hood up."

I could not help but notice that, now that we'd stopped and he no longer needed to hold the reins in either hand, his palm still rested on my thigh. I also couldn't help but notice that I still made no move to brush his hand away.

I complied with his request, flipping up the hood of my cloak over my head. Emrys dismounted Stardust and reached up to help me down. Even though I didn't need the help, I accepted, and his hands went about my waist and gently lowered me to the ground.

"You keep Stardust calm. I'll do the talking," Emrys said, his hands lingering on my waist longer than they probably should have.

"Halt. Identify yourself!" a guard shouted down from a tower window several stories up. Emrys released me and stepped forward to speak as I stroked Stardust's muzzle.

"I am Emrys Abrynth, of the king's court."

"Oh, Emrys!" the guard called back. I couldn't make out his features from the ground. "I almost didn't recognize you. Who is the female in the red cloak?" The guard whistled down at me. "Oy, why don't you speak, miss?"

"She is no concern of yours. That is a matter to discuss with the king," Emrys replied simply.

"A bounty, eh? You don't usually bring 'em in on horseback." I could hear the smirk in his voice, and my cheeks began to warm.

"As I said, this is a matter I will discuss directly with the king."

Emrys didn't bother correcting the guard about the bounty part though. I wasn't quite sure if anger or anxiousness was winning out, but I had to trust Emrys knew best how to handle this situation. These were his people, after all. I said nothing and kept my head down.

"Alright then." I peeked up under my hood as the guard made a sweeping gesture out of the turret. "Enter at will. Take your horse to the stables."

The massive gates slowly opened with loud clacks, swinging wide. Emrys and I passed through unencumbered and guided Stardust inside.

The town itself once belonged to a human king who was eradicated decades ago, his court burned or strung up by the neck, if not already maimed in battle. The fae had their own castle—more than one, in fact—which were invaded by witches long ago. The faeries responded with force, overpowering human warriors and claiming this kingdom as their own. Ours was a complicated history.

We passed through a second arch carved from stone, and the thriving city opened up in front of us, all surrounding the castle in the middle that rose up like a stone sentinel watching over the land. The city was massive from my perspective, a labyrinth of streets and alleys winding in all directions, leading me to believe the fae had expanded after taking over.

"Stables first," Emrys said.

The stables were adjacent to the city gates, a stone's throw from them. The stalls went on and on, filled with more horses than I could count, more than I'd ever seen in my life.

"Everyone keeps their horses here, and they're all very well cared for," Emrys explained. "In this community, we share. If someone else's horse falls ill, and they require one for a journey, another available horse is volunteered."

"Do you all share everything?" I asked.

"In a sense. If someone is low on coin and unable to buy supplies or food, their neighbors step up and spare what they can. It's what keeps this community thriving. Granted, the king has the best of everything and the most of everything. But to his credit, he makes sure that none in his kingdom go wholly without. In that way, he is a good, just king."

"Right, *good* and *just,*" I said, unable to stop the accompanying snort.

In fairness, this *was* a good way to live. In human towns and kingdoms, there were often the poor who no one else seemed to care about, and while some communities were very generous with each other, there were others who only looked out for themselves and didn't much care who was starving. I had to give the fae credit for their sense of camaraderie. But that didn't stop me from being angry at all they had taken from us, either.

"You'll be alright, Stardust," I said, stroking his soft muzzle once more as Emrys led him into an empty stall. My hand shook—maybe I was speaking more to myself than the horse, terrified at the thought of being behind enemy lines for the first time.

"I know you're nervous. Your heart gives you away every time." Emrys spoke close, his breath tickling the shell of my ear, and I jumped, so lost in thought that I hadn't heard him sneak up behind me. His hand gently touched the small of my back. "Remember, stay by my side until we receive the king's blessing. You'll be safe."

His words were meant to soothe, but it was hard to find any reassurance under the circumstances.

I turned my attention back to Stardust; the stall already had a bucket of water and a pile of hay ready. The horses really were well cared for, which made me feel better—for the horse, at least. It was tough to find a silver lining for my own situation, other than the fact that I wasn't being led here in cuffs.

Once Stardust was settled, Emrys led me away from the stables into the thick of town, his hand resting at the small of my back to guide me, or maybe even to subtly demonstrate possession to any who might get ideas. I mostly kept my head down to avoid eye contact and conceal my features, though I couldn't help but steal glimpses at my surroundings.

Faeries were everywhere. They were a diverse bunch, coming in all shades, shapes, sizes, and forms. Some lighter skinned, some darker skinned, some tall, some short. Some looked relatively human aside from their ears, while others possessed strange eye colors, wings, or animal visages, if they were shifters in their shifted form.

There were rows of quaint homes behind rows of shops selling meats, trinkets, and various wares, along with the occasional tavern. Decadent smells wafted toward my nostrils from a nearby bakery. Rowdy music drifted across the cobbled street, played by a bard in the square. Fae were laughing and dancing and... I spent so much of my life in the woods, I'd forgotten what camaraderie amongst others of my people felt like. I was jealous of what these fae had. Envious that they could live so carefree now while my kind were still slaughtered. Emrys must have sensed this, because he shifted uncomfortably beside me and reached for my hand, but I snatched it away. The anger bubbled up inside of me again, threatening to boil over.

"I know what you must think of us," Emrys whispered. "But please do not withdraw now. We must present a united front to the king so that he will believe our union to be genuine."

I sighed and drew a deep breath as we entered a large, pretty square, surrounded by tall, evenly spaced trees that rose like a crown around the courtyard, with a fountain in the middle. The sculpture in the fountain was a depiction of who I assumed was the fae king. Indeed, underneath was an inscription that read: *High King Armynd*. His chest was puffed out, chin raised, leg propped up as though claiming the fountain itself in his name, impressive wings folded at his sides. I stared at the stone likeness, suddenly chilled that we would be meeting him in the flesh very soon.

As we continued down the cobblestone street, we were surrounded by small carts, fruit stands, and mingling faeries. Even some low fae flittered about, darting in the air between buildings. They'd obviously wandered too far from their clans in the woods and got caught in serving their high fae masters. They seemed to act as little messengers and errand runners, bringing things to shop keepers and buzzing about like busy bees building a hive.

"Explain the different types of fae to me again?" I asked, trying to distract myself from my nerves. I yanked my hood lower over my eyes again when we passed too near a group of chattering fae.

"Well, you met the low fae," Emrys said. "They are what they are. Whereas the high fae come in many different varieties. Glamourer fae are the most common—those who can create illusions. Shifter fae are the second most common, and conjurer fae are a bit rarer. Most enchanter fae often possess the ability to use glamours as well. But those are the rarest."

"And the fae with wings?"

"They typically also possess glamour abilities to hide their wings at will. Although, the wing trait is becoming rarer amongst fae. These days, it's considered somewhat of a privilege to be born with wings. The sign of descending from a truly pure fae bloodline."

I nodded like I understood, but my head spun.

A small leather ball rolled near Emrys's feet then, accompanied by the sounds of squeals and cheers. Fae children. Emrys bent to pick up the ball and tossed it into the air, catching it in his palm.

"And just who does this belong to?" Emrys asked, a playful twinkle in his gold eyes.

A small, adorable boy with pink cheeks wandered forward, head down, his pointed ears twitching beneath his mop of blonde hair. I peered at him under my hood, and while he cast curious stares in my direction, he said nothing to me, instead addressing Emrys directly. "I'm sorry to hit you. The ball is mine."

"Perhaps I shall teach you how to aim," Emrys chuckled as he stepped forward. He handed the child his ball back and affectionately ruffled the top of his hair, making the boy smile. "Now, run along. And watch where you throw."

The children squealed and ran off, chasing each other around the courtyard without a care in the world. The children did not pay attention to me, nor did anyone else. That was good. I knew that feeling would not last, but I was somewhat comforted for the time being. I kept my hood drawn up around my face.

Close by, a faerie child fell and scraped his knee. His mother ran over to soothe him, something very human. It seemed a common thread amongst all species, caring for one's young—no matter how otherwise despicable that species, as a whole, may have been.

The town appeared to be set up in a sort of giant semi-circle. Rows of homes, then rows of shops with a central square in the middle, with the tall, dark stone castle not too far from the central square. The castle was surrounded by a wide moat, crossable only by a drawbridge. I craned my neck to look up at the towering, sprawling structure dotted with multiple, wide turrets, its upper walls jagged like teeth that could likely conceal archers too.

When we approached, once again, Emrys identified himself. The drawbridge slowly lowered with stiff clanks of metal and wood until it was level for us to walk upon and cross the moat. As we entered the castle itself, I began trembling anew.

The king—and my fate—awaited.

Emrys led me inside, taking my hand. As we walked, I was stricken by how beautiful the castle was. Whereas the outside was nothing but cold stone, the inside was decorated rather warmly, with plenty of windows around the sides—that had not been visible from the front—to let in light, multiple, flickering wall sconces, and brightly colored, marble flooring. The hallways twisted and turned, going on forever. A grand, sweeping staircase curved off to the right, and Emrys led me away from its base down a narrower corridor.

"What is it?" he asked, observing my expression.

"The town is so bustling and everyone seems so happy. As you said, no one goes without here. The castle is beautiful, and I imagine your quarters here are quite nice as well."

His eyes narrowed and he cast a sidelong glance. "What are you trying to say, Red?"

"I just don't understand how you can live in such opulence and still wish to die."

Emrys halted abruptly at that, spinning on his heel to look me directly in the eye. "Do you think all I care about is material goods? Do you think I wouldn't trade all of this for one more day with my family? Because I would. In a heartbeat."

He spun again and strode ahead of me, and I had to jog to keep up with his long legs. "Please, don't be cross with me. This situation is hard enough on me without my fake husband being unhappy with me as well."

"Not fake."

"You know what I mean."

He sighed as though attempting to exhale his annoyance. "Well, we are almost to the throne room now. Do not fear. And remember, we must convince him to accept our union."

With those words hanging in the air, we entered the throne room.

And I had my first real glimpse of the high fae king.

17

Rose

THE OPULENCE ALL AROUND ME MOMENTARILY took my breath away. Everything dripped gold, with statue busts and bold art lining the walls along with dozens of marble pillars. The art and statues depicted fae, while stunning green and gold trees grew up the walls behind the pillars, spread in even increments between the art, their branches and leaves snaking up towards the ceiling. The overall impression was that of an art exhibit in the middle of a gilded forest, one fit for a high king.

Up a set of ten steps at the far end of the room sat an ornate throne occupied by the king. Its high back was also made of gilded metal that had been twisted into the likeness of a tree, the branches curving over King Armynd's head. He was flanked by two guards on either side. Where was his queen? I would have to ask Emrys later.

Our footsteps clacked on the marble floor as we approached across the long room, and I couldn't help but keep my eyes trained on the king.

Unlike Emrys, the king had wings, which he didn't bother hiding. In fact, when we entered the throne room, his black wings—which looked like fine, slightly worn leather—were fully spread, nearly spanning the length of the room on either side behind those who flanked him. My guess was he often kept his wings out while seated in his throne as a means to demonstrate how powerful he was. Much like a person trying to make themselves large to scare away an animal. This was a show of intimidation, and it was working. The king—and his wings—were larger than any faerie I'd seen so far. His angular face was calm and astute, his brown eyes wide set and a shade lighter than his skin. His nose was sloped on the bridge yet pointed at the end, almost beak like, which seemed fitting for a creature with wings. Atop his head, to complete the look, sat a glinting, spiked crown.

Perched on either side of the throne were two large hawks. Once we stopped walking, they sprang up and promptly transformed into two faerie guards mid-air. Their nimble feet landed in unison like this was an act they had performed hundreds of times. The pair were clad in polished armor and held swords at the ready. A step or two up from them, off to the side of the throne, stood the two brutes Callum and Talyn. The sight of them made me bristle.

Finally, to the king's right stood someone who was his spitting image, and I could only imagine that to be his son; the resemblance was too striking to be coincidence. Same wide-set, brown eyes, same dark hair, same nose, except slightly less pointed at the end, his features all just a little softer than his father's. That must make him the prince, though he also lacked his father's wings, and something else seemed a little off about his face. There was a shimmering just above the skin, and I had to wonder if I was looking at some sort of faerie glamour.

"Come closer!" King Armynd waved us forward. His voice boomed.

Emrys stayed close by my side as we finished crossing the last stretch of the long room. Once directly in front of King Armynd, Emrys took a knee and gestured for me to do the same. I complied, bowing my head, grateful to not have to make eye contact with the intimidating king just yet.

"Your highness," Emrys said, addressing him formally.

"You may rise and speak," the king bellowed, and I obeyed, subconsciously edging closer to Emrys on wobbly knees.

My mouth was dry; this was the moment I had been dreading most. My life was now cradled in the king's large hands, his to decide whether to save or crush.

"Tell me of your latest quest, Emrys. And tell me who this person is beside you. Remove your hood, please." King Armynd addressed me directly. With shaking fingers, I brushed back my hood, fighting the urge to cringe as the fae king laid eyes upon me for the first time. I drew a deep, trembling breath and finally met his gaze. The king's mouth fell open at the sight of me, and I felt dangerously close to losing my breakfast right there on the polished, marble floor.

"I will explain," Emrys said, and the king nodded.

"Yes, you had better. I'd heard a rumor, and not a good one. But I had to see it for myself. So, tell me in your own words."

"This is my wife." Emrys's fingers circled my hand and gave a squeeze. Surely, he heard my heartbeat and sensed how utterly frightened I was.

The king scoffed. "I send you out to collect bounty, and you come back married. What am I to think?"

"I ask only that you keep an open mind," Emrys said.

"And the witch knows what you do, and she's fine with this?" His gaze shifted pointedly to me.

"She is quite aware," Emrys said.

"Let her speak," Armynd scolded.

I cleared my throat and forced myself to reply in a voice barely above a dry squeak. "I know all about Emrys's profession, and his past, and I entered into marriage with him willingly and with my eyes fully open."

The king tipped his head. "Why ever would you do such a thing?"

"Because we have seen past each other's differences," I explained. "We... saw each other's hearts." I prayed I sounded convincing.

"You catch me off guard." The king's attention shifted back to Emrys. He threw up his hands, lips pressed together. "Well, since you two have seen fit to elope without my blessing, I know nothing about your bride." His gaze snapped back to me again. "Tell me something of yourself, em..."

He trailed off, and I realized that he was waiting for me to supply my name.

"Rose," I offered. "I am twenty human years old and I have lived in the White Woods with my grandmother for the past eight years."

"Rose what?"

"Rose... Abrynth?" My eyes flicked to Emrys beside me, whose mouth curved a little at my statement. Maybe he liked hearing his name next to mine. But when one was married, one usually took their husband's last name, and I assumed that the king wanted to know I was dedicated to Emrys wholly.

I assumed wrong.

"No, dear. Your maiden name."

"Oh." I blinked in confusion. "Doyle."

I swore his eyes widened as though recognizing my name, but he masked the emotion quickly. "And where might your grandmother be now, Rose Doyle?"

My stomach clenched. "D-deceased, highness." In my mind's eye, I saw her slit throat all over again, her lifeless body lying in a pool of blood... No, I could not revisit that moment now. I must stay strong.

"Hm." The king's head bobbed as he eyed me up and down, assessing. "Well, Rose Doyle, as the blood-bound wife of one of my most trusted advisors and favored hunters, you are welcome here, so long as you agree to refrain from using any and all magic or wielding weapons of any kind. Is that understood?"

I tipped my chin down, quickly nodding. The king continued.

"And the second condition is this: you are forbidden from ever leaving the castle grounds and village. My late wife, gods rest her soul, believed that tradition is part of the glue that holds a kingdom together. That vows and ceremonies are sacred and meant to be respected. I honor her legacy now by upholding her values when I can."

Callum spoke up then, startling me. For a moment I'd almost forgotten he was there. "Really, highness? You mean to accept this sham of a union?"

My face heated at his words while the king glared at the brute. "Now, you know how much I hate being interrupted, Callum."

"But, highness—"

"You dare question my judgement?" King Armynd jumped to his feet. His booming voice, even louder now, echoed throughout the cavernous room such that it made even Callum bow his head and wince.

"No, highness."

"Good." The king reclaimed his seat slowly, rolling his eyes at Callum all the while as though the faerie were a petulant child. I could not help but feel a small sense of satisfaction at hearing Callum put in his place. King Armynd caught me in the beams of his piercing stare once more. "Now, all that said, I do not care whose wife you are. If you are ever caught wandering beyond the village walls, you will be executed on the spot and without delay. I cannot have a witch wandering loose where I can't keep an eye on her now, can I?"

ROSE RED

I hesitated, unsure how to respond to that. The king's long fingers tapped the arms of the throne one by one, thrumming a steady rhythm as he examined me with a now-stoic expression. Suddenly, he leaped to his feet again, folded his wings in and began to disrobe. He stripped off his shirt to expose a thick, powerful body, and I gasped as he spun to give me a good look. For the king's entire chest and back were covered in hundreds of eye tattoos identical to the ones Emrys and I sported. Many of them shifted and blinked, giving the appearance that the king's skin was crawling, and I shuddered.

Holding my gaze pointedly, the king touched one of the tattoos on his side, which glowed red beneath his finger. It must've been the mark that corresponded with mine, right there on the king's own body, because at once, I felt the back of my neck begin to warm and tingle as though Armynd were laying his hand on me instead of himself. He held my gaze pointedly as he released the tattoo, and the tingles on the back of my neck ceased immediately. With his point adequately demonstrated, he pulled his shirt back on and reclaimed his seat on the throne.

"I wanted you to see, Rose Doyle. You understand that you are marked and that I am always keeping track of you, should you get any ideas of grandeur."

I swallowed hard, my throat dryer than ever. "Yes," I croaked. "I understand."

"And mark my words, this mingling of the species ends with the two of you. May the gods help any child you conceive. Unless you want to see its brains dashed out in front of you, I suggest you find a tonic that will prevent conception. In fact, one will be provided for you. I would hate to make an example of your child, but I will."

The very thought of conceiving a child seemed absurd, nonsensical. But the way he said this was chilling, as though he had experience killing children.

I swallowed my anger to keep it from breeching my tone as I replied, "Yes, your highness."

I hated posturing myself before a faerie, but I had little choice. And truth be told, he frightened me greatly. I was all too eager to comply if it meant leaving this room—and his presence—sooner.

"Very good." The king's head swiveled. "Now, Emrys, coming back with a witch as a wife... I will accept this union, but you have also brought me no new bounty when you promised me a bounty. In fact, you seem to have off and married the witch who was meant to *be* your bounty. This cannot go unpunished." The high king clapped his hands three times. "I order one hundred cuts."

That did not sound good at all. I remembered Callum mentioning that as well back at the tavern, and it seemed I was about to find out what it meant. I tensed, wishing I had my sword should things get ugly. Was Emrys being punished for not bringing home a bounty... or was he being punished for marrying a witch? From the way the king looked at me, I was fairly certain it was more the latter.

"Remove his shirt." The king clapped once more, and the two shifter guards stepped forward to grasp a paling Emrys, who dropped my hand and accepted his punishment without a word of complaint. His shirt was removed, and I nearly gasped at the number of scars littering his well-muscled torso.

The guards led Emrys off to the side of the room adjacent to the throne steps, his wrists shackled between two columns to hold him upright. The king gestured for two more to come forward—Callum and Talyn. I watched in open-mouthed horror as the pair drew their daggers.

"Commence cutting," the king said.

Callum and Talyn exchanged a conspiratorial grin and immediately took turns slashing at Emrys as hard and deep as they could, opening cut after cut on his back, his chest, his stomach and arms.

I could not prevent the small yelp that came out of me.

"W-what is happening?" I sputtered.

This was absolutely barbaric. I turned toward the throne area and briefly locked eyes with the prince, whose expression remained impassive, though I could swear there was the hint of sadness in his eyes. He averted his gaze and made no move to intervene, however, and I looked to King Armynd in desperation. But the king's focus was already on me, as though he had anticipated my reaction.

"Be calm," he murmured to me, and suddenly, the fight left my body. I was under a faerie enchantment, which should make me angry, yet the anger could not win against the overwhelming calmness I was compelled to feel.

Meanwhile, Callum and Talyn kept hacking and slashing. I didn't even know if they made one hundred cuts, but there was an alarming amount of blood pooling on the ground around Emrys's feet, marring the pristine, shiny floor.

Soon, he slumped over, lifeless from the blood loss, his body smeared with so much red that one could hardly tell the color of his skin beneath.

"Emrys," I gasped in shock, yet I still felt disproportionately calm thanks to the king's enchantment.

The guards uncuffed Emrys, and his body dropped to the ground like a stone. It was over, and Callum and Talyn looked all too pleased with themselves. But when they turned to shuffle out of the throne room, the king stopped them.

"Where do you think you are going?" he barked at them. "I'm not finished with you two, either."

The pair exchanged a questioning look. But then the king walked over toward where Emrys was still lying on the floor, and I realized that my husband wasn't just unconscious.

He was dead.

18

Emrys

LONG AGO, I HAD A TWIN BROTHER, A YOUNGER sister. A mother and a father. My father was a boastful faerie who took great pride in his work, never afraid to peddle his wares no matter where he went. Not that he needed to peddle much. Most customers found *him*. Word of mouth was a powerful thing in East Sythea.

He specialized in leather making. He'd had his own tannery of the finest leathers, so well-regarded throughout East Sythea that even the high fae king himself took notice and placed special orders. Orders for sheaths and belts. For saddles and boots. He'd send his couriers to pick them up frequently and paid Father handsomely for his troubles. Because he was such a frequent customer, King Armynd invited my father to the castle on more than one occasion. It always became a family affair. My mother would join, because my parents were inseparable. I remembered our holidays at the castle being most lavish. I would bounce with excitement whenever the time came.

Father attempted to teach me the leather-making trade when I was very young. But I had no patience for it. Whereas my brother, Merys, was a natural. He was fascinated by the process and a shoe in to be my father's apprentice. Even at his young age.

I had the same penchant for storytelling as my mother and I was far more content to tell stories to my little sister, Merium. Tales of grandeur. Of swashbucklers and thieves and adventures on the high seas. Stories of our fae ancestors and the Otherworld. Of haunting sprites. Merium would listen with wide eyes until my mother told me to stop filling her head with nightmarish things.

"You are old enough for those stories, Emrys. But not Merium. Not yet. Let her enjoy her innocence for another year or two."

Merium would not get that chance. Little did I know, the nightmare was just about to begin.

A fortnight before my family was slaughtered, we'd heard whisperings of a human town being razed to the ground. A town filled with witches. Many fae were on their guard, fully expecting retaliation.

But never had I dreamed they would come for me and my family personally. Never did I expect to walk through puddles of their blood in my bare feet while I tried to contemplate the fact that I was utterly alone in a cruel world.

Now I heard the screams of my family in my nightmares. I smelled the tang of their blood on the air. Felt the dried crust of it on my cheek. And when I died, I knew my family waited for me with my name upon their lips. But I could never reach them. Because life would drag me from the dead once again. The curse's claim.

Now my hundred cuts were over and I was caught in that familiar tunnel. The plane between the living and the dead. I was a beggar seated at the threshold of the Otherworld, praying for admittance. I ran hard. But once again, I was denied entry so cruelly. So harshly. The opening at the end of the tunnel closed, swallowing the light and becoming nothing but a solid wall again. I collided with the wall with full force and grunted my frustration.

ROSE RED

The painful healing process began as always. Life's claws sunk into my leg. Refusing to waver.

The curse's iron grip dragged me back through the tunnel, clawing at the ground and yelling as my soul was sucked back into my body. Taken from my family once again. Only this time, I could hear Rose whispering to me as I approached my body.

At least this time, I was returning to someone. My wife.

19

Rose

"EMRYS." I PUSHED SOME HAIR FROM HIS forehead, which was clammy. I never imagined I'd find myself this concerned over a faerie. But then again, my very life depended on him waking up right now. He had to.

"He is healing now. He will awake soon," the king said for my benefit.

He was right. The cuts on Emrys's chest and abdomen began to close, skin fusing to itself until every wound was healed, one by one, as though they never happened. He began to stir with life once again.

"Emrys," I whispered. His eyes opened, a flash of gold that could've blended in with our gilded surroundings, and he blinked up at me.

"Rose?"

"You're alright," I said. Emrys sat up stiffly, and the king moved forward, bending over us both.

"Here, my boy. Take my hand." How the king could act like a caring father after what he had done to Emrys was beyond me. But Emrys accepted the offered hand and the king pulled him to his feet and patted him on the cheek. "Now, it is your turn," he said.

Emrys frowned. "My turn?"

"Yes." The king bellowed over his shoulder then. "Guards, please present Callum and Talyn to me."

With that, Callum and Talyn were dragged to the side of the room, their shirts stripped, and held into place between the same two posts where Emrys had been shackled. The king crossed the room, grabbed a whip—I didn't even know where it had been hiding—then came back and handed it to Emrys, who still looked a little confused.

"Callum and Talyn," the king said, addressing them directly. "If I am to recall correctly, you both pressed your wrist marks some time ago. Yet you returned with no bounty, either. Explain yourselves."

That bounty they'd marked must have been my grandmother. My breathing grew shallower at the thought, pulse picking up a little speed, though not nearly as much as it would were I not still under the high king's calming enchantment.

"The old witch killed herself," Callum said, his tone defensive. "It was not my fault."

"He is right," said Talyn. "She took us both by surprise."

King Armynd clucked his tongue admonishingly. "And yet, she killed herself on your watch. You *allowed* that to happen. Therefore, you will each receive twenty lashes. Emrys, are you feeling strong enough for this?"

"Oh, yes," Emrys said, looking pleased at the prospect of getting even with his two main antagonists.

"Then, begin."

The king stepped back and Emrys stepped forward. He swung the whip again and again, alternating between Callum and Talyn, who both hissed but bit their tongues to keep from crying out any louder. It seemed the king believed in enabling vengeance and corporal punishment as often as possible. Was this, too, *good and just?*

Emrys sported a predatory grin on his face as he swung and swung, his back muscles rippling, and I was reminded how powerful he was, how much he seemed to hold back that power with me.

When Emrys was done, Callum and Talyn's backs were both streaked with blood. Emrys sniffed and handed the whip back to one of the shifter guards, satisfied with his work.

"Callum and Talyn, you may go. The rest of you may leave as well. And next time, you had better deliver all you promise," said the king.

The remaining fae in the throne room shuffled out, all but King Armynd, Emrys, and myself. Once we were alone, the king turned back to Emrys. "I am sorry for the hundred cuts as always, dear boy. But I cannot have people thinking I've gone totally soft on you, can I?"

Emrys shook his slowly in reply. "No, your highness."

"Good." The king smiled. The smile was a bit unnatural, almost as though it pulled his face too tight. "I will have extra supplies sent up for your... new bride." Something about the way he said that—and the way the king acted around Emrys—did not sit well with me. "Now, show your bride to your quarters."

Once he left the room, I rushed back over to Emrys. With the king gone, the calmness granted from his enchantment had worn off, and I was left feeling angry and disgusted by what I'd just witnessed.

"Are you alright?" I asked as Emrys bent to retrieve his shirt and pull it back on over his head, concealing the scars and now-dried blood.

He waved it off like the whole thing was no big deal, his mouth twitching at the corners. "I am feeling quite fine for someone whose guts were just rearranged."

"Oh, no. Are you using humor to distract from how you're really feeling?"

"Now, why would I do that?" The curve of his mouth fell, lips pulling into a tight line. "I am *fine*."

I shook my head, unable to wrap my mind around all that had just transpired. "I thought you said the king loves you like a son?"

Emrys frowned at my question. "He does."

But that made no logical sense to me at all. "He just *killed* you! Or, he had Callum and Talyn do it, who looked like they were enjoying that *far* too much, by the way." Though in fairness, Emrys had enjoyed doling out their punishment with equal enthusiasm. "Why doesn't the king just have you flogged like Callum and Talyn?"

"The king knows I cannot die. They *all* know I cannot die."

"But you still feel pain! And one hundred cuts? That is a little excessive, is it not?"

He shrugged. "The number is more symbolic than anything. And it wasn't *all* that bad compared to how it could have been." From the strain in Emrys's voice, he was downplaying the severity. I'd heard his barely restrained grunts of agony while the brutes were cutting.

"Aside from having your guts rearranged," I said, throwing his words back at him.

"You'd be surprised the things you can grow accustomed to, Red. And the king was being merciful just now."

"How was *that* showing mercy?"

"He gave me the chance to get even with Callum and Talyn. And he could've placed me in the stocks and had me flogged in front of the whole village. He could've prolonged my torture a lot longer than that."

"But, Emrys, he *is* prolonging your torture. Every time he kills you like that, knowing you heal… it is just a reminder of the curse he's purposefully not breaking, a reminder of the night your family…" I trailed off and drew a deep breath. "I'm sorry. I should not say such things."

He caught his bottom lip between his teeth, and for a moment, I couldn't tell if he was lost in thought or biting back a retort. But finally, he said, "Perhaps you're right." With a sigh, he changed the subject. "Now, my wife, shall I take you to our room? Or would you prefer to stay here and argue about which knife Callum should use next time?"

Next time? Stars, I hoped I never had to see that again.

Emrys led us out of the throne room, and I followed close behind. He must've had pent-up anger simmering within, because he started walking so fast, I had to almost jog to keep up with him as he strode through the cavernous corridor. His mood swings were almost as hard to keep up with as his long legs.

"Now that I've been accepted by the king, can you remove this tattoo from my neck?" I asked.

Emrys stopped abruptly at that. "No one can, and you mustn't try, wife or not. Tampering with these marks would be a capital offense. If I were to try and the king found out, I would be severely punished. And you really do not want to find out the consequences if *you* try, as a witch within fae walls. Trust me."

I scoffed. "I still resent you for putting that mark on me. I imagine I always will." The mark did not pain me, yet I knew it was there, and that knowledge made me shudder at the violation.

His expression softened. "I *am* sorry. But apologies don't remove magic tattoos."

My scowl deepened, but Emrys redirected the conversation by resuming his walking—slower this time—and giving me a brief tour of the castle on the way to his quarters.

"The kitchens and the ballroom are to the right," he said, pointing down the corridor that winded in the opposite direction past the throne room. "Just beyond that is a small set of steps that lead to the servants' wing."

We moved toward the grand, curved staircase, which was also covered in a fine green carpet that resembled grass. At the top of the steps, we turned right and approached another, smaller set of stairs, very steep, narrow, and curving.

Emrys's room was located in the top of one of the turrets. We arrived on a small landing and he swung open the lone door there. The room was nice, with a pretty view over town. Not quite as opulent as I'd imagined, but far nicer than anything I had ever lived in. He had everything he needed in here, along with a quite inviting four-poster bed.

When I moved forward to step into the room, I found myself swept off my feet into Emrys's arms.

"What are you doing?" My hands instinctively wound around his neck. He chuckled, the sound rumbling in his chest.

"I believe it's customary for a husband to carry his new wife across the threshold of their quarters. Best we not break yet another long-standing tradition and risk worse luck than we both already have."

He stepped forward with me in his arms and set me down just inside the door. I found myself drifting toward the bed, running my fingers along one of the bed posts just to keep my hands busy. A nervous habit.

"We've only one bed here, obviously. Since it has only been me until now," Emrys said. He tilted his head, clearly gauging my reaction.

"We have already shared a bed together. We're married, as you said, so I suppose we can share for a little while longer." Even as I said the words, I heard the hesitation in them. Not that it mattered. "Besides, you have no intention of sleeping on the floor, anyway," I pointed out, thinking of our wedding night.

"True." He grinned, though it faded quickly. "Well, fair warning, Red. You've heard my nightmares. Sometimes they can be a little troublesome. Sometimes I talk in my sleep and thrash about."

"You haven't had any nightmares since before our wedding night."

He blinked as though that hadn't occurred to him. "You're right, I haven't. Maybe having a witch in my bed is far better than I'd ever dreamed."

Suddenly, he stood before me, staring right down into my face, and my breath hitched in my throat. For some inexplicable reason, I felt powerless to tear my gaze from his. My entire body shook again. It was finally sinking in that I was stuck in a faerie castle for the foreseeable future, that I was sharing a room—and a bed—with my blood-bound fae husband, and I could not predict what my life was about to become. Emrys frowned as he stared down at me.

"That heart is racing again." He pressed his palm over my heart, his long fingers curving over the top of my shoulder. "You can calm down, Red. You're safe now."

I nodded, trying to breathe deep, to slow my pulse.

"What do you think I'm going to do to you? What do you think will happen?" When I hesitated to answer, he sighed, and his hand drifted upward to gently cradle my jaw, urging me to look at him. "You know that I do not lie, so hear this. You are my *wife* now. I will never harm you... Unless you ask me to." He smirked, but the smirk turned serious quickly. "Your safety and well-being—so long as I still draw breath—will remain a priority. Understand?"

"I do." But did I, really? Now that we were within the castle walls, I was feeling especially vulnerable.

The ghost of a smile curved on Emrys's lips. "I would like to give you something as a show of good faith."

He withdrew his hand and stepped back, and my brow raised. "Give me what, exactly?"

"A wedding gift." Emrys crossed the room toward a large, wooden wardrobe, rounded at the edges. He yanked the brass knobs to open, reached inside, and pulled out a sword sheath that looked brand new. The leather was shiny and braided around the back. He handed it to me and said, "My father made this."

I ran my hands over the leather, marveling over how pristine the condition was. "This must be hundreds of years old, like you. How is it still in such great condition?"

"My father's skill was unparalleled. And now, I want you to have it."

I immediately shook my head. "I cannot accept this."

"Sure, you can. I've no cause to use it. I have my dagger with its own holster. I don't use a sword, but you do, and your own sheath is quite tattered."

"But—"

"Oh, for the love of—just *take* it, Red." He curled his hand around mine, forcing me to clench the leather while rolling his eyes all the while.

"This is very kind of you. Thank you."

"You are quite welcome." He cleared his throat. "Of course, the sword and sheath will both have to stay in this room, locked in the wardrobe, as long as you're living on castle grounds. You cannot wield your weapon. But they will both waiting right there for when you leave."

With that, he walked over to the window and leaned against the sill, gazing outside. He grew silent, contemplative. I felt compelled to break the silence as I grasped the gifted sheath in my hands.

"Back in the swamp, you asked me why I saved your life—or tried to—when I could've run away. Do you remember asking that?"

Emrys nodded and turned his head toward me. "Yes."

"When I heard you having your nightmare before that... It triggered something inside of me. I recognized a person in pain, a person who had *lost,* because I am one, too. I knew you had more layers than you let on, another clue being that stupid rabbit you refused to kill."

He laughed at that, but again he sobered quickly. "I didn't tell you that I had a pet rabbit as a child. Last thing my mother gave me. It ran away after my family passed."

It was a foreign concept to me, keeping an animal like a rabbit as a pet rather than food. But from Emrys's tone, it had meant something to him. "Did you ever find it again?"

"Nah." For a moment, he appeared lost in a memory, his gaze growing far away. He shook his head as though to clear it of unwanted thoughts. "Rabbits make poor company, anyway. All legs with a mean kick."

I cracked a smile which faded on the next breath. "You've done horrible things, Emrys. But I suppose I have too. I've killed plenty, and without guilt. What must that say about me?" I paused to draw a breath, frowning as another thought occurred to me. "Speaking of killing; do you think the king knows that I slaughtered quite a few of his bounty hunters?"

"You have not slaughtered any of *his* hunters. Most bounty hunters operate independently and are not in the direct employ of the king. They just pop in on occasion with a bounty, collect their coin, and go back home. Callum, Talyn, and I are the only members of the high court who also double as bounty hunters."

"Oh."

"So, tell your heart to relax."

That would be hard to get used to; I needed to learn to control my pulse around Emrys. He grinned crookedly, his arms crossed over his chest, booted feet crossed at the ankles and eyes fixated on me. "So..."

"So..." I shifted uncomfortably, unsure what else to say now that we were alone, other than, "I suppose there is no time like the present. Why don't we start right now?"

"Start what?"

"Attempting to break your curse."

Emrys quirked his scarred brow. "Right now?"

"Do you not want to?"

"I do. I just thought you might want a little time to get settled first."

In all honesty, I couldn't wait until I could get out of the castle. I couldn't help but feel like—despite what the king said about me being accepted as Emrys's wife—as a witch, I would never be fully welcome and would always have a target painted on my back. So, the sooner I could break Emrys's curse and get out of here, the better.

Strangely, the thought of breaking Emrys's curse and leaving him behind to kill himself filled me with a surprising amount of sorrow. But that was silly. Emrys would have handed me over for torture and death at the hands of the king in a heartbeat if not for our truce. And yet... something had undoubtedly changed in the way Emrys treated me ever since I saved his life—or attempted to—when the thieves attacked in the woods. There was a softness towards me that I would have never expected from a faerie, something that ran deeper than hate and distrust.

"You will need to sit." I perched on the edge of the bed and patted the empty spot next to me.

Emrys's lips twitched, but he promptly left the window he was leaning against and came to sit beside me as asked. "Now what?"

"We just need for you to remember how the witch placed the curse on you so that I can figure out how to reverse it."

"Do what you must." Emrys was sitting close to me, so close I could feel the warmth of his body leaping to mine. I turned to him and took his hand, placing it on my lap, palm facing up. My fingers stroked the lines of his palm. His skin there was a bit rough, calloused. The worn hands of a hunter.

"Alright," I said. "Close your eyes. Listen to the sound of my voice."

He closed his eyes at once. Truth be told, I had no idea what I was doing, but I figured we could experiment. One time, when my mother wanted to quit a nasty habit of pulling out her own hair whenever she grew anxious, my grandmother had spoken to her just like this. And whatever she did, it had worked; Mother stopped yanking on her hair. I figured it was worth a shot with Emrys, as well.

"Now, I want you to picture the night that your curse happened. Visualize that room. What you can hear, smell, taste, touch. Can you see it?"

"Yes," Emrys murmured.

"Good. Now, describe the room for me."

"It's a quaint home. My siblings and I slept in the same room, my parents in another. But that night when I came home and entered the living room, I sensed something was wrong. I can smell the remnants of supper—the duck my mother had cooked. And the fire is still crackling in the corner. And... my feet are bare. I am standing on the wooden floor."

I drew a deep breath, let it out, forcing my voice to remain calm as I spoke to him. "And then what?"

"And then..." Emrys frowned and his eyes popped open. "*Shit.* I'm sorry, I don't think I am in the right frame of mind to continue at the moment."

"That's alright." In all likelihood, I would have to try something more effective, like a memory tonic.

"Besides, that heartbeat is distracting me again."

His palm pressed over my heart; I hadn't realized how much my pulse had increased again at his closeness. Nor did I understand *why* it increased. Emrys tilted his head as he studied my expression, golden eyes scanning my face with a curious look to them. His gaze dropped toward my mouth...

Just then, loud taps on the window made me jump, interrupting the moment. My hand went to my heart; now I *knew* it was thumping uncontrollably. "What on earth is that?"

Emrys looked over toward the window and laughed a little. "It's alright. It's just Goro."

"Who?"

Without replying, Emrys stood and walked back to the window. He unlatched the glass and swung it open. There was a squawk, and a large raven popped inside, perching on the window sill. A dark black bird with a small patch of gray feathers on its breast. He had something in his beak.

"A raven?" I asked.

"Yes, a most trusted messenger within the castle. King Armynd has sent us a note, I believe."

"And he couldn't have had someone walk up here and hand us the note in person?"

"Well, as you've likely seen by now, the king has a flare for the dramatics. Plus, Goro doesn't mind." Emrys accepted the paper from Goro and spoke directly to the bird. "Thank you for bringing this."

"You are most welcome," Goro said in a friendly chirp as he flew away. "You know I am always at your service, Lord Emrys!"

Wait, *Goro* said? I shook my head in disbelief.

"Emrys."

"Yes."

"Did your pet bird just talk?"

"I think Goro would take issue with being called my pet. But, yes."

"It was not just repeating words. It was saying full sentences."

"Ravens are excellent linguists, actually."

"Not like this."

"I suppose you're right. To Goro's credit, he is a bit... special."

"How so?"

Emrys scratched his jaw. "Well, there once existed a small group of shifters who believed the gods would bless them if they remained in their animal form."

My brows knitted together. "I don't understand. Why?"

"Their belief was that, if the gods had deemed it fit to bestow an animal visage upon them, then remaining in their fae form rather than their animal form would be akin to rejecting a great gift. They believed that remaining shifted would keep them closer to the gods. Goro is very old. His family was very devout in this belief. He doesn't believe this to be true himself now. But the longer a fae stays in their animal form, the more animal-like they become. Eventually, the animal visage becomes normal and the fae visage requires conscious shifting. In Goro's case, it was like he had forgotten how to be a regular faerie. Frankly, I don't even know if he would remember what it's like to have *hands* anymore."

With Goro now gone, Emrys relatched the window and walked back over toward me, unrolling the small scroll that had been in the raven's beak.

"Well," he said as he scanned the words on the paper, "it seems we can put aside curse breaking for one night. The king has invited us to a banquet with the rest of his court."

"He has?" I asked.

"And we are the guests of honor to this celebration."

"We are?" That was the last thing I expected.

"Of course. He wants to officially announce our union. Publicly."

I frowned at that, wondering if there was some sort of catch. "It's quite last minute to be announcing an extravagant dinner this late in the day, is it not?"

Emrys narrowed his eyes at me like the notion was absurd. "He is the high king. When he demands something, it is done. And by whomever he demands it of."

"Oh." But then I thought of something else, and a bubble of panic rose in my chest. "What will I wear? I possess nothing fancy enough for a dinner with the king. In fact, I possess nothing *at all* anymore aside from the clothes currently on my back."

"Not to worry," Emrys replied with a smile. "The king will be sending up his own personal tailors for us both."

"Oh," I repeated, blinking rapidly. Again, I could not help but feel as though there was some catch.

"Perhaps try to get some rest first. A bath as well if you feel so inclined. It's been a long journey." Emrys gestured toward the bed, then the fancy claw-foot tub in the far corner of the room. "I will return in a bit, after I've attended to some business of my own. The tailors should arrive in a couple of hours. And, Red?" He looked down at me pointedly, placing two fingers under my chin to ensure I met his gaze. His scarred eyebrow rose as he said, "Be good."

With that, Emrys left the room.

After a quick soak in the tub, I pulled my dress back on—for lack of anything else to wear at the moment. I sauntered over to the standing mirror in the room and lifted my hair, trying to angle myself to see the eye tattoo on the back of my neck. I quickly gave up, realizing I would need another mirror to do so. It was still unsettling, thinking about that eyeball moving on the back of my neck. Yet oddly it was also the least of my worries.

I was about to attend a *banquet* to celebrate a witch and faerie marriage. Inside a fae castle in the midst of a sea of other fae. This could go very, very badly.

With lack of anything else to do at the moment, I gratefully slumped onto the bed. It *had* been a long journey, and Emrys had pushed us to keep moving on the last leg. Sleep was exceedingly hard to come by on a horse's back.

Now, I felt drained, exhausted, overwhelmed, and confused. Frightened of what was to come, as well. I had not realized it was possible to feel so many things at once.

Doing my best to push unwanted thoughts from my mind, I tried to relax and take a much-needed nap. But being inside the castle of one's enemies did not make for an ideal sleeping environment.

Soon, I gave up trying, pulled my knees to my chest, and stared out the window.

Dreaming about home.

A home that was now empty, and would remain so forever.

Until the forest claimed it for its own.

20

Rose

THE TAILORS ARRIVED A COUPLE OF HOURS later just as Emrys said they would, waking me from my nap. My exhaustion had won out in the end, and I'd managed to sneak in an hour of rest, at least. Which would have to do.

Sharp raps on the door woke me. When I opened the door, the tailor brushed past me without saying a word. It seemed *my* tailor arrived. Emrys had not returned, so I could only assume he was getting ready elsewhere.

My tailor was stunning, with raven-colored hair, pale skin, and full red lips curved into a permanent pout. She smelled of honeysuckle. She wasn't exactly kind to me, though she wasn't mean, either, just no-nonsense. She circled all around me, looking me up and down with her pointer finger tapping her chin as though lost in thought about what she should do with me.

I cleared my throat to break the silence. "I don't believe we've been formally introduced yet. My name is Rose."

The tailor's head snapped up; her mouth twisted as though confused as to why I was talking to her. After a long moment, she finally said, "I'm Rhea."

"It's a pleasure to make your acquaintance," I replied formally.

This time, Rhea said nothing. Apparently, it was far from a pleasure to make the acquaintance of a witch. But she was at least done circling me now. "Yes, I think I've got it," she said with a brief smile. "Now, take off your clothes."

My mouth opened and I let out a little squeak, caught wholly off guard. "Right now?"

"Yes," she said, rolling her eyes to communicate her impatience with me. "I've decided what I want to do with you, but I can't dress you if you still have your regular clothes on now, can I?"

I flushed, but what should I be embarrassed about? This *was* just her job, after all. I had never been very uncomfortable with nudity before, but it was a little bit different when nude around your own kind as opposed to your enemy, just as with Lysia.

I disrobed quickly, refusing to make a big fuss about it, and then I stood there feeling incredibly exposed and trying my best not to hunch over and cover myself. Part of me couldn't help but compare myself to Rhea. Whereas she had ample curves in all the desirable places, I felt like nothing but a bag of bones in comparison, unable to keep much weight on living in the woods.

Thankfully, Rhea didn't leave me naked for long. And it seemed this tailor possessed strong powers as well, because with a single wave of her hand, I was suddenly wearing a gown made purely of her own glamour.

Rhea shoved me in front of a full-length mirror in the corner of the room, and I gasped at the sight. I hardly recognized myself. The fabric felt luxurious on my skin, and the gown was beautiful, somehow accentuating my body in the most flattering way possible, giving the illusion of curves where there were none. The dress was a shimmering gold, the bodice fitted and a little low cut, exposing my decolletage. The sleeves and flared skirt were decorated with golden feathers, and my hair was swept up atop my head, capped off by a crown of gold feathers around the bun.

"Thank you so much, Rhea. This is gorgeous," I gushed, resisting the urge to twirl around.

She nodded in reply. "This is my job. You should have seen the outfits I used to dress the queen in before she was murdered by *witches*." I bristled at that, uncomfortable with the way she emphasized *witches*, but Rhea kept talking. "I used to dress her in the most elaborate gowns. Yours had *better* be gorgeous, or else that would mean I've lost my touch entirely, and I should be fired."

"Well, you certainly do your job well."

Her mouth twitched again at that. "I am glad you like it."

"But, how is it that I can *feel* the fabric? I thought faerie glamours were all illusion?"

"This is more than a glamour. I am a conjurer. I can create tangible things that exist even with me out of the room. Now, enough questions. Go be spectacular. Give them all a good show, witch." I frowned at her wording, which was odd. Not insulting, not threatening, but not precisely cordial, either.

I was unsure how to respond other than to say, "I will do my best."

"You are lucky to have Emrys as your husband, you know. There are plenty around town who fancy him despite his whole *brooding fae* act, whether he knows it or not."

Now I frowned and fiddled with the feathers on my skirt, unsure what else to say other than, "Thank you?"

I could not help the upward inflection at the end, and it did not go unnoticed. Rhea's mouth twitched fully upward into what I could only describe as a mischievous smile, her full lips curved almost wickedly.

"Your *husband* awaits." She put an extra emphasis on the word *husband* such that it had a strange connotation, and the crease between my brows deepened at her tone.

She made a sweeping gesture toward the door, and I stepped out onto the landing just in time to spot Emrys approaching up the stairs. He looked more handsome than ever as well in his dress attire. I was used to his bounty hunting clothes, and this outfit was something else entirely, even nicer than what he had borrowed from Aegan to wear at our wedding. His shirt was a pristine white inlaid with a weaving, shimmery gold that matched my dress, a cape made of the finest silk clasped at his throat, trailing down his back. His trousers were fitted to perfection, his boots polished and shiny, hair neatly combed.

He smiled warmly when he saw me, his eyes widening, lips parting. "You look..." He trailed off, searching for the right word.

Stunning?" I supplied.

"I was going to say *delectable,*" he replied with a sly wink, and I tried to control my pulse at not only his words, but the hungry way he said them. "But *stunning* will suffice."

"You're welcome," Rhea said from behind me, stepping out onto the small landing. Emrys's jaw tightened at the sight of her.

"Rhea," he greeted her with a curt nod.

"Emrys," she returned as she pushed past me and descended the steps toward Emrys, pausing to squeeze her body past his in the narrow stairwell. Once she was gone, Emrys shook his head and turned back to me, extending his arm.

"Shall we?"

I took his offered arm and we walked down the wide, green-carpeted stairs, turning left to pass the throne room and head to the grand dining hall together. Voices echoed down the corridor as we approached, and when Emrys held the door open for me, I gasped as the room was revealed. It was every bit as opulent as I'd expected.

The room was massive, ornate, even more so than the throne room. Everywhere there were grand murals and gilded candelabras and crystal chandeliers. The ceiling was painted to resemble an evening sky and the murals on the walls depicted lush woodland scenery. So much wealth in one place. I couldn't help but wonder if the castle was always this opulent when ruled by humans, or if its opulence has grown since the fae took over.

All around us were long tables filled with laughing, chattering fae, a cacophony of voices, sounds, and strange sights. One younger fae at a nearby table seemed to have trouble retracting his wings and kept poking his neighbors in the eyes and comically knocking over cups of wine.

A large group of low fae fluttered about, dragging dishes and food that looked much too heavy for their little bodies out of what I assumed was a kitchen. They had to operate in teams, with three faeries needed to transport a single, loaded plate.

I leaned in toward Emrys, gesturing toward the laboring low fae, and whispered, "Do they cook the food as well?"

Emrys laughed it off as though he thought I was joking, though he quickly realized I was not. "I should hope not. Cooking is considered an art; we have high fae chefs who take great pride in their work. However, the king considers serving at banquets to be beneath the high fae, so he calls in for the low fae to serve whenever we have gatherings like this."

I nodded, pretending to understand. Fae hierarchies were still foreign to me.

Off to the side of the room, adjacent to the tables, was a low stage for entertainment. One faerie performed a flame swallowing act that did not seem to impress the audience very much, although magic wasn't unordinary to the fae as a whole. Beside him, a bard played a lute and sang... and my eyes widened when I noticed the bard's features. Long, blond hair, a dimpled chin, ice blue eyes, and his ears... I gasped and, without even realizing I was doing it, gripped Emrys's wrist.

"The bard is human?"

Emrys nodded, his gaze briefly flicking down to my hand on his wrist before moving back up. "His talent is what saved his life. He's non magic, so not considered much of a threat. Plus, he has a pleasant singing voice that the king hated seeing go to waste. His name is Jasper, I believe."

That didn't sit well with me, but I could do nothing right now. The noma bard did have a wonderful voice. He sang of a sprite in the woods, a most intriguing tale, and I found myself captivated by the sound.

Soon, a hush fell over the room like a wave rolling in, including the bard, when King Armynd noticed our presence and stood. It was time to make our grand entrance, it seemed, and I must put on a good show for the king.

Armynd stood behind a long table at the head of the room, fully decorated with an array of colorful flowers and candle centerpieces. His wings were folded in completely such that they were not even visible from my angle. Maybe he only displayed them when attempting to intimidate new arrivals to the castle. Beside him sat his two shifter guards, along with his son, the prince.

The king made eye contact with Emrys and I, clapped his hands, and bellowed, "My guests of honor have arrived. Please, come forth, Emrys and his new bride, Rose! Join us at the head table, for we must celebrate."

There was no turning back now. My cheeks flushed and I grasped Emrys's arm to keep from collapsing. As we moved up the aisle through the center of the tables toward the head of the room, I felt the glares of the fae like many little daggers poking me. I kept my head held high and implored myself to not trip and fall on my face. I lifted my chin and did my best to quell the trembling in my legs.

Do not trip, do not falter, I repeated the words over again in my head. These fae wanted to see me fail, and I would not give them the satisfaction.

Emrys and I took our positions at the head table. Once we were seated, the king called for the feast to officially begin.

"Hello," a voice said from beside me, and it was only then I realized I'd been seated next to the fae prince. Up close, his glamour was even more apparent, much too shimmery all over his face as though his skin was laced with diamond powder. But despite the off-putting glamour, his brown eyes seemed genuinely warm and sincere.

"Rose, I don't believe you've been formally introduced to the prince yet," said Emrys from the other side of me.

"You can call me Korvyn," said Korvyn as he grasped my hand in a pleasant greeting. His skin was warm, his grasp firm.

"Pleasure to make your acquaintance," I said formally.

Korvyn broke eye contact and turned away abruptly. I did not perceive it to be a slight. Rather, it seemed more like a surprising lack of confidence, coming from a prince. He was more lively speaking to Emrys, however. Maybe he simply took a while to open up to someone, a trait with which I could relate.

Emrys fell into an easy banter with those around him, seeming at ease amongst most except for Callum and Talyn, who were seated too close for comfort. My tailor, Rhea, sat in between them, looking highly bored by the festivities as she cradled her chin in her hand and tapped her long fingernails on the tabletop. The three of them mostly spoke to each other and ignored Emrys and I altogether.

We were presented a delicious feast and it was, frankly, the best thing I had ever eaten. There was roasted pheasant, golden brown potatoes, sweet carrots, and even a decadent honey mead that complemented everything perfectly. For dessert, we were served slices of cake with chocolate shavings on top. Eating like this, I may actually start gaining some weight, which I was quite looking forward to.

I ate until my belly felt like it would burst. But then I felt guilty for eating in such excess when others of my kind went without, angry that the fae were allowed to *possess* such excess. In the hollowed-out shell of a human castle, no less.

Emrys spoke in my ear. "Your heart's thumping fast again and your face is as crimson as a tomato. Is everything alright?"

Before I could answer, the bard resumed his song across the room, playing his lute. His voice was silky like the honey mead, the prettiest I had ever heard. His long, wispy blonde hair skirted his shoulders as he gently swayed to his own music. But he sang with his eyes closed, his expression one of distinct sorrow. Beside me, the prince stared at him rather intently, leaning forward on his elbows, his glamour shimmering more all the while.

I waited until the prince was distracted in other conversation and grasped Emrys's elbow. "Are you sure the bard is in no danger?" I whispered.

"As I said, the king keeps him around because of his musical talents. He doesn't possess magic, so he's not considered much of a threat. As long as he keeps agreeing to share his talent, he's treated fairly well."

I wondered what *fairly well* meant. The bard was being kept as somewhat of a slave, even if it was just a slave who was forced to sing.

"Am I considered a threat? Being a witch?" I asked, unable to tear my gaze from the bard.

"You are my wife," Emrys said simply. "And they shall view you as such. Nothing more, nothing less. If the king accepts our union, everyone else must, also. Now, *relax*."

"Easier said than done," I hissed. *He* wasn't the one currently stuck in a room filled to the brim with beings who loathed his very existence.

"Well, try your best. We will be expected to share at least one dance as a married couple, Red."

"Wait, *what?*" I inhaled sharply, terrified at the prospect of dancing in front of all these people—no, *fae*—who hated me, a *witch,* by default.

"Just follow my lead and you will be fine," Emrys said. "Your heart sounds like it's ready to burst free of your chest and do its own dance in the center of the room."

"You dance?"

He lifted an amused brow. "I said I don't sing. I never said a thing about dancing."

Without another word, he stood and offered me his hand, which I had no choice but to accept. My heart thudded louder in my ears and I did my best to tune out the chatter of the fae and focus on the bard's song—and Emrys—as I was led to the center of the room. The bard switched his tune to a slower one about love, and I felt a moment of sheer panic, frozen in place.

"Calm yourself, Red," Emrys said, his voice soothing. He gave a deep bow before me and straightened back up, his gold eyes meeting mine. "Chin up. Just keep your eyes on mine and do as I do."

I nodded, and Emrys pulled me close and led me in a simple dance. All the while, his eyes remained trained on mine. I did my best to follow him step for step and soon, I had the hang of it, gliding across the floor in his arms as my dress swished about my ankles.

A smile twitched upon his lips as he stared down at me, gaze never wavering, his large hand cupping my shoulder blade. I even found myself smiling back when Emrys twirled me.

I spun, finishing the twirl pressed against Emrys's chest. He held my hand and, with our hips still connected and his other arm supporting my weight behind my back, he dipped me low. So low I nearly yelped for fear of falling— I simply had to trust that Emrys would not let me fall. And he didn't.

When I straightened back up, I found my gaze drawn to his lips, the very lips he ran his tongue over now as he stared back down at me.

"Emrys," I whispered, transfixed.

But then the song ended and I cleared my throat, spell broken.

My attention drifted for a brief moment, landing on Rhea, who was scowling at both of us. I frowned at her reaction, but did not have a chance to think on it further as Emrys led us back to our table to the tune of some very half-hearted applause.

"Lovely," the king said, and then he gestured for Emrys and I to stand next to him. "Bring your glasses for a toast."

Reluctantly, I followed Emrys to stand beside the king, with my glass in hand as requested. I hated being put on display for any length of time, especially now.

"I would like to propose a toast to my dear Emrys on the union to his wife, Rose. Let us all welcome her to our kingdom as one of our own. May their union be blessed, and may the gods smile upon them." King Armynd lifted his glass. We all raised our glasses in response, and I tried to keep my hand from shaking as I did so.

The room let out very begrudging *cheers* and I noticed that very few of them actually drank, most of them just held their glasses and stared, judging me.

ROSE RED

But then something felt wrong, *very* wrong. A cold, stiff breeze blew up and down my body all at once, making me shudder

Just before the entire ballroom erupted into loud guffaws, laughs, and jeers. And I very quickly learned why.

I looked down and realized with horror that I was naked.

Totally naked, and in full view of the whole room of fae.

21

Rose

My gasp was nearly an inhaled shriek as I hunched over to cover myself, dropping my glass in the process. It shattered on the marble floor and splashed my ankles with cold wine.

Emrys's face flushed with rage and he dove in front of me to shield me as best he could, immediately stripping off his cape to wrap around my body. I looked around the room wildly. King Armynd aside, the prince was the only other faerie in the room with the decency to not laugh. Rather, his eyes narrowed in a troubled frown.

That's when my gaze landed on my tailor, Rhea, at the end of the closest table. Her outfit was blood red, matching both her lips and her delight in cutting down others, it seemed. My dress was her conjuring, her creation, and right here, in front of everyone, she tore the magic away, leaving me bare and exposed. Apparently, Rhea could also take away anything she conjured in the blink of an eye. She was never being kind to me, but rather was just waiting for the prime moment to embarrass me as completely as possible.

Now, the tailor was smirking, her lips twisted up at the corners. She sarcastically raised her glass toward me and took a sip of her wine, brow raised. Thoroughly proud of herself.

"Cheers," she mouthed.

That bitch.

Suddenly, I felt like I couldn't breathe. Panic rose up in my chest, tightening like a vice under the incessant, judgmental stares of the fae around me. I could feel their hatred, their sheer joy at witnessing my misery.

Their jeers were like bee stings, their insults like needles poking me incessantly. All their voices bled together, their laughter all but deafening. "So, that's what a witch looks like naked," someone said. I didn't see who, but it didn't matter. I could not take any more of this.

"Emrys," I gasped.

Without another word, Emrys scooped me up into his arms to further shield me with his body, and then he carried me out of the grand ballroom. Even as the king called after him, he did not slow, his strides long and even as he carried me toward the large doors at the end of the room. I couldn't bear to look at anyone else, keeping my head buried against Emrys's neck and mortified by the sounds of laughter following me down the corridor.

"The king will have the tailor reprimanded. What Rhea did was unacceptable, and she knows it," Emrys murmured in my ear once we were a good distance away from the ballroom.

My head was still buried against his neck. He carried me through the castle and up the turret stairs to our room as though I weighed nothing, sitting us both on the bed. Then, he held me in his lap, and I was still too flushed with shame to climb away from him. His arms tightened around me, holding me steady until the tremors subsided.

"I am so sorry, Rose," he said after some time.

I sniffled. "This isn't your fault."

"It is. I should've known Rhea was plotting something. That she would be jealous."

I finally raised my head to look up at him. "And why would she be jealous?"

Emrys lifted an arm from around me, freeing his hand to scratch the back of his head, suddenly seeming bashful. "Rhea and I used to be... involved. But that was a long time ago. Though I don't think she has ever fully gotten over it."

That explained a lot; she still carried a flame for Emrys, and now a witch of all beings had taken the lover that scorned her. Maybe on some level she still viewed Emrys as hers, and her former beau wedding a witch as some prime insult. "That makes sense. Why didn't you warn me about her?"

"I never imagined she'd stoop this low. I had thought she would be over this by now, but I suppose not." He sighed rather loudly, like the winds of a storm lived in his lungs. "I should've insisted she use real fabric in lieu of her conjuring."

"As you said, you didn't know she would do this. And again, it's not your fault." I finally disentangled myself from Emrys—still wrapped in his cape—and climbed off his lap to sit beside him on the bed. "And it doesn't matter. The damage is already done, and I'm sure Rhea will just get a slap on the wrist for this." The worst part was that I had thought we'd gotten off to an encouraging start. I had thought that she took pride in her work, pride enough to make even a witch feel her most beautiful. But it had all been a ruse, just another reminder of how manipulative the fae could be.

Emrys's brows pulled together, mouth twitching as though choosing his words carefully. "Rose..."

"I am tired," I interrupted. "I would like to go to bed."

He studied my expression for a long moment before jerking his chin to point toward the wardrobe. "They will have left you some nightgowns there. They should be in your size."

"Are these *actual* nightgowns, or do I need to worry about those disappearing in the night, as well?"

"They are made of real, non-conjured cloth. You should be fine."

Pulling the cape tighter around my body, I crossed the room toward the wardrobe and opened it, gasping at the array of nightgowns, dresses, and cloaks in various colors and luxurious fabrics. Emrys had his side of the wardrobe, and I had mine. My hands skimmed over the outfits on my side. I had never owned anything this nice before, and certainly not in this kind of abundance. I selected a white dressing gown and frowned as I looked to Emrys.

"Turn around," I said.

It might have been a ridiculous request—I was certain he'd just seen all of me along with the entire court at the banquet, but still... I required *some* dignity. Emrys's lips pressed together at the request, looking somewhat bemused.

"Are we not husband and wife?"

I shot him a withering look, and he relented, lifting his hands. "Fine."

He spun around, and I dropped his cape on the floor before quickly sliding on my nightgown over my head. "You can turn," I said once finished, and I felt Emrys's eyes on me as I walked toward the bed and slid under the covers. They, too, were quite luxurious and so soft. This part, I could get used to.

I said nothing else to Emrys, though I felt the bed depress behind me when he finally climbed in and pulled up the covers. I could feel the heat rolling off his body. This bed was softer than the one at the inn—softer than anything I'd ever slept on in my life—but at the same time, it was a bed built for one, not two.

I found myself suddenly wide awake. Flustered, I turned over to find Emrys staring at me in the dark.

"What is it?" I asked. He was so close I could feel each breath he drew and expelled.

His voice was husky as he spoke, his eyes reflecting the moonlight streaming through the window. "You're my wife. Despite what you might think, I take my husbandly duties seriously. I failed to protect you tonight."

But we'd already been through this. "Emrys..."

"I will not fail again." It was a whispered vow. In the near darkness, the room lit only by the moon outside, Emrys lifted a hand and gently ran his thumb along my cheekbone, his knuckles skimming my jaw. "I promise you."

I wanted to remind him not to make promises he couldn't keep. He couldn't always keep an eye on me here, and I knew I was on borrowed time. But I said nothing except, "Good night, Emrys."

"Sleep well, Red," he whispered in reply before lowering his hand and shifting into a comfortable position.

I tried, I truly did, but sleep was hard to come by as I relived the events of the evening over again in my head. Maybe I would not come to physical harm, but the fae were also likely to push the boundaries in making my life as miserable as possible. And I knew now, beyond a shadow of a doubt, that I could never let my guard down here.

Not for a second.

I AWOKE THE NEXT MORNING TO EMRYS shuffling about the room. I rolled over, eyes still heavy with sleep.

"Good morning," he said without turning, having heard me stir.

"How long have you been awake?" I asked.

He turned to face me then. His eyes looked especially gold in the morning sunlight streaming through the window. "A while," he replied.

"I didn't hear you get up." I sat up and stretched my arms, fighting a yawn. Though I had eventually fallen asleep, I felt far from refreshed.

"I can be very quiet when I wish to be." A shadow of a smile crossed his lips. He sat at the edge of the bed beside me to pull on his boots, and continued to speak as he laced them. "Also, you were sleeping like the dead."

"I was?" That surprised me, as I hadn't thought I would come by any sleep at all given the events of the night prior. Though I *had* been exhausted after the arduous journey and this was my first chance to recover.

"I must attend to matters around the castle," Emrys said.

"Which matters?"

He paused as though he hadn't been expecting such a question, but he replied, "For one, dealing with Rhea." I almost blanched at the hated name, but I let him continue. "I am also meeting with the king. I owe him a status report from my last journey, along with a lot of other boring court matters that likely mean nothing to you."

"Alright," I replied. "And what should I do while you are gone?"

"Whatever you wish." He shot me a pointed look then, eyes narrowing. "Within reason."

"What does that mean?"

Emrys's expression could almost be mistaken for concern, and I leaned forward, waiting for him to answer. "I'd never deign to imagine I can tell you what to do without an argument. But I would very much like it if you wouldn't roam about today, considering what happened last night."

I flushed as I was reminded of my embarrassment once again. "So, what am I supposed to do, stay up in this room all day?"

"I would very much like that, yes. I'll see to it that you are brought up whatever you need."

"I thought I could do whatever I wish?"

"I changed my mind."

My mouth pinched, expression souring. "No, Emrys. I refuse to live in fear and cower in my room. That would be letting Rhea and the others win. They wish to keep me on edge, and they might have succeeded, but they must not *know* that. Plus, I need to go into town to gather items for a memory tonic. To help you."

"What items do you need? If they are mostly herbs and spices, I can have that sent up from the kitchens."

"Some herbs, but some of these ingredients are not things usually kept in a kitchen. I imagine I may even have difficulty finding them in town, but I must try."

Emrys blew out a long breath and ran a frustrated hand through his dark hair. "Fine. But at least promise me you will never visit the dungeons. The guards there are a whole other breed, and who knows what they might do to you if they catch you alone."

I swallowed and fiddled with the soft sheets, unable to stop fidgeting. "I promise, I won't visit the dungeons."

I hadn't even been thinking of the dungeons, though I should, especially if there were witches in the dungeons who I should know about and try to help. I had a sneaking suspicion that I would likely break my promise at some point, no matter what Emrys said.

"And be careful in town," he continued. "Keep your hood up. I swear to the gods, Red. If you get yourself into trouble, I am not above chaining you to this bed."

I rolled my eyes as I thought about how we met. "I am well aware of your fondness for chains," I fired back.

Emrys pointedly ignored me and continued. "Should you have any issues, send for me immediately."

"And how shall I send for you? Is there someone I can notify?"

"As a matter of fact, there is." Emrys smiled fully at that, a slight twinkle gleaming in his eye. He stood, walked over to the window, unlatched it, and gave three sharp whistles. A few moments later, there was a telltale squawking noise, and Goro swooped in, landing on the windowsill. Emrys gave the bird's head a friendly pat. "Thank you for coming, Goro," he said.

"You are welcome, Lord Emrys," the raven replied. I still had to get used to that.

"If Rose has any trouble, she will whistle for you. You will come and get me immediately. Is that understood?"

Goro nodded, a rapid bobbing of his feathered head as he clacked his nails on the ledge. "I will be there for my lady. I vow it," he said before flying off once again. I was still seated on the bed, my knees drawn up to my chest.

Emrys relatched the window and returned to me. "Remember, three sharp whistles. Goro is possibly the only one on castle grounds with better hearing than me. He can pick up on a whistle from the other side of town." Emrys paused to shoot me a questioning look. "You *can* whistle, can't you?"

I rolled my eyes. "Of course, I can."

That, I could do, though I hoped I didn't need to. I knew that going into town would be risky and I wouldn't feel very welcome, but I had to try. Besides, not everyone in the village saw my awful display yesterday at dinner, only the few invited by the king and his court. Word might have reached the village of what transpired, but most would not have *seen* it in person, at least. Regardless, I would not cower in fear and shame.

"I believe you'll find Goro to be adequate company," Emrys said. "He's quite a good listener, and cheeky to boot. A master pick-pocket as well. Though he will never volunteer that information."

I couldn't help but smile at the thought of a bird pickpocket. How did one even do that without fingers?

"Here's some coin, should you need it in town." Emrys placed a small brown pouch onto the bed, and I grasped it, feeling the coins inside clink together. "I will return this afternoon."

He hesitated, frowned, lifted his hand to the back of his neck, seeming quite off kilter.

"What is it?" I asked. "Is there something else you wish to tell me?"

"No." He lowered his hand with a sigh, his movements stiff. "Forgive me. I find I'm still not quite used to having a wife, and I am still trying to figure out how to handle all of this."

"You seem to be doing fine so far," I offered with a tight smile. "Mostly. For a bounty hunter."

He smirked at that. "And you're not so bad yourself, Red." He leaned close and whispered, "For a witch."

His lips brushed my ear as he spoke, and I couldn't help the shudders that coursed through me at his proximity—such a curious reaction. He leaned back and mercifully did not comment on my increased pulse this time.

"Breakfast should be sent up for you. You will hear three knocks and they'll leave a tray outside. It's safe to eat," he added. I thought Emrys would say more, but he simply stepped away and with one last, lingering gaze, he left the room and swung the door shut behind him.

I got dressed quickly in his absence, anxious to explore. I picked a long-sleeved green dress from the wardrobe and a complementary tan cloak to wear atop it.

Three knocks sounded on the door and I frowned. Surely, it wasn't Emrys back already. When I opened the door, there was no one, just a tray of various breads and colorful jams with some form of juice—the breakfast Emrys had promised. I picked up the tray and set it inside on the small table in the room. I took little nibbles, since I *was* rather famished, and it was all rather tasty. A small vial on the side of the tray drew my attention, and I wondered what it could be. I shoved the vial in my cloak pocket once I finished eating, intent on finding out what it contained before I did anything with it.

After, I crept down the winding stone steps of the turret and peeked around the corner of the wide corridor. Thankfully, I did not encounter any fae until I made it out into the village, save the ones guarding the drawbridge, which was already lowered when I reached it.

In town, I noticed immediately that I was getting stares. When I paused for a moment to steel my courage, I felt a tug on my cloak and looked down to see a fae child with silver curls, her eyes wide and innocent.

"Why aren't your ears pointed?" the girl asked, a question of pure curiosity rather than rudeness.

"Well," I began to explain, crouching to her level, "it's just because we were born a bit different, that's all—"

"It's because she's a filthy witch," another voice interrupted me. I looked up to see an older faerie—clearly the child's mother—glaring back at me. The faerie scolded her child. "Do not talk to her. I don't care who she is married to. As far as I'm concerned, witches are all trouble." She grabbed the child's hand and roughly dragged her away from me.

I remained rooted to the spot for a moment, shaken by the encounter, before finally convincing my legs to work again. But I had only walked several more paces into town when my gaze was pulled toward the side of a shop where crudely scrawled words practically screamed at me. Two very bold, telling words, etched in fresh, still-wet paint.

WITCHES HANG

22

Emrys

I KNEW, BEYOND SHADOW OF DOUBT, THAT LIFE at the castle was about to get very bloody complicated. Firstly, no one would disrespect my wife the way they did last night and get away with it. Not even Rhea.

And I knew just where to find that bitch.

She would be doing her morning garden walk just about now. Rhea was a creature of habit. When we were sleeping together years ago, I could always find her in the gardens the next morning. Today would prove no exception.

"If you can only choose to be one thing in life, Emrys, choose to one day be a good husband." That's something my father said to me once upon a time. Rose would likely be the only wife I ever had. I owed it to her, and my father for that matter, to treat her with respect. Witch or no.

That started with defending her honor.

Just as I suspected. When I arrived in the gardens, I spotted Rhea. She stood amongst the carefully manicured flowers, at the end of a row of trimmed hedges. She faced an ivy-covered wall, deep in thought. The sight of her physically nauseated me. I strode toward her with rage simmering in my gut.

"I ought to strangle you where you stand, Rhea," I said through clenched teeth.

She spun, startled at first. Her pouty lips curved up when she saw me. She looked rather proud of herself, which further fueled my anger in a truly visceral way. Only Callum and Talyn got under my skin more when it came to me wanting to smack the life from them. Currently, I fought the strong urge to shift into wolf form and cut Rhea deep with my claws.

"Go ahead, wrap your hands around my throat. I might even enjoy it. You do remember the fun games we used to play together, Emrys?" She reached out, fingers skimming my forearm. I grasped her hand roughly and pushed it away from me as though it were a snake about to bite.

"You are nothing but a thorn in my side. And I will see to it that you are properly punished for what you did to Rose."

She threw her head back and laughed. Her expression was one of challenge as she crossed her arms over her chest. "I have been the personal tailor of the queen, and a high-ranking member of the king's court, as well as the king's only *niece*. We both know he won't do a thing to me. The only reason your witch is even still alive is because my dear uncle adheres to outdated traditions, to a fault. But tradition says nothing about having a little fun at the witch's expense."

"What you did was unacceptable. I will not let it stand. Consequences be bloody well cursed."

Now her voice grew a mock tone of sympathy. Her eyes widened to doe size and her lower lip jutted out. "Oh, did I embarrass your poor little witch?"

"Watch your tone. And if you so much as *look* at Rose the wrong way ever again—"

"You'll what?" Rhea challenged. She lifted her chin so her gaze could meet mine more evenly. She was taller than Rose but still several inches shorter than I. "You won't kill me. You don't have the stones for that. Best you will ever do is report me to the king, which as we have already established will do nothing."

"Oh, that's where you're wrong, bitch. If you ever do anything like that to her again, I *will* kill you. And I will make it look like a not-so-tragic accident."

Her expression soured further. Lips pulled into a sneer. "You might believe that to be true now, but one of these days you will come to your senses. Once you get tired of your little witch toy."

"Fuck you, Rhea." My hand darted out, catching Rhea around the throat and under her chin. I slammed her back against the ivy-covered wall and lifted so she was eye level with me, balancing on her toes.

"Go on, squeeze. Hurt me, darling. *Choke me*," Rhea wheezed, her voice strained. My fingers tightened of their own volition. "There's the Emrys I knew. You miss… what we… had…"

"You are *delusional.*"

I released her and she collapsed against the wall, gasping for breath. She braced her arm on the wall to steady herself and looked back at me. "You know, you used to be so much more fun when we were fucking."

I took a step back. "And that was the biggest mistake of my life."

She scowled as she stood up straight, gingerly rubbing her neck. "The witch has changed you."

"Better her than you."

"Keep telling yourself that."

I turned my face toward the sky, rubbing my temples. This bitch was giving me a headache. But I still knew how to get under her skin. "You know I used you, right?" I looked back down at her pointedly. "I *used* you, Rhea. Get that through your head. I only agreed to warm your bed because I believed it was the distraction I needed from my own misery. But obviously, you weren't a good enough distraction. And you never will be. In fact, you were *part* of my misery."

Rhea drew a deep breath, her upper lip twitching. For the first time, she even looked a little wounded. It seemed I'd struck a nerve. But the crack in her exterior was short-lived and her countenance hardened again. "Tell me, Emrys. Has your witch seen the true extent of the damage you've inflicted upon her kind? Show her the full truth of what goes on here and see what she thinks of you. See if she's still willing to play the part of your doting wife after that."

My jaw clenched tight, but I did not acknowledge her rant. Instead, I said, "Stay away from Rose. Stay away from *us*. This is your final warning."

With that, I turned away and strode out of the garden.

23

Rose

FOR A WHILE, I COULD NOT TEAR MY GAZE FROM the hateful words.

WITCHES HANG

"Stars, how am I going to survive here?" I muttered under my breath.

I pulled my cloak hood up to conceal my features and kept walking, refusing to allow myself to be bullied.

"I don't like those words," a voice said from nearby.

I turned my head left to see a lady standing inside the door of a shop. She was fae, of course, and wore a blue dress with an apron tied over the front—she must have been cooking or mixing something. She was curvy, face rounded, skin brown. Everything about her was all soft curves except for her pointed ears. She had thick, curly brown hair that flowed down to her waist. "I am ready for peace between our kind. Always have been."

"As am I. My name is Rose," I said, extending my hand. She nodded and waved my hand away.

"I know who you are. We all do now." She breathed deeply as though searching for a specific scent upon the air. "My name is Feyleen, and this is my shop. Would you like to come in?"

ROSE RED

I hesitated for a moment; her shop might contain the ingredients I needed for the memory tonic, and despite having my guard all the way up, I did not wish to be rude if someone was genuinely offering kindness without strings attached.

I entered the shop, which was quite small inside, the confines cramped with shelves and tables lined with trinkets. The pungent—not unpleasant, just pungent—scent of spice tickled my nostrils.

"Do you make all of these?" I asked as my fingers skimmed a small statue on one of the main shelves. Upon closer inspection, it was a wood carving of a wide-eyed, winged low fae, right next to a carving of a cat.

"Yes," she replied. "I am quite fond of whittling."

All around were images of more cats. Felines of all kind littered the walls in paintings, in tiny sculptures. It seemed a common theme. "Are you a shifter?" I asked, and winced at my own brashness. "I'm sorry, I don't know if that's too much of a personal question to ask a faerie or not—"

"I am," she interrupted. "And I take on the form of a feline when I shift. If you hadn't already figured that out."

My attention shifted back to the well-stocked rack of herbs and spices. Rosemary—I would need that. And I was surprised to see Feyleen had all the other ingredients, as well. Sage leaf, lemon balm, peppermint oil, lion's mane... It was a favorite recipe of my mother's when we lived in Astyrtown, meant to help boost memory. Sometimes, she would set up a little stand in the town's market to peddle her potions for spare coin on the side. Innocent tonics that helped focus or relax the mind.

Feyleen's was a fully stocked shop; my mother would have been impressed. I picked up two vials and three small pouches and held them up.

"May I purchase these?"

Feyleen nodded. "Of course."

I placed them into my satchel and held up the pouch of coins Emrys had given me. "How much?"

She waved a dismissive hand. "No need."

"But—"

She cut me off. "Your payment will be staying for tea and a snack cake." When I hesitated, Feyleen smiled kindly. "I am not planning to poison anything, I promise. I heard what that tailor did to you and I think it's horrid."

My cheeks reddened at that; word really *had* spread fast. But Feyleen seemed honest enough. Besides, faeries were not supposed to be capable of outright lies, were they?

"I just don't want to impose."

"It is not an imposition."

"But if anyone sees you consorting with a witch, they might accuse you of being... I'm not even sure. *Bewitched* by me?"

The fae seemed unbothered. "They all know me. None of them will do a thing to me."

"Alright," I replied with a smile. "I would love to stay for tea."

Feyleen proved to be a kind host, and we spoke for a good while. I drank her tea and ate her cake, both delicious. The tea was herbal and the cake was spongey and honey-flavored. It took me a while to take comfort in the fact that she wasn't being falsely kind to me, that she didn't plan to deceive me the way Rhea had. I found myself enjoying her company and the conversation. We spoke of the forest, of Sythea, of family. She seemed genuinely interested in learning about me, my people.

"I am far older than I may appear to a human," Feyleen said, taking a dainty sip of her tea with her pinky finger popped out. "And I have lost many. Though most beings left alive on this earth have lost many at this point, I imagine. I am not unique in that; such is just the unfortunate world we live in."

"That is true," I replied.

We were perched on two stools inside the window of her shop, watching passersby throw the occasional questioning glare our way. When I expressed concern, Feyleen waved it off. "I am trying to lead by example," she said simply.

"Oh, I have one more thing to ask you," I said, thinking about the vial in my cloak. "This was left for me on my breakfast tray this morning. I would like to know if you can identify what's in it, or what it's used for."

Feyleen took the small vial and popped the cork, holding the opening under her nose and sniffing. Her nostrils crinkled, and she took another sniff. "Ah, yes, I recognize this. It's a tonic to prevent pregnancy."

That made sense based on what the king had said. It seemed he was quite serious about eliminating any chance at procreation and expected me to take the concoction. Of course, he also likely assumed that Emrys and I were doing the usual things husbands and wives did that we were not, in fact, doing.

"Thank you," I said, pocketing the vial again.

Soon after I finished my tea, I stood to leave, not wanting to impose any longer. I thanked Feyleen profusely for her hospitality—it felt good to know I at least had one ally in town—and she insisted on sending me with some extra tea cakes for the road, which I packed in my satchel.

On the way out, I flipped my hood back up. I passed by the awful words—WITCHES HANG—and once again felt stares directed my way like bee stings, but I held my head higher now as Feyleen's kindness remained fresh in my mind, comforting me like a warm blanket.

I approached the main town square where some beautiful music drifted toward me, sung by a familiar voice. It was a welcome sound; I'd found the human bard, someone who I knew would not treat me as an outcast. Maybe I could manage *two* pleasant conversations in a day.

The bard sat on a small stool near the fountain sculpture, his long blonde hair pulled into a small bun at the nape of his neck. His eyes were closed, lost in song. Before I could approach, he switched to a familiar tune and I froze as the familiar lyrics drifted across the courtyard.

> *"She walks above the dampened soil,*
> *Runs naked 'mongst the trees.*
> *Her raven hair flows past her waist,*
> *Skirting 'top her knees."*

I allowed him to finish the song, fighting a wave of emotion in the back of my throat at the memories it called to mind. When he was done playing, I walked up to him.

"Hello. Is your name Jasper?" I asked.

He looked up with wide-eyed astonishment, likely stunned that someone not only spoke to him, but knew his name.

"Yes, it is." He blinked rapidly, ice blue eyes narrowing.

"Where did you hear that song? I wasn't aware it was widely known in noma circles." I shook my head, unsure if he was familiar with the nickname. "I mean, non-magic human circles."

Jasper frowned, but then he leaned in close and spoke at a whisper. "I used to be a traveling bard. I often played for witches as well and heard some of their songs in the process. I was very young then, perhaps even younger than you now, and my mind was like a sponge, absorbing everything. But that was over two decades ago. Time sure does move at a gallop."

The bard appeared significantly younger than he was, it seemed. He only sported the faintest of lines around the corners of his eyes. He couldn't be more than nine and thirty, perhaps forty at most.

"I thought bards wrote their own songs," I said.

Jasper shrugged, his expression a bit sheepish. "When you're forced to play as much as I am, sometimes you run out of material and have to borrow from others. But don't tell anyone. Wouldn't want to ruin my reputation." He grinned cheekily, the lines at the corners of his eyes deepening a little. It was surprising—yet good—to see him able to make light of his situation. Some would say when humor was lost, hope was lost.

"No, wouldn't want that." I offered a small smile in return. "But the fae don't have a problem hearing witch songs?"

"They don't know the song's origin, and I don't believe they much care about the lyrics. They simply like to hear my voice." He flashed his teeth again. "In short, what they don't know won't kill me."

"I heard you play at dinner last night. You do have a lovely voice. I can see why the king is so enamored by that sound."

"Thank you, you are too kind. I saw you last night, too, Rose." He flushed then and started to fidget, fingers squeezing the strings of his lute. "I mean, I didn't see... well, I *did* see, but I didn't... I looked away when—"

"It's fine." I waved a hand. I didn't bother asking how he knew my name, either, because it was obvious he'd heard it at the banquet. "I must laugh it off or else I will go mad. What happened is done, the whole court saw me naked, and now we need to move past it."

"Right." The tips of his ears reddened, and suddenly he seemed desperate to change the subject. "If you don't mind my asking, how did you come to know Emrys? And how did you two, well... It's not every day you hear of a faerie and witch marriage."

"Let's just say that things turned out far differently than I had thought they would upon our first meeting."

Jasper did not reply to that. His gaze drifted across the courtyard as though conjuring a daydream. I crouched close, keeping my voice low.

"Tell me, Jasper... are you alright here? Truly?"

Jasper looked to the ground, clutching his lute tighter, and he wouldn't meet my eyes this time as he spoke. "When the fae invaded, my people were slaughtered right in front of me. I had taken no wife, and I had no children. For the first time in my life, I was grateful that I had no attachments, grateful that I didn't have to watch anyone I love die before my eyes. And now, well... I play because I have to, yes. But also, because I've finally been given something to live for."

I was about to ask what the *something* was, but Jasper shifted uncomfortably again. I realized at the same time he did that others were staring at him expectantly, and he lifted his instrument back to a ready position.

"I must keep playing now, Rose. As you can see, my legions of fans are waiting."

He smiled, but made it clear I was being dismissed. I took the hint, giving Jasper his space to play, and continued to wander through town while contemplating his words. I passed through the other end of the bustling square when I felt something... peculiar.

It felt like my blood was roiling in its veins, warming and pulling me in a distinct direction. I instinctively knew that I had to follow it on pure, blind instinct.

I moved through the now-crowded streets, ignoring the wayward glares as I followed the strange tingling. I rounded a corner, passing into a more desolate part of town, and the raucous sounds began to fade behind me. The tingling grew stronger the farther I ventured from the thick of town, almost like I was being led somewhere by an invisible force.

My blood heated more beneath my skin, beckoning. Relentless, it pulled me past the rows of small homes beyond the thick of town, leading all the way to just inside the stone walls surrounding the perimeter. It was a remote corner of the village, behind all houses and shops. There, I followed the tingling in my veins to a little alley within distant sight of the stables. And then...

The sensation stopped all at once. No more heating, no more tingling. There was nothing to see there, nothing of any significance. So, why was every part of my body begging me to keep exploring this dull, empty alley?

But then I heard someone coming, the distinct clomping of heavy footsteps nearby. I had the uncanny feeling that I shouldn't be here, that I'd ventured somewhere I shouldn't have. I rounded the corner out of the tiny alley quickly, eager to distance myself.

And collided right into Callum's chest.

"Well," he said, glowering down at me. "Fancy meeting you again, witch."

I bounced back with a yelp; it had been a little like hitting a stone wall. As big as Emrys was, Callum managed to be even a little bigger. He stood a couple inches taller, his shoulders broad, neck and chest thick like barrels.

"What are you doing outside the castle, witch? And what are you doing over here in this lonely back alley, of all places?" Callum glared down at me, chest puffed out. His blonde hair—slightly darker and shorter than Jasper's—was pushed behind his pointed ears, the ends curved up around the lobes, further showcasing his wide features. His thick brows somehow appeared even lower across his eyes today, nostrils flared like a bull and lips curved into a permanent scowl. His square jaw sported a splotchy blonde stubble. I held my chin high, refusing to cower from him.

"I wasn't told any areas were forbidden."

"The king told you not to leave, and you are dangerously close to the city walls."

"I am still within its boundaries and therefore I am not breaking any rules."

"I suggest you don't go wandering around. For your own sake."

"Is that a threat?" I tried to control the trembling in my voice.

"Make of it what you will," he replied.

I huffed, lifting my chin higher and balling my hands into fists at my sides. "I am Emrys's wife, not a prisoner. The king ordered everyone to welcome me, not punish me."

"Well, the king will say what he must to ensure Emrys's complacency. But make no mistake, *witch.*" He loomed over me, staring down his nose. "Your presence may be tolerated for now, but you are very far from *welcome.* And you may not be Emrys's prisoner, but considering that the king has expressly forbidden you from leaving the village... you are certainly still *his* prisoner."

My mouth flapped open and shut. I knew he was right and felt my face begin to warm.

"You are positively *crimson.*" A devious grin stretched Callum's features. "I could see it plainly last night too. You were very red in places I've never seen a person grow red before."

My face flushed hotter. "You will not win, Callum. You will not make me cower in fear and shame."

"No, but I know what will put the appropriate amount of fear in you. You will follow me now."

The words seemed to reverberate throughout my skull. Immediately, I knew I was under a fae enchantment. While the last thing I wanted to do was follow this brute, I found my feet stubbornly moving one in front of the other, acting independently of my brain. When I tried to fight, sharp, stabbing pains shot throughout my body, making me grunt.

This was what made the fae so dangerous. Witch magic was elemental. We could manipulate the elements to our favor—fire, wind, water, earth. We could use all these elements of Mother Earth to confound, to locate, to sense, to trap. However, what we could not do was *force* someone to do anything against their will. We could not *control* actions or influence emotions. Unlike the fae. Their magic was most treacherous.

"You enchanted my grandmother like this." I said it through clenched teeth, speaking to Callum's broad back. "You put her under your spell."

"Your grandmother?" He threw me a look over his shoulder. For a moment he blinked in confusion, but then his eyes widened in recognition. "Oh, right. The old woman in the cabin who slit her own throat. What a mess. Old witch stole money right out of our pockets and got us flogged. That would make *you* the witch who created the ring of fire in her own kitchen. I must say, that was magic I had not seen before. Impressive."

It made me physically ill knowing that all he cared about us was what extra coin he could fetch for his bounty, but arguing with him would not accomplish anything good. I just wanted to be free of this enchantment that made me feel violated in every way possible. "Where are you taking me? Please, at least tell me that."

He was silent for a long while before responding. He met my gaze again, licked his lips, and said, "I am taking you where you belong, witch. To the dungeons."

24

Emrys

I WAS STILL FUMING AFTER MY ENCOUNTER WITH Rhea, not quite sure how well I'd gotten through to her. Rhea was indignant and proud. Unrelenting. A dangerous combination. But if she came for my wife again, she'd regret ever being born.

I returned to the castle and paced corridors for a while. Desperate to blow off steam before my meeting with the king. I'd just passed the grand staircase when I heard a peculiar noise float down the hall. It was coming from the servant's quarters. Was that... moaning?

Curious, I followed the noise and soon realized where it was coming from. Jasper the bard's little room, tucked away in the far corner of the servants' wing. The door was ajar. The moaning sound grew stronger. What if the bard was being attacked? I could hear Rose's voice in my head expressing her concern for the human. She would demand I check on him.

How was my wife already rubbing off on me like this so soon? More importantly, why was I allowing it to happen so readily?

The thought of Rose aside, I could not stop myself now. Even if I had any inclination to. And when I peeked into the open door, I spotted something... unexpected.

"Well, shit," I muttered under my breath.

Jasper the bard and Korvyn the prince were locked in a distinctly passionate embrace. Their mouths latched onto each other. The vast majority of the court including the king himself knew Korvyn preferred male company. However, no one knew he had started an affair with the bard. With a *human.* I suspected he never intended for anyone to find out.

I turned to walk away quickly, pretending I didn't witness a thing. Korvyn must have spotted me. The door creaked on rusted hinges and rapid footsteps gave chase. When the prince caught up to me, I realized that he didn't even sport his facial glamour.

"Emrys," he said, visibly breathless.

I held up my hands as though surrendering. "This was my fault for sticking my nose where it didn't belong. But in fairness, the door was ajar. Significantly."

"Jasper was just taking a break from playing his music in the square. He actually said he spoke to your wife for a few minutes, and..." He cleared his throat. His breath came in short spurts. Panicked. "Emrys, please, you cannot tell my father."

"I was not planning to," I replied.

"It is bad enough that his favorite advisor has married a human witch, but if he found out his son was having a dalliance with the human bard, I fear how he may react. He already feels me unworthy of the crown, of being his heir."

Korvyn's glamour briefly flickered back into place then fell once more. It often did this when he was feeling particularly emotional. His glamour and enchantment powers were not quite as strong as others in the king's court. It was another thing that disappointed Armynd about his son. Now, his scars were exposed, encompassing half of his face. The skin on that left side was rough and ridged in several places of slightly different pigmentation, like a patchwork quilt. He'd obtained the scars during a battle involving witches years ago. The same skirmish that killed his mother. Unlike his father, Korvyn didn't seem to hold a grudge.

The prince felt along his face and sighed before sliding the glamour back into place. The skin on the scarred side was once again smooth. Though it was never perfect, always a little too lustrous.

"Korvyn, you've always been decent to me. Even when you did not have to be. I wouldn't divulge your secret to anyone. But if you wish to not be discovered, conducting your affairs in the bard's room with the door ajar is not the most inconspicuous course of action."

"Yes, you are right." He smiled a little. "Thank you, Emrys."

I clamped a hand on his shoulder and offered a friendly squeeze. "No need to thank me. Just be more careful."

With that, I turned to walk away down the hall from the way I came. I still had matters to attend to with the king. I had become derailed from my normal obligations because I had allowed Rhea to ruffle my feathers. Even now, her wretched voice was the worst kind of echo in my skull.

"Show her the full truth and see what she thinks of you."

Perhaps I would do just that.

"Lord Emrys!"

There was a flap of wings and a flurry of black feathers. Goro flew through the hall and landed at my feet. He spoke quickly, clearly worried about something. "I was circling the village and, well... it is my lady. *Your* lady, I mean."

"Rose?" Now my interest was piqued. "What's wrong?"

"I think you'd better come with me," the raven said. He took off back down the corridor toward the drawbridge, beckoning me forth.

Without hesitation, I followed.

25

Rose

"YOU'RE TAKING ME WHERE?" I DEMANDED AS Callum continued to steer me with his enchantment.

Callum shook his head. "Are you deaf? I said *to the dungeons.*"

"But why?"

"To show you what you need to see."

"You're not planning to lock the door and leave me there, are you?"

He chuckled cruelly. "As tempting as that sounds, I am not allowed to do such a thing. Not yet, at least." The pointed look he tossed over his shoulder chilled me to my core.

"So, you're taking me to the *witches'* dungeon, right?"

"Where else?"

"And there are witches in there now?"

"Perhaps."

I nibbled my lower lip, pondering, then said, "You don't have to use your enchantment on me. I will follow of my own free will, if you so insist." If I was being honest, part of me *wanted* to see the dungeons, no matter what Emrys said, especially if there were fellow witches inside. What if they were people who happened to know me from long ago, in Astyrtown? That wasn't outside the realm of possibility.

"Now, where's the fun in that?" Callum replied, his amused grin widening further. When I shot him a withering look, he rolled his eyes, but relented. "Fine."

The enchantment and compulsion faded and I nearly cried in relief. No wonder my grandmother would rather die than risk falling back under its control. While every aching muscle in my body tried to convince me to run in the opposite direction, I decided to keep my word and follow instead. Best just get this over with because Callum would force me to see whatever it was he wanted me to see one way or another.

He hurriedly led us through the winding castle corridors, snaking this way and that. We moved down a narrow set of steps into a cold, dark tunnel, a wing that smelled earthy and stale, the air damp. At the end of the tunnel sat a single, black door: the dungeons. A guard stood beside the door, clad in black armor and holding a sharp spear. He was so still, I'd almost thought him a statue at first.

Callum squared his shoulders, looked straight at the guard, and commanded, "Let us in. Now." He jerked his chin toward the dungeon door.

The guard shifted his gaze toward me in question, but it seemed whoever he was, Callum outranked him. He obeyed, opening the door with a jangle of keys and swinging it wide.

I craned my neck to peer inside but could not see much, and then I was shoved, hard, as two large hands hit me square on the shoulder blades. I stumbled forward, almost tripping, and Callum slammed the door shut behind me.

"Hey!" I shouted, banging my fist on the door. "You said you wouldn't lock me in here!"

He spoke to me through the little barred window at the top of the thick door, looking smug as ever. "Spend a little while here. Go and see the conditions you witches belong in. I will be waiting when you cannot take anymore. If it were up to me, I would leave you in here indefinitely. But Emrys and Armynd would eventually find out, and I'm not ready to stir that pot just yet."

He backed away from the barred door. I had no choice but to step forward into the poorly lit dungeons. The confines were narrow and dark with no natural light and very feeble flames flickering on scattered torches on the walls. It felt so cold and so oppressively stuffy at the same time, the air laced with dampness that made my dress stick to my skin.

As I passed by empty cell after empty cell, their dirty floors stained and overrun with rats, I understood that this was a place of sheer, unmatched misery. The thought sent a shudder through me that went from my head down to my toes. I stared at the rusted shackles and chains in the desolate cells, picturing witches there, so lonely and afraid, awaiting the inevitable time they'd be tortured or killed. Bile stung the back of my throat and tears pricked the corners of my eyes.

Stay strong, Rose, I told myself. It was very easy to picture myself being locked in here, as well. This was what my fate would've been if Emrys hadn't found a use for me. At any moment, this could *still* end up being my fate if I wasn't careful. I hugged myself, fighting a wave of chills.

My ears perked; there was a shuffling noise up ahead. Something bigger than rats and... was that *voices?* On edge, I wandered deeper still and found one of the cages occupied. I was not alone in here. As I drifted toward the cell, I realized the bars were enchanted, just like my cuffs had been. I could sense the magic pouring forth from them.

"Hello," I called out. "Is anyone here?"

Two sets of hands grabbed onto the bars from the depths of the cell, and two dirty faces peered out at me from the darkness.

"You are not fae," one of them observed. The pair were of equal height and build, their dark hair matted, their skin so caked with dirt it was hard to tell what color it once was. Both of them also sported a thick band of metal around each of their necks, some sort of collar with symbols etched into the outer ring.

"No, I am not. I am a witch like you, sisters." My voice cracked as I said it.

The stench of unwashed bodies and human excrement gathered in the buckets behind them—provided as latrines—wafted forth, and I fought the urge to gag. These were horrendous conditions to force anyone to live in, especially for any extended amount of time. A large rat scurried forth through the bars, darting past my feet.

"My name is Ophelia, and this is Orinthia," said the witch who had greeted me.

It was difficult to tell them apart, especially in the near dark when I couldn't even make out features like eye color. But the one who had just spoken—Ophelia—had a long, pink scar on her cheekbone.

"I am Rose," I said. "And I... Stars, this is..." I slapped a trembling hand over my mouth, unable to find the proper words. I raised my hand to my throat. "What are those?" I asked, indicating the collars.

"Another means to control us," said Orinthia. "They suppress our magic, even when we leave the dungeon."

Just like the cuffs Emrys had once slapped upon my wrists. Now, all I could muster was a muffled, "I am sorry."

Ophelia fiddled with a trinket around her neck that dangled below her metal collar—a silver pendant curved into delicate knots. I was surprised the fae hadn't snatched it away when she'd been captured.

"How are you walking freely here, sister?" Ophelia asked, tilting her head as she regarded me with slight suspicion.

"I, um..." I licked my lower lip, bit down, then spoke the truth in a quick burst as though the whole sentence were one word. *"I married a fae and the high king gave our union his blessing."*

Orinthia grabbed the bars tighter, her expression turning to disgust. "How could you do such a thing?" She spoke at the same time Ophelia asked, "Is your husband on the king's court? He must be rather high ranking to secure your protection."

I chose to answer Ophelia's question. "He is." My ears heated. On some level, I felt ashamed by the admission, especially seeing how other witches were really treated here by my husband's people.

"I hope he is not one of the bounty hunters who brought us in," said Ophelia, recoiling. "They were utter brutes."

"No," I replied quickly. "He was not one of them."

"But, why, sister?" asked Ophelia, echoing Orinthia. "Why marry a fae?"

"It was a marriage of convenience," I explained. "We... agreed to help each other."

I refused to look the witches in the face and admit that, on some level, I had even grown to care for Emrys. In fairness, there was more to him than met the eye. But he was still a faerie, a being towards which Ophelia and Orinthia currently felt no good will.

"Surely that can't be true." Orinthia shook her head. "Fae may not outright lie, but they certainly know how to bend the truth and deceive. It is a trick to get what he wants."

"I thought the same at first. But he is different than them. He was... actually very wronged by our kind, and I know he is sincere, sisters. I saw him relive his memories. I heard him cry in the night."

"I refuse to believe that," Orinthia said. "Faeries deserve whatever they get."

"Not him. Not all of them."

Ophelia had lapsed into silence, but she spoke again now. "The bad blood went on for longer than any of us know, and it is true that travesties were committed on both sides. I suppose the bloodshed has to end eventually. We cannot carry on like this, can we?"

"But, the Outerlands," Orinthia began, and Ophelia shushed her.

"Watch what you say, sister. Anyone can be listening," she snapped.

I lowered my head closer to the cold bars, ignoring the smell wafting from within. "What about the Outerlands?" I asked.

Ophelia looked to Orinthia as though they were silently deciding what to tell me. After a moment, Orinthia said, "Rumor has it that witches can find safety at the other side of the Void."

"But how do you get through the Void? Is passing through even possible?" I asked. The two witches exchanged another look.

"Perhaps," Ophelia said, though there was a twinge to her voice that seemed to indicate she knew more than she let on.

Orinthia interrupted before I could question further. "Our ending is coming soon, I fear." She sighed, wistful, mourning what was lost.

"No." My tone was resolute and I immediately made a solemn vow. "I promise, if it is the last thing I do, I will free you both."

No sooner had I said those words than something in the room changed. At once, the close confines felt even closer, as though the walls were closing in on us. A tickle traveled along my spine like cold fingers dragging up and down. Whispers in my ear grew louder, harsher, like so many buzzing bees. Something was coming. Something terrible.

"What's happening?" I asked, clinging tighter to the bars.

"Oh, no. Not again." Orinthia groaned as the dungeon came to life with a flurry of voices, some familiar, all of them vying for my attention.

"Duck down and cover your ears, sister. Close your eyes!" Ophelia warned as she heeded her own advice, hunching on the floor and placing her palms flat over her ears, curled up next to Orinthia beside the bars.

I could not comply because those voices... those *voices*. I looked around wildly, desperate to find the source.

And then... through the darkness, my grandmother walked toward me from the main dungeon door.

26

Rose

I NEARLY COLLAPSED ON THE SPOT AT THE SIGHT of her, choking back a sob.

"Gran?"

But she didn't look like the warm woman I knew in life. Her face sported no smile, her expression cold and not at all happy to see me. A line of blood formed around her neck, the wound where she sliced herself now opening up all over again like when it was freshly cut. Behind her, two more shadows emerged, stepping into the flickering sconce light. My knees threatened to buckle.

"Mother? Papa?"

They also showed no warmth toward me, their faces bloodied masks of disappointment. "We died protecting you, and it was all in vain. Look at you, surrounded by the fae," Gran said. Her eyes were glazed over now—the look of the dead.

"You have a darkness in you, Rose," my father said. His dark hair was greasy, unkempt, so unlike him. His broad shoulders were hunched as though the weight of my very existence had pressed upon them with leaden fists.

"You will dig up our family secrets and give in to the ancient darkness. You will fall to evil," my mother added. All the beauty she'd had in life was long gone now, her skin gray and pocked like a wight. Her spark that had always gleamed brightly within was now dulled, like a candle snuffed out and cold. All three of them stood side-by-side in one judgmental row.

"You will bring shame to us all," my father said.

"We should have let you die rather than allow you to consort with the fae," said my grandmother. They converged on me, circling, taunting, pointing accusing fingers.

"You have betrayed your fellow witches," they accused in unison. *"Traitor, traitor, traitor!"*

"No!" I shrieked, dropping to the dirty floor and crouching into a ball. "Stop. *Stop it!"*

My palms slapped over my ears. I felt their hands upon me, their icy fingers grabbing, clawing. I whimpered, but then...

All became still. Quiet. Nothing touched me anymore.

Though I was too afraid to move until I felt a hand nudging me. I opened one eye cautiously to see Ophelia poking me through the bars.

"It's over for now," she said. Slowly, I unclenched my body from its curled-up position on the ground and sat up.

"What on earth was that?" I was still trying to slow my heartbeat, which hammered like a drum.

"That was another faerie trick that occurs in the dungeons to torture us," said Orinthia. "Some sort of glamour meant to expose us to our greatest fears."

"We have learned to tune it out," added Ophelia, "but it's always rough the first time. It plays with your mind quite effectively."

"How often does it happen?" I asked, and Orinthia shrugged.

"Often enough. Whenever they think we're getting too comfortable."

"What triggers that sort of magic?"

"We are not sure," replied Ophelia. "As Orinthia said, it is obviously some kind of fae glamour."

"Time to go, witch. Emrys will be looking for you soon," a voice called from somewhere behind the main door, echoing down the narrow dungeon corridor and making me jump. Callum.

I sighed and stood on legs that felt wobbly enough to rival a newborn deer. "I must be going. But I promise I will see you both again."

"Our coven leader said she would see us again, too. So long ago. And here we are," Orinthia said miserably.

"Where is she?" I asked.

Orinthia exchanged a look with Ophelia, who shrugged and replied, "We do not know. But I do know what she would always say. *Keep your faith, sisters. Time is the prize.*' She would say it every time we were sure the fae were going to catch us. She always did her best to keep our spirits up." Her punctuating sigh was sorrowful.

Callum banged the door again; I needed to move. Before I could, another thought occurred to me. "Do they give you food and water?"

Orinthia chuckled mirthlessly. "Enough gruel to keep us alive for now. It is barely edible, and we are often left wanting. But yes, I suppose."

"Well then, how about a treat?"

I pulled the two tea cakes from my satchel that Feyleen had packed for me, placing one into each of their palms through the bars. I could hear the rumble in their bellies.

"Enjoy, sisters," I said. "And please take care as best you can, until I can come back for you."

They had barely managed a mumbled *thank you* before devouring the cakes.

I headed back toward the main door to meet Callum, who waited impatiently, pacing back and forth. Once I exited the dungeon, Callum closed the door and boxed me in against the cold stone wall, refusing to let me pass. Each of his meaty palms touched the wall on either side of me such that his arms formed a barrier.

"Enjoy the show?" Callum asked. He knew I'd just been exposed to that awful glamour. I did not reply, and the brute continued. "Do you know why I brought you to the dungeons to show you all this?"

At my continued silence, he spoke again.

"I showed you this to remind you what you married. These were not Emrys's bounties, but dozens like Ophelia and Orinthia passed through here before, brought in by Emrys himself. At his core, he will always be fae, no matter how you try to sink your witchy claws into him. He will never turn his back on his own kind, and if it comes down to it, he *will* choose us over you."

"No." I shook my head. "That is not Emrys anymore. You act as though you know him, yet all you do is berate him. Maybe you never really knew him at all."

But how could I be so sure? Truthfully, I did not know that for certain—we hadn't known each other very long, after all. We had only met in the first place because he had *captured me* for bounty.

"I have known him a lot longer than *you,*" Callum pointed out, and I could not argue with that. "I am telling you not to trust that husband of yours. He has much to hide, Rose."

I snorted. "Don't tell me you're pretending to look out for me."

"I would never look out for the interests of a *witch.* I am just reminding you that your days here are numbered. *No one* here truly wants you. Don't get too comfortable."

"Noted." I didn't care what he said at the moment. All I knew was that I did not want to spend another second here, trapped in this hallway with Callum. I realized that the guard who'd been there earlier was now suspiciously absent, so it was just us two in the dungeon corridor. Probably so Callum could have privacy to harass me. "May I go now?"

"Just one more thing. These witches *will* hang when it's their time. Do not even *conceive* of trying to help them escape. If you do, I *will* find out, and so will the king. You will be executed for treason without question, and it will be *your* legs dangling from the gallows, joining your own kind just as you deserve. And you will hang with Emrys as witness."

Not wanting to hear anymore, I ducked under his arm and ran past him as his words festered in my mind. Thankfully, he let me go and did not attempt to stop me with another enchantment.

I knew that, no matter what Callum said, I had to do what I could to free Ophelia and Orinthia. He was probably *hoping* I would so he would have a reason to get me executed, but I did not care.

No matter what it took, I would find a way. I had a duty to save those women.

"Witches *all* hang eventually!" Callum's voice bellowed after me down the hall, fading into the distance as I broke into a sprint.

UNSURE WHERE ELSE TO GO, I RETREATED BACK towards the turret room to find Emrys descending the stone steps. Hearing my approach, Emrys's head jerked up. I paused at the base of the stairs.

"Where were you?" he demanded. "Goro told me he was worried about you. I have been looking everywhere, but your scent trail went cold."

Scent trail? Shifter senses were still difficult to comprehend. Also, I had not even noticed Goro following me. "I was in the dungeons," I replied casually.

Emrys looked at me sharply, scarred brow flexing. "Did you just say you were *in the dungeons?*"

"I was."

His gold eyes narrowed. "Despite my distinct warning *not* to visit the dungeons."

"I had not planned it."

From the way his jaw clenched, I could tell he was angry with me. "You will not go there again, Rose. I forbid it."

My nostrils flared and I lifted my chin in defiance. "You cannot forbid me from anything."

He stood tall and stared down at me, even more imposing in height since he was still a step above me. "You are in my village. My castle. Amongst my people, under the ruling of my king. I serve as high-ranking member of his court. I most certainly *can* forbid you."

"Must I remind you that this castle and the entire village once belonged to humans and was forcibly taken? And I am your wife, not your prisoner. Maybe the king's prisoner, but not yours."

"I know that." His tough façade faltered just a little. "You just do not need to be throwing yourself into dangerous situations."

"My being here in the first place has always been dangerous. Why are the dungeons any more dangerous than the rest of the castle?"

"Because there are often guards in the dungeons specifically trained to detain witches. Let's not tempt fate with you."

"There was only one quiet guard who gave us no trouble when Callum asked him to open the door. He barely even glanced at me."

Emrys's mouth tightened. "Callum?"

"Yes, Callum was the one who took me to the dungeon. He was the one who wanted me to see how witches are really treated in the kingdom."

"And explain *why* you were with Callum?"

"It was not by choice."

Emrys came down the final step and gripped my shoulders tight. "He is vicious, Rose. Especially toward your kind. You of all people should know not to go near him."

"He cornered me and enchanted me to follow, and I am not able to resist a fae enchantment just yet."

"He enchanted you?" One of his hands lifted from my shoulder, reaching toward my face. "Did he hurt you?"

"No." I batted his hand away. "He just made me follow him."

"That bloody twat," he mumbled. He sucked in a sharp breath through his teeth, clearly fed up with Callum's antics. "He should not be enchanting you at all. He *knows* that. And given that this is no longer Aegan and Lysia's inn, I believe it is time to remind him."

His gaze darkened. Immediately recognizing his intent, I grasped his arm to stop him from passing me on a vengeance mission. "He dropped the enchantment once I agreed to follow him willingly," I said.

Emrys's head tilted, gold eyes bouncing around as he assessed me. "And *why* would you agree to follow him willingly?"

My own anger began to resurface then. Now he was shifting blame to *me* somehow? "Tell me, do you really wish for me to not visit the dungeons for my own safety... Or is it because you don't want me to see the deplorable conditions the witches are kept in? So that I don't think less of you for dragging them to their doom?" I couldn't help but reflect on Callum's words, because there was some truth to them.

"Callum said something to you, didn't he." It was not a question.

"He did. He told me that you had much to hide. He said I shouldn't trust you."

"And you believed him?"

No. But instead, my head tilted, and what came out was, "Maybe. Should I?"

Emrys looked a bit wounded by that, though the brief glimpse of vulnerability soon turned into something feral. I wasn't sure if the anger he harbored was directed more at me, or himself.

"You want to see what a monster I really am, Red? Would you like to see *all* that the witches must endure? Because Callum was right; there *are* things I wished to keep hidden from you. To spare you from seeing."

"I... I..." I sputtered, unsure how to reply to that.

"Come." Emrys pushed past me and grabbed my wrist in a vice-like grip, yanking forward.

"You are hurting me, Emrys," I protested, suddenly flashing back to the woods when he dragged me around in tight shackles. Maybe we weren't as far past that stage as I would have liked.

"Then don't make me drag you."

He released me and I followed, unable to stop myself. This was the second time getting dragged around by a faerie today, and I didn't like it at all. Though I needed to see whatever Emrys was about to show me, I suspected. Morbid curiosity festered within me, a burning ache that wouldn't be quelled until I knew all that I was up against.

We crossed the drawbridge, veering away from the bustling town center and following the cobbled streets around the edge of the moat until we were fully behind the castle. There, the cobbled stone streets became no more than dirt. A vast field came into view in front of us and Emrys halted us at its far edge.

"The witches' fields," he said, gesturing widely.

"This is an empty field." All around me were patches of torn-up grass, many open holes in the dirt, some mounded over as though something was freshly buried. "What do the witches do here?"

"Dig." Emrys jerked his head towards the dozens of holes in the field.

"Why do they dig?"

"So there is a reason to beat them," Emrys replied simply. "The witches work for no purpose other than to *make* them work. And when they tire, they are beaten or placed in the stocks."

Emrys pointed across the field at two sets of stocks streaked with blood. Next to the stocks stood something that made my mouth dry and my blood run cold in its veins. A taller wooden structure, a sentinel of doom.

The gallows.

"Yes," Emrys said, following my gaze. "They also work knowing they are bound for the gallows. Standing feet away from the very thing that will kill them. And then, they are buried in this field. You are standing on top of the bones of witches right now. I suppose that's part of what the witches dig—their own graves."

I stepped back on instinct, clutching my stomach and fighting a sudden wave of nausea. "I thought you said the king keeps them around for a while to use them however he sees fit."

"Oh, he does. He often forces them into labor around the castle as well—jobs none of the other fae want—while heavily guarded. When they aren't working or in the dungeons, they are here. Digging. For no good reason."

My eyes refused to turn from the gallows. I could picture the witches who had been hanged there, their feet swinging, their faces purple and necks broken. I could not stomach the sight, nor the thought. My breathing became labored as my chest tightened.

"Do you understand now?" Emrys said. "Now, you know everything. You know the full extent of how witches are really treated here."

From the corner of my eye, I saw Emrys turn to face me, but I refused to look at him. "Why are you showing me all this?" I cried, unable to stop the traitorous tears from running down my cheeks.

"So you know who I really am. I turned witch after witch over to the king knowing that this would be their ultimate fate. And while I did not relish in their deaths, I also did not care. And I did not care because I knew that if I did as the king asked of me, he would eventually break my curse. I did it all for personal gain. Nothing more. Look at me, Rose."

"No."

"Look at me." He grabbed my chin and forced me to look up at him then. I swore there was a flash of regret in his eyes as he saw my tears, but he hid it behind an impassive mask. "There was even a time when I would watch witches hang, and Rhea and I would go fuck later that night like it meant nothing. *Nothing.* I am a selfish bastard. Do you understand now?"

I could only hold his gaze, his eyes fiercely golden in the sun. My chin quivered in a way it hadn't since I was a child. "I understand everything. Callum wanted me to see the dungeons too, to know... everything you've done."

"Callum, for all his faults, is right about me. And should you ever feel yourself softening towards me, then hear this. Death is not only what I want. It is what I *deserve.* You should want nothing more than to break my curse. For when my curse is broken, and I finally end my miserable existence, my decaying body will serve the earth better than I ever could in life. Never forget that."

"I won't." It was a vow. My voice was barely a croak. Callum also said Emrys would always choose his own kind over me, and now, I was beginning to feel like that was true. No matter what he said about "protecting" his wife.

His fingers flexed around my chin, tightening just a little. "Tell me, Red, what do you think of me now?"

"You want me to hate you," I whispered.

"And do you? Because you should. Very much so."

I did not answer him. Instead, I freed myself from his grasp, turned, and ran away from the field, finding the cobbled path that led around the side of the moat back to the thick of town. All the while, I tried my best to force the image of the gallows and the graves from my mind.

Unable to slow, I ran through the main square, past its many shops and carts and fountain, not stopping until I reached the stables. I entered, passing horse after horse in their stalls. Some of them lifted their heads and huffed in my direction, more preoccupied with their food than anything else.

"Hey, Stardust," I said once I reached his stall.

His head hung over the side and he let out a soft neigh in response. Bending, I grabbed some lone pieces of hay off the ground and offered them to Stardust, who nibbled happily.

"Remember me?" I gently stroked the soft bridge of his nose and, finding myself otherwise alone in the stables for the time being, allowed myself a moment to lean my head against the side of the horse's neck while I cried. Stardust hung his head over my shoulder, the closest thing to a hug that a horse could give, I imagined.

After I had cried myself out and left Stardust to his food, I found a quiet corner of the village behind the stables to curl up in and whistled three times. I wasn't sure why I summoned the raven, but Goro arrived promptly, landing by my feet.

"Thank you for coming so quickly," I said. "I'm not in trouble. I just needed to ask you something."

Goro looked up at me with his little black eyes and said, "Ask anything you'd like. I am also a good listener, my lady."

I idly picked at the hem of my dress as I spoke. "Emrys says you are loyal to him."

"Yes, I do serve Lord Emrys loyally."

"Why?"

"Because he saved my life once."

That wasn't the answer I'd been expecting. "He did?"

"Yes, my lady."

"May I ask how?"

The raven sighed. "Some time ago, I had grown into a fit of despair. My family was very devout in their belief that remaining in shifted form was honoring the gods. A very outdated way of thinking, indeed. By the time I decided I no longer shared their beliefs... well, the thought of becoming fae again was overwhelming. I had grown accustomed to being a raven, you see. At the same time, I also was tired of being considered an abomination for choosing to stay in animal form. I was caught in a terrible limbo. One day, I found myself attempting to rile up an eagle to attack me. Emrys stopped me. He talked me down, and we became allies."

"I had no idea. I am very sorry."

He waved the feathers of his right wing, the equivalent of a human waving a hand in a dismissive gesture. "It was a long time ago. I am much better now." Though his tone still held a hint of sadness.

"I am glad you're better. You're wonderful as you are, Goro." I paused and changed the subject, sensing that Goro might not want to speak about this any longer. Additionally, I did not want to hear more, content to just remain angry and disgusted with Emrys for a while. His good deeds were inconsequential to me right now in the wake of learning of all his horrible ones.

"So, you serve Emrys loyally, but how about me?" Goro regarded me with a tilted head, black eyes blinking, and I clarified. "As Emrys's wife, would you serve me loyally, too?"

At that, Goro flapped his wings and flew out of sight for a moment. At first, I thought I'd been given my answer. He was loyal to Emrys, not me, and now he was probably off to tell Emrys everything I just said. I pulled my legs to my chest and sighed, resting my head atop my knees.

A few minutes later, my head snapped up at the sound of a squawk. Goro had returned with a bright orange flower held in his beak, freshly plucked from the castle gardens. Once he landed, he laid the flower at my feet—a clear peace offering.

I laughed and picked the flower up, twirling it in my fingers before bending to smell its sweetness. "Thank you."

"You are welcome, my lady," Goro said. He looked skyward as though hearing something I did not. "I must be going. But call again if you need me. Any time."

He flapped away, leaving me alone with my thoughts once again.

Thoughts that quickly turned back to the gallows.

27

Emrys

ROSE MUST HAVE HATED ME NOW. AS WELL SHE should. We would be going our separate ways soon enough. I could not forget the original purpose of our alliance, despite my subconscious screaming at me that I was a fool. A coward.

I hadn't meant to frighten her and I could not shake a deep feeling of regret. Remorse, too. Nor could I ignore the unrelenting urge to throw myself at Rose's feet. To beg her forgiveness. To taste her...

I had been given my first taste at our wedding, but I was a greedy bastard. I wanted more. I wanted all of it. All of *her*. But that was something I could not have.

"Bloody imbecile," I muttered to myself.

Rose was my wife. I would continue to do all I could to protect her, as promised. But I had no gods-cursed business wanting her the way I did.

Now, I made my way to the familiar little meeting room adjacent to the throne room. Inside was nothing more than undecorated walls and a single, rectangular table with the high-backed king's chair at the head of it.

Around the table were six other chairs occupied by myself, Prince Korvyn, Callum and Talyn, and the king's two highest ranking guards, Rogyn and Pery. The latter were hawk shifters. They both possessed deep-set, violet eyes and olive skin. They had a penchant for answering their questions in unison as though the two shared a single mind. My brother Merys had been my twin, as well. But we were also individuals with our own interests. Rogyn and Pery, on the other hand, acted as one. The only way I could tell them apart was by the slight scarring on Rogyn's face. A single slash through the middle of the brow where hair refused to grow.

They weren't cruel, just a bit mindless. They did what the king asked without hesitation. Probably why King Armynd valued them as guards. If he needed a head chopped off, he'd snap his fingers. Rogyn and Pery would jump with axes in hand, not batting an eye.

I sat between Korvyn and Pery at the table. Glared back at Callum and Talyn across the way. They seemed more perturbed and unpleasant than usual. If that was possible.

The king took his seat at the head of the table and nodded to each of us in turn. "I'm afraid this session will need to be brief," he said. "I will need to speak to Emrys separately after this."

My brows pinched together. Wasn't sure I liked the sound of that. But Armynd changed the subject before I could ask what he had in mind.

"Tell me, what do I need to know?" He leaned forward on his elbows, fingers steepled. "Pery, Rogyn, any news?"

"Yes," they replied in unison before taking turns finishing each other's sentences. Like the odd sorts they were.

"The Spring and Winter courts," Pery said.

"They are still speaking of gaining independence," said Rogyn.

"They are quite unhappy at the moment."

"They plan to attempt a negotiation with you as soon as possible."

"They want you to grant them land in East Sythea."

"Both North and South."

"They wish for the ruling courts to be as they were before."

Once, there were four courts named for each season. During the war, the courts took irreparable hits and consolidated into one for safety. Now, some of the courts wished to break off again and be granted the land and resources to do it. The king felt we were stronger united, which caused some unrest from the fae who wished to operate independently once more.

Armynd sighed, seeming weary to his bones. The king was quite old. Sometimes the weight of a long existence shined through in his mannerisms. "I assume they are none too happy with me at the moment. Perhaps they even trust me less now given that I am allowing a witch to roam free on castle grounds without chains."

Before I could protest the king's words, he snapped his gaze to Callum and Talyn. "Have you also seen this unrest?"

The pair exchanged a look before nodding. "Yes, highness," Callum replied. "The majority of the populace loves and trusts you. But there are some who are growing increasingly..." He searched for the right word, finally settling on, "Discontent."

Talyn nodded his agreement. "There's more, as well. It seems Bryock, the former Lord of the Spring Court, snuck out sometime during the night. Scouting land and rallying his sympathizers, I suspect."

"And why am I only just now hearing about this?" The king's palms slammed to the table.

Promptly, he stripped off his shirt and stood still. His feet spread to shoulder width apart. The eye tattoos all over his torso and back twitched and blinked. One of the eyes shifted its position to the middle of his chest. The mark connected to Bryock. King Armynd also liked to keep track of any potential troublemakers, often forcing marks onto any he deemed problematic.

The king pressed his fingers to the eye. It lit up like a little red lantern in the center of his chest. He closed his own eyes to concentrate, rubbing his finger into the tattoo. His lips parted slightly. Once satisfied with what he'd discovered, he opened his eyes. That tattoo immediately stopped glowing when he pulled his hand away. The eye slid back to its starting position at the lower side of his torso before stilling altogether.

"He is headed toward his former castle ruins in the southeast," Armynd said with confidence. "Rogyn and Pery, after this meeting ends, go find him and bring him back immediately."

"Yes, highness," the shifters replied in unison.

"There is something I would like to say," said Korvyn.

I cocked a brow. The prince rarely spoke up at these meetings.

The king's attention half-heartedly turned to his son. "By all means, speak your mind."

The prince's head was tipped down, staring at his hands folded on the table. He cleared his throat and continued in a voice far quieter than his father's. "You may have to compromise with the court lords, Father. Or else they will grow increasingly restless, which may result in a less than optimal outcome."

"I believe compromising to be a show of weakness," the king replied. Instantly dismissive of his son's proposal.

"But we cannot allow discontent to fester. Perhaps you can promote Bryock to a member of the council as a means to appease him. Perhaps some of the other former court lords, as well. In my opinion, we could use—"

"An opinion I did not ask for." The king scoffed, cutting him off. "When you are king, dear boy, you will have free reign to make these decisions. But it is I who still wears the crown, is it not?"

Korvyn sighed at the dismissal, visibly frustrated. Eyes still downcast toward the table. Korvyn usually did not take a strong stance against his father. Though in fairness, Armynd left little room for argument.

"Thank you all for reporting," the king said. "Now, I must end this session early. Leave and give me time with Emrys." He flicked his fingers toward the door like he was swatting flies with them.

When the others filed out of the room, I noted that the king had not asked me to speak. He still didn't. He simply gestured for me to follow him out of the small meeting room and into the throne room. Once we were alone, he wasted no time in sharing his utter disappointment. It seemed I did that quite often—disappoint. Though I was sure Korvyn felt the same way.

"You know I don't like to be kept waiting," the king said without turning. He clasped his hands behind his back. "You were supposed to meet with me privately before the council meeting, not after."

"I do apologize. I had an issue to address first."

"With your wife?"

"Yes."

A single, humorless chuckle jerked his chest. "That is an issue, as well."

"What issue?"

"She was spotted entering the dungeons. Tell her she is forbidden from visiting the dungeons again—I made sure Callum was aware of that fact as well. I don't want her getting any ideas, conspiring with other witches. No good can come of it."

"I... will remind her to avoid the dungeons," I said cautiously. My eyes narrowed as I read into the king's tone. "But there's more, isn't there?"

There was a long pause before Armynd turned toward me with judgment apparent in every line of his expression. "A witch, Emrys? I still do not understand."

The king wouldn't look me in the eye. I couldn't blame him for questioning this either. Not from his perspective. It was difficult to explain such an abrupt turn-around without sounding suspicious. The situation was complicated, just like my feelings for Rose. I decided simple redirection to be the best course of action. "Are you not happy for me? You held a banquet for us."

"I adhere to tradition, Emrys. Like my wife did. But that does not mean I understand. Witches took your entire family. Witches took Maeve, the love of my life." His fist thumped his chest hard. Right over his heart as though reminding himself that a piece of his wife still resided there.

The queen had always possessed a larger streak of kindness than her husband. Though one could argue it was her compassion that got her killed.

"Again, Rose is—"

"Different?" he supplied.

"Yes. She is."

His tone remained skeptical. "Maybe so, but we shall see. In the meantime, you must keep her in line."

"I know."

He shot me a look to match his tone. Brows raised. Lips pursed. "Do you?"

"I do. But she *is* my wife. I made a vow before the gods to protect her from harm, and there is still the matter of Rhea."

"What about her?"

"She publicly humiliated my wife at her own feast. Surely you remember. It happened right in front of you."

"And she will be reprimanded."

"It is not just Rhea, either. Talyn threatened her. Callum enchanted her to follow him. He has threatened her more than once."

His brow crept higher. "Did any of them hurt her physically?"

"Well, no. But—"

"Then you already know my answer. Words do not equal actions."

"With all due respect, did you miss the part where I said Callum *enchanted* her?" I knew the frustration was becoming more apparent in my voice. "Enchantments go beyond mere words."

"I enchanted her to be calm during your hundred cuts. Callum enchanted her to follow. She wasn't hurt in either scenario. So, what's the problem?"

"The problem is that none of you have any business *enchanting my wife,*" I snapped before I could stop myself.

The king glowered at me. His patience was worn thin to the point of breaking. He puffed out his chest and his wings began to unfurl. "Might I remind you to remember your place and watch your tongue?"

"Apologies, highness." I did know my place. And I knew better than to deliberately upset the king.

Armynd rubbed his forehead. "You are giving me quite the headache, boy."

"I don't mean to. But you must understand, Rose is my main concern now."

"And I promise you she will come to no real harm so long as she follows the rules. Do you not trust my word?"

"I trusted you completely, highness." It was a twist of words, using the past tense. I had certainly trusted Armynd with my whole being once. Now? Not so sure. And regardless of what Armynd said about Callum and Rhea, I would not wait for the king to decide their punishment. Should any of them lay a hand on my wife, I would kill the fuckers.

"Then relax, Emrys." The king tilted his head. His wings settled back into place. "There is something else on your mind. You have a similar tell as my son. So, out with it. You may as well finish exhausting me." He crossed his arms tightly over his chest and waited.

"I have served you loyally for decades."

Armynd's eyes narrowed as he interrupted. "Before you say something else you regret, might I remind you that you had nothing when I took you into the castle?" The king's expression grew thoughtful, even slightly wistful. "Do you remember when I first brought you here from Aegan and Lysia's?"

"I do."

"Sure, they found you in the wreckage of your own home, bloodied and afraid, and they cleaned you and fed you for a time. They cared about you, but they could not care for you the same way *I* could. Because who can care better than a king? And when I found out your entire family had been killed—including your father, a true talent whom I'd once considered a friend—I did not hesitate. I welcomed you with open arms."

"I know," I replied.

King Armynd had given me everything when I needed it most. Despite our differences, I would never forget that.

The king's tone grew clipped and his gaze darkened once again. "I brought you by my side as a high-ranking member of my court, made you a Lord when you had no nobility in your blood. I even gave you a beautiful room with a view. And you question me?" He shook his head. Clicked his tongue. "I have cared for you as though you were my own son. Korvyn considers you his brother."

"I know, and I am eternally in your debt for what you did for me. I wish to continue to serve you loyally, as a member of your court. However, I can no longer be your bounty hunter."

"If it is the blood bond with Rose you are worried about, you know that there are ways to ease the pain of separation when you are out hunting, yes?"

"It's not the pain I'm worried about. I just cannot hunt witches anymore out of respect for my wife."

Of course, there was more to it than that. The king required that Rose stay on castle grounds so that he could keep an eye on her. And if Rose was required to stay on castle grounds, then *I* would stay on castle grounds as well to keep an eye on *her*. Leaving her alone here for any length of time was absolutely out of the question. Too much could go wrong. Not to mention that every day I was gone was one less day for Rose to attempt to break my curse.

The king let out a long, weary sigh. "I had a feeling that was coming. Very well, I accept that. Because I suspect most, if not all of the witches are long gone from Sythea at this point, anyway."

That stood out as odd phrasing. "Long gone? Where—"

"But," the king interrupted, "I only accept your terms as long as you do not interfere with our other witch prisoners."

"Of course not."

"Also, I hope you do not plan to ask me about breaking your curse anytime soon. I still require your services."

"Understood." I had anticipated that as well. But now I had Rose, so it would be no matter.

The king narrowed his eyes, clearly expecting more of an objection. Perhaps he wanted to get a rise from me, which I would not give him. His mouth tightened and he gave a quick exhale through flaring nostrils. "Good. Also, I still require a report from your travels."

Thank the gods. This was the easy part. "Of course, highness."

I quickly summarized my travels, speaking of my encounters with the low fae and thieves. Armynd appeared bored by my report thus far. He made a show of fighting a yawn. His foot clicked out impatient taps on the marble floor.

"Finally," I continued, knowing just what would pique his interest, "I also encountered a Void pocket."

Now I had the king's undivided attention. His brow perked and he leaned forward. "That far west?"

"Yes. I was quite surprised."

"Was the witch in your company then?"

I did not much care for his phrasing. "My *wife,*" I emphasized the word, "was with me."

"And what happened? Tell me everything, dear boy." He strode forth. His hand rested upon my shoulder.

It often baffled me how quickly the king's tone could change. "A wight came out of the pocket. We clashed. The pocket disappeared." I left out the part about Rose entering the pocket. Somehow, that seemed dangerous for the king to know.

Armynd bobbed his head as though he'd expected that answer. Sometimes, I wondered if his spiked crown was permanently sewn to his scalp, given that it never budged no matter his motions. He squeezed my shoulder. "Valuable information, Emrys. Thank you."

When I started to turn away, he stopped me. His fingers curved like claws, digging into flesh. "I have not dismissed you yet."

"There's more?"

His head tilted, brown eyes scolding. "You know I cannot let your indiscretions go unpunished."

I frowned at his words. He had already given me a hundred cuts, what more was he planning?

He clasped his hands behind his back and sighed. "The others cannot think I've gone soft, and it is well known that anyone who abandons their post does not do so without consequences of some form. Therefore, you will receive one hundred cuts twice a day for a fortnight, then once per month for the entirety of the next year, through the next winter solstice."

My eyes widened. That was the harshest punishment he had ever doled out. He was making an example of me, and I had no choice but to accept it. Consequences were ironclad. Complaints accomplished nothing. "Very well, highness."

His fingers unclenched. He patted my shoulder again. "I'm sure you barely feel the cuts anymore, Emrys. You are one of the strongest lads I know."

Truthfully, I felt every cut. Every slash. One could only grow so much of an immunity to pain.

Armynd summoned Rogyn and Pery while I dutifully stripped off my shirt. At least it wasn't Callum and Talyn today. Thank the gods for small victories. The twins strapped me between the pillars near the throne, all business as usual. They gave no apologies. But at least they would take no real pleasure in my pain.

I knew this part all too well. Gritted my teeth in preparation. Just before the cutting started and the first burning wounds spread across my chest, the king held up a hand.

"I want our dear Emrys to understand the severity of his actions, so we will do something differently today. Your cuts do not have to stay upon his torso, back, and arms as normal. Cut wherever you wish to inflict pain. He will heal."

My mouth fell open. There had always been rules for my cuts before. No face, nothing below the belt. This was not true today. We were entering new territory, and the king's expression chilled me. It was the first time I had ever seen a hint of satisfaction in his eyes. Like he truly believed his punishment was just...

Rogyn and Pery exchanged a puzzled look and shrugged. They would do as the king asked of them without question. It was what they knew best.

This time, when the cutting started, I could not help the screams that followed.

28

Rose

A BREEZE WOKE ME UP, GENTLY CARESSING MY face. I frowned in my sleep, shoving some hair away from my eyes and wondering when the window had been opened. I distinctly remembered it being closed when I went to bed.

I blinked awake and my eyes took a moment to adjust to the dark surroundings of the room. My gaze settled on the window, which was open, and the moonlight was blocked by a large, shadowy form.

Emrys.

His side of the bed was empty, cold. He sat rigid on the window sill, his back facing outside, his eyes closed. I called his name. He did not open his eyes, did not stir or acknowledge me in any way. Maybe he had been walking in his sleep?

Drawing a deep breath, I swung my legs over the side of the bed and sat up.

"Emrys?" I called again, fighting a yawn. What hour was it? "What are you doing?"

He remained motionless in the window, feet flat on the floor, palms resting upon his knees. It was actually quite eerie, and an unsettled feeling grew in the pit of my stomach. I set my feet on the ground and stood, approaching with caution. Maybe Emrys just needed to be woken up and did not realize what was happening.

Before I could reach him, Emrys leaned forward and braced his hands on either side of his thighs on the windowsill. His lips curved into an isolated smile, eyes still closed.

Then... he pushed himself backward out the window.

"Emrys!" I shrieked in horror as he fell.

His feet went out last. I raced to the window and leaned on the sill to look down, reacting on instinct.

"*Talamh!*" I shouted, picturing exactly how I wanted the earth to respond.

The ivy that grew up the side of the castle darted out and snatched one of Emrys's ankles, halting his free fall. With my last bit of concentration, I pictured the ivy snaking farther up the turret, dragging Emrys along foot-first back to the window.

He awoke just as he was passing back across the sill.

"What the—*oof!*"

The ivy unceremoniously dropped him on the floor. I knelt beside him as the ivy retreated back out, spell broken. Emrys leaned up on his elbows, legs stretched out in front of him as he shook his head like a dog trying to dry itself.

"Gods. The fu—what?" he sputtered. "What just happened?"

"I should be asking you the same thing," I retorted, only just realizing how fast my heart pounded in my ears. "I think you were sleepwalking. You just pushed yourself out of the window and I had to use my earth magic to save you."

"Ah." Emrys squeezed his eyes shut and tilted his head skyward, nostrils flaring. His lips parted to emit a low groan. "Not again."

"Not *again?* You mean, this has happened before?"

He nodded slowly and tilted his head back down to meet my gaze. His gold eyes flashed in the moonlight. "On occasion."

"Why?"

He blew out a breath. "Let's just say I have cheated death frequently and sometimes death gets angry. I told you death is attracted to me. It even tries to come for me in my sleep. Obsessed with what it cannot have."

"I thought the nightmares had gotten better."

"They have. But that wasn't a nightmare. That was... death guiding me in a targeted sleepwalk."

"And how often does that happen?"

"Not all that often. Used to be more but I suppose death grows weary, too." Before I could ask more, Emrys frowned. "Did I hear you say you used earth magic to save me just now?"

"Yes."

"You shouldn't have." Now Emrys looked angry. "It was foolish to risk anyone seeing you using magic to save someone who cannot die."

I felt my ears heat. "No one saw. It is the middle of the night. Oh, and you're welcome."

"If anything happened to you because of me..." He trailed off and blew out a long breath. "I mean it, Red. Just let me fall next time."

That was the last thing he said to me before climbing to his feet, shutting the window, and storming out of the room.

EMRYS RETURNED SOMETIME DURING THE NIGHT after I had fallen back asleep. He was walking quite stiffly the next morning when he got ready as though feeling some lingering pain. But I did not ask him about it, nor did I say a word about his sleepwalking.

Before Emrys left, he turned to me, clearly hearing I was awake. "I must attend to more matters with the king," he said. "Goro will accompany you today. No more dungeons."

"Uh huh," I replied. I flipped to my other side, facing away from him.

"Rose." Emrys came around to the other side of the bed and knelt, staring pointedly into my eyes. His own looked especially vivid that morning, though I could not stand their assessment. I tore my gaze away and Emrys sighed. "Rose, I need you to look at me and acknowledge that you will not visit the dungeons again. The king has forbidden it. You do *not* want to test the king's limits."

I merely nodded in reply, and Emrys sighed.

"I said *look at me.*" His hand darted out to grasp my chin, holding my head still. My eyes flicked back to his, and his mouth tightened at my irritated expression. "Promise me, out loud, that you will not visit the dungeons again."

"Fine. I promise," I said curtly.

"Good." He released my chin and stood.

"Wait." I pushed myself to a sitting position. "I worry about them, Emrys. The witches in the dungeon. They are my *people.* And the least you can do is help me with something in lieu of my visiting the dungeons personally."

He cocked a brow. "And what something is that?"

"You can check on the witches. Or if you going there might arouse suspicion, you can find someone who you trust to check on them. Just so I don't go mad wondering what's happening to them."

"Red..."

"Please?" My eyes were wide as I pleaded, but really, it *was* the least he could do at this point after how he treated me.

He sighed. "I will see what I can do."

For a moment, he hesitated, fists clenched, as though he wished to say more, but he did not. Instead, he left the room, closing the door behind him. I was on my own once again.

After getting dressed, a tapping sound from the window made me spin. Frowning, I looked over to see Goro perched on the sill outside. When I opened the window, the raven lowered his head, pushed a foot forward, and swept a wing in front of him just like a person taking a grand, flourishing bow.

"My lady," he greeted.

"Hello, Goro."

"I am at your service today." Goro straightened back up and fluffed his feathers out, shaking his tail. The feathers looked a little damp; it must have been raining earlier, though the sun was out now. "Lord Emrys has asked me to stay with you."

"I know." I wouldn't complain about Emrys's request, and I somehow felt better with Goro keeping an eye on things. It was rather strange, having a bird as a bodyguard of sorts.

"Where are we off to today?" he asked.

"I haven't quite decided yet."

"Well, an adventure it is then. Shall we?"

Goro leaped onto the floor, walking with steady little hops in front of me. He led through the castle to the drawbridge. We crossed into the thick of town and soon passed by Feyleen's shop that sat right at the far edge of the main square.

"Look." Goro gestured with his wing toward the shop. "I love Feyleen; she is always very generous."

Outside her shop was a small pile of seeds and bread crusts stacked near the door, seated atop a piece of cloth to keep it all dirt free.

"She always leaves some out for me," Goro said. He hopped over to the pile and began munching happily, seeds spraying all over the place.

As he chewed, Feyleen poked her head out. She wore a pink apron today. "Rose!" she greeted with a little wave. "Lovely to see you again. You too, Goro."

The raven waved a wing in reply, his mouth too full of seed to speak.

Feyleen turned her attention back to me. She crossed her arms over her chest and leaned her hip against the door jam. "Did the memory tonic work?"

"I haven't gotten a chance to test it yet," I admitted. "But I promise I will let you know as soon as I do."

"Please do. I'd love to know if my ingredients are potent enough. You know I do most of my gardening right out back, behind the shop? It's a lot of work, but I find it quite fulfilling."

Goro hopped back over then, having eaten his fill. Feyleen bid us a quick farewell before disappearing back inside her shop. As we continued onward, I thought about what Emrys had said before and tossed a sly smile in Goro's direction.

"Emrys tells me you're a pick-pocket."

He waved a wing. "I *was,* my lady. My family was quite poor growing up and I learned certain skills to help us get by. Regrettably, some of those skills were not always so legal."

"How, exactly, does a raven pick-pocket? If you don't mind my asking."

"I can show you." Goro nodded toward a female faerie walking across the far end of the square. "I will steal that shiny comb from her hair and she won't feel a thing."

Goro flew away before I could respond, swooping across the courtyard like a breeze. He buzzed above the unsuspecting fae, glided down, and plucked the comb from her hair, effortlessly grasping it in his feet. He redirected his path of flight, circling back around toward me. Once he reached me, he dropped the comb into my outstretched palm and I laughed.

"That was something to behold. Although, you didn't exactly pick her pocket."

"She did not have pockets, my lady."

"Regardless, it was still quite impressive." I turned the comb over in my hands, admiring it. It appeared to be gold inlaid with pearls, and I wondered how much something like this would cost. At the ground beside my feet, Goro shifted uncomfortably, dancing around in nervous little hops. "You want to give it back, don't you," I said knowingly.

"Yes, please, my lady. I do not like to steal anymore."

Smiling, I bent to hand Goro back the comb, which he accepted in his beak. The faerie he'd stolen from was distracted by a fruit stand at the far end of the courtyard, and just as she started perusing some citrus, Goro dove back over her head and dropped the comb.

"Beautiful accessory, miss!" he shouted as the comb bounced off her head.

She looked up in shock before feeling the back of her hair and frowning in confusion. Goro swooped back over toward me and made a panicked motion with his feet, gesturing me to *shoo.*

I ran beside him as we fled, until we were safely away from the courtyard and out of sight of anyone who might accuse us of thievery. I bent, my palms on my knees as I rested, letting out a tremulous belly laugh all the while. The raven landed near my feet.

"You are wonderful company, Goro," I said when I'd straightened back up and caught my breath. A month ago, who would have guessed my closest ally would be a bird?

"You as well, my lady," he said.

"May I ask you something?"

"Yes, my lady?"

"Would you happen to know where to find Jasper? The bard?"

Goro looked up at me over his shoulder and swiped the tips of his wing feathers across his beak like a person scratching their chin. "You wish to visit the bard?"

"I do," I replied. "If you wouldn't mind."

"Of course, my lady. Follow me." Goro waved his wing to beckon me forward.

He flew at first, circling back around toward me, but once we crossed the drawbridge, he landed on the stone floor and waddled through the winding corridors. He made a left at the end of the first corridor, then a right, leading towards a much less picturesque wing of the castle. No tapestries, no marble, tiny windows, some walls gathering a thick layer of dust where no one bothered cleaning. I remembered Emrys pointing in this direction and mentioning the servants' quarters when he gave me the initial tour. It would make sense that they stuck the lone noma there.

My footsteps clacked on the flattened stone as I traipsed behind the waddling raven.

"The bard's room is this way," Goro said. He stopped. "Ah, seems we arrived just on time!"

Jasper had just stepped out of his room, and when he spotted me and Goro, he froze, blue eyes wide. I waved to him, and he lifted his hand in an awkward return wave as though he hadn't expected to see me again, at least not so soon. "Are you busy, Jasper?"

"No, I was just going for a walk," he replied, tucking some stray blonde locks behind his ear. "I usually go for a walk before I start playing. Gets the blood flowing, keeps the senses sharp. I must keep the old ticker as nimble as possible, you know." He tapped his head.

"I can come back, if you'd prefer to be alone," I offered.

"No need. I have another hour before I am scheduled to play, and I would quite appreciate some company."

"Great." I peered down at Goro, who still lurked near my feet. "Goro, would you mind giving me a little bit of time alone with Jasper?"

He narrowed his black bird eyes, tilting his head. "Lord Emrys asked me to keep an eye on you."

"You can still keep an eye, just at a distance for a few minutes? There are a few things I would like to speak to Jasper about in private." It wasn't that I didn't like Goro, or didn't trust him. But Goro was still, at his core, *fae*, and I was seeking another strictly human perspective.

"If I allowed you to wander alone, Lord Emrys would not be happy with me at all. Do you promise to stay in this corridor with Jasper?"

"I will not leave this corridor," I replied sincerely.

After a long moment, the raven nodded. "Very well, but I will not stray far. I will speak to you soon, my lady."

Goro waddled down the hall, staying within sight at the end of the corridor so that I would not be able to sneak past him if I decided to vacate the servants' wing. I turned my back to him, facing Jasper. The raven proved to be a wonderful distraction that morning, but in his absence, my careful façade crumbled. When Jasper noticed this, his features pinched with concern.

"Are you alright, Rose?" he asked.

I paused to draw a deep breath, head shaking. "Not really. I saw the dungeons yesterday, and the fields."

"So, that means you also saw—"

"The stocks and the gallows," I finished for him. "Yes."

Jasper nodded knowingly. "It is tough to stomach. I was shown the same thing when I was brought in the service of the high king as a reminder of how easily my life could be snuffed out if they so choose. I did not expect anyone to throw me a welcome party, but their hospitality certainly left something to be desired."

My trembling increased and I wrapped my arms around my middle in an attempt to self soothe. "Why do they hate us so?" I echoed the words my grandmother had said to me the day before her death.

"They don't *all* hate us. I happen to know that for a fact. Goro seems to be quite fond of you, for one," he pointed out.

"That's true, and I am very fond of Goro. He is different, though."

"It is a start. Who else?" He leaned against the wall and crossed his arms over his chest, shoving his hands beneath his armpits as he listened.

I thought for a moment. "There is also a faerie shopkeeper in town who was very kind to me. She gave me tea cakes."

"Feyleen?"

"How did you know?"

"Because she's given me a cake or two as well. Even brought me tea with honey when my throat grew a bit sore after an extended session in the square."

"She's very kind."

Jasper held his hands up as though to say, *I told you so.* "There, you see? And are you not married to a fae?"

"I am, although it is… complicated."

"And I…" He licked his lips and trailed off, flushing. "Never mind."

"Jasper." I managed a conspiratorial smile once I'd composed myself, and nudged him with my elbow playfully. "Are you secretly seeing a fae?"

Jasper said nothing, but he blushed an even deeper shade of scarlet. That was all the confirmation I needed, and he quickly changed the subject. "I have something to show you. Perhaps it can help with some of the feelings you've been having." The bard waved his hand, beckoning me to follow into his room.

Being in the servants' quarters, his room was far smaller and more threadbare than Emrys's. His mattress was thin and his sheets rough, his furniture made of unpolished wood that looked as though it might give one splinters if sat upon the wrong way. Jasper crouched next to his narrow bed and slid something out from beneath one side of the mattress.

A leatherbound journal.

"A kind faerie gave me this shortly after I had been captured by the high king, and I have been keeping records in it. Some speak to poor treatment, but many of them recount acts of kindness. You would be surprised just how many there are." He opened the journal to a specific page and slid it over to me to read. His handwriting was a neat, flourishing cursive

"On this day, a shopkeeper in town offered me some hot tea with honey, a most delightful treat, its aroma like the sweetest mead," I read. His words were every bit as flowery as his penchant for storytelling through song. "Would that be Feyleen?"

"It would be." Jasper flipped to another page.

"Today, the fae prince told me a most wonderful thing. He declared that my voice was the first thing to make him smile since his beloved mother's death," I read, running my finger across the paper. I looked up, brow raised. "That is very sweet. Prince Korvyn does seem a good deal nicer than his father."

The tips of Jasper's ears were red. He bit his lip. "Let's move on to another page, shall we?" He thumbed through another couple of entries before turning the book back towards me. He thumped his pointer finger on the page. "Here."

"Today, three rosy-cheeked fae children danced in the square to my music, a lively little jig. Their grateful mother

255

tipped me with a delectable, fresh slice of bread. It was warm as a summer's day," I read.

"And the one directly beneath that," Jasper prompted.

My eyes scanned down the page. *"Today, I had a private audience with the high king Armynd. At first, he seemed quite morose, but then he taught me a hauntingly beautiful song that he loved when he was younger. He asked me to play it, and I obliged him. At first, I was frightened, but the king seemed impressed with my rendition, and the song flowed out of me like a serene river."*

I peered up at Jasper, brows furrowing with skepticism. "I am frightened of the king as well. I never quite know what to expect with him."

"Nor do I," Jasper admitted. "But he has not raised a hand toward me yet, so I suppose that must count for something."

"Are you asked to sing privately for him often?"

He nodded. "Usually once a week, sometimes more. Particularly when he's feeling nostalgic about the queen."

When I slid my finger beneath the page to turn to the next one, Jasper pulled the journal from my grasp and slammed it shut. "There are some things in here I wish to keep private—my innermost thoughts are enough to make one's brain bleed in large doses—but you get the idea. It's not *all* bad."

"Thank you for showing me this, Jasper." It did help to ease my mind a little.

"He's hiding something else."

The voice came out of nowhere as though spoken directly into my ear, and I whirled around. There was no one in the room but the bard and myself, and the door was closed. Had the voice come from inside my own head? There was also a tickling at the base of my skull, a tingling in my veins, and then the voice spoke again.

"*Ask him what else he is hiding,*" the voice demanded, and I jumped.

Jasper stared at me in question. "What's wrong?"

"You are hiding something else in here," I said, repeating the words of the voice in my head. It was a statement, not a question. Somehow, I knew this to be true.

Jasper immediately paled, jaw slackening. "How did you—"

"Because I think whatever it is might be calling to me, somehow."

"*The bard possesses a witch artifact,*" the voice hissed, and I paraphrased its words.

"It is something that once belonged to a witch."

Now the bard's ice blue eyes widened, and I could tell from his expression that I was right. Jasper bit his lips together and slid on his knees at the far corner of the room. He grasped a loose stone on the wall and pulled, revealing a small, hollowed-out space containing a book. He carefully pulled it from inside and dusted it off before placing it face up on the bed.

The book was dark brown with gold lettering, bound in worn leather, with strange symbols etched around the border and on the spine. I knew immediately that this book had power.

A grimoire.

I did not believe this was the one my family once possessed. I didn't remember much about it, but I distinctly remember different binding. Grimoires were quite rare, but more than one did exist in the world, and now, I had found another.

"Korvyn had salvaged it from a previous excursion to Astyrtown and gifted it to me," Jasper said.

I flipped the pages, one after another. Each page had a gold border inlaid with more peculiar symbols, and spell details meticulously written out. Every page included an illustration that was, to say the least, unsettling. The illustrations depicted the intended effects of each spell. This was the first time I'd ever gotten to look inside a grimoire, as my parents had always forbidden it. I could understand why now.

The spells in here made me uneasy. Spells to shapeshift into another person, or to bring great wealth. There was also a multitude of curses and hexes, their accompanying illustrations depicting endless suffering in gut-twisting detail. Curses to bring plagues upon entire households, to erase memories, even to whither crops and kill livestock. The energy this book gave off was far from positive and fairly overwhelming. I flipped page after page and did not see anything about an immortality spell. But even after I had perused every last page, I found myself transfixed, unable to put the grimoire down, its energy sending tingles up my limbs, into my chest. I felt possessed.

"This noma dared to hide a witches' book after the fae laid their filthy hands on it. Kill the noma. Kill the fae prince. They have no business touching a witch's things."

I knew the voice in my head was not mine. Was it the book speaking directly to me, trying to convince me the ideas were my own?

"You've been reading for quite a while, Rose. I have to go soon," Jasper said, interrupting my thoughts.

I frowned; how long *had* I been reading? I'd gotten so lost in the book's pages that I had completely lost track of time.

When the bard reached for the grimoire, I yanked it back and snapped at him. "Does it look like I'm finished?"

Jasper blinked, taken aback.

"Kill the bard and take what's yours," the voice said. This time, I could picture myself setting Jasper aflame, cackling as I watched his skin char to black and the flesh

ROSE RED

peel from his bones, dusting the floor with ash. My skin warmed. I raised my hand.
And prepared to summon my fire.

29

Rose

IT WAS JASPER'S WIDE-EYED LOOK THAT stopped me, the distinct look of trepidation. It horrified me, the thought of being *feared*. Stars, what had I been doing? With a gasp, I slammed the book shut and jumped back.

"I am sorry. Put the book away," I whispered.

Jasper's eyes narrowed, but he slid the grimoire back into its hiding place nonetheless. "What happened?"

"Did the grimoire ever call to you, Jasper? Did it ever make you... feel things?" I hugged myself, rubbing my arms to relieve a sudden chill.

He stood and turned back to face me, expression puzzled. "What kinds of things?"

Awful things. "I don't know, just... things."

"No," Jasper said. "The book never made me feel any sort of way, other than saddened by how much human and witch history had been lost during all the fighting."

I chewed my lower lip in thought. That meant the grimoire only spoke to other witches. "I think this book might be dangerous," I said.

"How so?"

"It seems to influence thoughts. I—does anyone else know about the book?"

"Only Korvyn."

"Promise me you will keep it that way." When he hesitated for a moment, my voice rose a couple of octaves. "Promise me you will keep it hidden!"

"I promise, Rose." He held up his hands in surrender. "No one will find out."

"Good."

"I must be going now," he said. "It is my time to play in the square. But this was... Well, this was *something*."

He seemed eager to get away from me all of a sudden and I could not blame him. He left the room and I moved to make my exit as well. But in his wake, I heard the grimoire whispering to me again.

"Do not leave the book here. It belongs to you. Take it. The noma has no business keeping it."

It took every ounce of strength I possessed to leave the room behind, close the door, and flee down the hallway. The book wanted me to *kill*.

True, I had killed my fair share of fae, and I may have done so without much guilt, but I only did what I must to ensure our survival. After reading the grimoire, I could see myself not only killing, but taking great pleasure in it. *Laughing* about it and seeking more destruction to quelch my own bloodlust. That frightened me more deeply than I cared to admit.

"Come back!" the grimoire demanded. I was so eager to get away that I rounded a corner without looking and crashed directly into Emrys's solid chest.

He grasped me by the upper arms, preventing me from stepping back on instinct. "Where are you going in such a hurry, Red?"

"Do you care?"

"Of course, I do." He frowned. "I was worried you might've done something rash and gotten yourself into more trouble after what you saw. Goro told me you were with the bard and I came to find you."

"Worried?" I snorted, shaking his hands off me. I wasn't ready to make amends. Not quite yet. But as I turned to walk away and put distance between us, Emrys stopped me.

"Rose, wait." His hand darted out to grip my elbow before I could get far, and I instantly yanked it free.

"Stop acting like you care enough to worry about me after the way you treated me. All that talk about wanting to protect your wife, yet your actions *wound* me, Emrys."

His expression softened. "I won't apologize for worrying. But I *will* apologize for snapping at you after you saved me from falling out of the turret. And for... showing you the fields the way I did."

"Don't. I needed to see it." The fields served as a further reminder to never let my guard down here. As a witch, I would never *not* be in danger, that much was apparent.

Emrys's golden eyes grew pained. He pushed a hand through his dark hair, almost a nervous gesture. "I want you to know that I am not that person anymore. I will not be taking anymore bounties no matter what punishments the king doles out for it. In fact, that was part of the matters I discussed with Armynd. I informed him that I would continue to serve on his court, but not as his hunter. He agreed, though I was given a hundred more cuts. I will continue to receive cuts daily for a fortnight."

I cringed at the admission, but did not relent. "That sounds awful. But do you just expect me to forgive you for everything else because of it?"

"I also spoke to Korvyn. He owed me a favor or two, and he agreed to check in on the witches periodically."

"Thank you," I said sincerely. "But as I said, that was the least you could do."

Now, Emrys's patience seemed to be wearing thin. He grabbed my arm to keep me from storming off, tighter this time. His jaw twitched as he spoke, eyes flashing and pink rising to the tips of his pointed ears as he attempted to bottle his clear frustration with me.

"You can be angry with me all you wish, Red. But we *do* still have an agreement, and you *will* honor it. You will come back to our room and make your first true attempt at breaking my curse. *Right now.*"

I saw no sense in arguing and followed Emrys back down the corridor without further objection.

On the way back to our turret room, I asked Emrys to make quick pit stop to the kitchens to borrow a mortar and pestle—an essential in any tonic, potion, or poultice making. Now, I had everything I needed, and as soon as Emrys closed the room's door behind us, I set to work.

I had him sit on the bed while I mixed the items for the memory tonic quickly—ironically working from my own memory. First, I poured drops of oil and balm into a little bowl, and used the mortar and pestle to ground up the leaves and lion's mane before mixing everything together. The sludge didn't look very appetizing, but hopefully it would do the trick. If not, I had enough of each ingredient for multiple doses to try again should this attempt fail.

Once finished, I handed the bowl to Emrys. "Drink," I instructed, and he wrinkled his nose.

"Dear gods, what is in this?" But he obeyed, throwing his head back and downing the liquid in one gulp. He blanched at the taste, the scar around his brow twitching. "How long do we wait?"

"It should work pretty quickly." I sat beside him on the bed. "Now, this memory tonic is meant to call to mind all the details you might have forgotten—or made yourself forget—about that night," I explained. I looked up, trying to quell the waver in my voice. "But I've heard your nightmares and it sounds like a horrible thing to relive."

He shook his head, his mouth pulling up at one corner. "I appreciate the sentiment, Red. But it's not necessary.

This may be revisiting old wounds, but it must be done. I remember every detail about that night except for how it ended. It seems the curse also put a block in my memory."

"That's the point of the tonic. But what you are about to see—"

"I see them every day, without fail. It does not matter." The sheer heartbreak in his voice made my own heart ache by extension—no matter how angry I remained with him—calling to mind my own deep sense of loss.

"Alright," I said, forcing my voice to steady. "Close your eyes. Remain still."

He obeyed, his eyes sliding closed. Emrys's breathing began to quicken. I did not like having to do this—knowingly causing mental anguish.

"Emrys," I whispered. "Listen to my voice and remember this is just a memory. I need you to skip ahead. Picture the witch who cursed you. See his face and focus on it. Focus on the words he said to you that night."

"I see him," he said, eyes still closed. I placed my palm atop his scarred brow to ground him; his skin was clammy under my touch. "He has a crooked nose with an indent on the bridge. Wide, condemning eyes. A cross between green and blue, I think."

"Good. Now, what does he say to you? What does he do?"

"He is killing them all." Sweat beaded on Emrys's brow, his hands trembling. I never imagined I'd ever see a faerie this emotionally vulnerable, breaking down in front of me. I couldn't help but feel guilty that I was the one to put him in such a state. "I'm hiding. I am doing nothing. I am just sitting there doing fucking *nothing* while he's killing them. Stunning them with magic before they can react and slashing their throats. Every single one of them."

Oh, dear goddess. What he went through was horrible beyond words. "Focus on the *after*. When he sees you, when he approaches you. What happens then?"

"He…" Emrys trailed off, his body stiffening. "He's dragging me to my feet. He is making me look at the bodies, showing me all the blood. He grabs my head between his hands to force me to look, and… the blood of my family is on his hands, too. Now it's all over my face."

His words made my stomach twist, and I mourned his loss of innocence right with him. "Now what is he doing?"

"He is telling me that their deaths are my fault. I led him right to them. He says he doesn't plan to kill me. Instead of killing me, he will curse me with an eternity of knowing what I brought upon my family. He is starting to chant. His hands are warming. They are hot now, like kindling."

Now, we were getting somewhere. "How does he curse you?"

"I don't…" His face pinched in concentration, sweat dripping down his temples now. "I cannot understand the words he is saying. I feel blinding pain, especially around my eye—my scar. But just as he starts my vision goes dark. I cannot see, I cannot hear anything…"

Emrys's eyes flew open. "Did that help at all?" he asked, turning toward me.

"That is progress, just not enough quite yet. We'll just keep trying until we figure this out."

"We still have time, I suppose." Emrys shifted on the bed. "Not right now. I need to see the king again soon."

"What matters does he have to discuss with you this time?"

"Another hundred cuts."

I frowned. "He is having you cut twice every day?"

"A hundred cuts twice a day for the next fortnight, and then once per month for the next year, through the winter solstice. That is my punishment for abandoning my hunting duties, and for bringing no new bounty when I'd clearly marked one."

"Does the king *hate* you?"

"No," Emrys replied quickly. "He is just a complicated faerie." I had no idea why Emrys would continue to feel loyalty toward such a monster.

I could not stop thinking about what Emrys had just laid bare to me, the horrors that he went through. Both then when he was a child at the hands of witches, and now at the hands of the king who claimed to love him like a son. And for a moment as I thought about Emrys's past and my conversation with Jasper, I felt connected to him through grief.

I realized Emrys's gaze was upon me then, golden eyes crinkling at the corners. He still sat so close. "What's on your mind?"

"I am thinking..." I trailed off and shook my head, leaping to my feet. Suddenly, I was shoving down a very strong urge to do something I should not.

"Rose?" Emrys said my name huskily. He stood beside me, gently turned me to face him. His eyes drifted to my lips, and I found myself staring at his full mouth. I wanted... *I wanted...*

Without thinking, I rose up on my toes. He must've realized what I meant to do, because he bent to meet me halfway. And I pressed my mouth to his.

I couldn't explain my actions other than sheer compulsion, one not created by any enchantment. Emrys didn't seem to mind, judging by how he immediately responded, kissing me back with fervor, hard and deep. He groaned into my mouth, his tongue parting my lips, and drew my body closer until there was no space left between us. His large hands slid down my sides, grasping my hips. And then he was walking us both forward until my back met with a solid wall.

His roaming hands found my backside, my thighs. He gripped me tight, lifting until my legs hitched about his waist. Stars, I felt every hard inch of him between my legs and I was starving for more. I *wanted*...

But suddenly, I tasted salt upon my lips, and only then did I realize it was tears.

My own.

Emrys tasted them too because he pulled back, his eyes hooded with desire and laced with confusion. When he saw the shiny trails on my cheeks, he frowned. "Is something wrong?"

He still held me upright, clutching my backside, my legs wrapped around his waist. "It's just... What you went through as a child was so terrible. I suppose it made me emotional."

"It was, but..." The crease between his brows deepened. "Gods, Red. Is that why you wanted to kiss me?"

"I..." I licked my swollen lips, but when I did not deny it, he rolled his head about his shoulders, exasperated, and lowered me back to the floor. I couldn't help but feel a loss at his distance. "Is it not customary for a wife to kiss her husband?" I finally said, but it was too late. I had paused too long in my response.

"Perhaps. But we are far from customary." Emrys inhaled a deep breath, let it out, and turned away from me to face the window. "I am a bloody pathetic creature at times, I imagine. A broken thing."

"No. You're hurting, Emrys. And you never get a chance to recover from that hurt here in the castle. The king does not treat you as well as you believe."

"That may very well be. But hear me now." He spun, pinning me in his intense gaze. "I don't want you to *ever* do what you just did out of *pity.*"

"Then when *do* you want me to do it?" Why was I asking such a question as if I planned on kissing him again?

He closed the distance between us again and stared right down into my face, eyes gold as flames. "I want you to," he murmured, lifting a hand to trace my jaw with his finger, "when you desire to."

"And if I never desire you that way?"

Even as I said the words, they sounded hollow in my ears. I was already feeling things I shouldn't, if I was being honest with myself, and that was... so incredibly confusing.

I could swear Emrys flinched a little at that, though he maintained his expression, his finger still skimming my jaw. His eyes followed the simple movement before meeting my gaze again. "Then I suppose I shall remain wanting. That might be for the best, anyway."

His finger lowered until it rested over my heart, which beat wildly. I knew he heard it too. My own body was betraying me.

"This always gives you away," he said, lips curving into a knowing smirk. "I can be patient, Red. But I don't suspect I'll remain wanting for long."

Cocky bastard. And yet... my heartrate increased even more at his proximity. I opened my mouth to reply, but the words died in my throat as Emrys leaned close and dropped a kiss upon my cheekbone, soft as an eyelash. Then he released me and turned to leave the room.

"Wait," I said.

He froze in the doorway, but did not turn.

"If I could find the right ingredients in town, I could make you a tonic for the hundred cuts. To help ease the pain."

"No," he replied, his voice low. He turned only his head to catch my gaze over his shoulder. "I need to feel it. All of it." A ghost of a smile flickered upon his lips for a brief moment. "But thank you for caring."

He left the room, letting the door click shut behind him.

30

Rose

"THAT WAS QUITE DELICIOUS," GORO SAID. HE pointed the feathers of his left wing inward to pat the lump under his neck where he stored his food.

"Quite," I agreed.

I was back in our turret room with Goro eating the lunch that had been left for me. It was far too much for one person and I was more than happy to share some with the raven.

Goro burped—a noise I had certainly never heard coming from a bird before—and I threw my head back and laughed. I was still laughing when the door swung open.

"Glad to see you two getting along so well," Emrys said as he walked into the room. His lips curved in amusement, dark hair a bit more tousled than normal. I had been at the kingdom for over a week now. It had been a solid week since Emrys and I had kissed and the tension—and resulting awkwardness—between us seemed to be at an all-time high.

"Goro is wonderful company," I said.

"Oh, stop." The raven waved a wing. "You flatter me, my lady."

"Well, I hate to interrupt, but King Armynd has summoned your presence," Emrys said, looking surprised by those words even as he said them.

"The king wants to see me?" I swallowed hard, my palms already starting to sweat at the prospect. "Right now?"

"Yes."

"It is alright, my lady," Goro said. "We will meet after." He wiped his beak once more with the tips of his wing feathers and hopped to the window sill, flying away as I stood to join Emrys.

"Should I be afraid?" I asked as I followed down the turret steps.

"The king will not harm you." Emrys kept his eyes trained on the path ahead. "That much I know. He will not go back on his word of honoring our union."

"Then what does he want to speak with me about?"

"I have no idea. But your heart is pounding again." He paused to face me in the corridor, gold eyes peering down into mine. He lifted a hand to gently brush some stray auburn strands away from my face. "I will not let you come to any harm at his hands, Rose. Do you trust that much, at least?"

I could only nod. Emrys's eyes bounced around my face for a moment, thumb resting against my chin. I thought he might say more, but his lips pressed together, and he turned to continue leading me through the corridors.

I followed Emrys to the throne room, his hand on the small of my back to guide me the rest of the way. Once there, we waited outside for a few minutes until the door swung open. To my surprise, Talyn and Callum walked out, and I scowled. They strode past Emrys as though he wasn't there. I wondered what they'd been talking about and why, as one of the king's advisors, Emrys hadn't been invited to this meeting. Judging by Emrys's troubled expression, he didn't know why, either.

"Come in, Emrys." King Armynd's voice floated from within. Now, I was even more nervous.

"It's alright, Red," Emrys whispered into my ear. He pushed gently on the small of my back to encourage me, and we both walked inside the room together. Our footsteps clacked on the marble as we crossed the large, extravagant room, passing all its columns and gilded trees on the way to the throne. The king did not occupy the throne this time, but stood in front of it at the base of the steps. He approached as we did, meeting us in the middle.

"You may leave, Emrys. Thank you for fetching Rose," the king said, and panic clenched my stomach like a fist. On instinct, I reached for Emrys's hand, terrified to be left alone with the high fae king.

Emrys squeezed my fingers and stood rooted to the spot. His gold eyes clouded with worry and indecision. "You wish to have a private audience with my wife?"

"Yes, Emrys," the king replied. "Will that be a problem?"

"I just—may I ask why?"

"No, you may not."

"I would much prefer to stay."

"That is not up to you," Armynd snapped. "But do not worry, I promise to keep her safe in your absence. I just wish to have a little chat with her. Surely, you trust me enough to know that she will come to no harm in my presence today. You know I speak only truth."

Emrys cast me a sidelong glance, eyes slightly pained, and I nodded to give him my assent. He leaned close and whispered right into my ear, "You'll be fine. I will be right outside if you need me."

He reluctantly left, footsteps clacking away. The door clicked shut, and then I was alone with the high fae king. My knees shook as he approached. Everything about this fae exuded confidence and power, his walk predatory, his voice deep and commanding. He was tall, broad, his gaze dark and piercing as though nighttime lived within it. I understood how a being like this was able to get anything he wanted with the snap of two fingers; I could only hope he would never snap his fingers to order my own execution. He had said he would not harm me today, and faeries could not tell outright lies. Moreover, I had to trust Emrys would not leave me with his king right now if he thought me in any immediate danger.

"First of all, I would like to say that I am sorry for what happened with Rhea at the banquet." The king straightened to full height before me, his wings not in sight today. "I have reprimanded her. My niece is very strong-willed, but Korvyn and I are the only family she has left. She does seem to rebel quite a bit because of it."

"If I may, your highness, at least she does have you and Korvyn. My entire family is gone. All... Dead." I nearly choked on the last word. I was already shaking like a blade of grass in a stiff breeze, as it was, and I hated showing weakness before any faerie much less their high king. But I was well aware this fae had the power to behead me with his own bare hands if he so chose.

His astute brown eyes did not blink as he assessed me, mouth pulled into a tight-lipped smile of amusement. "You and Emrys already have much in common."

"May I ask why you wanted to meet with me today?"

"Do not fear, Rose Doyle. This is just a meeting to get to know you a little better." He tilted his head, hands clasped behind his back. He began to slowly pace around me, unsettling me further. "Tell me a little more about yourself."

"Tell him nothing," the voice in my head hissed. I blinked against a sudden headache at the intrusive thoughts. Ever since reading the grimoire, they popped into my mind randomly. *"You are alone with him. This may be the only chance you have to overpower him. Kill the high fae king. You are not weak; you have your magic. KILL HIM! NOW!"*

Wincing, I drew a deep breath and did my best to ignore the voice, for the voice was quite reckless in its demands.

"What would you like to know?" I heard myself saying instead, resisting the urge to rub my temples, to tell the voice in my head to *just be quiet* out loud.

"You said your name is Doyle. I have heard of a coven of Doyles before. Notoriously powerful, from my understanding."

"I have heard the same, but my family and I have been living in isolation for so long, it is hard to tell how others perceived us. We only wanted to live in peace. Nothing more."

"Peace is gone. Kill the king," the voice snapped, and I gritted my teeth.

"What elements do you harness, Rose Doyle?" the king asked out of the blue.

"Wh-what?" It also was not lost on me that he seemed to love using my full name. Additionally, that he seemed to refuse to call me *Rose Abrynth.* As though he had some strange attachment to my maiden name.

At my sputtering, the king smiled, which was neither warm nor reassuring as smiles usually were. "Do not look so surprised. Is it really so hard to believe that I know how witch magic works? I have seen my share of it. Such magic killed my wife, after all."

"I... was very sorry to hear about the queen," I said, praying I sounded sincere enough for his liking.

His halted his pacing, gaze snapping to mine and expression darkening for a brief moment. He came back to himself with a quick shake of his head. "She had a good heart, my dear wife. Perhaps better than she should have," he said. "Now, what elements have you mastered?"

I bit my lip hard. *"Tell him nothing,"* the voice in my head warned. But telling him nothing was not an option, was it?

"I master fire and earth, your highness," I eventually replied.

"Fire?" King Armynd's eyes widened in slight surprise. "One of the rarer mastered elements, no?"

I tipped my chin, eyes narrowing a bit. "It is."

"Perhaps the most treacherous of all."

"Yes, most treacherous. Use it against him now," the voice said.

"I do not wish anyone here harm," I replied, panic once again churning inside me. My head throbbed even worse as the unwanted thoughts bounced back and forth in my mind, refusing to be ignored. "Truly, I don't."

"And I believe you."

I raised a brow. "You do?"

"I know Emrys, and he wouldn't bring someone into my kingdom unshackled unless he knew they were not a threat. Now, show me."

"Beg pardon?"

"Your magic." He gestured inwardly with both hands in a *give it to me* motion. "I want to see."

"But." I hesitated, licking my lips. "I thought I was forbidden from using magic."

"Not if I directly request it. It was I who forbade it, so I am also the only one who can ask to see it. And now, I require a demonstration. This is not a request."

"Do not do it. He is trying to trick you," said the voice in my head.

But again, what choice did I have? I certainly was not prepared to make a stand, nor would I win one inside this castle with all the king's forces within shouting distance. This felt like a situation where I would be wrong no matter how I chose, but I was obligated to do as the king asked. He waited expectantly, watching, one hand grasping his elbow and his other hand lightly tapping his chin. I inhaled deeply to summon strength.

"*Sorcha,*" I muttered, and my fingertips sparked with glittering light, like little embers about to start a fire. I held up my hand for him to see. The king leaned forward to observe, and smirked.

"You can do better than that. Dig deep. Show me more."

I cleared my throat and planted my feet. "*Talamh,*" I muttered, and the trees lining the room began to shake. Whenever I used an elemental power, aside from the spoken command, I also had to picture my intent. And now, I pictured the branches in the room growing and extending outward. A branch shot out and grabbed the column in front of it, winding around the marble like a snake. Then another branch shot out, and another, until the column was covered in so many branches it looked like another tree itself. Once finished, I allowed my concentration to break, and the tree snapped back as it was, retreating from the column until all was back to normal.

"Also impressive," the king said, tapping his chin, head bobbing. "Quite a show you put on. But I need to see more."

"*Show him more. Much more. Hurt him.*" The voice in my head was relentless.

Instinctively, I knew which power he wished to see most, because it was also the one I was most reluctant to show him. But I could not delay any longer. I lifted my hand.

"*Teine,*" I muttered.

31

Rose

AT ONCE, A FIREBALL GREW IN MY HAND, hovering above my palm.

The king's face lit up, his eyes reflecting back my flame. His hands fell to his sides. "There it is. *Fire.*"

After a moment, I extinguished the fire by clenching my hand into a fist. "I am terrified, your highness," I admitted.

His thick brows furrowed. "Of what?"

"That you feel threatened by my powers, and I do not want you to feel threatened. Again, I mean no harm to anyone. I swear it."

"Yes, you do. You should. Kill the king. Kill him now."

The king laughed heartily at that. "I feel threatened by no one."

"See. He laughs at you. He disrespects you. Kill him." I winced.

Now, the king eyed me almost warily, as though noticing my internal struggle. "Is everything alright?"

"I am fine," I replied quickly. "But now that you have observed my power first-hand… Do you still plan to honor my union to Emrys?"

"Why would I not? Have I not showered you with every hospitality and welcomed you with open arms?"

"I am grateful," I said carefully before licking my lips and trying my luck. "If you are so readily accepting of me, could you also see it in your heart to grant the same mercy to the witches in the dungeons?"

His expression soured, chin tilting down to look me square in the eye. "My, you are a bold little thing, aren't you." His tone darkened, and I cowered, bowing my head. "You are shaking so badly I can hear your teeth rattle from here, Rose Doyle. Do you wish me to calm you?"

He meant to use an enchantment like he did before, and I wanted nothing to do with any faerie magic. "No. Thank you."

"As for the witches in the dungeons, there is already great unrest amongst my people. Many are still terrified of your kind. Letting those witches go would further fuel this unrest. They were caught red-handed having killed one of our own, and that cannot be forgiven. They *will* face the consequences, and any intervention on your part would be... most unfortunate for you. Do you understand me?"

I shivered at his words. "Yes."

"Now, you seem to please Emrys, and that must count for something. I plan to reiterate to my court that if any harm comes to you, they will have to answer to me. You are too important, Rose Doyle."

My head snapped back up. "Important?"

But the king did not elaborate. When he finally dismissed me, I was unsure how to feel and entirely confused. Emrys was waiting for me just outside the throne room doors, true to his word. He immediately grasped my arm when he saw me and guided me to a quiet corner.

"The throne room is rather sound proof by design, but I was able to hear a little. Thank the gods for heightened shifter senses. Did Armynd make you demonstrate your powers?"

I nodded. "He also asked me about my family. He said that he will see to it that no harm comes to me. He also said I am important."

"Important for what?"

"I'm not sure."

"Hm." Emrys frowned. "I suspect Armynd is up to something and I'm going to find out what."

Emrys led me by the hand back to our turret room. He followed close on my heels as I went up the winding stairs. They were so steep that I was quite certain my behind was eye level with Emrys's face more than once.

When we reached the top landing, I was so distracted that I somehow completely missed the tray of food that had been placed just outside the door. My foot slid on the tray and I fell like a sack of potatoes. Emrys caught me, but his toe also got hooked on the edge of the tray I had just inadvertently kicked toward him, and we both clattered to the floor. I landed on my back and Emrys landed on top of me, knocking the wind from my lungs. He was *heavy*.

"Are you alright?" he asked.

"I am fine," I replied when I'd caught my breath. "But I thought faeries were supposed to be graceful creatures."

He grinned. "Says the human witch who tripped over a tray of food and dragged her husband down with her."

"Said husband should've broken my fall rather than land on top of me."

"You," he shook his head in mock admonishment, "are impossible."

"Maybe," I said, and then I was laughing, and Emrys was laughing with me.

When we both sobered, I noted that Emrys had not moved, although he'd lifted some of his body weight off of me by bracing his hands on the floor, caging in my head, his knees straddling me.

"How are you feeling?" he asked. The muscles in his forearms were corded, tense.

"I..." My chest heaved as I looked up at him, his body pressed to mine.

He moved his hips a fraction of an inch, just enough to make me feel... something. A sweet tingling between my legs that made me gasp. His jaw clenched and his eyes slid to my lips hungrily, to my chest where my heart beat wildly. He rolled his hips again, very purposefully this time, forcing a telltale bulge to rub between my legs with just the right amount of friction that made me hiss.

"Emrys," I breathed.

He shifted his hips a third time and I found myself quickly losing all sense of reason. Quite soon, we would be past the point of no return. But was I ready?

His head dipped down, gently nipping my jaw, working back up my chin. But just as his lips had barely brushed mine, I froze. And panicked.

"We should really get some sleep," I whispered.

"Fuck." He murmured the word against my lips, so low I could barely hear it, and then he pulled back. His jaw clenched, eyes narrowing as though fighting an internal battle. Meanwhile, my chest was still heaving with uneven breaths. He emitted a huff that came out as a low, mirthless chuckle. "Sure. Whatever you say, Red."

He stood and reached down to grasp my hand, pulling me to my feet with ease. But he did not let go and remained still for a moment, staring down into my face. His fingers tightened around the hand he had still not released.

"Please," he murmured, his breath fanning my face, "control your excitement. You make my own self-control near impossible to maintain."

I blinked in confusion. "My excitement?"

"It's not just your heart going crazy. No... I can smell your arousal too."

"You can smell... Wait, no, I'm not..." I was sputtering, instantly flushed with embarrassment.

"It's an intoxicating scent, you know." His breath tickled my ear as he leaned closer still. "And it is driving me absolutely mad with need, Red." He pulled back, swallowed hard, eyeing me up and down.

"My heart drives you crazy. My scent drives you crazy. I can't control any of those things. What do you expect me to do, Emrys?"

"Maybe it's just you that drives me crazy, Red. I've never felt..." He trailed off and shook his head. "Never mind. I just... I need a moment." He released me and left the room, pulling the door closed behind me. Even in his wake, my heart continued to hammer in my ears.

In an attempt to calm myself, I stepped back, crossing over toward the window and leaning my head out for some fresh air. I was far more frustrated than I cared to admit, the throbbing between my legs now an ever-present ache, demanding to be acknowledged.

I sat in the chair beside the window and stared out into the night as a gentle breeze brushed my face. But no matter how many deep breaths I took, no matter how I tried to picture anything at all in my mind that would distract me from my sudden lascivious thoughts, I found myself failing.

All I could think about was the feel of Emrys on top of me, grinding himself between my legs, how good it had felt. And that was with our clothes *on;* I could only imagine what more would feel like. I thought about the feel of his lips on mine, the warmth of his hard, thick body pressing into me, and the aching between my legs reached an all-time high.

This was just... lust. I was still too confused, too conflicted to do anything more *with* Emrys yet. But I also could not take this feeling anymore without a resolution.

Before I could stop myself, I found my hand drifting down, sneaking under my nightgown as I was desperate to find relief. I had only done this a couple of times before, by myself in the woods. It was only natural to be curious about one's own body, but it was far from a frequent occurrence because constant fear of capture did not leave much room for lustful thoughts. Now, however, it was different.

With the first circle of my fingers, I let out a low moan. This. *This* was what I needed right now. My head fell back on the chair as my fingers increased their movements, applying more pressure, and my moans grew in volume to match.

But a sudden noise from outside the door made me stop. A loud bang, a snarl.

Emrys.

My hand, still wedged between my thighs, froze.

"Don't you dare stop now, Red," he growled.

My face flushed crimson. Stars, he had never left the landing outside the room. He could probably still smell my arousal. And being a shifter, he could *definitely* hear my moans. He'd heard *everything* that I'd been doing.

"Rose..." His voice was strained as it floated through the door again, louder this time. "I said... do not *stop.*"

Truthfully, I did not want to; I needed to finish what I started or I feared I would be awake all night fighting the ever-present ache. My fingers resumed their work, rubbing faster as I neared my peak.

Another moan escaped my lips, and I heard Emrys grunt in response from outside the door, leading me to wonder if he was touching himself the same way I was right now. I could not help it; I found myself picturing him with his hand wrapped around his length, stroking up and down. The thought only fueled my desires further, and in that moment, I felt wild, reckless, uninhibited. I did not care about anything but my own blinding need.

When at last my release came, I heard another bang and a groan from outside, like Emrys had slapped his palm against the door as he found his own release.

Oh, my...

Now that I was coming down from my high, I felt a flood of relief but also a creeping embarrassment. Unsure what else to do, I climbed back into bed and curled up under the covers, willing my pulse to go back to normal. Though for a long while, I could only stare ahead, reliving what had just happened in my mind.

The door creaked open behind me sometime later as Emrys slipped back into the room. He did not climb into bed with me, however. Instead, he sat in the chair I had vacated and inhaled deeply. I wondered if he could still smell the lingering evidence of my arousal. Likely, he could.

"Go to sleep, Red," he ordered from behind me, obviously knowing I was still awake from my still-erratic heartbeat. His voice was still strained. "It'll be a while before I'm safely able to join you."

Even though my back faced him, I could feel his eyes upon me in the darkness until I finally felt the pull into sleep.

32

Rose

WHEN I'D WOKEN UP THAT NEXT MORNING, Emrys had not returned to bed. Or if he had, he'd already left, and we had not spoken of that night again. Though I could not lie; I'd thought about it often, and I could tell Emrys did too from the hungry way I often caught him looking at me. But somehow, we managed to keep our impulses under control.

Every night, Emrys started leaving and coming in after I had fallen asleep. Sometimes when I would wake during the night, he'd be asleep in the chair beside the bed. I didn't ask why, but I think it was so he could control his own primal urges.

Strangely, part of me didn't want him to.

Now, two more weeks had passed without any cursebreaking progress. We were well into Autumn, and the leaves around the castle had begun to hint at changing. Soon, they would erupt in a barrage of colors which would float like confetti to the ground before only the pines were left green, and then frost would set in. I wondered how different the castle and grounds would be in the winter—if I was still here, of course, which I very well may not be.

We were trying to break Emrys's curse every day but getting nowhere, and I'd already exhausted my full supply of ingredients from Feyleen. Every time Emrys got to the part where the witch cursed him, his memory would go dark, no matter how much tonic he was given. Emrys would leave to receive his hundred cuts, and that became his cycle: memory retrieval followed by punishment. Though the memory retrieval could be easily misconstrued as a different form of punishment in itself. All of this seemed very draining for him, and he was growing wearier by the day.

At least Emrys was now done with his daily cuts, and down to monthly cuts for the next year—or however long he remained alive.

After our latest attempt to break his curse failed yet again, Emrys seemed agitated. He rubbed his face hard and stalked over to the window, leaning against it to look out.

"Maybe the memory block has nothing to do with the curse at all." I walked up behind him, deciding to test the waters. "Maybe you are somehow subconsciously blocking *yourself* from remembering."

His gaze snapped to mine, brows knitting in a questioning frown. "Why would I do that?"

I drew a deep breath. "Because, deep down, you no longer desire death?"

Emrys crossed his arms over his chest and sighed. "What I *want* is no matter."

"What does that even mean?" When he didn't reply, I sighed. "You really do blame yourself for your family's deaths, even after all this time." I shuddered at the horror of it all. I leaned next to him, peering out the window also. Below, passersby traipsed along the cobbled street skirting the moat, heading into town. "I know it's not the same as your curse but for what it's worth, my family's death haunts me, as well."

He turned to me in interest. "I never asked, what happened to make your parents venture so far from the cabin?"

I swallowed hard as I recalled the day; it was still so fresh in my mind. "It was a rough winter, and we were dangerously low on food. My parents left to find what they could. Before my mother went out the door, she kissed me and said, 'We will never allow ourselves to be taken alive by the fae. Their questioning could lead them to you and your grandmother. So, if we do not return, promise me you will not come looking for us. Promise me you will stay and look after your grandmother, my Rosey.' I begged to go with them, but they would not let me. They said it was too dangerous. I should have fought harder to go. Maybe I could've helped somehow if I had."

Emrys was very quiet as he listened, allowing me to continue. His gaze met mine with a distinct look of empathy.

"My mother made me promise not to look, but I broke that promise. I went looking. I ventured the farthest I had ever ventured from the cabin on my own, a full two day's walk. And that's when I found evidence of the ambush. I saw the blood, a lock of my mother's hair and a piece of her cloak... and my father's sword, lying in some bushes. I collapsed, knowing for sure they were gone forever. And my grandmother... well, she slit her own throat right in front of me, to protect me. Just as my parents died to protect me. I am sure of it." I squeezed my eyes shut. "It is awful to think about, but despite the fact that I often blamed myself, I know they wouldn't want that. Just as I'm sure your family would not blame you." My eyes opened again, and I looked back to Emrys, who bristled beside me as his expression grew infinitely more pained.

"But their deaths were different. Their deaths were not your fault. They *chose* to protect you. You don't even know for sure what happened to them. Whereas I unknowingly led those witches right to our home. Because of that, they died right in front of me."

I touched his arm. "You *unknowingly* led them, exactly. How could that be your fault?"

"Because I was a bloody fool!" he snapped, standing upright suddenly, fists balled at his sides. In a quick movement, he punched the wall beside the window so hard that several small cracks formed in the stone. When he withdrew his fist, there was a slight indent and blood streaked on the wall. He hung his head against the stone above his fist mark. "I should have known better. My father had told me not to sneak out at night. To stay away from the markets. That it was dangerous because the witches were out for blood and closing in fast. But I just couldn't listen to him. Why couldn't I just *listen?* Careless little shit, I was."

"No. You were a child, Emrys. Part of being a child is *not* knowing any better, and I'm sure you had no idea you were being followed." Unafraid despite his outburst, I stood beside him and placed a hand upon his arm again, not letting go this time. "Let me tend to your hand." I gestured toward his bloodied knuckles, but he flexed his fingers and shook his head.

"I am fine. It will heal. In fact, it's healing already." After a moment he turned to meet my eyes, and he lifted his uninjured hand to rest upon the curve of my jawbone, his thumb stroking gently, all anger having left his body for the time being. "It's important you know... Me wanting to die isn't just about choosing death, Rose. It's about choosing to rest with my family after hundreds of years of torture. Can you understand that?"

"Yes," I replied.

If someone were to give me an opportunity to reunite with my own family, I may not be able to pass it up, either. But my voice hitched with unexpected emotion. I shook my head and stepped away from his touch, turning my back to him and hugging myself. His words deflated something inside of me, and I could not help but feel a wave of sorrow knowing that my husband was still choosing death.

ROSE RED

GORO STOPPED BY THE ROOM ALMOST immediately after Emrys left that day. "Where are we off to today, my lady?" he asked, hopping in through the window.

"I thought I might walk into town and visit Feyleen." Feyleen was still one of the few in the kingdom who had been genuinely kind towards me, and I needed more supplies for my tonic, as well.

"Oh, I love Feyleen!" Goro bounced with giddiness. "She always leaves me a treat."

"I know," I said, having seem him indulge in those treats once already. In fact, we'd already spoken about Feyleen extensively on multiple occasions, but Goro's memory wasn't always the best. Strange, because I had always thought ravens had excellent memories. Though Goro was far from a typical raven in many regards.

We left the tower, crossed the drawbridge, and entered town together. Goro was especially chatty, telling me about all his favorite shopkeepers, but I found myself tuning him out. For some reason, I had a pit in my stomach telling me something was about to go very wrong.

"Where to now, my lady?"

The answer came to me very quickly, because I felt it again. That strange tingling in my blood. I had not felt it in a while, yet it suddenly beckoned so distinctly, someone may as well have been screaming right in my ear, "Follow me!"

With Goro at my heels, I allowed my blood to direct me forward. We stuck close to the village wall, following the tingles until we arrived at the same little alley I'd been drawn to before. As before, there was still nothing to see here.

"Why are we standing in an empty alley?" Goro asked after I'd been silently staring for several long moments.

I wasn't sure how much to tell him, so I settled on asking him questions that must have seemed rather odd without context. "Do you see anything here? Anything out of the ordinary? Have you *heard* anything unusual about this place?" I gestured widely, indicating the whole alley.

Goro tilted his little head up toward me. "About a little alley? No, my lady. I see nothing but a dirt path and stone walls. There is nothing at all back here to my knowledge."

Unsatisfied, I walked forward and scuffed my feet in the dirt, whirled around, shuffled some more. I walked to each wall enclosing the alley and ran my fingers over stones, looking for any signs of seams, any signs at all that something was hidden here. But there was nothing. I sighed; my blood must have been wrong, the tingles just meaningless jitters. I felt foolish.

"Let's go visit Feyleen now," I said once finished. "I need to restock my memory tonic ingredients."

But when we reached the main square and Feyleen's shop, Goro and I both stopped dead in our tracks.

Her store had been vandalized, her window broken, and horrible words painted in red, sloppy letters across the door. They taunted me.

WITCHES HANG

The blood drained from my face.

"Oh dear," said Goro.

"Feyleen," I called, stepping into the shop, careful to avoid broken glass and fallen trinkets littering the ground.

The inside of the shop, frankly, looked as though it had been caught in a maelstrom. Goro hopped in beside me, also careful of where he stepped so as to not cut his feet.

"Oh dear, oh dear," he repeated, shaking his feathered head.

I gasped when I spotted more writing on the back wall, echoing the same words as outside:

WITCHES HANG

My stomach hurt, churning as bile climbed my throat. This was not right.

"Feyleen," I called again.

She stepped out from a back room then, looking worn, her hair disheveled. "Rose," she said in greeting, setting the broom in her hand aside and rubbing her hands on her apron.

Evidently, she had been in the process of beginning to clean up. Or at least trying to, though the number of things broken and thrown to the floor was fairly overwhelming.

"Feyleen, I am so sorry."

"This isn't your fault," she said.

"Let me help you clean."

But when I reached for the broom, she placed a hand on my arm to stop me.

"I do not blame you for this, but I also cannot have you in my shop any longer. This damage was unexpected, but it was also enough. I don't think I could stomach anymore of this. I am sorry, but I must ask you to leave."

"I understand," I said, though her words were like a punch to the gut.

Feyleen drew a deep breath and offered a small, melancholy smile that trembled at the corners. "I wish you all the best, Rose."

"You as well, Feyleen."

Feyleen let out a sorrowful mewl and shifted into cat form, hunching down on all fours and shrinking, sprouting fur and a tail—I wondered if it was a form of comfort for her. She scampered off to the back of the shop and out of sight.

Goro and I took that as our cue to leave.

"That's terrible," Goro said, hopping beside me. He took off in flight then, circling near my head. "Poor Feyleen. I wonder who did this."

As we rounded a corner and exited the main square, I soon learned the likely culprit. They were facing me, hovering beside the wall of the shop next door to Feyleen's, staring right at me with matching, wicked smiles.

Rhea... and Talyn.

They wanted to isolate me from anyone who treated me with kindness. It was clear they didn't want me here and right now, they were winning.

Before I could snap out of my stupor long enough to react or even think about confronting them, they exchanged a smug look and disappeared into the shadows beyond the buildings.

33

Rose

AFTER GETTING SENT AWAY FROM FEYLEEN'S shop, the pit in my stomach continued to churn and grow. If Feyleen was targeted for simply showing kindness to a witch, I had a bad feeling that Ophelia and Orinthia were in grave peril more immediately than I'd realized.

Surely, Rhea and Talyn weren't the only ones trying to make me feel as unwelcome as possible, and if there were others, they may have been even more dangerous. Callum came to mind.

Goro chased after me when I strode toward the castle with angry stomps. "Where are you headed?" he asked, flying after me.

"To check on Ophelia and Orinthia. Personally."

"Lord Emrys said the king forbade you from entering the dungeons. It could get you both into big trouble."

"I do not care."

"Besides, the witches were moved."

I halted abruptly, head swiveling around to look at the raven who landed breathlessly beside my feet. "To where?"

"To the fields, my lady. Just this morning. I saw it."

"Well, the king may have forbidden me from the dungeons, but he said nothing about the fields."

"I am not sure that's a good idea, either." Goro flapped in front of me. "Lord Emrys will not like that at all."

"Emrys does not need to know then."

Goro sighed. "You know I must advise him, my lady."

"Then advise him. I am still going."

"But, my lady..." Realizing his argument would be fruitless, Goro fell into silence. He followed me around the cobbled street that skirted the moat, circling around the back of the castle to the fields.

And once we arrived, I gasped at the scene unfolding before us.

Ophelia and Orinthia were there this time, digging away. They were not even given the benefit of tools to help, but were rather forced to dig with their hands like dogs. And apparently, they were not working fast enough. A stern-faced guard slapped Orinthia across the face—it looked like the same guard who had been standing watch at the dungeons when Callum enchanted me to follow him—and dragged her to the stocks. He forced her into an uncomfortable bent position between the two wooden boards, her neck locked in place alongside her wrists.

The sharp crack of a whip pierced the air, and I directed my attention back toward Ophelia, who was now being flogged right next to the hole she had been digging. It must've been pure agony for them, and I refused to stand by and watch this atrocity continue to unfold.

"Perhaps we should not interfere," Goro whispered from beside me. But I would not just stand here and do nothing.

As I marched forth onto the field, I realized that the guard flogging Ophelia was none other than the brute Callum. Of course. He seemed to enjoy inflicting pain far too much. What if he and the others had even coordinated their attacks to send me a message?

Callum dropped his whip and shoved his own dagger into Ophelia's palm, handle first. She looked to it in confusion, though she did not have to wonder what he was planning for long. Ophelia's body went rigid, her face turning redder than my hair. And then, with a loud cry... she stabbed herself in the leg.

I slapped a hand over my mouth to keep from crying out. Ophelia yanked the knife free from her thigh with a wet sloshing sound that nearly made me gag. The now bloodied dagger shook in her hand. I could see how hard she was trying to fight it, but I knew better than most how hard it was to break one of Callum's enchantments. Unable to resist the compulsion, Ophelia stabbed herself a second time. She sobbed in agony.

"Please, no!" Ophelia begged. "No more."

"Again!" Callum commanded, and this time, she stabbed herself in the other leg and screamed toward the sky. Orinthia called out for her sister from the stocks, pleading with Callum to stop this madness.

"Oh, dear. I see where this is going," Goro said. He flew off, darting into the sky across the field, undoubtedly to alert Emrys.

I hardly registered his exit, too busy watching in horror as Ophelia and Orinthia were beaten, humiliated, slashed... These women did not deserve this, and I refused to stand idly by and watch it happen, regardless of the consequences.

Stop!" I cried, running in front of Ophelia. But Callum ignored me entirely.

"Again," he said, stepping around me like I was little more than a slight nuisance, a buzzing gnat.

Again, with no choice but to comply, Ophelia stabbed herself just above her knee. Tears streamed down her face.

"I said *stop!*" I screamed two words at the top of my lungs.

"Make me," Callum challenged, eyes brimming with malice as he finally acknowledged me.

"Yes, make him," said the voice in my head. And this time, I could not stop myself.

"Talamh," I muttered under my breath.

The grass beneath Callum's feet shifted suddenly, like a rug being yanked. Caught off guard, he fell to the ground, his massive body thudding loudly. He glared up at me, seething, lips curling back from his teeth that looked surprisingly sharp for a non-shifter. With the enchantment broken, Ophelia opened her hand and dropped the bloody dagger, still crying.

"Did you just use magic, witch?" Callum demanded. He propped himself up on his elbows.

"I did no such thing," I said, staring down my nose at him. "Looks like you just tripped over your own oversized feet."

His jaw twitched. "You will regret that. Now pick up the knife."

The words seemed to echo in my skull, and I gritted my teeth. I had already experienced how painful fighting an enchantment could be, but today it seemed even more severe. My entire body protested my movements, my muscles screaming in agony. That quickly, Callum had me fully under his control, even as he still lay on the ground.

"Stop this." Every muscle in my body trembled, and I had no choice but to grab the knife. Callum climbed back to his feet, never taking his eyes off me for a second.

"Be still," Callum ordered once I had the knife in hand, and I froze. Stars, I loathed this. Loathed *him*.

Ophelia had sunk down on her side in the grass, still crying softly, knees bent.

"I should have you flogged for interfering," Callum spit. "Or perhaps placed in the stocks to cool down."

"You will do neither. You will let me go and release these women back to the dungeons. Now." But even as I said the words, I knew they were futile. Of course, Callum had the upper hand. In point of fact, I had already picked up the bloodied dagger just because he'd commanded it, and now I stood frozen and holding the weapon at the ready against my will.

"You are very bold for someone who is currently my puppet," Callum said.

"Let me out of this enchantment and I will show you just how bold I can be."

Callum stepped forward menacingly, never taking his hate-filled eyes off of me. "Are you threatening me, witch?" He clucked his tongue, shaking his head mockingly. "A witch threatening to attack a faerie in their own kingdom? What would the king think? Except that you deserve a swift trip to the noose."

He jerked his chin toward the gallows at the other end of the field. I bristled, jaw clenching. My palms had grown clammy where I gripped the knife, and my own sweat combined with Ophelia's blood made the handle slippery in my hand.

"Just let me out of this enchantment, Callum." I tried to wriggle my body free. Again, the simple attempt at movement sent protesting waves of pain throughout every muscle and bone I possessed.

"If I do release you, will you immediately leave this field and allow me to continue punishing these witches as I see fit?"

Ophelia whimpered behind me, defeated, but I held my ground. I would not abandon these women in their time of need, and I replied with an even, "I will not let you hurt them anymore."

Callum chuckled cruelly. "Just remember you brought this on yourself. And since you're here, you may as well make yourself useful. Now, stab the other witch with that knife."

"No!" I cried, though my legs were already moving to comply with Callum's command.

I struggled against my own body that was now trying to force me to stab this woman who was already in poor shape on the ground. My muscles felt aflame, and I yelled from the strain.

"I am... so... sorry," I managed to say as I bent closer to Ophelia, fighting with the knife.

But just as I raised the blade to plunge it into Ophelia's side, I felt Callum's enchantment bend the tiniest bit. Like his enchantment was a spun cocoon surrounding my body, and my mind a new wing poking a hole in its impossibly strong, confining silk. I gained just enough control to direct my blade to the ground, stabbing the grass right beside Ophelia's arm, my entire body shaking from the effort.

Without warning, Callum kicked me in the side, so hard I feared a broken rib. I exhaled a shriek.

"Leave them alone, you bastard!" Orinthia shouted from the stocks across the field.

The dungeon guard near her cursed in response and thumped the back of her head with an open palm.

Callum ignored her completely. "Pick up the knife again, witch," he commanded. "And this time, cut *yourself.*"

I was too weak to even try to fight it this time. It took every ounce of strength I possessed to break free before, and now I was wholly depleted. Crawling on my knees, I yanked the knife from where I'd stabbed the ground and lifted it.

"Cut yourself!" he shouted again.

With no strength left to resist, I slashed the knife across my forearm. It felt like a thin line of fire dragging across my skin, and I hissed.

That was when a growling mass of muscle and fur flew through the air from behind.

Emrys.

My husband knocked Callum to the ground and, while straddling him, shifted back to his regular form, still baring his teeth in a wolfish, almost maniacal grin. His eyes were pure fury. Enchantment broken, I dropped the knife and let out a long breath.

"Did I just see you enchant my wife?" Emrys snarled, hand curving around Callum's throat and squeezing. "I told you before if you ever laid a hand on her, I would tear out your tongue and feed it to you. Perhaps I shall just tear out your throat, instead."

"Let your fae husband tear out that brute's throat. You know you want to watch it happen."

In my mind's eye, I could see Emrys in wolf form sinking his teeth into Callum's neck, pulling stringy strips of wet flesh away from his windpipe as I stood by beaming with glee.

"Make your fae angry. Watch him kill his own kind," the voice said.

I had never felt anger quite like this before. It was powerful and refused to be ignored.

"Emrys," I said, giving in to the voice in my head. "Callum didn't just compel me. He *hurt* me. He kicked me in the stomach first, and then he made me stab myself right after threatening me again. My back was facing you so you did not see the injury, but here it is."

I held up my arm to show Emrys the depth of my forearm wound. As soon as he laid eyes on the blood, his teeth clenched, making his jaw jump. His face clouded over with the scariest expression I had ever seen him make.

"You made my wife *bleed?*" he barked down at Callum.

"Just to make her stop interfering. It was a warning."

Emrys didn't care for that explanation. He immediately began punching Callum in the face again, and again, and again, his fist connecting with loud crunching noises that quickly became wet *thwacks.*

"Yes, let the hateful fae die. Let your husband kill him. He deserves it. He deserves to die choking on his own blood," the voice in my head said, cackling.

But it was the sound of Orinthia's guard shouting that brought me back from the brink. What was I doing? If Emrys killed Callum, that could also lead to nothing good, especially not when there were witnesses. The king might even have us hanged side by side, for all I knew.

"Emrys, stop!" I pleaded. "Think about the consequences!"

"I do not care," Emrys said, his tone feral. "This is worth it."

Another punch. Another. I gripped his shoulder from behind. "If you kill him, the king might blame me for putting you up to it. You are being watched *right now.*"

I pointed toward the dungeon guard standing dumbfounded next to a stock-bound Orinthia. That seemed to get through to Emrys because finally, he lowered his fist. Callum moaned, his face a battered pulp, barely recognizable. But he was alive. His chest still rose and fell with shallow breaths. Slowly, Emrys climbed off of him.

"You are lucky my wife is keen on showing you mercy today. Because if it were just me with no witnesses, you would be dead right now," Emrys spat down at the prone fae. Then he leaned close to his bloodied face and spoke low. "But don't get too comfortable. When you least expect it, I am coming for you, Callum. Your days are numbered."

Emrys strode over to me then, lifting my arm to examine the wound. It honestly was not that bad; I suspected it just looked worse than it was. But I was still shaken.

"Goro told me where you were and I came immediately. Are you alright?" he asked, brows knitted with genuine concern, and I nodded.

"I'm fine, but Ophelia and Orinthia need our help. They are badly hurt, Emrys."

On cue, Ophelia groaned on the ground behind me. Even before she had been forced to stab herself, she'd also been flogged too hard, the flesh of her back shredded. She would not last much longer like this, not with that much blood dripping down her back and legs. Orinthia was in better shape despite the stocks, at least coherent and not in excruciating pain, but she was crying openly for her sister. Emrys looked to them, his jaw tightening.

The dungeon guard next to Orinthia was still just standing there staring. He'd been watching the whole spectacle with Callum unfold, waiting to see what happened. "The witches have had enough," Emrys shouted to him. "You may go."

Emrys outranked the guard just as Callum had. He nodded at Emrys's request and freed Orinthia from the stocks. It also seemed he did not possess the same need for violence as Callum—nor the same vendetta—and he left without further protest, striding across the field. He half jogged, seeming content to put the situation behind him.

Now Callum stirred on the ground, groaning in pain. He spat out blood, maybe even a tooth.

"When the time comes," he said weakly from the ground, staring pointedly at me, "I will take great pleasure in peeling the skin from the witches' bones while they beg for mercy." He pushed himself to his feet, sneering at me all the while. "I will skin them strip by strip, until they draw their final breaths in agony."

Now, I shook with pure, unfiltered rage.

"He has said enough. Kill him, already!"

"Teine," I said.

And I whirled around with fireball in hand.

34

Rose

THE FIREBALL QUICKLY GREW IN SIZE. IT morphed into a large raven made of flames, flapping its wings and hovering above my palm—I had never seen my fire magic do that before. But I did not even bat an eye at the oddity, ready to let it fly. Before I could hurl it at Callum, a large hand gripped my uninjured forearm and Emrys stepped between me and the brute. This time, it was my husband talking *me* down.

"No, Red," he murmured down at me. "You were right to stop me before. The king may recognize our union for now. But if he catches you using magic inside the city walls, especially if he catches you harming a fae with your magic, there is no telling what he might do to you. Put the fire away. If one of us is going to give Callum what's coming to him, it has got to be me." He bent close to whisper in my ear, "And he *will* get what's coming to him if it is the last thing I do. I promise you this."

He was right, and I willed myself to calm down. Reluctantly, I lowered my arm and extinguished my fire. I could not let my anger get the better of me, not until Emrys and I had accomplished both of our goals.

Emrys bent to haul Ophelia over his shoulder as gently as he could to not aggravate her wounds. Orinthia leaned on me as we helped them across the field, back toward the castle.

"You must get us away from here," Orinthia begged me as we moved across the drawbridge. She limped, having injured her back in the stocks. "The king has been doing odd things. I fear his intentions."

I lifted a brow. "What kinds of things?"

"Like taking us into separate rooms and removing our collars to test our magic."

"The king tested my magic as well. He made me demonstrate which elements I had mastered."

"Why would he do that? Unless he is trying to learn how to harness our power for himself."

I fell into silence, troubled by Orinthia's admission. I wondered if Emrys knew about Armynd's secret sessions with his prisoners, but it seemed the king had been keeping him in the dark about a lot these days.

Ahead, with Ophelia still in his arms, Emrys steered us away from the corridor that led to the dungeons, and I frowned.

"Where are we going?" I asked.

"We cannot go to the dungeons. Not yet. The king has expressly forbidden you from returning there. And seeing me like this would rouse suspicion."

I realized then where Emrys was leading us: the servants' wing. Together, we walked up to the bard's door and I knocked, since Emrys's hands were otherwise occupied.

Jasper opened the door, his face a tableau of shock as he saw who all was standing in the corridor. His blonde hair was loose about his shoulders today, and he tucked it behind his ears.

"Please," Emrys said. "May we enter? We need a quiet place to tend to some wounds."

"Let them in, Jasper," another voice said, floating from somewhere in the room behind the bard.

It was Korvyn.

We entered the room and Jasper shut the door behind us, his blue eyes narrowed in question. It was tight quarters inside. Emrys gently set Ophelia down upon the bed, and I helped Orinthia sit in the single wooden chair beside it.

Once Ophelia was settled, Emrys turned to Jasper and barked orders. "We need food, water, items for a poultice. Go fetch them."

Jasper's expression soured and Korvyn spoke on his behalf. "Just because he is human does not make him your servant."

"I know." Emrys pinched the bridge of his nose as though fighting a headache. "But we do need these items and I can't exactly whistle for Goro; gathering all we need is a tall order for a bird." He lowered his hand with a sigh and turned to me. "I suppose I can go, myself. If you'll be alright here."

"Of course, I will." I grabbed his wrist before he could leave. "Wait. Do you even know what's needed for a poultice?"

I wasn't sure why I was so skeptical, but Emrys looked almost offended that I would ask that. "I am not *that* hopeless, Red. I'll be right back."

He slipped out of the room then, closing the door behind him, and that was precisely when I heard it again.

The grimoire.

It amplified the voice inside my head. Though I was quite sure the voice in my head had always been the grimoire, ever since I had first come into contact with it.

"Perhaps you could find a spell to help them. Use me. Take me," the voice said. Suddenly, I was sweating in the tight confines of the room, and I hoped Emrys wouldn't be long.

Jasper spoke softly to the moaning witch on the bed, trying to keep her calm. It was Korvyn who had his eyes on me all the while.

"You don't look so well, Rose. Are you alright?" he asked.

"Fine," I replied.

Korvyn lifted a brow, seeing right through my bravado. His face glamour flickered, dark skin shimmering.

I wasn't sure who the grimoire might endanger, and I didn't feel comfortable speaking about it right now. Ophelia seemed too far gone at the moment, too lost in her pain for the grimoire to affect her. But Orinthia was looking around the room with a puzzled expression on her face. The grimoire might've been whispering to her, as well. It seemed to have a pull of some sort on all witches in its vicinity.

Thankfully, Emrys wasn't long. He returned with a loaf of bread, a pail of water, and poultice supplies cradled in his arms. Emrys and I set to work applying poultices to Ophelia's wounded back and legs. All she could do was moan as we moved around her.

Korvyn and Jasper tended to Orinthia in the meantime, even though she looked bothered by the prospect of another fae—the prince no less—touching her. But to her credit, she said nothing to protest.

I was also eager to get out of here, as the grimoire still beckoned to me. *"You know what you need to do,"* the voice said, even though I really did not know what it wanted, other than sheer destruction.

Orinthia frowned, too. She heard what I was hearing, no doubt. Her eyes locked on mine, but I looked away quickly.

When we finished with Ophelia, Emrys turned his attention to me. In my haste, I'd forgotten that I, too, had been wounded.

"Let me see," he said, reaching out with palm open.

"I'm fine."

"You are not fine. You're still bleeding. This wound needs to be tended, also."

"Emrys—"

"One more word of protest and I'll be forced to strap you down while I apply the poultice. Don't test me, Red."

I snapped my mouth shut, knowing it was no idle threat. Though I resisted the urge to roll my eyes, I relented.

He gripped my arm and gently laid the poultice. I hissed at the initial sting. Emrys's fingers could be so gentle—for a *wolf shifter,* no less—and his brows creased in concentration as he worked.

Orinthia's gaze darted between Emrys and myself as he fussed over me. She studied us as though attempting to put some puzzle pieces together, to solve the mystery of why we acted the way we did toward each other. I was still trying to solve that mystery, as well.

"It should heal just fine," Emrys said once he'd finished with me, offering a tight smile that crinkled his scarred brow. He turned his attention back to the other witches. "You must go now. I am sending you with some bread and fresh water, and extra poultice supplies should you need them."

Emrys shoved the items into a spare satchel provided by Korvyn and handed it all to Orinthia—save the bucket of water, which would have to be carried separately.

"I am so sorry we can't get you out of the dungeons now," I added, feeling a pang in my chest.

"Wait," Ophelia spoke up from the bed, her voice weak. I didn't even realize she had woken up.

With Orinthia's help, she sat up. I ducked down so that I could hear her, and she removed the pendant from around her neck, the one that sat beneath her collar—its silver spotted with blood—and handed it to me.

"Please take this." Her voice was trembling from pain as she spoke.

"I cannot accept this, Ophelia," I said, but her trembling fingers closed my hand around the metal.

"Something to remind you of me," she said. "Should I not make it out of here alive, and should you ever find more of our people... this will be something to show them. To prove that you saw me, that you knew me."

More of our people. Was that even possible?

Tearfully, I accepted the charm and hung it around my neck, the silver cool against my skin. "I will," I said.

"I will escort them back to the dungeons. I can carry the water, as well," Korvyn offered as Orinthia helped Ophelia stand from the bed. "If you can walk," he said to Ophelia, and she nodded weakly.

"I think I can make it," she said despite the pain apparent in her tone.

"Of course, the fae prince offers to take them to the dungeons," the voice in my head sniped. *"Do not let them leave. Kill the prince. Break the witches out now. He will deceive you. They will hang."*

"Stop!" I shouted.

One of my hands darted out and yanked the material of the prince's shirt, the other hand raised as though to summon fire, to *hurt* him. All in the blink of an eye. It was like my body had lost itself to another enchantment for just a moment, only this had been an enchantment of my own making. My own mind betraying me.

"Hey!" Jasper yelled. "Let him go!"

But I did not let go. My hand shook, my jaw clenched. I could feel the magic pumping through my veins, begging to be let out, begging me to burn the fae prince. His glamour flickered, revealing the scarred half of his face.

"Make it even," the voice said. *"Burn the other side too."*

Emrys grasped my arm and hissed in my ear, "What are you doing, Red?"

Gasping, I lowered my arm and shook my head rapidly, pulse pounding. "I'm sorry. I don't know what came over me," I said. "Please, just take care of Ophelia and Orinthia."

I raced out the door to put distance between myself and the grimoire. My grandmother had been right—it *was* a bad influence. Outside the room, I could breathe a little more, and Korvyn and the witches went the opposite way down the corridor while Emrys followed me.

"What happened in there?" he asked.

"It's hard to explain. There is something in the castle influencing me. A grimoire."

His mouth tightened and he narrowed one eye at me. "A grimoire?"

"Yes."

"Here in the castle?"

"Yes." I paused. "You've heard of them?"

He shrugged. "Only stories. That the most feared witches drew their power from such books."

"That is true, and no one else can know about the grimoire here. Such a thing can be dangerous in the wrong hands. Emrys, you mustn't—"

"Relax, Red." His hand cupped the side of my neck, catching me off guard. His fingers cradled the base of my skull, applying gentle pressure as he looked down upon me with a reassuring gaze. "I have no interest in the grimoire. Nor in telling anyone else of its existence. Alright?"

I exhaled a deep breath, nodding. "There's more."

"I figured as much."

"As for Ophelia and Orinthia, I must know… how long before their execution?"

Emrys looked contrite, gaze drifting. He dropped his hand as he explained. "They haven't been here very long. Just over a month now, by my count. The king typically forces labor upon the witches for several months before…" He bit his lip and trailed off. "It is typically months before execution, sometimes even a year or two. So, they still have some time."

"We have to get Ophelia and Orinthia out of here. I cannot allow them to die."

His eyes squeezed shut, reopened, mouth tight. "It would be extremely difficult to sneak them out past the city walls. They are marked. If we try to run with prisoners, the king's guards will kill without discrimination. That is considered an act of treason against the king. That would be stealing his property."

"They are not property; they are people," I reminded him, disgusted by the prospect.

"I know, but the king feels differently."

"If you know, then *help* them. You said it would be extremely difficult to break them out, but not impossible."

"I did say that." He let out a long breath as his tired eyes searched mine. Finally, he said, "Very well. But we cannot do it now. It will have to be after... after you keep your promise to help me and you are ready to flee the castle as well. They can leave with you."

"If you have a plan for getting them out, then why can't we do it now? Why do we have to wait for *me* to get out?"

"Think about it, Red. Once the king realizes the witches are gone, he is going to need someone to pin the blame on. You as the only other witch in the kingdom would make the perfect scapegoat. I cannot risk your safety. I *refuse* to." Emrys began pacing anxiously. "We will need to move under the cover of night, and I will need time to think of a plan." His gold eyes snapped to mine. "Understand that I cannot promise we will succeed, but I can promise I will do my best to help you save them."

I decided to press my luck. "We could get the bard out too."

"Absolutely not. We cannot complicate things further. Really, Jasper is treated quite well, all things considered. As long as his voice stays in shape, he will be fine."

"And what if he should become ill and temporarily lose his voice? What would the king do then?"

"Wait until he felt better, I would assume. Wait until his voice came back."

"And if it didn't? Because with the way he is always forced to perform, his voice might not last forever. In fact, it might wear out sooner than later."

Emrys's pause was all the answer I needed. "Let's not jump straight to worst scenarios, Red. We can only do what we can do, and Ophelia and Orinthia will be a big enough risk as it is, to both of us. The bard stays. That's final. Besides, he has Korvyn."

"Are they... An item?" I asked.

"Yes."

"How long have you known?"

"Not long, but I was sworn to secrecy. The king would be furious if he found his only son having illicit trysts with a human. But you understand why he would do everything in his power to keep Jasper safe."

I did; anyone would do the same for the one they loved.

As Emrys and I walked back toward our turret room, I grasped the charm from Ophelia and rubbed it as though for luck. In my mind, I repeated the same words over and over as though my fellow witches could hear me.

I will save you, sisters.

35

Emrys

ROSE'S HEARTBEAT SOUNDED FASTER THAN IT should have. It woke me. I rose up to my elbows and peered across the room.

"Can't sleep?" I asked.

"No." She shook her head. Her voice sounded strained. She sat in the cushioned chair with her knees hugged to her chest, staring out the window. "I cannot stop thinking about Ophelia and Orinthia. What they're going through."

"I understand." I could not imagine what Rose must be thinking now. Of faeries. Of this kingdom.

Of me.

Her eyes glistened with tears when she looked up. "Would you check with Korvyn to make sure Ophelia and Orinthia made it safely to the dungeons?"

"I will ask him," I assured her. I would promise anything to dry her tears. The sight of them troubled me greatly.

"Thank you." She sniffled, rubbed her nose on the back of her knuckles. "I can't explain it but somehow, I feel responsible for those women. They remind me so much of myself in so many ways. And they are so frightened. I just… I need…"

Her voice trembled. On instinct, I climbed out of bed and went to kneel beside her chair.

"I know," I replied. "You are my wife, and seeing you like this... Well, I don't much care for it. And I want to fix it."

"Some things can't be fixed," she whispered.

My brows furrowed and I reached out to touch her cheek. A tear escaped her eye, trailed down. My thumb brushed it away. I lowered my hand, clasped her forearm.

"What I do know is that I don't have any court matters to attend to today. My daily cuts are done for the time being and I'm not scheduled to knock on any doors. We can spend the day together, if you'd like."

"I would," she said.

Those two words brought with them a peculiar sense of relief.

"It's a good thing I can avoid Armynd's company today, because I imagine the king will not be happy when he sees Callum's face. Not that I care. He's got more coming. When he least expects it." I tilted my head, examining Rose's expression. "Do you trust that I'll protect you from him? Because I will. He will never hurt you again, Red."

Rose was silent. I stood and peered out the window. The sun hadn't even risen yet. It still slumbered, as we should have been.

"Perhaps we should get a little more sleep before we start the day? At least try. You need it."

Another stiff nod. "Alright."

She sniffled and rose from her chair. Crossed the room toward the bed and slid under the covers. I climbed in beside her.

"Emrys?" she said.

"Yes?"

"When you hurt Callum today... When you say you wish to protect me... Is it because he threatened the only thing that could break your curse?"

"That's ridiculous."

"No, it's not," she interjected. "It could merely be the blood bond at work, too."

"Red—hey, look at me." I turned to face her. Reluctantly, she turned to her side as well. I lifted a hand to skim my knuckles over her cheekbone. "You may be the only thing that can break my curse, but you must know by now that you mean more to me than that. I feel protective over you. Fiercely so. Every bone in my body aches to shelter you. To keep you safe."

She bit down on her lip. "I am scared, Emrys." Her voice sounded so small. Recent events had slowly drained the confidence right out of her. I loathed the thought. And fuck this place for dulling her flame.

"Come here."

I reached out to tug her arm and encourage her to move closer. She obeyed without resistance and rested her head atop my chest. This felt good. Too good. Perhaps that was a dangerous way to think.

"Try to get some sleep," I whispered. "You're safe here."

I almost added, *with me.* But was she? It was I who put her in harm's way in the first place.

She nodded against me. Soon, her breathing evened out and she drifted off to sleep.

It was a long while before I followed.

"YOU SEEM MORE QUIET THAN NORMAL," ROSE observed as she stood to dress the next morning. "What are you thinking about?"

I stretched my arms wide and pillowed my palms under the back of my head. Watched her with a smirk. "Trust me, Red. It's better you don't know." Truthfully, I was thinking thoughts I should not. As always.

She lifted a brow, but said nothing. I took three deep breaths and stood to dress as well. Rose always stepped to the other side of the wardrobe and turned her back to me to change. I did my best to respect her space, even when that was the last thing I wanted to do. Even when I wanted to charge right over there and kiss her until her knees buckled.

"Where are we off to today?" Rose asked once she was ready.

She wore green today, which brought out her eyes. I cleared my throat.

"I thought we'd go take a walk through the gardens first," I replied. I strode to the window, stuck my head out. Breathed in the fresh air. "Seems like a nice day for a walk."

Together, we left the room and walked toward the gardens. Rhea was an early bird and I had slept later than normal. So, the gardens should be bitch-free for the time being.

"The flowers are beautiful," Rose said as we entered. "I'm surprised I hadn't spent any time in the gardens yet. It is so much more peaceful back here."

"It is."

She walked ahead a little, pausing to sniff some buttercups. The Autumn sun lit her auburn hair like a red halo. "My grandmother kept a beautiful garden at the cabin," she said. "She loved tending to her flowers. She said it helped her focus."

"My mother loved flowers as well," I said, smiling at the memory.

She used to pluck wildflowers to make crowns for herself and Merium. I could still smell the blooms as the pair sat side by side near the fireplace weaving them together. The thought brought a wave of melancholy with it.

Rose returned to my side, walking close. Her hand looped through the crook of my elbow. "You said your mother liked to tell stories?"

I nodded. "She did. My mother was the storyteller and my father was the joke teller. I think he inadvertently offended his fair share of nobility. He didn't always have appropriate timing. But they loved his leather work so much they didn't mind."

"Your family sounded lovely," Rose said. Her fingers flexed on my arm.

"They were."

I paused at a noise from up ahead in the gardens. Two voices floated across the trimmed hedges. My hand covered Rose's on my arm, dragging us both to a stop.

"Be still for a moment," I whispered, listening intently. Making sure no threats loomed ahead.

I stopped abruptly when I smelled a familiar stench behind me. Yes, another heartbeat.

"Hello, Emrys." Callum stepped from behind the bushes.

"You are either very brave or very stupid," I hissed at the sight of him.

Callum chuckled. I was quite proud of the number I had done on his face. One eye was swollen shut. His nose was crooked, obviously broken. Every ounce of skin on his face was one big bruise. By now, Rose had heard the commotion. She came up beside me. Her heartbeat pounded faster at the sight of Callum. His eyes shifted to Rose briefly, and I snarled louder. I didn't want the fucker so much as *looking* at her. Callum held up his hands. "I come in peace. But the king wants to see you."

"Now?"

"Oh, yes."

I whirled around when Talyn's scent wafted forth. He rounded the corner of the bushes behind us such that our path was cut off in both directions.

"Talyn, won't you escort our dear Emrys here to see the king?" Callum said.

"Emrys..." Rose said from beside me.

"It's alright," I murmured. Then to Callum, "I'll go with Talyn. But you stay the fuck away from us."

Grabbing Rose's hand, I begrudgingly followed Talyn out of the gardens and whispered in my wife's ear. "Go back to our room. Close the door. Don't leave for anything, not until I'm back. Barricade the door if you feel threatened. Do you hear me?"

"But—"

"Go!" I shouted.

She turned and fled the other way, headed toward the drawbridge. Thank the gods, she actually listened.

"Don't want your little witch to see the show?" Talyn said, shaking his head.

He led the way not inside the castle to the throne room, but to the fields, and I knew the king was about to have a lot to say about what occurred yesterday. And when the king was in a punishing mood, I did not want Rose anywhere within sight.

Once at the fields, Talyn made a sweeping gesture forward. "The king awaits."

His grin spoke volumes. Of course, he wanted me to be punished as severely as I could be. Thankfully, he didn't linger, leaving me alone with the king.

King Armynd stood facing the gallows, hands clasped behind his back. I grew more uneasy with every step I took.

"Tell me, Emrys. What do you see?" he asked without turning his head as I stopped beside him. He nodded toward the vast space in front of us, and I frowned.

"An empty field."

"Oh, but it is not empty. What lies at the opposite edge?"

I swallowed. "The gallows."

"Precisely. And what do the gallows represent to you?"

"Highness?" Sometimes Armynd had a habit of growing rather philosophical at times. Sometimes Insufferably so. But I was still baffled by this line of questioning.

"Come, now. When you see the gallows, what do you think of? Do not hold back."

I licked my lips. "I see an instrument for death."

"Is that all?"

"I am not sure I follow."

He sighed. Shook his head. "The gallows are not merely an instrument for death, boy. They are an opportunity. They represent hope; a means to weed the faerie population of any who wish to cause them harm, whether from outside or within. Only then can we have the true peace my wife always wished for."

"With all due respect, I'm unsure that is the sort of peace the queen would have wanted."

His head snapped to the right so he could pin me in his glare. "You dare infer that you know my wife better than I did?"

"No."

His wings were out again. They flapped a little in the wind that had begun to pick up around us. The scent of dirt, decaying earth, and stale blood was carried to me on the breeze.

"Know that I do not take pleasure in the pain or death of anyone. Not even our enemies. But—just as I always have—I will do what I must to protect my people. Even if it is your wife they need protection from."

"Rose is not—"

"Save it, boy." He held up a fist. "I explicitly told her *not* to interfere with our prisoners, and she did. I explicitly told her *not* to use her magic, and she did. I tried to be a hospitable host, being that she *is* your wife. I gave her every opportunity to show me she could abide by my rules. Not only did she break them, but then *you* beat Callum to within an inch of his life. All in an effort to defend your witch who should have never been interfering with the prisoners in the first place. Something *must* be done about this."

It felt like an icy fist slowly crushed my stomach. "Like what?"

He turned his body toward mine and spoke. Voice deep. Resolute.

"Emrys… I want you to collar her."

36

Emrys

MY JAW SLACKENED AT ARMYND'S WORDS. "You want me to *collar* her?"

"Yes."

"Like the witches in the dungeon."

"Rose has proven she cannot be trusted. And as such, she will be treated as hostile, and collared so that her magic is nullified."

I shook my head slowly. Tucked my tongue in my cheek as I contemplated his words. "Perhaps you could just punish me on her behalf. I *was* the one who injured Callum, after all."

"Callum wouldn't have received that beating if it weren't for your wife. You are lucky I'm not immediately having her taken to the gallows. It is either the collar or the noose. Your choice."

"Rose will hate the collar."

"Do you want your wife to stay alive?"

"Of course."

"Then collar her. Do it today, my boy. Or your wife will meet the gallows instead." He reached inside the folds of his jacket. His hand emerged with a cold metal collar which he slapped into my palm. Along with a key. "I believe you know what is right, Emrys. And I am trusting you to do the right thing. Just know that if Rose is ever caught without the collar, if she is ever caught using magic again without my prior knowledge, I *will* be forced to have her hanged. And that will be on you. So, I suggest you do not waste this final chance."

He smacked me on the back. Too hard. I stumbled forward a step. Then he turned on his heel and left me alone in the fields. My attention slowly drifted from the gallows to the metal collar in my hands. I turned it over, studying it.

While wondering exactly how I was going to break the news to my wife.

ROSE LEAPED TO HER FEET WHEN I ENTERED the room later. Thankfully, she had listened and stayed put until I returned. While the king's verdict was bad, it could have been much worse. I only hoped Rose saw it the same way.

"What happened?" she asked, wringing her hands nervously the way she often did. "The king summoned you about what happened at the fields, didn't he. That was my fault. I just couldn't let Callum keep hurting them like that."

"I know," I said.

"What's that?" She nodded at the collar I held in my hands. I sighed. No use delaying the inevitable.

"I understand why you did what you did, Red. And it didn't help that I beat Callum with witnesses present. But you had to know there would be consequences for this."

Her mouth slackened, eyes widening a little as she swallowed hard. "And what consequences are that?"

I held up the metal in my hands. "I must collar you."

Her eyes opened further. She recognized the collar. The witches in the dungeon each wore an identical one. Her hands jumped to her neck as though protecting it.

She shook her head adamantly. "Absolutely not."

"This is the alternative to keeping you out of the noose after you were spotted using magic on the fields."

"Callum reported everything?"

"Yes. And I am sure the other guard corroborated his story, too. Hence the collar. But," I held up the small silver key, "only I have the means to open it, as well. Armynd is trusting me with it. The caveat being that if your collar ever comes off, you will be executed. I am sorry, but it must stay on until the day you leave."

"I won't—"

"Do you wish to die, Red?" I snapped. "I can only protect you if you work with me. And follow the bloody rules."

She eyed the collar for another long moment before she spoke again. "Alright." But as she said the word, her lip quivered a little.

I cleared my throat. "There is something you should know. Something that cannot leave this room. These collars… They're actually quite easy to alter before they're snapped into place. Once the symbols on the inner metal circle touch the witch's skin, their powers are suppressed. But as a faerie, I need only put a deep scratch or two through some of the symbols to make its binding powers ineffective. As those marks are inside, no one will know better."

Her eyes widened with a little hope. At least she had the knowledge that the collar was for the king's benefit only. That her magic would not be truly bound. Though I desperately hoped she still understood the gravity of the situation. "By doing this, Red, I am trusting that you will never use your magic unless the situation is literal life or death."

"Or unless I need it to break your curse."

"No, I—" I pressed my teeth into my lip. "Perhaps we should put the curse-breaking on hold for a while. Just forget any attempts until the hostility towards you dies down."

"It never will, Emrys. Surely you know that."

"Well, so far you haven't needed to use magic in any of your reversal attempts. The tonics don't count."

"The tonics are also not *working*. And if they did, and we figured out how the curse worked from your memory, I would still need magic to *reverse* the spell. Remember?"

I sighed. She had a point.

"Do you not want me to break your curse anymore?"

"I do. Just not when it can put you in danger. Which is why I am merely suggesting you lay low for a while."

Rose's gaze had shifted back to the collar. "What are these things made of? Iron?"

I chuckled. "Gods, no. Faeries cannot touch iron. These are silver. Now turn around."

Reluctantly, Rose did. Her shoulders slumped with defeat. I used the key to open the collar, sliding it into the tiny keyhole on the back. I lifted it over her head and pulled it back until it was snug against her neck. Then I snapped it shut, locked it with the key. Hating the sight of it on her, I bent down. Pressed a soft kiss to her spine just below the collar. She shivered. Her skin tasted sweet, and I resisted the urge to taste every inch of her right now.

But my mouth dried as I laid eyes upon her eye mark as well, another mark she had because of me. It sat just above the collar, nestled near her hairline. It was unmoving now.

Rose stepped away from me then, out of my grasp. She walked to the full-length mirror to examine her new accessory. Likely feeling just as violated as the day I had branded her.

"I'm sorry," was all I could say before I left the room.

37

Rose

ANOTHER THREE DAYS PASSED. ANOTHER three days of getting used to my collar. Of adjusting to being the infamous pariah, now equipped with a shiny, new reminder for the whole village that I couldn't be trusted. My sleep had been restless, haunted by dreams of Ophelia and Orinthia hanging from the gallows, of buzzards feasting on their dead eyes and picking their bones clean.

I knew I would have to figure out how to break Emrys's curse as soon as possible. If Ophelia and Orinthia were meant to leave with me, then the sooner we could get me—and by extension, them—out, the better.

But we were at an impasse. The memory recalling sessions with Emrys had not worked, which meant I needed to try another tactic. I knew the logical next step, even though it was something I had been hoping to avoid at all costs. I simply did not see any other options right now; I could only pray I didn't lose myself in the process. This also meant I would have to use magic despite my promise to Emrys not to; I had to be extremely careful to not get caught, or it was over for all of us.

Emrys had been summoned away again with more court matters to attend to, and I was on my own with Goro. First, I needed to get the raven to stop following me, or else he might try to put a damper on my plans.

"Would you send a message to Korvyn for me?" I asked. "I just want to make sure Ophelia and Orinthia are alright, and ask if he's checked on them yet today. Please?"

He didn't know that Korvyn had already reported to Emrys late last night, who in turn reported to me, and I intended to keep it that way.

"Very well, my lady. But please do not stray far until I return."

I did not move until he flapped out of view. With Goro gone, I was now free to enact my plan.

But first, I needed something.

The grimoire.

As much as the book terrified me, I remembered seeing one spell that was exactly what I needed now, and it seemed to be one of the more benign ones. Surely, I could tolerate one of the less malicious spells without losing myself.

After navigating to the servants' wing, I softly rapped with my knuckles on the bard's door.

"Jasper?" I called.

No answer.

Satisfied that he was gone for now, I turned the knob and entered.

Jasper must have been playing for the king—or elsewhere in town—because the room was indeed empty. I closed the door quietly behind me and dragged the single wooden chair across the room to wedge it under the knob, just in case anyone should try to come in. I could not risk being interrupted.

My hands shook; not only was I scared of the grimoire, but I shuddered at the thought of what might happen should I get caught using magic. The collar around my neck was a stark reminder of the borrowed time I was on here. Emrys had been kind enough to modify it for my benefit, but he was trusting me not to use magic unless I required it to defend myself... or break his curse.

I approached the grimoire's hiding place in the wall, removed the loose stone, and grasped the cool leather of the book. With a deep breath, I pulled it out of the wall and laid it upon Jasper's bed, kneeling beside it.

"Yes, use the magic inside you. Magnify it," the voice in my head said. *"Give in to the darkness."*

"I will give in to nothing," I answered out loud, feeling quite mad as I opened the book. "I merely require a simple locating spell, and you are going to provide me with one. I know you have one; I have seen it."

In response, the front cover of the book flew open and plopped itself onto the bed, making me jump. I leaned back on my knees, watching as the pages began to flip rapidly as though moved by an unseen hand. The flips stopped abruptly, and I cautiously peered at the page it had landed on. Sure enough, the book had opened right to the locating spell I needed. How convenient.

A cold tingle skittered down my spine. I knew I should not be doing this, but I had no other options anymore.

"I am your only option," the voice said. *"Do not fear me."*

The grimoire seemed desperate for me to use it, which set off warning bells inside my mind. Yet the book's influence was also rubbing off on me and strangely, even though I *knew* I was being coaxed, I could not bring myself to look the other way.

"Goddess, help me keep my heart pure," I whispered toward the ceiling, praying this would not send me down a path of no return. My grandmother would surely stop me from doing this.

But Gran was not here. Not anymore.

I directed my attention to the words on the page. Surprisingly, no ingredients were needed aside from one: blood. Because of course, it was blood. That was, after all, the basis for all dark magic.

"*Choose an object to use as a vessel for guidance,*" I read aloud. "*Anoint it with your blood to complete the bond with your vessel. Picture what you wish to find and speak the words below.*" This led me to two questions. Firstly, why did this seem too easy? Secondly, what was I going to use to cut myself?

Quickly, I looked about the room. The small desk, the chair, the bed...

"Come on, Jasper," I whispered.

Then it occurred to me. If Jasper kept his journal hidden under his mattress, maybe he kept other things hidden under there, as well.

Without further ado, I shoved my hand under the lumpy mattress. My fingers bumped the journal, but nothing else of note, just stray feathers and dust bunnies. I walked around the bed to feel under the other side of the mattress and then... Yes, I felt something wooden. I pulled out the object, realizing that Jasper was keeping a paring knife handy. Likely to use for emergencies or self-defense if he needed it. And as a human in a faerie castle, it was probably smart of him to always be on his guard.

I pricked my finger with the edge of the blade and pressed the drop of blood to Ophelia's necklace, which still hung around my neck, careful not to get any blood anywhere near my collar, just in case. It was the only thing I could think of to use as my locating vessel. Once the metal was saturated with my blood, I slid back toward the grimoire and read the spell out loud in a language I did not recognize, though it felt ancient. Like the grimoire, it also felt powerful. I could only hope I was pronouncing the words correctly, though they seemed quite derivative of modern vernacular in many ways—or, modern vernacular was more likely derivative of *it*.

After finishing the last line, I clutched the soiled necklace and focused on my intent: finding out how to break Emrys's curse.

"*Find the reversal spell,*" I said inside my head. "*Find whatever can help me break Emrys's curse. Show me where the answer hides.*"

The spell responded almost immediately. I felt hot and cold at the same time, the sensation moving down my entire body, bubbling straight through to my core until I feared power would burst right out of my belly. The metal of the necklace heated around my neck until my skin felt close to blistering. But the sensation died down quickly, leaving me to wonder if the spell had failed.

In answer to my question, the necklace lifted off my neck. It jerked forward, floating mid-air and pointing to the door as though raised by a mischievous sprite intent on getting me to follow its lead.

I paused only long enough to tuck the grimoire safely back into its hiding place, and then... I followed.

The floating necklace tugged me forward. I tried to conceal its movements under my cloak—which would be a clear indication that I was using magic—as it led me through the castle corridors, across the drawbridge, through town and the central square. My chest tightened when it drew me toward a now-familiar alley within sight of the stables. The stench of horse dung was especially pungent today, permeating the air, but I paid it no mind.

Because it seemed my blood had not been wrong, after all. And unlike the last two times I came here, the alley was no longer empty.

The ground at the back end of the alley was at first smooth and unbroken, but a moment later, something appeared on the ground as though it had been conjured from the air. It looked to be a grate of some sort covering a wide opening. The image would flicker back and forth between smooth ground and grate-covered hole; surely an illusion meant to camouflage, one that my locating spell allowed me to see right through. No villagers seemed to venture here, and if they did, the opening would be hidden to them, and whatever it contained would remain concealed, as well. My necklace pointed forward once again.

Clearly, I was meant to enter.

Upon closer inspection, the grate was held in place by a thick chain. I looked all around to ensure I was alone—no Callums lingering close by this time—and I whispered, *"Teine."*

I wrapped my fingers around the chain until the fire in my hand softened the metal enough to become pliable. Keeping as quiet as possible, I yanked the chain to pull the links apart. The grate was a bit trickier, having likely rusted shut over years of not being used. Who knew the last time this was opened?

With my tongue clenched between my teeth, I yanked with a grunt and the metal grating finally gave way with a rusted groan. Wincing, I peered over my shoulders, listening to ensure no one had heard the noise and planned on coming to investigate. But all was silent, still.

Sighing in relief, I peeked inside the opening, which led down a steep set of stairs into a dark cellar. Even now, my surroundings flickered. One moment I saw the carved stone and steps, and the next, there was nothing but a dirt hole in the ground. That sort of illusion would certainly be effective if working properly, but the grimoire's spell continued to cut through the glamour quite effectively.

I crept down the steep stairs into the damp cellar, watching my step. The stone had started crumbling in small patches, making the descent rather treacherous, and the inky blackness became darker still the farther I moved from the opening.

"Sorcha," I whispered, holding up my palm. Bright sparks appeared at the ends of my fingertips, casting a warm glow off the tunnel walls and allowing me to see better.

The stairs eventually flattened into a damp tunnel that snaked and narrowed, growing steadily chillier the farther I ventured. I shivered, pulling my cloak tight around my body as I continued down the winding corridor. It finally dead-ended at a narrow, arched door, also locked. When I moved forward, Ophelia's necklace yanked me backward.

"What are you doing?" I said out loud on a harsh whisper.

I took another step forward with the same result, the necklace all but strangling me in its ceaseless efforts to stop me moving forward. The locating spell was supposed to get me safely to whatever location it sought, so maybe it knew something I did not.

The necklace lifted again, this time pointing up over the top of the door. My eyes narrowed as I realize the door was equipped with some sort of booby trap. A thin line ran from the doorknob to a pulley system above the door. Opening the door would trip the booby trap, and I was not eager to find out what it was. Arrows? Knives? Poisoned darts? The possibilities were endless.

"Teine," I muttered, directing my fire at the string.

It snapped rather quickly, and without any force to pull the line downward, it dangled, useless, beside the door. With a deep breath, I gently eased the door open, exposing a rather large, cave-like chamber. Empty.

A scuffling noise arose at the far end of the room, just beyond where my light could reach. Likely rats or some other small vermin—though maybe not. Cautiously, I moved forward, feet scuffing the dirt floor. I kept walking until I saw where the noise was coming from.

There was an old wooden chest perched on top of a stone slab, fastened shut with another thick chain and lock. I moved my palm and its light forward, illuminating writing of some sort on the trunk lid. I leaned forward to swipe my free palm over the trunk, clearing away the cobwebs to get a better look and coughing as I sent a cloud of dust flying into the air. This trunk, whatever it held, had not been opened in a very long time.

My fingers traced the words and symbols etched into the wood. Before I had time to attempt to decipher any of them, a clunking sound from within the trunk made the thick chain and lock around it rattle.

"Stars," I whispered as I jumped back in shock, clutching my chest.

Was this the point of the chain, to keep something from getting out? Maybe this box should not be opened... but I had come this far, and it had to be for a reason. The locating spell had guided me here after I asked it to help me break Emrys's curse, and whatever was inside this box... it must have been the solution. However, it seemed I would need a key for the lock first.

Or, would I?

"You are already more powerful than you think," the voice in my head said. I had my magic and I knew what I had to do, though I was terrified to do it, and my pulse pounded in my ears at the prospect of what I was about to reveal when I popped the trunk lid open.

My need to know won out over my fear.

"Teine," I murmured again.

The simple light extinguished and my hands heated up until my fingertips were red, hot enough to snap a chain link free, just as I'd done with the grate. The thick chain clattered to the ground at my feet. There was no turning back now.

ROSE RED

With my palm held up as a light, I swung the trunk lid open with my other hand. The lid clattered backward. A musty smell greeted me as I looked down...

And gasped in shock.

For looking back up at me, clear as day, was a severed head. Even worse, the head looked up at me. It held my gaze as it opened its mouth and spoke.

"Well, lovely to have a visitor. And who might you be?"

38

Rose

HIS EYES WERE WIDE AND WEARY, A BIT glazed over such that it was hard to tell what color they once were. Maybe a cross between green and blue? His forehead—carved with a strangely familiar symbol—and cheeks were lined heavily with age, his hair salt-and-pepper in color, his eyebrows overgrown. He had a sharp chin and a turned-down mouth, a crooked nose with a crease down the middle. And he sat upon the stump of his neck, possessing no body. I slapped a palm over my mouth, suddenly feeling bilious, and shrieked.

"Good heavens, child," the head said, visibly perturbed. His voice was thin, high and raspy, wheezing with each word. I half expected moths to come flying out of his dusty mouth. "I do not need the first sound I've heard in years to be screams. Give my poor ears a rest, will you? It has been a long decade in the dark. Or *decades*. It might have been a hundred years; I am not quite sure anymore. It's easy to lose track of time inside a trunk, isn't it? And I get no visitors, either. Such a lonely existence."

My fingers slowly unclenched from around my jaw, and I lowered my hand. "How are you still alive in such a state?"

"A curse, I'm afraid."

"Immortality." I bit my lip. "Where is the rest of your body?"

"The terrible fae king had it burned—*haha!*" I frowned at his ill-timed laughter. Though spending decades as a severed head in a box was enough to make anyone a bit delirious. "So that way," he continued, "there would be no possibility of reuniting it with my head. Very sound thinking, I must say!"

Would this be what happened to Emrys if his head were ever separated from his body?

But a more pressing question remained... why was my family's crest carved into the middle of the witch's forehead? It took me a moment to make out the crudely etched drawing—cut into flesh with a knife—but I recognized it. A teardrop-shaped tree and the outlines of two dragons at opposite sides of the trunk facing inward toward each other, breathing fire in an arch over the treetop.

"Who carved my family's crest into your forehead?"

"*I* did, to complete a spell used to amplify bloodline magic—*haha!*"

A grimoire. Of course, he'd used one, and this must have been one of its spells.

The head frowned, eyes narrowing. "Hold on, you just said this is *your* family crest? Who are *you?*"

"My name is Rose."

"Rose who?"

"Rose Doyle. A witch. My parents were Devin and Lilly Doyle. My grandmother was Evelin."

The head gaped in recognition at the names, so wide his chin nearly touched the trunk bottom. "Child, I believe you are my granddaughter. Great, great, great granddaughter. I am a Doyle, and my mother's name was Evelin. I can only imagine that same name got passed down through the years."

Now I was the one gaping. How could that be?

"Tell me," Grandfather continued. "If you are truly a Doyle, then how many of the elements have you harnessed?"

"Two," I replied.

"*Bah!* Disappointing," he fired back immediately.

"Which two?"

"Earth and fire."

"Hm, well, fire is one of the rarest, at least. How about your parents? How many for them?"

"They each harnessed two elements, as well."

"It is still quite disappointing that my descendants have never mastered more than two elements. We have become weak."

"How many elements did you harness?" I asked out of curiosity.

"All four, of course." He stated it so casually, then added another *"Haha!"* for good measure.

Now I knew why the Doyles were once considered so powerful. It was very rare for a witch to master three elements and almost unheard of for one to master all four.

I shook my head. "You had so much power. You could have used it for good, and yet you used it for petty revenge, to hurt his family."

The etching on his forehead wrinkled as he arched a brow. "Hurt whose family?"

"Emrys said a witch followed him to his home at night, killed his entire family, and then cursed him. Was that you?"

"Hm. Who is Emrys and why should I know that name?"

"Emrys Abrynth, a faerie. A witch killed his brother, sister, and parents, slaughtering them in the night, then cursed him with immortality, leaving a crescent-shaped scar around his eye. I am asking once again... Was that witch you?"

"Ah." The head squeezed his eyes shut for a moment and blew out a deep sigh. "Yes, it was me."

I clutched the lid of the trunk as my knees threatened to give out. The locating spell had worked, but this meant it was my own kin who hurt Emrys and killed his family. My own flesh and blood was a monster.

"I remember that night very clearly," my grandfather continued. "It was a case of mistaken identity, I'm afraid. Fae burned down my village, killing so many people I knew and loved, without mercy. We spent months attempting to root out those who carried out the crime. The noma king at the time was so thoroughly frightened by the attack, he made me put the princess and her betrothed in a trance for their own protection. All humans were in a panic. And we believed the fae boy's father was one of the sadistic, bloodthirsty fae who led the raiding party, but we were mistaken. I only found out my mistake years later, when it was far too late to fix anything."

"You killed the whole family. The *children.*" My tone was laced with sheer disgust, bile once again stinging my throat. "You cursed an innocent boy."

"No fae are innocent—" He cut himself off and cleared this throat, blowing out another breath with puffed cheeks and flapping lips. "Apologies. Old habits, older vendettas. You are right; the boy did not deserve that."

"Of course, I am right."

My grandfather looked down toward the dusty bottom of the trunk, visibly ashamed. His tone was more somber now. "My need for vengeance back then was unparalleled; I had given myself over to the dark arts readily. But when one spends as much time as a severed head locked in a box as I have, one has all the time in the world to relive their sins and realize just how horrendous they could be. I have many regrets, none for which I can properly make amends. But I *can* help you now. I can tell you how to reverse the faerie's curse. I assume that is what you came searching for?"

"Yes. But how can I trust you?"

"Because I would never lie to my blood kin."

At my skeptical look, he amended his words and tried again, returning to the strange, bubbly tone he'd used before.

"Because you will test the reversal spell on me first. Long ago, I too was made immortal. I am more than ready to leave this plane now. Oh, yes. More than ready—*haha!*"

My head spun as I thought of all I had learned. The head in the box who killed Emrys's family was my great grandfather, an immortal witch who was once evil. Sometime after he killed Emrys's family and cursed Emrys, he was captured by the king. I didn't think my parents knew the full truth, or if they did, they took it to their graves.

But something else was bothering me. "How did you become immortal? Who cursed you? Only other witches would be able to do such a thing, correct?"

My grandfather eyed me warily. "Yes."

"So, what witch cursed you?"

"No other witch. I cast immortality upon myself—*haha!*"

My jaw fell open. "You can do that?"

"Yes."

Stars. "*Why* would you do that?"

"*Oh-ho,* I purposefully granted myself immortality because I wanted to stay alive to fight fae for a long time to come. I used to think that immortality couldn't be *that* bad. I thought I was being merciful and letting the boy off easy compared to his family. But then I became immortal, got held captive as a severed head in a box, and I understand now how truly horrible life eternal can be when the best you can hope for is death."

"Did the spell come from the grimoire?"

"Yes—*haha!*"

"There is another grimoire here, you know. Inside the faerie castle."

"Bah. That is troubling, indeed. Because that book is powerful and it could very well change the course of an entire war. Should it fall into the wrong hands—"

"No offense, Grandfather," I interrupted, "but I believe yours *were* the wrong hands to begin with, given what you did with it."

"Fair enough. I was so desperate to find help against the fae that I turned to blood magic too quickly. And reading the book might have changed me, but casting spells from it tainted my soul, corrupted me down to my marrow. My moral compass broke a long time ago, and I think that book stole what was left of my humanity. Its influence has worn off now, but it is too late for me to redeem myself."

My face drained of blood. Now that I had used the grimoire, was my soul already tainted, too? I was silent as he continued.

"Now, listen carefully, child. Let us begin."

"How?"

"First, you will need to draw your own blood."

I blinked. More blood?

"Blood spells have more power," he explained, sensing my reluctance. "And Doyle blood is perhaps the most powerful of all."

"How so?"

"Not very many witches possess the ability to give immortality nor take it. But Doyles do. Oh yes, we do. *Ho-ho!*"

"We do?"

"Yes. Now, cut yourself."

With a sigh, I looked around for something sharp to cut myself with, only finding the jagged edge of the lock I'd melted. Cringing, I swiped my finger over it—a different finger than the one I used for the locating spell—and hissed as blood beaded up. It made sense that blood magic called for blood in order to work, but it was already getting quite old.

"Now, press the blood to the top of my head. Rest both of your hands there."

At the request, I wrinkled my nose but complied, first smearing the blood. What was left of his hair felt dry and crunchy under my palms, caked with dust. Then I laid my hands flat.

"Now what?"

"Now, you'll repeat some words after me."

My brows rose. "That's it?"

"You misunderstand, Granddaughter. This kind of magic—blood magic—has everything to do with intent. To curse someone, you have to truly *want* to do it, and to free someone of a curse, you must genuinely desire their freedom."

"Why do all the grimoire spells seem so simple?" I asked. In fact, it was frighteningly easy to curse someone.

"Because most witches know that such spells are corruptive, and avoid them," my grandfather replied. I swallowed, fearing I was already on a path with no return, but I could not stop now. "Now, test the reversal spell on me. I am ready to go from this life."

"I will try," I replied, though my mouth felt dry as kindling.

With hands still on his head, I listened to the words he spoke and tried to repeat them exactly.

I barely knew my grandfather, and what little I knew was far from positive, but I *did* genuinely want to free him of his curse. Mainly because spending decades as a severed head in a locked box of a lonely cellar was already quite a stiff punishment.

"Repeat the words twice more. There is always power in threes with spells like this. And keep your intentions focused," he instructed. I nodded, closing my eyes to concentrate.

Soon, I could feel power rising up within me like a wave in my gut, spreading out toward my limbs like the tide itself, heating up my hands and flowing through them to my grandfather.

You're using dark magic, I reminded myself, suddenly nervous.

Although, technically, I was *reversing* dark magic. Surely that wasn't the same thing? Though, it was still blood magic, and that made me nervous.

When it was done, I lowered my hands, and my grandfather sighed with relief. My eyes opened, and I peered down at him once more.

"Oh, it does feel good to be free—*haha!* I wish you well, Granddaughter," was the last thing my grandfather said before the skin and flesh began melting from his bones like candle wax. A surge of pure white energy left him and jumped to my skin, warming me, as though I was absorbing some degree of his magic. Maybe because it was family magic—Doyle magic.

And then, it was done. All was dark, and I was staring down at a lifeless skull in a box, its sockets hollow and empty.

But all was not quiet. A sudden howling made gooseflesh erupt down my arms. The sound seemed to be coming from the dingy tunnel, getting closer and closer until it swirled into the room and knocked me right off my feet.

"Gaoth!" a voice shouted. It could have been my own.

The wind made my eyes blur with tears, forced my mouth open and choked me, whipped my hair across my face. It was relentless, holding me to the ground, whistling around me, making my skin prickle everywhere it touched me.

And then, just as suddenly as it had come, it left. There was nothing around me but silence, and I gasped in a sharp breath, my limbs tingling.

My grandfather had mentioned he'd harnessed all four elements. Had I just somehow absorbed his *wind power?*

"Yes, use it," the dangerous voice in my head said. *"Create a cyclone. Kill them all."*

The voice seemed even louder now, refusing to be ignored, Ophelia's necklace heating against the skin of my chest. I hushed the voice, suddenly overwhelmed and also fighting a massive headache.

"No," I said out loud, answering thoughts out loud that were surely not my own. Maybe I *had* gone mad. "I am *not* creating a cyclone."

But if I *had* just harnessed wind, I *did* want to test my new power eventually—sooner than later. Though, the air in this tunnel was stagnant, stale, and I felt wholly depleted at the moment. It would have to wait.

I had done what I came here to do, and the locating spell had worked, though I was determined to make that the last time I consulted the grimoire. The king had not been lying about having a means to break Emrys's curse, but who knew how long he had planned to dangle it over Emrys's head and not actually *help* him?

But now, I had a dilemma.

When, exactly, to tell Emrys I knew how to break his curse?

And that my own grandfather was the madman who cursed him.

39

Rose

ALL DAY, I FRETTED ABOUT WHAT I WAS GOING to say to Emrys when I saw him later. Goro had returned, displeased that he had spent so long looking for me, but I assured him I had not gotten into trouble. He had also brought another invitation for Emrys and me, freshly distributed by the king.

"What's this banquet for?" I asked the raven as I read the note scrawled in sprawling gold.

"It is the anniversary of the queen's death. The king honors her memory every year with a big feast. It is customary for his whole court and their kin to be in attendance."

"Do you ever attend these banquets, Goro?"

"Me?" His black eyes widened at the question. "No, my lady. I do not imagine I would feel very welcome."

His reply saddened me. "Well then, should you ever decide to attend, you would be in good company with the lone witch at the party."

I looked more closely at the note. This invite was for the following night, and immediately, I decided to wait until after the banquet to tell Emrys what I had discovered. I feared how he would look at me when he found out it was my own kin who made his life miserable.

Just one more day. That was all I needed.

But the next evening came far quicker than I had anticipated. By the time Emrys came back to the room, I was already getting dressed for the banquet. Or, attempting to. Mainly I was just lifting things up and putting them back down, examining each article of clothing and accessory as I attempted to pick the most appropriate attire.

"How was your day?" I asked, and Emrys paused just inside the doorway.

"It was... fine," he replied after a moment. "The usual. Nothing you'd want to hear about. And you?"

I chose my words carefully. "Goro and I walked through town for a bit. And he checked in with Korvyn about Ophelia and Orinthia."

He raised a brow. "Again?"

"Yes."

"And? Any change?"

"No."

He nodded. "Good." His attention shifted towards the array of jewelry and garments I had splayed out across the bed, everything I had found inside the wardrobe. "I see you are already preparing for the king's celebration."

"I am trying, anyway." I frowned and set down the garment in my hands. "There is something I must ask about tonight's feast." Already anxious about the answer I blurted, "She was killed by witches, right? The queen?"

"Yes," Emrys replied.

I let out a quick huff of breath through my nose. "Well, I'm sure I will feel very welcome tonight."

"You will be just fine. I'll be by your side all night. And at least Rhea will not be your tailor. No more conjuring."

I did feel a bit safer and less likely to face public humiliation, and I would take what small comforts I could get.

Emrys's gaze flicked to the bed. "Blue," he said.

"What?"

He pointed with his chin. "You should wear the blue dress."

"Oh." I smiled. "Thank you. I was having trouble deciding." Truthfully, I had been leaning a little towards the blue garment, as well.

Now a smirk curved on his lips. "I know. I saw."

With that, we went to our separate corners of the room to get dressed. This had become our routine, and Emrys, surprisingly, was rather good at respecting my space.

I stood before the full-length mirror with my dress on and dragged a comb through my auburn waves, making a fuss piling my hair atop my head in carefully arranged curls. Emrys had finished before me and now he perched on the edge of the bed watching my movements with amusement. I felt his eyes upon me, and when I finally finished, I turned to find myself pinned in a rather intense golden gaze.

"What?" I asked as Emrys crossed the room toward me. He wore blue and cream, complimenting my own outfit.

He shook his head as though to clear it of lascivious thoughts. "You just look..." He trailed off. His fingers lightly traced the curve of my hip beneath the royal blue, fitted bodice of the dress, and I shivered. "I am a lucky bastard to call you my wife. For no matter how long."

But then a crease formed between his brows as his fingers moved back up, across my shoulder, until they hovered just below my metal collar. I had hung a dazzling blue sapphire necklace below it that rested just above the small valley between my breasts, but it still did nothing to distract from the ugly metal collar that would remind everyone at the party that the king viewed me as little more than a dog who needed muzzling. I felt a pang at that, and Emrys sighed at my expression.

"I have the power to take this off you right now, Red," he said. "The key is always with me. But you know I can't. Not yet."

"I know," I whispered.

As he'd said, the collar was the only thing standing between me and the noose. Frankly, I was surprised I'd been invited to this banquet at all, and part of me had wanted to lock myself in the room rather than show my face there. Maybe I was only invited because the king *wanted* everyone to see my collar. To see that he was *'keeping the witch in line.'*

"Red." Emrys's voice was husky as his lingering fingers dragged across my collarbone, following the line of the metal. "Stay by my side. The king will expect you to be there. But you, my wife, are a bold creature. You haven't let any horrible circumstance snuff that spark inside you yet. Don't start now."

I nodded and offered a half smile. "Is it time to head down?"

"It is." He grinned good-naturedly at that and moved to close his side of the wardrobe. "Shall we?"

He offered me the crook of his arm, which I accepted, gripping his elbow with both hands and holding on like he might float away if I let go.

Emrys and I descended the turret steps, the grand, green-carpeted staircase, following the flickering sconce light. This would likely be our last night like this before I broke his curse, before I got sent away and he died... and before he never looked at me the same way after finding out what my own great grandfather did to him. But I wouldn't think about that now.

No matter what collar I wore, no matter how many hateful glares caught me in their beams, I was determined to make the most of this night.

Jasper was just about to play by the time we entered the banquet and took our seats at the table. His hair was carefully combed and secured into a little knot at the nape of his neck, and he wore nicer clothes than normal—I wondered if the prince had a hand in that.

Before the bard started playing, he spoke. "This song is a tale of two lovers who cannot express their feelings for each other in the open, but rather must steal little moments to be together. It is called *Stolen Glances,* and it—"

"Just play, already," a voice shouted. An impatient faerie rolling his eyes from the side of the room.

Jasper snapped his mouth shut and clutched his lute. "Yes. Here it is."

As he began playing, I couldn't help but look over at the prince, who sat at a different table from us this time. He stared at Jasper with the most intense, loving expression, his glamour shimmering brighter than ever, and I swore there were tears pooling in his eyes. I leaned toward Emrys and whispered, "You don't think those lyrics are about—"

"Korvyn?" he finished for me. "Yes, I believe that's exactly who they're about."

"They are being quite obvious," I said, considering how they were currently staring at each other so intensely and openly. "I cannot imagine the king would be happy finding out his only son was taking up with a human at his wife's memorial banquet."

Emrys shrugged. "The king would never deign to imagine that his son would be interested in a human. So he will overlook the obvious until he can't anymore. But they do need to be more careful. I already told Korvyn as much."

"Seems they don't much care. And it is a beautiful song."

"It is," Emrys agreed.

Truly, it was so deep and meaningful, and I could hear the emotion in Jasper's voice as he sang, laced in his vibrato with every note. He meant every word; it was obvious he cared deeply for the prince, and that the opposite was true as well.

> *"Across the room their eyes meet,*
> *A moment lost in time..."*

As he continued to sing in his smooth, silky voice, I felt Emrys's hand rest on my thigh. At first, it felt somewhat innocent, but even that small touch made my pulse speed and my breath hitch in my chest. Emrys must have noticed my reaction, because he turned his head and caught my gaze with his lips curved into a crooked smile. Oh, how my body loved to tell on itself in his presence.

When his thumb began to stroke in gentle circles, my pulse sped even more, and when his hand drifted dangerously close to my groin, I couldn't help the little mewl that escaped my throat. At my reaction, Emrys's nostrils flared, his jaw clenching as though he was currently exerting a great deal of self-control.

"What are you doing?" I whispered, though I still made no move to stop him.

"What does it seem like I'm doing?" He leaned close, his lips brushing my ear. "I'm making sure my wife is having a good time."

Thankfully, those around us seemed oblivious to what my husband's hand was doing under the table, and I was glad of it. Emrys's thumb skirted the mound between my legs, rubbing in little circles. My dress was light and thin enough that I could feel the heat of him through the fabric, could feel the friction his little movements created at the apex of my thighs. I sucked in a sharp breath and grabbed his hand under the table, halting his movements. I *did* want him, no matter how much I tried to deny the feeling. But I wanted it to be when we were *alone*.

His hand flexed around mine. He bent to whisper in my ear again. "Do you have any idea how attractive you are, Red? You are driving me bloody *insane*."

He pressed a kiss just beside my earlobe, on the curve of my jaw, right near where my pulse continued to beat wildly. The feeling of his kiss lingered after he'd pulled away. I flushed and attempted to turn my attention back to the company around us.

Across the way, Rhea, Callum, and Talyn looked just as annoyed by my presence, judging by the way Rhea stared at me. Oh, stars, had she seen my reaction to what Emrys had just been doing and figured out what was going on?

I wasn't sure, but she tipped Callum's head her way and planted a deep kiss on his lips when she thought she'd caught Emrys's eye, but she hadn't; it was apparent he could not care less about her. Emrys's focus was on me, his large thumb now drawing lazy circles on the back of my hand.

"Are you not enjoying the food?" he asked, noticing my plate was barely touched.

"I am."

"Then are you not hungry?"

To appease him, I took a big bite of potato. Truthfully, my stomach was too full of the butterflies that currently flitted about—for many reasons—but I tried my best to eat. Around us was all pleasant chatter and the clanking of utensils on plates.

At the other side of the table, Rhea still fussed over Callum, making a big, obvious show of feeding him a strawberry, which he took between his teeth and laughed. It was a strange thing, seeing Callum laugh. Talyn whispered something to Callum from his other side, vying for his attention as well, and Rhea rolled her eyes. She didn't seem to have much patience for Talyn, no matter whose shop they vandalized together.

"They hate you. Kill them. Kill them before they can conspire against you," said the voice in my head, which I did my best to ignore.

Thankfully, my attention was redirected by the sharp clinking of a glass, and everyone looked to the head of the room where the king now stood. He wore purple today, laced with gold—the clear color of royalty. The shoulders of his jacket swooped up at the edges, coming to points that complemented his spiky, polished crown.

"Attention, all," said King Armynd. "I would like to propose a toast to my beloved wife."

But that was all he had a chance to say.

"Witches killed your wife in cold blood, and yet you allow one to roam free," a drunken voice interrupted from the back of the room, and my face instantly reddened. He appeared haggard and drunk, sloshing his glass. His face was also littered with bruises and swelling in their final stages of healing. "Collared or not, their kind are still dangerous."

"Fucking *Bryock,*" Emrys muttered under his breath, clearly recognizing this faerie. Now, Emrys squeezed my thigh beneath the table, hearing my heart thumping wildly in my chest for an entirely different reason than earlier.

"Kill him. Kill them all. You have the power. Show them what a witch can really do," the voice in my head said, and I tried to ignore it once again.

"Watch yourself, Bryock," warned the king, his brown eyes darkening. His wings unfurled rapidly and two faeries beside him had to duck to avoid being knocked down.

"Your wife would be rolling in her grave," the drunk faerie continued. "The courts deserve independence to run things the way they wish to run things, *Armynd*." It was a shock to hear the king addressed so informally, and a collective gasp resounded in the room.

"How dare you make such a spectacle at my wife's feast?" the king spat. His face was crimson, his wings starting to slowly flap up and down as though he was contemplating taking off in flight, plucking Bryock out of his seat, and dropping him from the highest tower. Spittle shot from between his teeth as he bellowed, "Take him away!"

He gestured for Rogyn and Pery. They immediately sprang up to remove the offending faerie who cursed as the shifter guards approached him. He struggled against their powerful grips even as they dragged him from the room and out the large double doors.

A hush had fallen over the crowd, with most faeries stunned and exchanging scandalized glances. A few whispered to each other; undoubtedly this would be the talk of the town for the next few weeks to come. But then, there was the sound of a chair scraping the marble flood as it slid out from a table, and I turned to see Rhea standing from her seat. "Is Bryock wrong, uncle?"

"Remember your place, Rhea." Another warning from the king. Darkness spread across his features.

"Sit down," Callum warned from beside her, tugging her elbow. "Don't do this."

But she did not want to hear it, wrenching her arm free of his grip. Talyn, who sat at the other side of Callum, rolled his eyes as though he'd been anticipating such tiring behavior.

"I told you she was trouble, Callum." Talyn did not bother to lower his voice, wanting the whole room to hear his annoyance.

But Rhea ignored them both, continuing to address the king. "You are losing control over your own people, Uncle. You know I'm right."

"Do not make me throw you in the dungeons, Rhea." Armynd clutched his glass so hard, it was a wonder it did not immediately shatter in his hands.

"No need. I will see myself out." She lifted her glass of wine, finished its contents in one gulp, slammed it down. Then, after throwing a quick, pointed glare in my direction, she stormed out of the ballroom.

When Callum stood abruptly with the obvious intent to chase her, Talyn gripped his wrist and leaned over to whisper something. If I had to guess, it was reminding him of his esteemed place in court and not jeopardizing his position. Whatever Talyn said, it seemed to have the desired effect of calming Callum, who reluctantly reclaimed his seat.

"Does anyone else have anything they would like to add? By all means." the king bellowed in a tone that meant he would entertain no such notion. That there was plenty of room in the dungeons and stocks and he would have no qualms about sentencing anyone to their isolation. Beside me, Emrys remained silent, stiff.

When no one replied, the king nodded. "Good. Now, I apologize for those wholly unnecessary interruptions." Armynd was still flushed red with anger, but he raised his glass to finished his speech nonetheless. "My wife had a kind heart. Perhaps the kindest of anyone I had ever known. She yearned for peace, wished for it every single day. But it was her kindness that led to her untimely end, for what my beloved wife did not realize is that peace first requires bloodshed. Much of it." My jaw slackened at his words, at how *wrong* they sounded. "My wife had my whole heart. She always will. And true peace for our kind is nearly upon us. All I ask is that you continue to believe in me, your king, just as you once believed in my wife, the queen. Keep her legacy alive. And together, united, there is nothing we cannot do. Now, enjoy the rest of the celebration!"

I could see him still shaking with thinly veiled rage. With the speech finished, he downed his whole glass of wine in one gulp and plopped back into his seat, wings folded in again, and the festivities continued.

The rest of the banquet went by without incident. Nobody said another word to me, and nobody tried to enchant me or ruthlessly embarrass me either, which was a marked improvement from the last feast. The music soon became livelier, and some faeries had taken to dancing in the middle of the room, spinning around in drunken little circles and giggling. Some couples twirled gracefully around us. Without a word, Emrys stood and gently tugged me to my feet beside him.

"Oh, you know I'm not a dancer."

He flashed his familiar crooked smile. "Who said anything about dancing, Red? Come, I want to take you to the best spot."

I raised a brow. "The best spot for what?"

"You'll see."

He led me toward the ballroom doors. A few of the other fae were already starting to file out of the room, too. Most of them ignored me, some of them glared, and others glanced at my collar and shook their judgmental heads. Suddenly, I was grateful to be getting out of this ballroom. But I was still curious.

"Where are they going?" I asked.

"Again, you will see."

"Where are *we* going?"

He shot me a look. "How many *you will see*'s must I repeat before you accept the fact that I am trying to surprise you with something nice?"

"At least one more," I replied with a grin.

He shook his head, though a smile played upon his lips. Clutching my hand, he led me down the corridor, up the grand, green-carpeted staircase. He turned as though headed toward our turret room, but continued past our spiraling stairs. The hallway here was extremely narrow, such that we had to walk one in front of the other. At the end of the hall was a single door. I had never bothered exploring this way before because everything important seemed to be in the other direction, down the grand staircase.

Emrys opened the door to expose a small yet cozy room. It was dark, unlit, with no bed, just several cushy chairs covered in dust, and an open balcony.

"This used to be where the queen snuck off to think," Emrys said. "When she was having a bad day or needed a little space from Armynd. They were blood bound and she loved him. She never wanted to stray far. She just... liked having a room of her own to think sometimes. Armynd could be a little overbearing. The queen swore me to secrecy."

I let my fingers trail over the arm of a cushioned, high-backed chair as we passed it on the way to the balcony, which was wide, with a low, stone rail. It had a gorgeous view over the town, even better than the one from our turret. Below, the lanterns in town had already lit up like glimmering stars.

And that's when I heard the first boom and jumped with a little yelp.

Emrys laughed. "It's just the fireworks."

"Fireworks?" Right in front of us, overtop the town, was a series of booms and splashes of colors that streaked across the sky. I had not seen fireworks since I was a small child in Astyrtown, and even then, only once. They were beautiful.

"The king always finishes the Queen's memorial banquets with a fireworks display. And this is always where I come to watch. It's quiet, with the best views. Like I told you," Emrys said.

He was right. The display was stunning, vibrant bursts of golds and greens and blues. Some of the fireworks even took on the shapes of different animals. A small trail of smoke climbed up into the air and popped, revealing a large, impressive burst of silver that quickly morphed into the visage of a wolf howling at the moon.

"For the shifters?" I asked.

"The king usually tries to honor all different fae as best he can." His gaze was trained up toward the sky, the light reflecting back in his eyes as he watched the wolf fade from view, dispersing into cloudy wisps carried away on the breeze.

I leaned across the balcony, my elbows on the stone rail, and Emrys leaned close beside me with his shoulder pressed to mine. My breath hitched in my chest when I turned my head to see Emrys staring right at me with fire in his eyes. At the sound of my racing heart, his lips curved into a smile.

"Breathe, Red," he whispered, echoing the words he'd said to me at our wedding.

Just like at our wedding, he tipped my chin with two fingers and gently pressed his mouth to mine while the fireworks boomed. Flashes of brilliant colors brightened the world around us, even with my eyes closed. I found myself lifted by the hips the next instant, so that I was sitting on the edge of the low balcony facing inward, Emrys standing between my legs and holding me steady to keep me from falling. My arms wound around his shoulders as he kissed me.

Soon, his lips left mine in favor of dragging across my jaw, and he repositioned his arms so his palms could cradle my shoulder blades, the weight of my body pressing into his forearms. He leaned me back ever so slightly to grant better access to my throat such that if he were to let go, I would tumble right off the balcony rail and fall. But I did not fear at all; I knew he would never drop me.

I hissed as his lips peppered heated kisses along the side of my neck, his teeth nipping gently, his tongue tasting the flesh of my throat just above my collar, following the line of the metal.

"Why is it," he mumbled between kisses, "that I just cannot seem to get enough of you?"

I did not know, nor did I care. Because at the moment, I could not seem to get my fill of him, either.

The booms grew louder, more rapid, and finally Emrys groaned. He pulled his mouth from my neck to whisper in my ear, "It's the finale. You shouldn't miss it. Spin around." He eased me back into an upright position. With his help, I did as I was told and swung my legs around so they were dangling over the outer edge of the balcony. Emrys stood directly behind me, his arms snaking about my waist and holding me in place. His chest was pressed to my back, his cheek pressed to my temple as we watched the grand finale. I stared in awe as boom after boom pierced the night air and color after color decorated the night sky, and then everything went dark and quiet.

"Is it over?" I asked.

Emrys nodded. "Are you disappointed?"

"A little," I admitted. "I could watch that all night."

"And I could watch *you* watching that all night." He paused. "Among other things."

There went my pulse again at his words.

With the festivities over, Emrys helped me down off the balcony, and we left the queen's secret hideaway to return to our room.

I began wringing my hands as soon as we ascended the steps of the turret and entered our room. Each revelation churned through my mind: I'd found my grandfather who killed Emrys's family, I finally knew how to break Emrys's curse, yet the words just sat there at the tip of my tongue, refusing to be spoken.

"Emrys, I..." I licked my lips, trailing off.

"Your heart is racing again, Red. What is it?"

But my breath caught in my throat at the thought of what I was about to say. Once I told him that I knew how to break the curse, our end would officially be beginning, and I was not ready for this to be over. Selfishly, I just wanted one night. One night to be with him in every sense that a wife could be with her husband, to do the thing that I had never done before, to experience it with Emrys for the first and maybe last time.

So, I did not tell him about my grandfather. I would, but not tonight.

Instead, I perched on the edge of the bed, prompting Emrys to sit beside me. He ducked his head down, his fingers reached up to trace the curve of my cheekbone. When I did not flinch away, his fingers shifted to cup my chin and tilt my head upward. I met his gaze, realizing exactly what he wanted right now, because it was what I wanted as well.

"I need you to kiss me again," I whispered.

And he was all too happy to oblige.

40

Rose

WHEN EMRYS CAPTURED MY LIPS, IT WAS SOFT at first, sweet. My stomach fluttered as he shifted his body to angle more fully toward mine. The kiss deepened as his other hand reached up to wind through my hair, creating a fist above my scalp before flattening on the back of my skull, his large palm holding my head in place as he consumed me, his mouth growing needier.

Gently, I reached up to trace the crescent shaped scar around his eye, moving my finger back to caress the shell of his pointed ear. Emrys hissed and pulled back immediately.

"I thought I told you what that does to me," he growled. "Do it again, and I may not be able to stop what happens next."

"I don't want you to stop," I said, pressing my forehead to his. "In fact, I think... I want to... make this legal."

With that, he pulled away, breaking our contact completely so he could examine my expression in full. "Don't play games with me," he warned, his husky voice almost a growl.

"I'm not." I cleared my throat, suddenly nervous. "Even though the king doesn't know we never made things... official, I want to, now. I do."

Emrys's nostrils flared. "You do..." His eyes flicked down, then up. "You aren't lying. I can smell how wet you already are, Red."

I couldn't help but flush at his words. "Then why are you hesitating?" I raised a brow. "Do you not want me?"

"Of course, I fucking do." Emrys looked at me as though I'd just asked the most ignorant question in the world. "Surely you must know." He leaned close; his lips touched my ear as he said, "I've wanted you from the moment I first laid eyes on you. Whether I knew it or not."

"Sometimes you run very hot and cold, you know."

He sighed. "I know. It is because I want what I shouldn't have. That's dangerous for us both."

"But... What if I said I wanted it too? How about then?"

His eyes were intense as he replied, "I would say... I am weak, Red. In fact, I find myself powerless against you." His forehead connected with mine again. "Say the word and I'm yours. Say the word and I will worship you the way you deserve to be worshipped."

His words did something to me, caused a twitching within, a throbbing between my legs.

"In that case, I am saying the word, Emrys. I want all of you. Tonight."

"Well, in that case," he grinned, "I shall lay the world at your feet, my lady."

With that, Emrys unbuttoned my cloak and slid it off me before working on the laces of my dress. My breathing came heavy, my pulse at its peak. He pushed my dress down my shoulders, yanking the material down to my waist and tracing my bare skin. All the way down to my belly. Once there, he paused, his fingers tracing a long, jagged scar on my side. He lifted a brow, since it seemed this was the first time he'd noticed it.

"A fae nearly caught me on one of my hunts a year ago," I explained. "I thought I would die, but I didn't."

Emrys hissed inward through his teeth, but said nothing. He placed his palm over my exposed breast, rubbing the hardened nipple, and I arched my back to press into him further. His mouth twitched, enjoying my sounds of pleasure. He bent to drag his lips across my collarbone, following the line of the metal collar before moving down to the small valley between my breasts.

"You still have too much clothing on," I rasped.

"That can be fixed," he murmured against my skin.

Once Emrys removed his shirt, I was reminded that he was covered in scars of many different shapes and sizes, all across his chest and abdomen. I had never seen them up close like this before. "How is it that you scar?" I asked. "I've seen the punishments you endure, but I've also seen the way those wounds can heal without a trace."

"They usually do," he said, but he didn't elaborate further.

Instead, his lips found mine again, his greedy mouth and tongue staking a claim. When he pulled back again, his pupils were dilated.

"Lay down on your back. Now," he commanded, and I was powerless to do anything but obey.

Then his mouth began to explore my body. He took his time, dragging his lips down my abdomen before pausing at my thighs, shoving them apart. He hooked his hands behind my knees and yanked me forward, staring at that part of me like it was water in a barren desert.

"Gods, have I been dreaming about this," he whispered just before his hungry mouth descended upon me.

His tongue parted my folds, finding that sweetest spot that made me arch my back off the bed. While his tongue never ceased its work, his hand lifted to slide a long finger inside of me. I cried out, fisting my hands in the sheets beside my body. Stars, I had never felt like this before. Then a second finger joined the first, and I moaned at the added pressure, unable to think straight.

"Tell me, Red. Has any man ever touched you like this?" he asked as his fingers continued to pump inside of me, pushing in, pulling out, curving just so. "Has any man tasted you?"

"N-no," I admitted, barely able to register his words.

"Then I'm the only one who knows what you taste like. And you taste..." He licked me once, the flat of his tongue running the length of my folds. "So sweet." His mouth latched onto me in full, and I cried out. *Oh,* this was...

"Emrys," I hissed.

"Hmm?" he said with his mouth still on me, the vibrations that little noise made upon his lips sending a shiver of pleasure up my belly.

My hands went to his head now, pushing through his dark, silky hair as his fingers stroked in and out, his tongue moving in the most perfect little circles, making me dizzy with pleasure, with need. And then... his lips circled around the hardened bundle of nerves at the apex of my thighs, closed. Pulled.

I squeaked his name again, hardly able to speak. He pulled harder with his lips and my legs shook; this was almost *too much.* "I want you. Now."

He looked up at me then, his eyes dark, pupils wide, voice husky as he replied, "Does it look like I've finished eating, Red?"

His large hands pushed against my thighs, further opening me to him, that part of me on full display. But I didn't feel exposed. I felt wanton, uninhibited, eager... and strangely safe. He breathed in deeply, savoring my scent the same way he seemed to be savoring my taste, his nose buried in my folds, his tongue doing the most incredible things that had my head spinning.

A low growl sounded in the back of his throat just before his tongue dipped inside of me in place of his fingers, piercing my opening, lapping at my inner walls. I had to bite my fist to keep from shrieking out loud. Oh, I was sailing toward a peak I wasn't ready for yet.

"Please," I begged. "Come up here."

His mouth pulled up at the edges, a crooked, devilish grin. "As you wish."

He pulled his fingers from inside of me and dropped a kiss on my pubic bone, my stomach, between my breasts, working up until he was on top of me, peering down at me. A crease formed between his brows and despite his heavy breathing—and likely using every ounce of self-control he possessed—he stilled.

"Red, you need to be sure about this," he said. "Once I start, I don't think I'll be able to stop." His voice shook with need, his self-control nearly to the point of breaking.

"Why wouldn't I be sure?"

"You're a virgin."

"Yes."

"And I will likely die sooner than later."

I felt a pang, but forced it away. "I don't care. I want this," I said, my voice raspy. "Please."

He said no more. His eyes locked on mine as he aligned himself with my opening, and I silently granted him access with a single nod. Without further fanfare, he entered me with one quick thrust forward. My body protested the intrusion for the briefest of seconds. It hurt at first, a sharp sting, and I hissed. Emrys stilled, allowing a moment for me to adjust to the foreign girth of him.

"I don't think there's any more room, Emrys."

"I'm not even all the way in." He dropped a kiss on my forehead. "You... Are. Just. That. Tight."

With each word, he rocked his hips forward just the tiniest bit, causing a delicious friction that mingled with the pain.

"Oh," I managed to say, the word a strangled groan, my eyes squeezing shut. And then Emrys's lips were near my ear, his words a whispered command.

"Come on, Red. Open for me."

And I did. Somehow, I did. The muscles deep within me unclenched all at once, and with one more long, persistent thrust, Emrys was fully seated inside me.

"Gods," he grunted, leaning his forehead against mine.

I'd felt nothing like it in my life. I felt stretched to the point of breaking, so full, so very full, and yet... Somehow, I wanted even more of him. And as he started to move in earnest, in that moment, I never wanted to be anywhere else but right here, right now, with my husband wedged deep inside of me, awakening pleasures I never dared dream existed.

"Oh, yes," I breathed.

I felt myself meeting him thrust for thrust, the initial pain gone and now only pleasure coursing through me in its place, pleasure bursting in never-ending waves.

Grasping Emrys's shoulders, I leaned my head up and gently ran my tongue along the top ridge of his pointed ear. Emrys's response was immediate, and I swore he grew harder still inside of me as he let out a gasp of pleasure.

"Fuck, Rose," he hissed in my ear before returning the favor of dragging his teeth over my earlobe.

"I think you already *are* fucking Rose," I tried to say, but I was not sure what came out because Emrys thrusted into me hard now, hard and fast, a frantic pace that rattled the bed frame.

I collapsed, throwing my head back. Pain mixed with pleasure. Goddess, help me, it was everything I could've wanted for my first time. Emrys hooked a hand behind my knee and lifted my leg, changing the angle of his penetration and somehow, if possible, it felt deeper still, as though he was reaching into the very core of me. I knew right then that I was about to fall apart.

What was I doing, making love with my sworn enemy? But I pushed the thought far away in favor of how good this felt.

"Emrys, *Emrys*, I... *Ah!*" I tossed my head back in pleasure as he touched that sweet spot deep inside me, and I writhed beneath him.

Emrys grunted through his teeth, and when I looked into his face, he was barely there. His eyes were wolf amber, fierce, pupils dilated and teeth bared. He was driven, relentless, feral, and yet... I never wanted him to stop.

He reached between our sweat-slicked bodies, his hand finding that hardened bud between my legs, rubbing it between his fingers as he thrust deeper still inside me, bumping my womb.

My back arched. My entire body erupted with the sweetest of tingling, a true, unabated pleasure like I'd never felt before.

Emrys mumbled a string of colorful curses, thrusting into me once more as he found his own release.

I laid there for a while on my back, my breasts exposed, my hand over my pulsing heart, chest heaving. I didn't know how long I lied there, but sometime later, I felt the bed shift, and Emrys propped himself up on his elbow to look down at me.

"How are you feeling?" he asked. His free hand reached down to idly fondle my exposed breasts, bending to press a kiss to the top of each in turn.

"Like I can't move," I admitted. "I feel positively spent."

Emrys laughed. "Well, then, it sounds like I did my job properly."

He pulled me to him, securing my back to his front, and I felt so many conflicting things. Shame for sleeping with my born enemy, for *liking* it. Though a bigger part of me did not care. Emrys was different; he was not evil. Both our kinds had bad in them. Mainly, what I felt was a bubble of hope. Selfishly, I did not want Emrys to die. I wanted him to choose to *live*. With me.

I knew that, come tomorrow, I would tell him what I discovered. I would break his curse and honor our agreement.

But tonight, I was content to stay wrapped up in his arms.

Maybe for the last time.

I WOKE UP SOMETIME DURING THE NIGHT. I DIDN'T know what hour it was, but I felt cold, the bed empty. Emrys no longer held me. In fact, he was gone.

When I rolled over, I gasped as I spotted him seated on the windowsill, just as he had done before when he threw himself out of the turret. Flinging the covers aside, I ran across the room and gripped onto his biceps, the muscles tense beneath my hands.

"Wake up!" I shouted. "You're sleepwalking again. Please don't jump."

Maybe he could not die, but a fall from this height would mangle his body in such a way that healing would take far longer than it did with mere cuts. I could not bear to see it. In response, his arms jerked up, shoving my hands off him. When I grabbed his shoulders, this time, his large hands wrapped around my neck below my collar, nails digging in. The muscles in his forearms were corded from strain, his jaw clenched but eyes still closed. I grasped his wrists.

"Emrys," I managed to choke out. "Wake... *up.*"

I released my grip on one of his wrists to slap him across the face, so hard my own palm stung from connecting with his sharp cheekbone.

That seemed to snap him out of his trance. At least, the falling to his temporary death part of it. But then it was like the nature of his sleepwalk shifted, because he still did not wake. While death had loosed its icy hold upon him for now, something else had taken over in his unconscious state: the feral wolf. He released my neck, growled. His arms darted out, palms catching me on the shoulders and throwing me off balance, and I fell.

He straddled me before I could move, pinning me to the ground. One of his large hands locked both my wrists in place above my head, his other hand somehow managing to divest himself of enough clothing to thrust inside of me without warning.

In one swift motion, he was seated within me, and I cried out. I was still sore from earlier and the tender, inner parts of me were currently being battered by Emrys all over again. Although my body responded to him immediately, like harp strings in the hands of a musician.

Emrys was still not awake. His eyes were half open, but his pupils dilated wide, gold eyes fierce yet still caught in the throes of sleep. His lips curled back to expose his teeth. The animal side of him was fully in control, undoubtedly driven even madder with need by the scent of my fear mixed with my arousal. He snarled down at me, and his thrusts were so hard my entire body jerked forward with every motion of his hips.

Yet my body was also greedy, constantly crying out for more. I knew it would always be drawn to Emrys like an ant to sugar.

When I cried out again, one of his hands slipped across my mouth. He rolled his hips, reaching a new spot inside me, and I bit down on the fleshy part of his palm. Unconscious Emrys growled at that, somehow finding a way to pump into me even harder, faster.

This was no soft lovemaking, but a primal joining that sought only release, and I welcomed it. The sharp tang of blood filled my mouth as I bit down harder. And I quickly followed Emrys over the edge when he bottomed out inside me, grunting.

His limp body collapsed on top of me, crushing the breath from my lungs. As if I wasn't already breathless enough. I needed him off of me.

"Emrys," I hissed.

Thankfully, he'd at least released my wrists, and I took the opportunity to box his sensitive ears. *That* ought to wake him up.

With that, his head jerked up, his eyes fully open, slowly adjusting to the moonlight. He saw me beneath him, flustered, breathless, and his eyes widened in horror.

"Rose…" He pushed himself up on his palms, lifting some weight off of me. "What did I do?"

"You were sleepwalking again," I said, catching my breath.

"And… did I hurt you?"

I bit my lip, released. "You didn't mean to," I said.

"Fuck!" He climbed off of me and stood, shoving his hands through his hair. He looked down, realizing his pants were down past his buttocks, and he pulled them back up. "What have I done?"

"I'm alright," I said. "Really."

"None of this is bloody alright!"

"Emrys," I whispered, forcing myself into a sitting position.

He knelt beside me on the floor, looking to my nightgown that was pushed above my waist, looking at my bruised wrists, the tender flesh around my neck. He lifted a hand toward me, made a fist, pulled back. His voice was raspy as he spoke. "No one has shared my bed before. No one has been in my room when I've sleep walked before, either."

"Not even Rhea?"

Emrys looked at me as though I had grown a third eye. "Do you really think I wanted her anywhere near me when I was unconscious, even in sleep? No, Red. She always left the room when we were finished and she certainly never got to spend the night with me."

Wow, so that meant I was the first.

"But I should have known better than to put you in danger like this. Apparently, when death comes knocking, the feral side of me comes out as well. Especially after what happened between us earlier. I just... *gods.*" He hung his head in shame. "I am so sorry."

"I said I was fine."

Emrys stood again, this time making his way toward the door. In a panic, I chased after him and stepped in front of him, blocking his path.

"Please, don't leave," I said. "I doubt you'll have another episode tonight."

"You don't know that."

"My first time was with you, Emrys Abrynth." My voice shook with emotion, unexpected tears springing to my eyes. "I wanted it to be with you, and it was... everything I wished it to be and more. And what came after... I refuse to let it ruin everything else for me. Please, don't..." I swallowed hard. "Please, just stay with me."

After a long while of his gaze following the shiny trail of my tears, Emrys finally relented with a jerky nod. Together, we climbed back into bed. But when I moved toward him, he stiffened.

"Red..."

"Do not shut me out and leave me cold, Emrys. Not now."

Once again, he relented, letting out a loud sigh as I laid my head upon his chest. His arms wrapped around me slowly, warm and solid. And despite what he might've thought, I felt safe. I knew he would never give me more than I could handle, even while unconscious.

For a long while, I laid there listening to Emrys's steady heartbeat, his even breaths, until it lulled me to sleep.

And as I drifted off into unconsciousness, I swore I heard Emrys whisper.

"None of this is alright."

I WOKE UP GLOWING AFTER THE NIGHT BEFORE, feeling thoroughly sated, and yet... a pit was growing in my stomach. A pit that started with Emrys's sleepwalk, his reaction after, my guilt over not telling him I'd learned to break the curse yet.

My muscles were stiff and there was a distinct yet pleasant soreness between my legs that reminded me of my night with Emrys. I flushed at the thought. When he'd sleepwalked, he bruised my neck and wrists. But he had not gone too far, and I knew how to wake him up now. I was more afraid of the thought of him never touching me again.

I reached behind me to find the bed empty, cold. Frowning, I rolled over and spotted Emrys staring out the window. He was clothed from the waist down, but his bare back faced me as he stood statue still, prominently displaying his scars.

"Good morning," I said, my voice raspier than normal.

He turned, mouth pulling up at the corners at the sound of my voice. His eyes caught the sun, making them glitter like the finest gold. Though they were weary—I wondered if he'd gotten any sleep at all, or if he'd stayed awake to ensure he did not sleepwalk again. "Good morning to you, as well."

I lifted a brow. "Is it not customary for a husband to kiss his wife in the morning?"

His smile deepened, tugging up more at the corners. "I suppose it would be."

"Then come here."

"With pleasure, Red."

Yet there was a slight hesitation in his step as he crossed the room towards me. He braced his knuckles on the edge of the bed beside me, depressing the mattress as he bent down to kiss me, and I reached up to curve my fingers around the back of his neck, drawing him close.

He pulled back far too soon, peeling my hand away from his neck and pausing to press a chaste kiss to the inside of my wrist before lowering it back to the bed. I couldn't help but frown, because his kiss, while sweet, had left me wanting in the sense that I could almost *feel* him holding back.

He turned to dress for the day, and I did the same, stretching as I made my way toward the wardrobe and feeling the evidence of last night's activities in every part of my body as I moved. Once again, I felt Emrys's eyes on me. The air between us felt thick, the silence heavy, and once I had finished dressing, I asked him what was wrong.

"Please, sit with me," Emrys said, pulling me beside him on the edge of the bed. My brows furrowed in question as Emrys took my hands. "Last night was..."

"Incredible?" I supplied.

He laughed. "It was. At least, the first part was, not what came after." His smile dropped quickly, and a creeping dread filled my stomach. "But I should've stopped it, as much as I wanted it. As much as I wanted *you*. It was wrong of me. My sleepwalk last night was just proof of why this all was wrong. Of how very badly I can *hurt you*. Just look at the bruises on your neck, Red. Your wrists."

"I told you I was fine." I sighed, then spoke knowingly. "But that isn't all. You still wish to die."

When he didn't deny it, I yanked my hands away, feeling like I'd just been punched in the stomach. Foolishly, I had believed our night together may have changed things. I was wrong, and I found myself inexplicably angry. "Do I really mean nothing to you?"

"You do. More than you know." He leaped to his feet, putting distance between us. "But we got married and came here with an understanding of what this all meant, did we not? I ensure your freedom, and you help break my curse so I can join my family. That was the deal. But, gods, I never expected for you to flood my every waking thought, Red. I never expected... any of this."

I threw up my hands. "Then why *die?*"

"Because I am tired of running toward something I can never have. I am tired of the pain of my soul being forcefully shoved back into my body again and *again*. I am tired of death never ceasing in its quest to take me when I cannot be taken. I am tired of *knowing* my family awaits me. Of knowing that I continue to fail them every day. I am just *tired,* Red. Also..." He licked his lips and trailed off.

"Also what?" I asked, my own voice hoarse with sorrow.

"Also, because *you* deserve better. I said I would protect you. But really, I should be protecting you from *myself.*" He gestured toward the marks he'd made on my neck last night when he tried to strangle me in his sleep.

I shook my head, fingers drifting toward my still-tender throat in response, bumping the cool metal of my collar. "That was nothing. You didn't know what you were doing."

"Doesn't change the fact that I *did* it." He tucked his tongue in his cheek and sighed. "And it was not *nothing.*"

"But—"

"No *buts.* Joining my family... it's best for both of us." He shoved an exasperated hand through his dark hair. "Gods, how could you even still *want* me after all this? Look at you, Red. Because of me, you are covered in bruises. Stuck in this castle harassed by my fellow fae. You've got a *collar* around your neck meant to suppress your magic. All of that is my doing, no matter how indirectly. You must understand; my life is an endless circle of pain. If I am not receiving it, I am giving it. Always. But now... I refuse to be the cause of yours. Even if you hate me for it. I implore you to see me for what I am and to realize all the reasons why you should not want anything to do with me."

"Do *not* tell me what I should want. In case you haven't noticed, sometimes I have trouble reigning in my anger, my power. Sometimes I fear I have given myself to darkness. That I'm a danger."

"You are far from a danger, Red."

"Neither are you! Not anymore. And I just... I thought that..." I trailed off, not knowing what I was saying. I thought that if we made love, that if he started to genuinely care about me, maybe he would not choose to die? "I was hoping that last night would change your mind," I admitted out loud.

His eyes narrowed and suddenly his tone became accusing. "Is this why you're having such a hard time figuring out how to break my curse? Because you are purposely sabotaging things to ensure the curse is *never* broken?"

I reeled back as though slapped. "How could you accuse me of such a thing?"

"You already *know* how to break it, don't you. You are just choosing not to share. You're only pretending with all your little tonics."

"I—what? No!"

Now his laugh was mirthless. "You're a bad liar, Red."

"How dare you question my integrity."

His head tilted. "Or perhaps you've known this entire time that there *is* no way to break the curse. Perhaps you've only been toying with me to get what you want. A clever little ruse. That's what you humans are best at, after all: lying."

I reacted blindly, unable to stop myself, and my hand darted out to slap him. His head turned, slowly swiveled back, eyes full of fire, practically glowing like embers.

The next instant, I was pushed back, my wrists pinned to the wall over my head. Emrys glared down at me, his chest heaving, the full force of the fae upon me.

"Tell me the truth," he growled. "Are you sabotaging my freedom?"

"Just because I was hoping you might change your mind doesn't mean I haven't been taking our agreement seriously. I *have* been trying, and I have explained to you very clearly the difficulties I've been having. I *will* break your curse."

"Are you very sure about that?"

"I plan to uphold our agreement." And I did; regardless, I had always been planning on breaking his curse, if he still chose as much, even knowing it would destroy me. But this conversation was making me so angry that I was now lashing out.

"I'm not sure I believe you anymore."

"This is rich, coming from someone who was turning my kind over for torture regularly until very recently for nothing more than coin and a bed. You *knew* the king never intended to break your curse. I think you hunted my kind for sport, for pleasure." The words were just flying out of my mouth. I could not stop them.

"Oh, so now I'm back to being the villain, is that it?" He leaned close and murmured into my ear. "Tell me, was I still the villain last night when you were begging me to fuck you?"

"No, but you're doing a fine job of being the villain now."

"*Good.*" His lips curved. "There's the anger I expected."

I bucked against his grip. "Bastard," I spat as he pulled back to stare at me.

"Oh yes, I am," he agreed. "But you've known it from the start."

For a while, we stared each other down in this position, chests heaving, daring the other to make a move. Emrys broke first. He bent and kissed me fiercely, capturing my lips with bruising force. And I responded, intoxicated by the scent of him, my lips moving with his, my mouth just as greedy. His fingers splayed open and laced with mine, still holding me firm to the wall. He pressed his body flush against mine, and I felt every solid inch of him through the thin fabric of my dress. Wanting more. Needing more.

"I'll show you *bastard,*" he rasped as his lips left my mouth in favor of trailing a line down my neck. Teeth nipped as he moved, sinking into the tender flesh. Not enough to break skin, but enough to make it clear that I was being claimed. I shuddered at the mixed pleasure and pain, dizzy with need.

His knee moved to separate my legs, rubbing the fabric of my dress against me in the most delicious way, and I couldn't help the moan that escaped my lips. His hands finally released mine, trailing down my body, my breasts, grasping my hips and pulling me firmly against him.

His teeth dragged across my throat, skimmed over my jaw. I pushed down onto his leg harder, writhing forward and back, and he lifted his knee higher, giving me what I wanted. And oh, did I want it. I wanted it *all.*

But why? Was this not only prolonging the torture?

"Stop," I said, muffled against his lips that had just returned to my mouth. "What are you doing?"

He pulled back, looking somewhat confused. "What does it seem like I'm doing?"

"Kissing me when I do not wish to be kissed."

"Bullshit. I didn't feel you protest, Red."

"You only brought me here in the first place to break your curse. I was silly to think this could be anything more. I'll bet you're counting down the days until you can be free of me."

Now his brows pinched together. "What? That's not—"

"Do you only wish to use me in every way possible? Is that all I am to you? An object to bend to your will."

"You know that isn't true," he said, but I ignored him.

"Now, let me go, or I'll use my magic in ways you really will not like."

I knew I was wrong to act this way. I did know how to break the spell, and I had chosen to keep that information from Emrys so that I could selfishly have the experience of making love to him, so that I could have one more night's reprieve from seeing the disgusted way he would look at me when I revealed who was responsible for his curse. And now... I was hurt that he was still choosing death.

After several long, tense seconds, he released me and backed away. I rubbed my wrists and sighed, eager to put distance between us. My lips still tingled from his kiss, and I was fairly certain my neck sported the impressions of his teeth.

"Don't worry. I told you I would do everything in my power to break your curse, and I will," I said. "Then you can finally be rid of me."

"Rose—"

But I was already gone out the door.

As I fled down the stairs, I brushed away tears of anger, of frustration. Maybe this was all my fault for ever allowing myself to feel something other than loathing for a fae.

41

Emrys

I HAD NOT MEANT TO HURT ROSE. I HATED SEEING her weep, and I'd been the direct cause of it. All the more reason I was not good for her.

Korvyn's voice interrupted my miserable thoughts.

"Fuck it all," he said, lifting his foot in disgust. I was not the only one having a bad day.

He had somehow managed to step in horse dung. Uttering another string of curses, he dragged his boot along the edge of a cobblestone to clear it. It was rare that Korvyn cursed. Or lost his temper.

Korvyn had intercepted me that morning on my way to the council meeting. Evidently, we had both been shut out of council proceedings for the time being in favor of tedious busywork. Knocking on doors. Looking for court independence sympathizers to report their names to King Armynd.

For the better part of the morning, we'd greeted bemused faces and asked each occupant the same questions. When interrogating for the king, yes or no questions were always asked. The interrogated were obligated to respond. Faeries may have been capable of avoiding the truth. But they were not capable of telling outright lies.

"Are you aware of any feelings of unrest amongst the town?"

"Do you believe courts deserve independence?"

"Do you believe the king to be a strong, just leader?"

"Would you ever consider overthrowing your king in order to obtain independence?"

Now, after knocking on easily our twentieth door, Korvyn was agitated. "My father just wants to keep us busy."

"I gathered that." I tucked my tongue in my cheek. "What do you think they're discussing?"

"I have no idea, but it must have to do with witches."

I did not care for the sound of that, being outside the king's circle, especially while he was discussing my wife's people. But Korvyn was likely correct in his assumptions. Troubling.

"Curses," Korvyn said again as he finished checking his boots for dung remnants.

"You alright?" I asked.

"No. Am I being that obvious?"

"A tad. Or perhaps my powers of deduction are simply unparalleled."

He scoffed. Scooted his boot over the stone again. Cursed.

"Is something else wrong?"

"You mean other than the shit on my shoe?" He sighed. "I checked on the witches this morning. They were being moved from the dungeons, but not to the fields. When I questioned the guard, he said Callum and Talyn were having them moved at the request of the king. No one would tell me, the crowned prince, where they were taking them, just that my father had questions for them. It all felt odd." He sighed again, the sound coming from deep within. "My father thinks me soft. Too soft. Like you, he's been keeping me out of the loop more and more. I think he wishes he had another heir to give everything to. But alas, he is stuck with me. Strange that I feel more kinship with you than ever now that we are both equally upsetting to the king."

"For what it's worth, I think you make a fine heir, Korvyn." I clapped his shoulder.

Though my gut grew unsettled at the prince's revelation about the witches. Rose wouldn't like it one bit. Nor did I. It couldn't mean anything good.

Now, I peered over the prince's shoulder and frowned as I looked ahead on our list. I read the next name and glanced at the dwelling in front of us. "Bryock's house? The Spring Court Lord?"

"Yes," replied Korvyn. "We are here to question his family. His sister, brother-in-law, and nephew reside in the same household. We are to determine their involvement in Bryock's affairs, if any."

I blew a puff of breath out. Already thoroughly irritated. "Let's just get this over with."

We walked up to the front door of the house nearly identical to its neighbors. All the houses in the kingdom sat close together in even rows, each with small patches of grass and trees out front. Each house was painted shades of green with white and brown accents. Bryock's door was brown. A pot of flowers sat just outside of it.

Korvyn extended his arm, knocked. Footsteps thumped inside and the door swung open. It was Bryock's sister, Brynne, who answered. She resembled her brother strongly. Same turned up nose, same plump, red cheeks.

Her eyes narrowed when she saw us. "I was wondering when the king would send someone to knock on our door."

"May we come in?" Korvyn asked. He peered over her shoulder inside the house.

"Be my guest. I've nothing to hide."

She swung the door wide and gestured for us to enter. At once, an unpleasant smell greeted my nostrils. A familiar one. Just when I thought my day could not get worse.

Sure enough, when we entered the living room, Rhea was seated in a chair near the fireplace. She drank a cup of tea casually, undisturbed by our presence.

"Well, well." She lifted her chin when she saw me. "To what do we owe this pleasure?" My jaw clenched tight, teeth grinding. Very much *not* in the mood for her bloody tiring antics today.

"We are here at the request of the king," Korvyn said.

Rhea set down her cup and saucer on a small end table. Ran her fingers along the back of the couch. She wore black to match her hair—and perhaps her soul. "Of course you are, cousin. And what might my dear uncle be inquiring about?"

"What do you think?" I asked. She raised a brow at my tone. I turned my attention back to Bryock's sister. "We will be brief. Had you known of Bryock's intentions regarding his quest for court independence?"

Brynne paused for a long while as she searched for the right words. "I had known he desired independence. I had no idea that he was planning to do anything behind the king's back, however."

Korvyn seemed weary. His shoulders slumped and he blew out a breath as he looked to his list of questions. He sounded bored as he asked the first one.

"Are you aware of any feelings of unrest amongst the town?"

"Yes," Brynne replied evenly. No hesitation.

"Do you believe courts deserve independence?"

She hesitated a bit longer this time. "Yes."

Now, Korvyn looked up with interest. He cleared his throat and continued. "Do you believe the king to be a strong, just leader?"

She squeezed her eyes shut. Well aware she was about to tell us a truth we would not like. "Perhaps once. Not now."

Well, shit. This just got interesting.

"Would you ever consider overthrowing your king in order to obtain independence?" Korvyn asked the final question.

Bryock's sister lifted her chin. Tilter her head a bit. "I hope it will never come to that."

I noted that the answer was not *no*. Now, the question was... what to do? I was merely here to fulfill an obligation. Court issues were currently the least of my worries and Brynne had always seemed a pleasant, logical sort. I would hate to see her bound for the dungeons or stocks. Or worse, the gallows. But we *were* obligated to report this to the king. Were we not?

Before I could speak a word, Rhea stood abruptly. She walked to Brynne's side. Crossed her arms over her chest. "Why don't you ask *me* how I feel about court independence? How I feel about my dear uncle? I do not believe you will like my answers, either. Now, what are you two going to do about it?"

Korvyn and I exchanged a glance. Rhea's smug, challenging look never wavered. She placed her arm around Brynne's shoulders. The shorter fae trembled. She was well aware of how she had just incriminated herself. She knew her mere answers were enough to get her reported for treason.

In the end, it was the prince who made the decision. He stepped forth and looked down at Brynne. "Two final questions. Given how afraid you are right now, I should think you most agreeable. Will you guarantee that you will table your notions for court independence indefinitely, and not cause any future problems for your king?"

Bryock's sister frowned, seeming confused. "Y-yes," she stammered. "I will try."

"And will you keep what we just discussed to yourself?"

Brynne's face was flushed. "Yes," she replied on a sigh. Barely above a whisper. Her head wobbled on her neck.

"We won't intrude any longer then," said Korvyn.

Thank the gods. It seemed the only one who wanted to be here less than I did was the crowned prince himself.

But before we could leave, Rhea left Brynne's side and darted over toward me like the snake she was. "How is your little witch handling things?" she asked.

I bristled. "What happens between my wife and I is none of your business. And if I thought for one second that turning you in would get you properly punished, I would. But being the king's niece has its benefits. And I won't watch Brynne hang for the mere sake of wiping that smug look off your face. Tempting as it is."

"Oh, you don't want to stay for tea?" Rhea called after us as we made our exit.

"Rhea is stirring something up, I know it," I said after we had left. We crossed down the front path and back onto the cobbled street of the village.

"I wouldn't doubt it. But we will speak nothing about what just happened in there. We will keep a closer eye on Brynne, but we will report nothing. Agreed?"

"Agreed. I'd rather not." If the king asked us a direct question about it, we might be in trouble. But hopefully it never came to that.

"At least that was the last house for the morning," Korvyn said. He blew out a relieved sigh.

But a noise from up ahead gave us both pause. Korvyn and I exchanged a look. It was the sounds of a scuffle, and we approached with haste. Quickly traversed the town square. Now I could see four younger male faeries standing in a circle. They heaved rocks at something on the ground.

"Witch sympathizing shifter," one of them said. He spit and kicked the dirt, sending forth a spray of gravel. Looked like a Callum type. A mini-oaf with low brows.

"You hate your own kind so much you'd rather stay a bird. Maybe you'd like to be able to shift into the form of a witch," said another. He tossed a sizeable stone.

"Oh, please, stop!" That voice was familiar.

"Hey!" I sprang forward.

Without thinking, I shifted into wolf form and growled at the boys. Loud, feral. I wanted them to shit their pants and from the looks of it, I was successful.

I bared my fangs and crouched. Pawed at the dirt. Muscles coiled to spring. "Run," I barked.

That did it. Their eyes widened. They dropped their rocks and fled in the opposite direction. With a throaty chuckle, I shifted back. Korvyn stood beside me.

"Are you alright, my friend?" I crouched beside Goro. He peered up at me with a dazed expression.

Goro stomped his feet and held up one wing, then another. His tail feathers were ruffled, but he seemed uninjured otherwise. He nodded.

"I was just eating the food Feyleen had left out for me like always when I got apprehended. They came out of nowhere. That hasn't happened in so long." His voice shook. "I did not like it, Lord Emrys. They frightened me."

"I am sorry." My jaw clenched, and Korvyn noticed.

"I can see in your expression that you are worried. Perhaps you would like to check on your wife," he said. "I think we have done enough for the morning, and I will keep an eye on Goro."

The prince bent to scoop up the raven, offering up his shoulder as a perch. I watched the pair walk back toward the castle.

And wondered exactly what this bloody town was coming to.

42

Rose

BY THE TIME I FINISHED EATING BREAKFAST, Goro had not shown up. He'd usually arrive soon after Emrys left in the morning to escort me into town, but there was no sign of him today, and I was starting to worry. I hoped he was alright, though I didn't much feel like going into town today, anyway. Because I knew just how to occupy my time instead.

I dabbed my mouth with the silky napkin provided on the tray. Even cloth for napkins was luxurious here; I almost hated to soil it. My attention was drawn to the small vial next to my juice cup. A fresh tonic was provided every two or three days since I had first arrived. Before Emrys and I made love, I'd been pouring the contents of the vial out the window to avoid suspicion. Any staff who found the bottle full might question why I wasn't taking it, and any explanation that might follow would not benefit me. But now, after what happened between Emrys and me, I would need it for the first time.

I uncorked the bottle and poured the contents down my throat, making a face at the bitter taste. I hoped it worked as it was meant to, because I could not imagine bringing a child into this horrid world.

With that done, I set the empty tray outside the door and shut it, pausing to wedge a chair under the knob. I crossed the room and latched the window shut, too, drawing the curtains. Sorry, Goro, but I could not risk an interruption today.

I frowned then, realizing I had no choice but to leave the window open. Because how was I to test wind power with no wind present? The power was far too new. Only once a witch fully mastered their element could they create it without nature's assistance, as I could with fire. Until then, however, a witch needed to be in the presence of the element itself to bend it to their will. And typically, a witch would only get to such a level of mastery with one element throughout their life.

Quickly, I opened the window again and sat cross-legged on the floor. The metal of my collar was cool against my skin, reminding me that I must be extra cautious about my magic usage. Our tower room was fairly isolated and the door was barricaded; I prayed that was enough.

"*Gaoth,*" I whispered.

A strong wind entered the room, making the billowing curtains flap wildly before tearing at the bedsheets as well, swirling them around me. I pictured myself being lifted by the wind. And then I felt the wind hugging me like so many arms, lifting up. I rose about a foot off the ground before my concentration gave out, as did the wind. I fell hard. But I refused to quit.

Determined, I repeated the process again and again with similar results. Each time, the wind would lift me, but then my concentration would break and I would fall. Though I also managed to hold my concentration a little longer each time, allowing my body to go just a little higher. Which also made the impact hurt worse when I inevitably fell back to the floor.

I was fairly certain I had been practicing for several hours by the time the door pushed open an inch and clunked against the chair. My concentration snapped like an uncooked green bean, the wind rushing back out the window and dropping me. I landed on the ground in a heap and groaned.

"Are you alright in there?"

It was Emrys, his voice muffled from the other side of the door.

"Fine," I replied, but he must have heard the strain in my voice.

"Open this door. *Now.* Please don't make me break it down. I don't feel like having to explain the damage to the king today."

"Coming."

After allowing myself one more moment to catch my breath, I crossed the room and moved the chair to swing the door open. Emrys's face was a mix between curiosity and... something else. Was he still angry, or contrite?

I flushed at the sight of him, thinking about our night together, the morning after, our heated argument. I wasn't sure how to feel now.

"Gods, what happened in here? Why are the linens scattered all over the floor?"

I peered behind me, surveying the damage the wind had done. Rags, curtains, and bedsheets were all strewn in various heaps on the ground. The wardrobe doors hung open, the table and chair tossed on their sides.

"Nothing."

Emrys lifted a brow. "That's not very convincing, Red. Did you loose a wild boar in here while I was out?"

"Do you need something?" I asked curtly. Emrys flinched at the coldness of my tone.

"I just thought you should know why Goro did not come today."

My stomach clenched. "Where is he?"

"Goro is fine, but he is shaken. He was being bullied in town today. I don't wish to worry you but feel you should know, given that he's your friend."

"Bullied?"

"He wasn't hurt. I scared off the little shits responsible."

I instantly wanted to set aflame whoever hurt him, young or not.

"Second," Emrys continued, "about the other night and the morning after—"

"You were right," I blurted. "I *was* hiding something."

A crease formed between Emrys's brows as he listened, waiting for me to continue. I drew a deep breath, finally ready to tell him the truth and bracing for the inevitable.

"I learned how to break the curse the day before the queen's banquet. It was wrong of me to not tell you immediately, I know, but I swear I was always intending to honor our agreement. And I *will* break it for you tonight if you wish."

Emrys contemplated my words for a long moment before shaking his head. "How did you figure it out?"

"I found the witch who cursed you."

Emrys reeled back, gold eyes wide. "You—*what?*"

"I noticed that I would get this strange tingling on the castle grounds that would get stronger in certain areas. One day I followed it towards this little entrance in a back alley near the village wall."

"Where?"

"Within sight of the stables. It was basically a hole in the ground with a chained grate over it."

Emrys frowned. "I've never seen such an entrance."

"That's because it was hidden by a glamour of some sort. The grate opened into an underground cellar, and there was a witch's head in a box. It turned out..." I licked my lips, palms sweaty as I worked up the courage to tell him. Stars, I hoped he could see it in his heart to forgive me once he learned the truth, that he wouldn't think me a monster like my grandfather.

"Just say it, Red."

I could not meet his eyes when I spoke again. "Emrys, he was a Doyle. My great, great, great grandfather was the one who cursed you, and I had no idea. I am so sorry."

Emrys paled and stepped back. His legs connected with the bed and he practically collapsed onto it. "Is he still there?"

"No. He's gone."

"I would have liked to have looked upon the bastard once more. You should've brought me there so I could have said my piece." His gaze snapped to mine, a cross between angry and wounded. "How could you take that opportunity away from me after everything he made me suffer?"

"I am sorry, but if you would have seen him, you would have pitied what a pathetic creature he had become. There would be no use torturing him, because he was already about as tortured as a being could get, trapped as nothing more than a head in a box, locked in the darkness for decades."

"That doesn't fucking excuse—"

"He thought your father was someone else," I continued. "He thought your father had led the siege of his town, but he only *looked* like another fae who had done so. He said that he regretted deeply what he had done to you and your family, and he showed me how to fix the curse. To prove what he said was true, by his request, I tested the reversal spell on him. He is very much dead now. Nothing more than a decaying skull in a box. It worked, proving that he spoke the truth."

"Do it then," Emrys demanded, though it was barely above a whisper. "Reverse it."

"You are truly ready to lose your immortality?"

"Yes," Emrys said.

The *yes* was weak, barely a whisper. Maybe he didn't feel as sure as he once did, now that the opportunity had finally presented itself. Or I was just reading too much into things, looking for another excuse to not do this, and I could not delay any longer.

I drew a deep, calming breath before sighing it back out and sitting on the bed beside him. "Hand me your dagger."

He hesitated, lips pursed.

"Please?"

His eyes narrowed. "For what purpose?"

"Because I am your wife." I held out my hand, palm up. "And I asked nicely. Hand me your dagger."

With a slightly bemused expression, he unsheathed his dagger from the holster on his hip and placed the handle into my palm. I immediately pressed the pointed tip to my finger, drawing blood.

"What are you doing?"

"Hold still and close your eyes," I said. He shot me a look. "Please," I added for good measure.

He nodded and stilled at once, eyes sliding closed. His lips twitched, but he swallowed any retort. I laid both hands atop his head, just as I had done before. The fresh blood on my palm blended into his soft, brown hair. He raised his brows with his eyes still closed.

"And you are sure you know how to do this?"

"Yes." I thought. I *hoped*. For Emrys's sake, not mine.

Reclaiming my focus, and with my own eyes closed, I said the words my grandfather had taught me. They were words in a language of old that sounded as though they had been lifted directly from the grimoire, which, in all likelihood, they had. I tried to forget that fact and remember my intent instead, doing my best to not butcher any pronunciations.

Remember, you want Emrys to be free. To be happy. To get what he wants.

But then, I also wanted him to want *me*. And that contradicted all of the above—didn't it?

My hands flexed on his head, still sticky with the warmth of blood. I repeated the words twice more. And then, it was done. Surprisingly fast and somewhat anticlimactic.

"Alright," I said once I had finished. "That should be all."

"That's it?" He opened one eye, then the other.

"Maybe." I frowned.

Come to think of it, I had not felt the power flow through me as I had before with my grandfather. Maybe because I wasn't absorbing any magic this time, just offering up my own?

"I don't like *maybe*. What does that mean?"

"I mean... how do you feel?"

Without a word, Emrys grabbed the dagger back from where I'd laid it beside me on the bed and pricked himself, just a small slice down the index finger. Blood beaded at first, but then the blood was sucked back into his flesh, the cut healed as though it had never happened. Emrys sighed and hung his head, visibly defeated.

"It didn't work," he said. "Perhaps the gods are simply trying to tell me something."

"Nonsense," I said. "This isn't any gods. The failure is on me."

"It's fine, Red."

"No, it's not." I knew I had to try again, to give my husband what he wanted above all. I cared deeply for him; I knew that now, Goddess help me. I did not want to let him go, but I must.

The hardest part of reversing the curse was the *wanting* it; my grandfather had said that intent was everything. While I did not want Emrys to die, I *did* want him to be happy. I only hoped that would be enough to break the curse.

"We'll try again," I said.

Quickly, I repeated the initial steps. With my hands atop his head and my eyes closed, I said the words my grandfather had taught me once more, spoken just above a whisper.

This time, I pictured Emrys laughing, the corners of his eyes crinkling with humor. Reunited with his family in the Otherworld. I *did* want to give him that, as much as it might pain me. Because it was his one wish.

I had never met his family nor seen the Otherworld. In my mind's eye, his family appeared faceless, floating in a land of nothingness. I simply focused on the emotion, on how I would feel reuniting with my own family. I, too, craved that feeling someday, and I wanted *Emrys* to experience that joy.

I repeated the words a second time. I pictured him telling jokes with his father, telling stories to his sister, their faces slowly coming into focus. Kind faces that matched Emrys's descriptions the best my mind would allow me, ones that loosely resembled Emrys.

I repeated the words a third and final time, my fingers flexing in his hair. Even when Emrys laughed, somehow there was still a distinct sadness behind his golden eyes. Now, in the image in my head, there was no more sorrow. I pictured him at peace, finally.

This time, when I finished the spell... something changed. As before with grandfather, I felt the wave within me, flowing out toward my limbs, heating my palms and transferring to Emrys. I heard him gasp and squirm a little beneath my touch. The surge of power rolled out like a tide.

After, I lowered my hands and slumped on the bed, thoroughly drained. Why did it seem so much harder now than it did with my grandfather?

Because convincing yourself to let go of your husband was never going to be easy, I reminded myself.

Emrys's hands were upon me the next instant, cupping my cheek, pushing hair from my face. "Are you alright, Red?"

"Yes." My voice was weak. "I just need a moment to recover. But... how do you not hate me now?"

A frown clouded his features. "Why would I hate you?"

"Because you just found out it was my family member who cursed you."

"Right." His eyes flicked down, back up, hand still caressing my cheek. "I can't hate you for something done over three centuries ago by a man you were generations removed from ever even meeting."

"You don't hate me?"

He smiled a little. "No. Of course not. Especially since—" His brows furrowed. "Do you think it worked? The reversal?"

"Something was definitely different this time. Did you feel it?"

He nodded, brushing his thumb over my cheekbone. "I felt *something.*"

"Test it," I encouraged him.

Emrys straightened up and this time, he used the dagger to slice himself down the front of his forearm, a long, deep cut. Blood immediately started gushing and dripping down onto his legs, staining the sheets in the process.

"Goddess, Emrys!" I gasped, having not expected him to do more than cut his finger like before.

I sat up, still feeling a bit woozy. I rolled on the bed, grabbing a cloth from the nightstand to press to his wound and stave the flow of blood.

"It isn't healing like it once did. I believe it worked," he said with a disbelieving laugh as I lifted the rag to reveal a still-steady stream of blood.

"It did, you mad bastard. But was stabbing yourself like that really necessary?"

I held the rag on his arm, putting pressure until the bleeding slowed. Then I carefully bandaged the wound, wrapping it tight.

"Thank you," he said.

I did not know if the gratitude was for breaking his curse or tending to his wound. His hand lifted to touch my cheek again, gentle at first. But then he curved his fingers behind my jawbone and pulled my lips to his, swallowing my soft cry of surprise. His tongue demanded entrance, and I granted it to him, winding my arms around his neck and kissing him back like it was the last time. Maybe it was.

In that moment, a wave of conflicting emotions washed over me: joy, desire, sadness, regret, longing, guilt. Strangely, I was not sure if the feelings were purely my own... or Emrys's, too. He must have felt it because a small questioning sound left the back of his throat and he pulled away.

"I probably shouldn't have done that," he said.

And he was right, for so many reasons. But in that moment, I did not care about any of them.

When Emrys stood, I cleared my throat and spoke. "You will have to be more careful from here on out. Until the day comes for you to... do what you must." Something else occurred to me then. "But what if death tries to claim you in your sleep again?"

"I believe death will be satisfied that I am a mere mortal now."

"But this also means your king will soon find out his pet head in a box is dead, and come to the conclusion that it must have been my doing. Meaning Ophelia and Orinthia are in more danger by the day, as well."

"It does seem Ophelia and Orinthia are being questioned with greater frequency. Which *is* troubling."

"Then I must leave, Emrys. As soon as possible."

Emrys nodded resolutely. His mouth flapped open and shut for a moment as though he wished to say more, his eyes adopting a sudden pained look, but whatever sat at the tip of his tongue remained there.

The silence was nearly palpable for a moment until he finally spoke again. "I will secure your safe passage immediately."

I desperately wanted to ask Emrys to leave with me, to flee with me, but he had already made it clear that he still chose death, to rejoin his family. I could not interfere with that, and any attempts on my part would only delay the inevitable and make it hurt worse in the end. So, I too held my tongue.

"Assuming Goro is feeling alright after today, I will send him with a message. He is very fast. He should reach Aegan and Lysia in about a day. They usually respond to me very quickly. I ask for favors very rarely, and have given back in return. They should be here within a week's time, if I had to guess."

"Then we need our plan figured out now."

"About that—"

"I have an idea," I said.

He raised a brow. "And what plan is that?"

"Well, first you must know that I have come into a new power. Wind."

The brow lifted higher. "You've mastered another element?"

"Yes."

"Since when?"

I wrung my hands together. "Since I found my grandfather and he passed his powers onto me upon dying."

"And you've been practicing those powers?"

"Yes."

"Gods, Red." He tilted his face skyward and sighed as though dealing with a petulant child. "If you were caught—"

"I wasn't."

"But if you *were* we would both be positively fucked. The king would know I tampered with your collar. You would be executed without question."

"That's why I had the chair wedged under the door, so no one could come in."

"And yet you had the window wide open. Goro is not the only bird shifter in the castle, you know."

I frowned because he was right; Rogyn and Pery were hawk shifters, as well. I would have to be more aware next time.

"So, what is your plan? Because mine was still a bit of a work in progress."

But I did not get a chance to answer. Emrys and I exchanged a look at the sound of a sudden commotion from down in the village. Was that... screaming? And just like that, I knew it in my bones.

Something was very wrong.

43

Emrys

"EMRYS, WHAT IS IT?" ROSE LOOKED OVER MY shoulder to peer out the window.

Screams and shouts floated up from below. Metal clanked against metal. Flames raged high, billowing in the wind. A battle was happening. There was no mistaking it.

"Stay here," I said.

But Rose immediately followed, sticking closer to my side than my own shadow. "You seriously think I would stay behind?" she huffed.

"I was hoping you would."

"Well, I'm not, unless you shackle me to the bedpost."

"That can be arranged." Rose crossed her arms over her chest, refusing to budge. I shook my head. "I am serious. I refuse to put you in harm's way."

"It's my choice. Leave me behind and I will never forgive you. Maybe I'll even learn some hexes just to spite you."

I grumbled at her stubbornness. The temptation to lock her in the room and keep her safe was strong. But if I'd grown to learn one thing about my wife, it was that her threats weren't idle. "Fine," I relented. "But if you're coming you will need to be armed."

I reached into my side of the wardrobe for Rose's sword.

She raised a brow. "I thought I wasn't allowed to be armed?"

"Rules change during a siege. Do you have your sheath?" I asked.

"Yes."

She dug into her own side of the wardrobe and pulled out her old sheath. When I lifted a brow, she spoke again. "I'm not about to sully the beautiful sheath you gifted me. Not just yet."

"I don't want you sullying anything," I said. "Remember, do not take the sword out unless you absolutely have to."

Rose nodded. "How about you?"

I patted my hip where I'd just buckled up my holster. "I've my dagger, and my wolf form as a weapon. Now, stay behind me and keep quiet."

Rose rolled her eyes. She didn't very much like taking orders. But she did so now without further argument. Which was good. Because if my wife put herself in any immediate danger, I *would* still find a way to shackle her for her own safety.

We descended the turret steps, finding the castle empty. Eerily so. It seemed most if not all the king's forces were concentrated in town.

As suspected, we emerged outside and crossed the drawbridge to witness utter chaos in the dark.

Void pockets had converged around the castle. They were everywhere, as though forming their own fog wall within our city limits. The pockets were *inside* the walls for the first time that I could recall. There were wights attacking innocent villagers. They forced their way into shops and homes, sank their rotted teeth into necks. Ripped away chunks of flesh.

"Gods," I muttered at the carnage.

Rose stiffened beside me.

Around us was pure madness. Ahead, Callum fought alongside Rogyn and Pery. A few of the other king's guards, too. The prince also had taken up his sword. He'd dropped his glamour so that the scarred half of his face was exposed, though that was likely the least of his worries. He yanked his sword free from the chest of a wight, dragging black goo and viscera with it. The wight did not even slow.

"You must wound the head," I bellowed. Loud as possible. I knew this from my last encounter in the swamp.

Korvyn nodded. With one hard swing from the prince, the wight fell in two pieces. Moving no more. Korvyn may have lacked his father's enchantment powers and wings, but the prince was no slouch in battle. Though now a voice across the courtyard pulled his attention.

"Korvyn, I will fight with you!"

Jasper.

The bard wielded a sword. Likely taken from a fallen king's guard. His face was a mix of determination and pure fear. The blade wobbled in his grip like he'd never held one before. He probably hadn't. He looked as uncomfortable with the sword as a toddler did on their feet for the first time, learning to walk. This was not about to end well.

"Jasper, don't. Get back inside the castle!" Korvyn shouted, waving his arms wildly above his head.

No sooner had he said those words than a wight tackled the bard from behind, dragging him to the ground. Everything happened too bloody fast. Even for my quick shifter reflexes.

"No!" Korvyn screamed.

Right as the wight sank its overgrown claws into the bard's abdomen.

"Stay here!" I shouted to Rose.

Of course, she did not. I heard her trailing right behind me, sword held at the ready. Thankfully, Korvyn and I were able to take care of the wight with two mirroring strikes. Its body fell to the ground. The prince cried out and dropped to his knees beside Jasper.

"Get him out of here, Korvyn. Take him to safety," I said.

The prince pulled Jasper to his feet with my assistance. Together, they hobbled back toward the castle.

"Do you think he'll be alright?" Rose asked.

I couldn't lie. Instead, I said, "I don't know."

All I knew was that I would not be taking my eyes off my wife for a second tonight. I knew I could never convince her to return to the castle with Korvyn and the bard. So that meant I would have to keep her by my side. But before I could turn to head back into town, she grasped my elbow tight. Her expression was one of panic.

"Emrys, please be careful," she said. "Remember, you are mortal now. You can die. I know you *wish* to die, but I could not bear to see it happen right in front of me."

For just a moment, the chaos seemed to fade. I brushed the side of her neck just above the cursed collar. "I must defend my castle, my king. But I do not intend to die today, Red. I will fight to stay alive until I know you are away from here and safe. I promise you this. You are my priority right now. Do you hear me?"

She nodded, a single jerk of her head. I smiled tightly.

"Good. And you must be careful too. If anything were to happen to you..." My voice trailed off, reflecting a surprising amount of emotion. I cleared my throat. "Just stay within my sight," I finished.

"I will."

No sooner had I said that than another wave of wights attacked, simultaneously jumping out of dozens of Void pockets. Their teeth clacked, tearing the flesh from any fae they could sink their teeth into. Two converged on me in a rush and I fell to the ground.

I shifted into wolf form. Jumped and sank my teeth into one of their throats. I gagged; the flesh was rancid. A low growl sounded nearby and I turned just in time to see the other wight standing directly behind me. Its pocked arms were poised to attack. It never got the chance.

Someone stabbed it from behind, right through its neck. That gave me the time I needed to knock it down and finish the job. Canines through temples; that should do the trick.

Rose stood there with her bloodied blade; I'd found the swordsman who stabbed the wight's neck. I shook the blood off my snout and attempted to smile up at her. Must have looked a little peculiar coming from a wolf. But the smile was short-lived as a wight charged at Rose full speed, knocking her off balance.

She fell to the ground with a little shriek. Snarling, I spun on my paws and dove head first to pull the wight off of her. My teeth sank into its spine, and it took everything I had not to retch. The creature howled, moving just enough for Rose to dislodge herself and roll away.

I would take care of the rest. I leaped at the wight, snapping my jaws. Another rancid bite.

After the wight was no longer moving, I shifted back to my regular form. Shook out the transformed muscles of my body and turned to my wife.

"Are you alright?" I examined her for any signs of injury, though it was hard to see in the dark.

"I am fine. Are you?"

"Yes. Still breathing."

Everything became very much *not* fine when more shrill shouting arose across the courtyard. This time directed at Rose.

"What is the witch doing out here?" Callum shouted. His face was still in the process of healing from my beating. "And why is she armed? I'll be sure she hangs for this."

The bastard had the audacity to threaten my wife again. Right in front of me. This ended right here, right now. "You will watch what you say to my wife," I snarled, advancing on Callum.

A shrill cry sounded nearby. A child. Tears ran down her small, round face. "Where are your parents?" I heard Rose say as she ignored Callum completely and ran for the child. She took her small hand to get her to the safety of one of the buildings. I hated taking my eyes off my wife, but this was my one chance.

Another wight attacked me then, swinging its arms to try to grab me. I dove out of the way at the last second. But Callum, on the other hand...

"Here's a tasty meal," I said.

I got behind the wight and shoved it as hard as I could toward Callum. Caught off guard, Callum stumbled back with the wight on top of him.

"Help!" he shouted. Callum fought. But he would not win this battle with the wight.

The creature was already horizontal atop Callum who struggled to keep its gnashing teeth away from his neck. Well, I would just give the wight a little help. I placed my boot on the creature's back and pushed. Callum wasn't strong enough to hold off the wight with me behind it, and teeth met flesh. The creature ripped into his cheek, devouring like an owl would a rat. The wight yanked his mouth away, pulling gooey strips of Callum's flesh with it.

It was not the most pleasant way to die, and I'd experienced plenty. But that was what he got for threatening my wife. For hurting her. I didn't like to kill, but I did like justice. And this felt just to me. Gruesome, but just. Callum howled.

"I told you it was coming," I mumbled down to him. "You will never touch my wife again."

Speaking of my wife... I whirled around. Where had she gone off too?

A Void pocket appeared across the village courtyard. This one was massive, the height of the castle. An ear-shattering shriek from within pierced the night, making my sensitive ears ring. Sounded like some large, furious creature. And then... someone was shoved right in front of the pocket, staggering and gasping in shock. They twisted their ankle and fell. Held their leg in pain.

Feyleen. The shopkeeper. In an instant, I knew exactly where my wife was. She must've already led the child to safety, and now her reckless tendencies made her leap right into more danger.

Reacting blindly, Rose ran toward the shopkeeper just as another wight attacked me. I had no choice but to defend myself. If any harm came to Rose, I would never forgive myself for taking my eyes off of her.

"Fuck... you..." I snarled at the wight. My hand gripped its throat, holding its head away from me. Its jaws flapped, teeth clanking. Putrid air wafted towards me from its mouth.

I attempted to shift, only to realize I could not. My magic suddenly seemed blocked, and I could only assume it was due to the arrival of the massive Void pocket. It had happened before, in the woods.

With no choice but to use my blade in lieu of claws and teeth, I unholstered my dagger. With a loud grunt, I stabbed the wight in the temple. It shrieked. Crumpled to the ground. I turned just in time to see Rose help Feyleen to her feet.

Then fire erupted from the pocket, bursting forth all at once.

"Rose!" I screamed just as she was wholly engulfed by the flames.

No. Oh, fuck, *no.* I should have never agreed to let her join me. I should've chained her to the bloody bed. Left her in the turret as my instincts had warned me to do.

The raging fire flickered, providing a small window. To my utter shock and relief, she was still standing. It was as though she repelled the fire. She had her back to it, ducking down with the faerie shopkeeper in front of her. The fire went around her like a rejected hug. Somehow, the wall of flames danced away from her. The hot wind it created whipped her hair around violently.

The fire stopped for just a moment. Perhaps whatever beast within was gathering its energy to send more our way. But in that split second of calm, an arrow flew from somewhere behind me out of the darkness. It sailed directly into the Void, disappearing.

Another shriek floated from within. A distinct sound of something in pain. The stray arrow had hit its target. Whatever that target was.

The flames did not return and all the Void pockets disappeared at once. Just like that, the siege was over as quickly as it had started.

"Are you alright, Feyleen?" I heard Rose ask. Feyleen could only nod. Rightfully stunned by what had just happened.

I ached to be by Rose's side once again to check on her. But my attention was drawn to a single, howling cry.

"What have you done!" the voice shouted.

It was Talyn. Crouching over Callum's lifeless body.

This was not going to end well.

Talyn jumped to his feet and pushed his way over toward Rose. I followed. He would not get near her without me present.

"You killed Callum," he accused. "You used magic to summon the void pockets and then you killed Callum, filthy witch." His voice dripped venom and trembled with emotion. I was surprised to see tears glistening in his eyes.

"No," Rose said, obviously confused.

"Then explain how the flames went around you."

"I cannot explain that. I don't know why that happened."

I grasped Rose's hand, standing tall beside her. No way was I letting her take the fall for Callum. "If my wife meant to harm this community, then why was she fighting alongside us to get rid of the wights? Why did she just save the shopkeeper?" I asked.

Talyn's eyes narrowed. "To throw us off her true intentions. Saving one fae to make herself look innocent while the rest of the town as a whole gets torn to pieces."

"That is absurd," said Rose.

"I agree," said Feyleen. She raised her chin defiantly as she stood beside Rose. "It was *my* life she just saved. And I for one will be forever grateful to her for it."

Talyn ignored her and spoke directly to Rose. "Fine. But if you didn't summon the Void pockets, you still broke the rules by using magic, on castle grounds no less, which is still a capital crime for a witch. You used magic to protect yourself from the Void pocket's flame. I know you are capable of bending flames to your will. I saw you produce a flame in your hand before you came to the castle."

"Watch yourself, Talyn," I warned. "Do you not see the collar Rose wears, you nitwit?"

He chuckled humorlessly. "How am I to know if either of you tampered with it? It is done easily enough."

I froze. Oh, shit. I hoped no one else directly inquired me about what I had done to the collar. Especially not the king.

But thankfully, no one questioned us further. And my wife seemed keen on defending herself.

"No. I did not use any magic at all to repel those flames," she insisted. "They just went around me of their own volition, I had nothing to do with that."

"Lies. You really expect us to believe that?"

"I am telling the truth!" Rose's tone was defiant now.

"Guards!" Talyn shouted, peering over both shoulders for backup. "This witch is a fae killer. Take her to the dungeons!"

"On whose authority?" I stepped in front of Rose. "Let me make one thing abundantly clear; no one lays a hand on my wife. No one takes her anywhere she does not wish to go. Anyone who feels otherwise answers to me." I half-shifted, enough to snarl and expose elongated fangs. "Who's first?"

Before anything could escalate, a hush fell over the crowd. Complete silence blanketed the square save for the faint cries or sniffles of injured or mourning townspeople. The crackling of dying flames.

The king was here now, surveying the damage. He held his favored bow and arrow that he rarely had cause to use anymore. I was quite certain I knew where the arrow that hit the beast had come from. The king was once a master with the bow, particularly fond of hunting large game. Deer, boar, always hitting his mark right through the eyes. He had not hunted since Maeve died, but it seemed he never forgot how.

Now, he looked every bit the warrior with said bow slung over his shoulder and his wide wings fully spread. He stopped right in front of Rose and me, stepped up onto the ledge of the square's fountain. Standing right in front of the statue bearing his own likeness.

"You are all grieving now, scared, and as your king, my heart breaks with you," he bellowed. "We have lost many of our own today. Good, strong fae, including Callum. A member of my own court who sacrificed himself to protect us from our attackers. But we are strong, and we will rebuild. Most importantly, we will not allow ourselves to forget this. Oh, no. Because as you all can see, the witch threat is still very much alive."

There was a cacophony of voices around the courtyard which quickly died out. King Armynd continued speaking.

Rose shifted uncomfortably beside me at the king's words. I squeezed her hand. Talyn had returned to Callum's side, crouching beside his body. I almost felt a pang of remorse, though not quite. I didn't like killing. But they had threatened my wife. Callum had *hurt* Rose. There was no way I would allow him to continue breathing.

"Now is not the time for dividing," the king continued. "It is not the time to seek independence, to break off the courts once more. Now is a time for unity amongst all fae, until we can be assured that the witch threat has been eliminated wholly and completely, for good this time."

A chorus of cheers erupted all around. That was my cue to leave and remove my wife from a situation that could very easily turn on her.

But as I grabbed her hand to direct her out of the village, I felt the king's eyes upon us both. Watching.

44

Rose

THE SIEGE WAS OVER, AND EMRYS AND I WENT back to our room, moving slowly, slightly dazed. After closing the door, Emrys's demeanor change from weary to frustrated, even a little angry. He strode across the room to stare down into my face.

"Never do anything like that again."

I blinked. "Like what?"

"Like leaping in front of a Void-produced inferno."

Now, I frowned. "I had to save Feyleen."

"That was reckless, Rose. And very stupid."

My arms crossed over my chest, unrelenting. "I will never apologize for saving a life."

"Then at least apologize for nearly giving me a heart attack. Gods, I thought..." He trailed off, pinched the bridge of his nose. Then he walked to the window and looked out, surveying the damage from above as he continued speaking. "It is becoming more dangerous here. Aegan and Lysia won't be able to make it for a little while still. You need to be extremely careful until then."

"I will try," I promised.

He met my gaze over his shoulder and smiled tightly. "Good."

"So long as I don't see another friend in trouble."

His smile fell.

"Emrys, you should know... I believe I saw the king push Feyleen in front of the Void pocket today. On purpose."

Now he blinked in confusion and turned to face me fully. "Why would he do such a thing?"

"I don't know. Maybe to test me? To see how I would respond?"

He growled. "I will ask him about it. Get the truth."

"You killed Callum." It was a statement, not a question, because I already knew the answer.

"Technically, a wight killed him."

"A wight you pushed into his path?"

Emrys's eyes narrowed, but he did not deny it. "Are you seriously mourning the loss of Callum?"

"Not at all." I shook my head. "I don't blame you. But... before, you wouldn't even kill a rabbit and yet I have seen you kill and maim your own kind now. What changed?"

He stepped forward and lifted to touch my cheek. "I always thought I had the animal side of me under control. Turns out, you make me feral, Red."

"That's what I was afraid of."

"Why?"

"Because before, you said you wouldn't kill unless absolutely—"

"It was necessary," he cut me off. "Frankly, Callum had it coming for a while."

When I opened my mouth to speak, his thumb pressed against my lips, silencing me.

"Protecting you will always come first for as long as I draw breath. I meant that." His hand fell then, his gaze redirecting toward the window again. "Though I am still convinced that sometimes, it's me you need protecting from."

"No." I wrung my hands together then, suddenly nervous. "I don't know where we stand at present, but I hope you have at least forgiven me for holding back the truth."

He turned back to face me, brow arched. "How could I not forgive you? It's not as though I didn't do terrible things to you before we entered into our union. Or even after."

I sighed. "I just want you to know that I... I have grown to care about you. Deeply. And selfish of me or not, I do not wish to see you die. I know you have made your choice, but I just want to make it abundantly clear how I feel. Because soon, within a matter of just a few more days, I won't be able to tell you anymore."

He was silent for a long while, so long that I began to fidget uncomfortably. "Aren't you going to say something?" I asked, and he sighed.

"You once asked me about my scars. Why I heal when stabbed by others yet my torso is littered with marks. It's because those scars were self-inflicted. All the times when I tried to join my family by my own hand. When I was injured by someone else, the wound healed without a trace. But if I did it to myself... Well, the wound still healed but left a distinct mark. I believe that was part of the curse as well. It was meant to taunt me."

I gasped, feeling my heart sink at how sad that sounded, and I suddenly fought a compulsion to bend down and kiss every scar, each one a reminder of how badly Emrys wanted to die.

"I am sorry," I breathed, stepping toward him and placing my hand on his chest.

His smile was characteristically crooked as he covered my hand with his. "I am not telling you this to make you pity me. I am telling you this so you understand all the reasons you should not want me to live. There are certain wounds that never heal, and I am littered with them. I have said it before and I will say it again: you deserve better than that."

"Please stop telling me what I deserve," I said, barely a whisper.

"Rose..." His voice, thick with some form of emotion, trailed off. He shook his head. "You are covered in wight blood and ash. I will draw you a bath," he said, changing the subject and effectively ending the conversation.

But when I began to shed my clothes, Emrys hissed as he looked at me, his face instantly concerned. "You are bleeding. Your shoulder."

I hadn't even known I had been stabbed; it seemed one of the wights had gotten to me with their claws after all, or that I had gotten cut somehow in the skirmish. Now that Emrys mentioned it and the initial adrenaline had worn off, I could feel the pain, the burning. Emrys sat beside me, examining the wound on my upper shoulder, and it was only then I realized I was mostly naked before him.

"You're wounded too," I pointed out.

"I don't matter. You do."

"No," I said. "Emrys, you matter to me. Very much."

But Emrys acted as though he didn't hear me, gently tending to my wounds, and after, he helped me into the bath, careful to not submerge my shoulder.

I had seen my husband wield a whip. I had seen him cut down others in battle, demolish Callum's face with his fists, tear the guts out of a wight with his wolf teeth, and yet with me... Emrys could be so gentle. Like now, with his touch making me shiver. And not just with wanting, but with a deep, resounding sadness that all too soon, I would feel his touch no longer. Never again. It was strange to think how far we had come. Sworn enemies to reluctant allies to where we were now. But all too soon, our story would end completely.

Emrys dragged a chair beside the bathtub, sitting right beside me. I whispered his name as he gently moved a rag over my shoulders, careful to avoid my wound.

"Hush," he said. "Let me take care of you."

I bit my lip and squeezed my eyes shut, doing my best to reign in my emotions. The rag moved lower, skimming across my breasts, my nipples peaking at his touch like flowers opening toward the sun. The rag slipped lower still, beneath the water line, over my stomach, between my legs.

I threw my head back, resting it against Emrys's knee, and moaned at the delicate little circles he made. The metal of my collar clinked against the lip of the tub, but I ignored the sound.

"Emrys," I whispered again.

"Let me take care of you, Rose," he repeated. *While I still can* was implied. But I tried not to think about that. Not now

And then the rag was gone, and it was just Emrys's fingers sliding into my channel, stroking my inner walls just so, his thumb finding that hardened bud and circling it in a way that sent shivers of pleasure pulsing through my belly.

Emrys must have knelt beside the tub at some point, because the next instant I felt his lips on my neck, skimming upward toward my jaw, whispering how perfect and beautiful I was in my ear, his fingers never ceasing their work. And it was the movements of his hand combined with the whispered sweet nothings that led me to find my release quicker than both of us had anticipated.

"That's it," Emrys murmured, peppering soft kisses along my cheekbone.

When the bath was over, Emrys applied a fresh patch to my wound, so gently, with such tender care. I dried off and slid my nightgown over my head, then laid beside Emrys in the dark, on the bed.

I could tell he was conflicted, so I lifted my head to kiss him on the lips and quiet him before he could decide to turn me away. As before, I *wanted* him, and I could not seem to stop myself. I fumbled to release him from his breeches in the dark. Before he could stop me, I kneeled before him to take the length of him in my mouth, wanting to taste him the same way he'd tasted me.

Emrys hissed in surprise, letting out a mumbled string of curses as I moved my tongue over him. I had no idea what I was doing, exactly, but I must have been doing *something* right, because I felt Emrys tremble.

"No," he said after a minute, shaking even more. "No. I need inside you. Now. Come here."

His voice was low and raspy as he grabbed me by the upper arms and guided me to a standing position. He laid back upon the bed and, taking me by the hands, guided me to straddle him.

I lifted my nightgown and lowered myself down onto his length inch by delicious inch. Once he was fully seated inside of me, he groaned and sat up, pulling my nightgown over my head, exposing me to him wholly. I shouldn't have even bothered putting it on in the first place.

He wrapped his arms around me, his mouth skimming across my collarbone before latching around my breast in the darkness, teasing it with his teeth and tongue as I arched back and sighed. Feeling full, feeling content, and feeling like my guts were about to be ripped out within a matter of a few days, all at the same time.

Emrys laid back on the bed, grasped my hands. He placed them flat upon his chest, and looked up at me with an intense expression.

"Take what you need," he said. His fingers sunk into my hips, holding me in place.

And I did. I moved as though I might lose everything if I slowed down, my pace nearly frantic until I was breathing as though I had just run the length of the White Woods without stopping. My eyes squeezed shut, the emotions too overwhelming, threatening to consume me whole if I let them.

Emrys grunted beneath me. For a moment, we were a frenzy of wet, slapping flesh, and I took him deep, each thrust hitting my womb. Exquisite pain mixed with pleasure. I didn't care if he bruised me from the inside out, I just never wanted this to end.

When I opened my eyes again, Emrys was looking up at me, and I knew he spotted my tears catching the moonlight streaming through the window. I could not fight them anymore. They streamed freely down my cheeks.

"Do not weep for me, Rose," he whispered. "Please."

His thumbs reached up to swipe the tears away. He flipped us so he was on top, his fingers lacing with mine and pinning my hands to the bed beside my head, moving between my legs in earnest. His lips found my throat, trailing kisses down and up, nipping my chin and jaw before capturing my lips once again. He quickened our pace now, faster, deeper, harder, clamoring for the sweet release we both desperately needed.

He released my wrists. My nails dug into his back and soon, I could feel him pulsing deep inside me. When at last we found our release together, he swallowed my cry with his mouth.

I swore I could taste the salt of his own tears mingling with mine.

45

Rose

ANOTHER SIX DAYS PASSED. EMRYS AND I HAD not made love again since the night of the Void siege, nor did we mention it, the wall between us firmly in place again.

Thankfully, he had not had any other sleepwalk episodes, either. Though I suspected he waited until I fell asleep and left the room more often than not, just to be safe. I had woken up to a cold, empty bed more than once, and I wondered where he went. Maybe the queen's hidden room. I did not like it, but I knew better than to say anything. What was the point?

Emrys had sent Goro with his message for Aegan and Lysia the day after the Void siege. Over the past six days, Emrys had gathered some provisions while I had spent more time exercising my new wind power. I knew it would be key for my eventual escape, and testing its limits was crucial—Emrys agreed now, too. He gave me his blessing to practice, so long as I secured the room properly before I did, with a chair wedged under the knob as before. At first, I needed the window open, but I began producing the wind on my own without nature's assistance much sooner than expected. My grandfather's absorbed magic was indeed powerful, and I feared I had only just begun to scratch the surface.

"*Gaoth,*" I'd say again and again, practicing with every spare moment.

Each time, the wind would streak through the room and surround me like a cocoon, levitating me higher and higher until I could touch the ceiling before setting me back down. The landing would need work; sometimes it was a little rough, and I had ample bruises on my shoulders and backside to show for it.

Mastering a new power in days like this was practically unheard of, and I could only assume it was a combination of my grandfather's strength and the grimoire's influence, both of which frightened me. That was not ideal; if I feared my power, I may be reluctant to rely upon it when needed. I had no choice but to lean on it because it was my best shot of getting out of this village.

Today, after I finished my last magic session, I decided to visit Jasper in the servants' wing to see how he was mending. I had just entered the familiar corridor when I heard it.

"*Come to me, Rose,*" a familiar voice said. I stopped abruptly. Gooseflesh overtook my arms. Since when did the grimoire call me by *name?* Moreover, the closer I got to its hiding place in the bard's room, the louder it became.

"*Come and get me,*" the voice demanded.

I inhaled a deep breath and ignored it. I could bear the voice for just a few minutes; I needed to check on Jasper. Once at the end of the hall, I knocked on the bard's door.

"Come in," a voice said. Not Jasper's.

I opened the door to see Jasper on his bed, tucked under the covers with pillows propped up behind his back so he could sit up. He was still in rough shape, patched up, pale and battered, but alive and recovering. His long, blonde hair was loose about his shoulders, some strands clinging to his forehead and neck with sweat.

"Rose!" the bard greeted as cheerfully as he could muster. "Welcome to the inn and please give my healer a warm *hello.*" He started to sing raucously, slurring his words a little. *"Oh, he whose hands are magic, he who*—oh gods, I forgot the verse."

The prince chuckled, shaking his head. "That would be the opium," he said.

"I can see that." I couldn't help but smile at the scene, myself.

Korvyn flittered about by his side, bringing whatever the bard needed, setting a jug of water by his bedside and sitting at the edge of the mattress to drag a bowl of soup to his lips.

"I can feed myself, my prince," Jasper said, but the protest was weak and he dutifully sipped his soup. His brows lifted and he went back for more. "What is *in* this. Delightful!"

I quickly felt like I was intruding, but before I could leave, Korvyn lowered the bowl and stopped me.

"Please stay for a moment, Rose," he said. His glamour wasn't even in place at the moment, his scars on full display.

"Oh, yes," Jasper interjected. "Stay for a spell." He frowned. "Is that an uncouth thing for a non-magic human to say to a witch?" But before I could answer, he started humming to himself, and the prince tuned him out to speak directly to me.

"I know what you are about to ask. I did manage to check the dungeons earlier, in between caring for our Jasper here."

"How did they seem? And did you give them my message?" I had asked him to deliver a very specific message the day before.

"They acted a little spooked, but unharmed otherwise. And yes, I told them exactly what you said. *'Keep your faith, sisters. Time is the prize.'* Though I still do not even know what that means."

"Time is the prize—Oh, I like that," Jasper giggled to himself, and Korvyn and I continued to carry on our conversation despite his babbled interruptions.

"I just wanted them to know I'm thinking about them. But thank you for passing on the message," I said.

The prince nodded cordially. "Of course. But after I gave them your message, the guards came to move them."

"Do you have any idea where they might be now?"

"I am sorry, Rose. They are likely being questioned, though I do not know why or where. My father keeps me in the dark almost as much as Emrys. He thinks me soft." Korvyn's gaze shifted back to Jasper, who still babbled, and he smiled fondly. "Perhaps I *am* soft."

While the plight of my fellow witches troubled me greatly, the thought of it faded from my mind far too quickly. My thoughts instead became singular. The grimoire called to me again, the voice growing stronger.

"Take me with you," it said. *"Take me from the fae prince and the noma. They have no business keeping what is ours."*

"The grimoire," I whispered, unable to ignore its cry any longer.

Korvyn raised a brow, surprised. "You know about it?" His gaze shifted back to Jasper, who shrugged almost sheepishly.

"Jasper showed me the grimoire. He said you rescued it from the ruins of Astyrtown."

"He did, did he?" Korvyn flashed another sidelong, gently chiding glance in Jasper's direction.

Jasper stretched his lips wide in an awkward grin. "Guilty."

"Korvyn," I continued, "I need both of you to promise me that you will keep it safe and hidden."

He frowned. "Well, perhaps if it once belonged to your kind, you should have it. That's only right," Korvyn said, but I shook my head rapidly, panic rising in my chest at the mere thought.

"No. That book is dangerous, and I fear what I might do if it stayed in my hands. The grimoire corrupts witches; that's what it does. It calls them to the Dark Arts, to blood magic. I imagined it escalated many battles far beyond where they needed to go. From all I had gathered, it is quite useless for fae and non-magic humans, but no witch can get their hands on it. Keep it hidden, keep it away from me and safe. Promise?"

"Of course," said Korvyn.

Jasper sang a prolonged, *"I prooooo-mise..."*

I looked to Korvyn. "Can you make sure he promises when he's more coherent and understands exactly what he is promising?"

The prince nodded, and I sighed my relief. The only beings who could do damage with a grimoire were witches, which was why leaving it in the fae castle was the safest place for it. As much as every fiber in my being wanted me to turn back and claim it, I could not and would not.

I left them to their healer and patient roles then, not wanting to intrude any longer, nor remain in the same room as the grimoire longer than necessary. I bid them well before continuing on.

Once I was away from the bard's room and outside the castle, the grimoire's grip—and persistent voice—began to fade again. I could finally focus on my other worries once more.

Ophelia and Orinthia were not in in the dungeons and we still had no idea where the king was taking them. That did trouble me.

Emrys and I had come up with a plan for getting them out as soon as Aegan and Lysia let us know they were here.

It involved Goro pick-pocketing the guards for their cell keys while Emrys distracted them long enough for me to sneak them out. We'd duck into a storage room near the servant's quarters where Emrys had already hidden changes of clothes, so they could blend in with the fae populace. And then we would wait until precisely midnight before sneaking toward the southern edge of the city wall, a time when the guards in the south tower would be changing shifts, granting us the break we'd need to sneak out.

The plan could only work if Ophelia and Orinthia were, in fact, in the dungeons, and I was starting to get nervous. Restless, I kept wandering, and soon decided to check in on Feyleen. She'd been overtly kind to me again ever since the Void siege.

As I walked, I surveyed my surroundings. There were still a few crumbled bricks and blood stains on the sidewalk as a reminder of the siege, though the town as a whole did a fine job recovering from the attack.

I kept walking, but I never made it to Feyleen's shop. Because as I passed through town, just short of the main square, I spotted something that made me nearly crumble on the spot.

I looked up and shrieked out loud, slapping a hand over my mouth to try to hold in the bile rising up my throat. Because hanging over my head were the swinging bodies of Ophelia and Orinthia.

Now dead.

It took me a moment to realize who they were, because they had been so badly beaten prior to their deaths that their faces were nothing but blood, their limbs caked with dried crimson puddles. I could not even imagine the amount of torture they went through for them to end up in such a state.

I had failed them. If I hadn't dragged my feet breaking Emrys's curse after discovering my grandfather's head, maybe we would've had enough time to get them out. The reality sunk like a stone in my stomach.

Hanging around their still-collared necks were two signs, each with one word crudely written in blood. The signs spelled out a single message while placed side by side.

WITCHES HANG

I cried and sank to my knees, chest heaving with shallow, spastic breaths. This was a message to me, a message to all witches. Unable to contain it, I turned my head to the side and retched, the contents of my stomach spilling to the ground. I could not fathom this, could not accept this.

"I am so sorry," I whispered to the hanging bodies above me, hugging my middle and rocking back and forth. "I'm sorry."

Ophelia's necklace still hung around my neck, hidden beneath my cloak and the neckline of my dress. Now, it was all that was left of her.

She would not be buried. Both of them would be left out for the vultures and crows to pick their carcasses clean down to the bone. Their bones would be cut down and scattered. There would be no official grave, just a hole dug in the fields. There would be no one to say words over them, to send them on in peace to the goddess.

Now, I positively seethed with rage.

"Oh dear. Oh dear, oh dear," Goro said, landing beside me. I hadn't even known he had returned from passing Emrys's message to Aegan and Lysia. He must have just gotten back.

When I looked up across the courtyard, I spotted Talyn, who stared at me cruelly. Talyn, who never liked me to begin with and who now believed I had a hand in killing my main tormentor—his best friend—and was out for vengeance. This was his doing. The witches never had a chance here, but he sped up their execution. He flayed them just as Callum once promised he would, and the king readily agreed as yet another means to remind me I was on borrowed time.

I stared back at the dark-haired fae with all the hatred I felt, shaking with rage, my jaw clenched tight. It took every ounce of strength I possessed to not use my magic right now, to not attack him in broad daylight and make him sorry he was ever born, no matter what collar I wore. Talyn's lips twitched into a smirk, a brow arching upward as he mouthed three distinct words.

"You're next, witch."

He dragged a finger across his throat, then gave a wave before turning on his heel to walk away. I clamored back to my feet and bolted forward, seeing red. I did not care what happened to me anymore. I wanted his blood; I wanted to *kill him.*

"Yes, kill him. Kill the nasty fae," a voice rasped in my mind, and I wasn't even sure if it was the grimoire this time, or my own. *"Go get the book. Find the perfect spell to make him pay."*

But there was no time to find a spell in a book. I wanted to kill him *now.* He did not deserve to draw another breath.

Just then, a black mass flew right in front of my face, a flurry of feathers hovering to block my path. "I know what you want to do, and I do not blame you," said Goro. "But you mustn't."

"Move out of my way, Goro," I said, but every time I attempted to move around him, he flew in that direction, once again blocking my path. If I tried to duck, he flew lower. Every second he stalled me was another second for Talyn to get away.

"Kill him," the voice inside my head said again. *"Rip his feathers out. He is, after all, a faerie at his core."*

"I cannot let you do something that will get you into trouble, no matter how much he may deserve it." Goro stubbornly refused to get out of my way, intentionally mirroring my steps to stop me. My rage suddenly and inexplicably went from a simmer to a rapid boil, spilling forth unchecked.

"I said *move,* you useless, stupid *fucking bird!*" I screamed the words at the top of my lungs, and Goro gasped, his beak flapping open.

"My... my lady," he muttered, completely taken aback by my outburst.

He landed near my feet looking utterly dejected, and it was his reaction that snapped me out of my haze of anger. I dropped to my knees beside the raven, horrified by my own behavior.

"Goro, I... I am sorry."

I lifted my hand as though to pat his head, but lowered it—I had never seen a bird look *sad* like this before. My pure, driving need to kill Talyn had passed, but my despair had not.

"I'm sorry," I whispered again.

I leaped to my feet and moved in another direction this time, at first unsure exactly where I was going as I sprinted through town. But I quickly realized who I was looking to find: my husband.

My legs and lungs burned as I fought another wave of nausea down.

"Slow down, my lady!" Goro called after me.

"I must find Emrys!" I shouted back to him.

I kept running until I rounded a corner and spotted Emrys approaching from the castle, crossing the drawbridge. My body flooded with relief, and I nearly crumbled at the sight of him. His face changed when he saw me, question and worry clouding his features. But I did not stop to tell him anything as I was still too breathless at the moment. Instead, I launched myself into his arms, crashing into his chest and burying my head there for just a moment while I trembled all over and caught my breath. I looked to him like a life raft on a stormy sea. His arms went around me on instinct.

"Rose, what happened?" When I didn't answer, he pulled back, gently gripping my arms so he could look down into my face. He saw my expression, the tears streaming down my cheeks, and his jaw clenched with preemptive anger. "Did someone hurt you?"

He turned my face this way and that, examining me for any signs of cuts as I struggled to find the words, to tell him what happened.

"I was not injured. Not me," I finally said once I had stopped shaking enough to speak. "But Ophelia and Orinthia were killed. I failed them. *I failed.*"

"If you've failed, then I have failed, too." Emrys drew a deep breath, squeezed his eyes shut. "Show me where they are."

"No. I cannot go back there. I cannot look at them that way again." I felt the sobs threatening to choke me again, but I swallowed it down as best I could. Emrys gripped my upper arms tight, listening intently as he allowed me to continue. "If you want to see for yourself, they've been strung up right in the middle of the town center. Hung by their necks. And from the looks of it, badly beaten and tortured first. They had signs around their necks that said *Witches Hang.* It was a warning to me; I know it. Talyn thinks I killed Callum and he's out for vengeance. He carried out what Callum said he would do on the witches' fields, and then he threatened me. He said that I'm next."

I hadn't realized how severely I was crying until Emrys pulled me back into his arms. I quickly soaked the material of his shirt through with my tears.

"Goro, please give us a moment," Emrys said over his shoulder, his voice rumbling in his chest as he spoke. I heard the distinct flap of wings as the raven flew away to give us privacy. When I was finally composed enough, I pulled back. Emrys's lips curled back from his teeth as he snarled his next words. "I will *kill* Talyn if he ever lays a hand on you. Just like Callum."

"No." I shook my head. "It's not just him. The king is sending a message, too. He doesn't trust me; the collar already made that much clear. He blames me for the Void pocket siege, like Talyn. And when he discovers his pet head in a box is gone as well, he will also know that was me, and he will end me. I don't even know that I can afford to wait for Aegan and Lysia anymore."

Emrys paled but nodded resolutely. "Then the time has come. Aegan and Lysia should be close to the castle by now, according to Goro. I'm sure they will be here very soon. We will get you out tonight, under the cover of moonlight. And you will get to a safe place and wait for them. I will send Goro with you."

He finally released me. His jaw clenched tight, and I swore I caught the faint glimmer of a tear welling up in his gold eye just before he turned away.

46

Emrys

TWO HALVES OF ME WERE AT WAR. THE PART OF me that wanted to stay with my wife, and the part of me that knew our union would forever be cursed. That I had done nothing but hurt her or put her directly in harm's path since the moment we'd met.

Laughter echoed down the hallway just as I passed the grand staircase. King Armynd turned the corner… with Talyn at his side. The two of them seemed *far* too friendly for my liking. That was never so before.

"Emrys." The king's voice floated down the hall. He paused, wings hidden from view. Any good humor from his conversation with Talyn vanished at the sight of me. "I need to speak with you. Come with me."

From his tone, the king was in no mood for pleasantries.

Shit. I swallowed hard. This could be nothing good. Talyn threw me the most threatening look he could muster before parting with the king.

Armynd beckoned me forth and I followed. He did not slow until we entered the small meeting room adjacent the throne room.

"Close the door," he commanded.

I did as he asked, though I could feel that my tongue was about to get the better of me. The words tumbled forth.

"You had the witches executed far earlier than normal. Why?"

I had once looked up to the king as a father figure after my own died. But now it was becoming increasingly difficult to remember the reasons why.

The king's large wings sprang from his back, unfurling. Sometimes, his glamour failed when he got emotional. Just like his son. "My decision to expedite the witches' execution is none of your concern. What *should* be of concern to you is convincing me why I should ever trust you again. Can you honestly tell me that Callum dying during the mysterious Void siege was nothing more than mere coincidence?"

I shrugged. "There were too many wights that night. You saw, they were everywhere." That part was not a lie. Though Armynd was no imbecile. He surely picked up on my intentional avoidance of answering the question directly.

"And why would I believe that? I already saw the beating you gave Callum even *before* the siege."

"As I said before, Callum hurt my wife." My voice raised an octave. Cracked. "I defended her, as a husband should. And I would do it again."

"We do not attack our own."

"We do if they deserve it."

Armynd lifted a brow. "Are you admitting to killing Callum?"

"I am admitting to nothing other than defending my wife. A wight killed Callum, not me." Again, technically, that was not a lie.

The king shook his head. "You have changed so much, Emrys. And it's because of her. Isn't it."

"Of course, it's all about her. From the moment we met... She floods my senses, highness. Every waking moment." It was true. *Fuck,* it was *so true.* The witch had gotten under my skin no matter how many times I had tried to deny it.

The king's brown eyes narrowed at my revelation, jaw tightening. "She cannot be trusted."

"She *can.*"

"And how do you explain the Void siege? Not long after she arrives, we are under an attack, the likes of which we had never seen before. You expect me to believe that was coincidence, too?"

"It was. She had nothing to do with that. In fact, she told me she saw *you* push Feyleen in front of the Void pocket. She thought that maybe you were trying to test her."

"And you believed her?" The king shook his head.

"I believe my wife, yes."

"Your judgment is clouded by her witchcraft," the king hissed. He advanced on me. An accusing pointer finger poked my chest. "By being blood bound to a witch, whether collared or not."

"No. It is not." I swallowed hard. Armynd lowered his hand but did not back away. His wings flapped idly behind him. "I may have changed, but I have always respected you. What you did for me is something I can never repay."

"Then prove it."

"How?"

He tilted his head. "Admit to me why Rose is really here."

"She is my wife—"

"And I am no fool!" He barked the words right into my face. A little spray of spittle hit my cheek. I tried not to cringe. "You think I really believe you suddenly fell in love with your bounty and decided to marry her without ulterior motive? Perhaps you even thought a human witch could break your curse. Isn't that it?"

Well, shit. Armynd knew more than I had thought. Panic's icy fingers dug into my chest. I drew a deep breath. Needed to bloody calm down. "Highness, I—"

"Do not insult my intelligence, Emrys Abrynth."

I swallowed hard. "And what would you plan to do if that were true?"

"You are still legally married, and you know I do adhere to tradition."

"Tradition isn't the only reason you honored our marriage though, is it?"

The king was silent for a long moment before he continued. "I recognized the name Doyle. There have been... whisperings of a notoriously powerful coven with such a name. Such a power may prove useful."

"Useful? How?"

He ignored me. "Perhaps you have genuinely grown to care for the witch. So, I will do nothing for now but remain disappointed in you. You and Korvyn could be brothers by blood. Now, it is time for your punishment, and I think I would like to perform the one hundred cuts myself this time."

My jaw slackened at that, falling slightly agape. "I thought the punishments were once per month now?"

"Not anymore."

This would the first time the king had ever raised a hand toward me. He had ordered me to be flogged and cut numerous times. But I'd always thought he didn't want to inflict pain on me by his own hand. Apparently, that was no longer true. I could not let this happen, not until I knew Rose was safe. Because the cuts would kill me this time and I would not come back once they did.

"Please, highness. No cuts today."

"And why not?" A knowing smile curved on his lips. He let out a humorless chuckle and clucked his tongue. "Ah, yes, she already broke your curse, didn't she?"

My silence was all the confirmation the king needed. I'd paused for too long while trying to search for the right words. *Bloody idiot.* The disappointment dripped from Armynd's tone as he spoke again.

"How did she do it?"

When I again declined to answer, he shook his head. "Did she find the witch in the cellar?" Armynd sighed. "That bastard was powerful. Took out ten of my best guards before we stopped him. We beheaded him thinking that would solve the problem, but the head kept talking. I'll admit, it scared me half to death. So, I shoved him in the deepest, darkest cellar. To let him think about what he did. I did that for *you,* Emrys. I punished him for *you.*"

Once again, I said nothing. Because I knew no matter what I said, it would be the wrong thing. Was I grateful that Armynd had taken me in and sought vengeance on my behalf? Sure. Was I happy he had also dangled the curse reversal over my head for so long to get me to do his bidding? Absolutely not.

The king clucked his tongue. "Oh, Emrys, what am I to do with you?"

For a moment, I stood rooted to the spot. Unsure what to do. The king had the power to have me and Rose hung side by side with the snap of two fingers. I had known this from the very first time I came to the castle, how much power this one being wielded.

"When exactly do you plan to die?" he eventually asked.

I had never before wished fae capable of telling direct lies more than I did right now. "Sooner than you would like, I imagine."

"Do not presume to know what I would like," he snapped. "How about you rejoin your family now, Emrys?"

My head snapped up. "What?"

"It was all you wanted before Rose came into your life, wasn't it? Well, let me give it to you now. You're right. I have denied you long enough. You deserve to be with your family."

I blinked rapidly. *No.* This could not happen. Was I being tested?

"Please, highness. Not today. Not yet."

"Why not? You have waited so long for this. To be put out of your misery." His jaw twitched. Without warning, he reached into his jacket. Pulled out a knife.

And stabbed me in the gut.

I grunted in shock, eyes wide. For a moment, Armynd clutched the knife handle, its blade still lodged in my stomach. He grabbed my shoulder. Held my gaze with his nose inches from mine as he spoke. "You have betrayed my trust, Emrys. This is but a taste of what is to come."

He yanked the knife free in one smooth motion and stepped back. I clutched my bleeding stomach. Sank to my knees. The king looked down at me coldly now. Cruelly.

"I believed I've missed vital organs this time. Go have your witch wife patch you up."

My hands shook as I lifted them to examine the extent of the damage. *Shit.* So much blood. I was used to bleeding, but not when I didn't have the curse to drag me back from the brink. I needed to get help. Fast.

I slapped a bloody hand on the meeting table. Left a sticky, red imprint. Dragged myself to my feet, dripping more blood on the floor. Gasping. I was still alive for now. I might not be for long, but I had to keep breathing for Rose. I had to stay alive long enough to ensure she left the castle and made it to safety.

I needed my wife.

The king turned away, disgusted. "Get out of my sight. I cannot even stand to look at you. And Emrys? There *will* be more consequences for this. And they will be coming soon."

He left the room without another word.

I dragged myself through the hallway with sheer determination and adrenaline. Left a blood trail behind me like a wounded snail. Somehow, I made it up the turret steps. I almost crawled up the stairs. Were there always this many bloody stairs?

Finally, I reached the landing. I pushed through the door, hands clutching stomach. I staggered forward. Rose stood from the bed when she saw me and gasped. Thank the gods she was here.

"Rose," I managed to choke out. I took one more step inside the room before I collapsed.

And the world went dark.

47

Rose

"OH, MY GODDESS. EMRYS!" I RUSHED OVER TO kneel next to his prone form.

He had come through the door bloodied, disoriented, grasping his stomach. Had the king cut him? He was supposed to be down to monthly cuts now, so why would he be cut again so soon? Had he gotten into a fight?

He whimpered, straddling the line between conscious and unconscious, muttering my name over and over. I lifted his head, but his eyes remained closed. I'd seen him like this before, although his cuts healed quickly then, within minutes. Now that he was mortal again, this wound would not heal without intervention, and I would need to help him mend it myself.

I could call for Goro to gather me healing supplies, but I would need several items that he may not be able to carry at once or identify properly. Not to mention, it may be too late by then. I must remain calm and think quickly.

Then it came to me. My fire.

It was something I had seen my grandmother do one time when Papa had gotten injured during a hunting excursion. I knew how to seal a wound to stop it from bleeding out.

Quickly, I grasped Emrys's shirt above his wound. The fabric was already cut, and I tore the hole wider, exposing the injury fully to me. Stars, it was bad. I drew a deep breath and pinched the wound closed with my fingers, which were now sticky with blood.

"Teine," I muttered.

My hands began to warm, growing hotter. I concentrated the flame on my fingertips, burning the flesh such that the ends of the wound closed in on itself. Even while mostly unconscious, Emrys groaned against the pain. Sweat dripped from his dark brow.

"I'm so sorry," I said.

But it had worked. I could only pray it was enough, and all I could do now was wait, though the wait was quickly proving to be pure torture.

Thankfully, Emrys began to stir. "Rose," he whispered, eyes still closed.

"It's alright," I said. "You will be fine."

He slid into unconsciousness again.

Emrys was too heavy for me to lift onto the bed, and I was drained from practicing my wind magic all morning even before I used my fire for healing, so a wind lift was out of the question. I simply slid a pillow under his head and sat beside him on the floor with my back against the bed.

Praying to the goddess that he would wake again.

EMRYS AWOKE BEFORE ME. "RED?" HE SAID questioningly.

"I'm here," I said, head still thick with grogginess. The sound of his voice filled me with sheer relief. I was far from ready for him to be gone yet; though I doubted I ever would be ready.

He winced and raised his torso up on his elbows, looking down at is stomach wound. "Not a single stitch," he marveled, gently running a finger across the puckered top edge of the wound. "Blistered, though. You used your fire."

"Yes," I said. I sat up beside him and winced, stiff from sleeping beside him on the hard flooring. "It was the quickest and most efficient way to keep you from bleeding out. Though in hindsight, maybe I should—or shouldn't have... I know you wished to die."

"Stop, Red." He gripped my chin between thumb and forefinger. "You did the right thing. I would never dream of dying until I know you're safe."

I smiled shakily. "I was going to visit Feyleen in a bit to get a salve for the burn."

"No need. I will be fine. Besides, there is no time."

He lowered his hand then and slowly climbed to his feet before striding across the room. I watched as he reached into his side of the wardrobe, quickly changed his soiled and torn shirt with a clean one, and grabbed a satchel. He returned to the side of the bed and dropped the bag near my feet.

"You should've left last night. You *would have* if it weren't for what the king did to me. He knows you broke my curse. He's too close to Talyn, convinced you're a threat. You must go *now*. To the west tower." He peered out the window, expertly telling the time by the position of the sun. "The guards should be changing within the hour. It won't be nearly as large of a window as it would be at midnight. You will have to move fast, Red."

I swallowed hard and nodded. We had spoken of our plans in great detail so many times by now, it would be forever burned into my mind, yet I was terrified at the prospect of things not going to plan.

"What about Stardust?" I asked. It was probably a silly question because I already knew the answer.

"You cannot take him. But if I know Aegan and Lysia, they'll be bringing their two new horses. You'll likely be able to ride one of them."

"Alright." My chest felt tight. I had prayed for this day upon first arriving to the castle. But sometime within the past few weeks I realized that I was no longer dreaming of this day, but rather dreading it. My, how things had changed. "Are you sure you cannot go with me?" I asked again.

"I cannot. The king and his guards will be more active now. I need to stay back to ensure none of them give you chase. I'll guide you to the tower and listen for any nearby heartbeats that might intercept us. I will make sure you get out of the village safely. But that is as far as I can go."

I nodded, my stomach twisting. Suddenly, I felt as though I was having my guts scooped out of me with a wooden spoon, like I was hollowing out and soon I would whither into nothing more than a dried-up husk. I was not ready for this.

He held up a small key then. "First, we need to get this cursed collar off you."

Oh, thank Stars. I was quite ready for this thing to be gone. I turned my back to Emrys and felt him slide the key into the little keyhole on the back of the collar, felt the little click as it sprang open. His fingers brushed my skin as he worked, lingering longer than seemed necessary. But then he pulled the metal away; I was free, and I instinctively reached up to touch my neck while turning back around to face Emrys.

"Goro will go with you. Send a note back to me when you are safely with Aegan and Lysia. You'll find a small strip of parchment, a quill, and ink in your satchel." He pointed his chin toward the bag he'd tossed by my feet. "I packed it yesterday before the meeting with the king. It should have everything you need, including two days' worth of food and water, and a note for Aegan and Lysia. Also, a vial of my blood."

When I quirked a brow, Emrys explained.

"The farther we get from each other, the more our blood bond will try to draw us back toward each other. Keeping a vial of each other's blood should help with that. Not fully, but enough to take the edge off."

"You need a vial of my blood as well, then."

He waved a hand. "I can handle pain. It will not be forever."

"No. Don't be stubborn."

"Red..."

"I'm serious." I grabbed one of the empty vials left over from the pregnancy tonic, tucked away next to the claw-footed bathtub. "Your dagger?" I held my hand out in an expectant gesture, palm up.

Reluctantly, Emrys handed it to me. Using the tip of the blade, I cut my finger before Emrys could protest further and squeezed it over the bottle. I had to cut a second finger to get enough to fill it. I corked the bottle and handed it to him with my non-cut hand, his fingers brushing mine as he accepted.

"It is the least I could do," I said, sucking my fingers into my mouth to stop the flow of blood.

"Oh, and one more thing. Your father's sword." Emrys handed me my sword from the wardrobe. He'd packed it away again after the siege per the king's rules, and I gratefully accepted it now.

"Let it keep you safe," he said, offering me his father's sheath as well and helping me put it on with the sword. "The sheath was one of the few items of my father's that had managed to survive. But a fine work of leather. Perhaps it even has a bit of luck to it, surviving all that it has."

My father's sword and his father's sheath. Somehow, it seemed almost poetic.

"I must say goodbye to you now. Because once we leave this room, we will have to be quiet. I'll need to listen for heartbeats and we might not get another moment to say goodbye properly." Emrys held my shoulders for a moment after that, but didn't look me in the eye as he spoke, instead choosing to lean his forehead against mine with his eyes closed, breathing me in. "So... Thank you, Red."

"For what?" I asked.

"For putting your trust in me. For helping me. For bringing some true joy into my life over these past few weeks." He leaned back and pinched a lock of my auburn hair between his fingers, transfixed by the small action. "For a long while, I was numb to everything. I jumped from one high to another searching for a way to simply *feel*. Hunting, fucking, sometimes even shoving my blade into my own gut. But I was a mere shell of a person... Until I met you. So, thank you. For giving me a little life in the days I had left."

Stars, this was hard. He tipped my chin and ghosted a kiss upon my lips, barely a touch. Emrys pulled back fully and I expected he had so much more to say, that something profound would leave his lips the next instant. But all that came out was, "I wish you well."

I blinked through a frown. That was it? But then, we both knew what he was going to do once he received word of my safe passage. A quick good-bye was best and Emrys was correct to show restraint, no matter how much it hurt.

"Emrys," I whispered. I did not know what to say. Really, I had a thousand things to say, but nothing seemed sufficient. So instead, all that left my lips was, "Goodbye," leaving so many things unsaid.

But when I turned to head down the turret stairs, Emrys's hoarse voice floated toward me across the room. A single command. "Wait."

I barely had a chance to draw another breath before he closed the distance between us once more and his mouth met mine, kissing me deep, his careful restraint gone. His hands framed my face, thumbs hooked behind my ears. I breathed in the woodsy scent of him, reveled in the dizzying feeling of his warm lips claiming mine. It was over far too soon.

"I'm sorry. I couldn't *not* do that. One last time," he said once he'd pulled away.

"One last time," I breathed, voice shaking.

I opened my eyes to find him staring at me so intensely I nearly gasped. I drank in the sight of him, those golden eyes, that scarred brow, forever burning it into my mind.

"OK," he whispered once he'd released me. "Now, stay close behind me and keep quiet."

I did as he asked, following him down the stairs and corridors, waiting until he listened for heartbeats and gave me signals to follow with quick waves of his hand. We stayed pressed against walls, hidden in shadows. We had made it all the way to the drawbridge when Emrys stiffened. He held out a hand to halt my forward motion and turned to speak directly into my ear.

"Rogyn and Pery are nearby. Wait for my distraction and then cross the drawbridge without delay. Go straight to the tower and don't look back."

I could only nod. This was it, the true goodbye. His gold eyes were sorrowful as he cupped my cheek once more, dropped a hasty kiss on my forehead. With one last, lingering gaze, he slipped out the corridor to greet Rogyn and Pery, stopping them before they could find me.

"What are you doing, Emrys?" I heard one of them ask.

"Just going for a walk."

"King Armynd wanted us to look for you."

"Well, you both are welcome to accompany me to the garden. I was just on my way there to clear my head."

"No," said the guard. "We are to ensure you stay in your room until the king summons you."

I paled. If they went back to our turret room, they would pass right by me, and I would have nowhere to hide.

"That's fine," Emrys replied, keeping his voice steady. "But might I at least get a little food from the kitchen first? I'm going to get a little hungry sequestered in my room all day."

There was a long, tense pause before, to my utter relief, the guard said, "Alright. But be quick about it."

Their voices faded and I took my cue.

I slipped down the corridor, refusing to look back. We had originally planned to do this at midnight, but now, the sun had just barely set, which was risky. There would still be fae out and about, and the guard change window would be much narrower. Thankfully, the drawbridge from the castle had been damaged in the siege and not yet repaired, so it remained open, which was one less obstacle to deal with.

"Don't leave without me," the voice in my head said. And for a moment, I fought the very real urge to turn around and grab the grimoire. But I would not; it was too dangerous.

Just up ahead, Goro was waiting for me. He swooped down and perched on my shoulder. "Hello, Goro," I said.

"Hello, my lady," he replied. "I am here to make sure you find Aegan and Lysia safely."

We made it most of the way to the western wall without being spotted or stopped. I was just beginning to think how smoothly things seemed to be going, which was a mistake, as my hopes were quickly dashed by Talyn. "Where do you think you're going, witch?"

I froze in my tracks at the sound of the hated voice. Of course, Callum's lap dog would be the obstacle to my freedom. Of course, it was always coming down to this moment. And I knew right then, in my very bones, that it would be him or me; one of us would not leave this encounter alive.

"I am leaving," I told him.

"Not before you kill him," the voice said, but I ignored it.

"You are in no position to make demands, witch."

My chin raised as I very pointedly unsheathed my sword from my back. "You *will* allow me to leave. Because if you try to stop me, I will—"

"Lower your arms and be still," Talyn commanded, and at once, I felt my stubborn arms comply with his enchantment. I fought, I fought hard, but his enchantment powers were equally as strong as Callum's. And here, I had thought Callum's were the strongest of his kind, aside from the king.

"Please, Talyn, just let me go." Now I was to the point of begging, and I hated begging this brute more than anything. The more I struggled against his enchantment, the more it hurt. My arms felt like wooden boards, stiff, my flesh full of splinters. "All I want to do is leave."

"You know I cannot allow that. What if you know of more surviving witches that you haven't told us about, that we *don't know* about, and you report back to them about all you've seen here? Although, if the Void pocket siege is any indication, perhaps you have already found a way to do that."

Talyn's eyes flashed with such pure hatred for me. Before, I hadn't perceived him to be quite as threatening as Callum. He was shorter, with softer features, lankier build, a less gruff voice. But right here, right now, I found him every bit as menacing and intimidating as Callum had been. Maybe because he felt he had little left to lose now.

"I already *told* you I had nothing to do with the Void pockets attacking!"

He chuckled mirthlessly. "And I already told you that I do not believe you. Just as I don't believe you had no hand in Callum's death. He was my *friend."* His voice broke at that. The brute had feelings, after all. He shook his head as though to ward off unwanted emotion. "You are a *witch,* and you've put my people in jeopardy, just as your kind has always done. And it is my duty to stop you right now. With Callum gone, I am Armynd's right hand now that he no longer trusts Emrys, or his son."

"Talyn, please. I know you are more reasonable than Callum—"

"Never say his name, witch!" He shouted it so loud, the tendons in his neck stuck out.

I snapped my mouth shut before licking my lips and trying again. "I am only asking you to let me leave. All you have to do is walk away." Tears pricked my eyes. My arms still would not budge under the enchantment.

"No." Talyn shook his head slowly. "You know what? Merely preventing you from leaving is not good enough. I gave you a chance, I really did. But you have proven that you are dangerous, and you will continue to be a danger to us as long as you keep breathing."

I knew where this was going, and my stomach heaved. "Don't do this…"

"Lift your sword," Talyn commanded, ignoring my pleas. "Kill yourself with it, witch. Slit your own throat just like your grandmother."

Now, the sword changed direction, the sharp end pointed up at me. I gasped, sweat trailing down my forehead as I struggled to break the enchantment. My arms shook from the exertion, muscles on fire. I could not hold this for long.

The tip of the sword edged dangerously close to the delicate flesh of my neck. Soon, the compulsion would win, and I would die…

With an enraged squawk, Goro swooped down from behind me and flew directly at Talyn's face, pecking him right in the eye and causing Talyn to cry out in shock, in pain. The enchantment dropped at once with the fae's concentration broken, and my body sighed with relief, my muscles flexing as they came back under their own power.

This was likely my only chance.

Talyn tore Goro off of his face, throwing the raven to the side so hard, I was terrified he had broken something. Now, I did not need the voice in my head to tell me to kill. Not only did I already *want* to, but I had no choice—it was him or me.

"Teine," I murmured, and a massive fireball appeared in my hand.

Wasting no time, I threw the fireball straight at Talyn with all my might, hitting him square on the head.

And setting him on fire.

He was engulfed by my flames immediately. He screamed and thrashed around. But then my shoulders were grasped from behind and I was thrown to the ground with the tip of a sword pushed against my throat. I groaned from pain of impact, trying to focus my now-blurred vision.

"You are coming with me, witch. I saw what you just did, and you will hang for it," the tower guard said, obviously having come to investigate after hearing the commotion. The sword trembled a little in his hands, his violet eyes round—this faerie obviously feared witches.

Before he could touch me, before I could even think about conjuring magic, a hand reached from behind him, stabbing a blade right into the side of his neck before he had time to react. The guard dropped his sword, gurgling on his own blood as he tried to stop his neck wound from gushing. He lifted both hands to his throat, but it was like a beaver trying to build a dam with one stick.

Unable to slow the flow of blood, he crumpled to the ground and fell over. Dead. Revealing the last person I expected to see standing behind him.

Rhea.

I looked to her in sheer bafflement. This faerie was the first to torment me upon my arrival to the castle, and she took great pleasure in helping to vandalize Feyleen's shop as a means to further traumatize me. So... "Why did you do that?" I asked. "Talyn blamed me for Callum's death, and now you saw me kill him. Callum was your lover and Talyn was your friend."

She laughed darkly. "Callum and I were nothing. I was only using him. The same way Emrys once used me, I suppose. And Talyn and I were never friends. He was an annoying prick, insufferable. All he did was follow Callum around like a fawn trailing its mother, looking to suckle a teat."

I shook my head, still failing to understand. "But why kill the guard to help me?"

"Oh, *I* didn't. *You* did; you killed all of them. At least, I will be telling everyone the witch destroyed Talyn before she fled, along with the guard who responded to the commotion."

"But you're letting me leave."

"Yes. Getting rid of you has always been my top priority, because the farther away from Emrys you are the better, in my book. And if you stay, you're as good as dead, too. Which, believe it or not, I do not want. There is a war coming, witch. My uncle knows this better than anyone."

"I don't understand. The war is over. It's been over for quite some time. The witches lost."

"And those Void pockets just appeared out of thin air too, did they?" Her mouth curved into a cruel, condescending smile that matched her tone. "Oh, you naïve little witch. There is so much you do not know. And I fear that when the war comes this time... well, I do not want to be on the losing side."

"I don't—"

"Just go, before I change my mind. You have until someone else discovers these bodies before the king sends his guards after you. It's getting later in the evening but that could be five hours from now or five minutes. So, I suggest you move if you want any sort of head start."

She didn't need to ask me again. I turned and fled toward the guard tower.

On the way, I scooped a limp Goro into my hands and raced up the steps of the now-empty turret, winded by the time I reached the top. Without wasting any time, I climbed into the guard's overlook window. Ahead was forest, looming black against the blooming colors of sunset. Stories below was hard ground. Fear gripped my stomach.

"Goddess, be with me," I whispered as I allowed myself to fall, clutching Goro to my chest and using every ounce of concentration I possessed to summon the wind, begging my new power not to fail me now.

The wind answered.

It howled, whipping around me so fast it nearly took my breath away. It wrapped around me like arms giving me a tight hug. The wind slowed my fall and I hit the ground with a solid thump, enough to jostle my joints but not enough to break anything.

We had made it.

Once safely outside the wall and out of sight of any guards, concealed behind the tree line, I looked to Goro in my hands and set him down on the grass.

"Goro," I whispered, gently nudging him with my finger. Thank the goddess, he shook his head and his eyes blinked open.

"That hurt," he said before hopping to his feet.

"Are you alright? Is anything broken?"

The raven carefully lifted one wing, then another, then stomped both of his feet and wiggled his tailfeathers. "Doesn't seem like it," he replied.

I sighed with relief. "I'm so glad. You just saved my life, Goro. How can I ever repay you?"

"No need, my lady. I was happy to be of service."

I jumped up at a noise coming from deeper in the woods, the distinct sounds of twigs snapping. Footsteps. Someone was headed this way.

With my sword once again held at the ready, I looked on with bated breath and then...

Aegan and Lysia appeared before me, emerging through the trees. They had found me.

I rushed over to them with Goro right on my heels, fighting the strong urge to throw my arms around both of them in a bear hug. They were dressed in full travel gear, the horses packed with loaded saddle bags, and they smiled tightly when they saw me.

"Thank you so much for helping me," I said, and Aegan nodded.

"Anything for Emrys. He is family to us."

"You're sure you know of a way through the Void?" I asked.

Aegan and Lysia exchanged a look. "We believe we do. We must warn you, however, that our route, our theory is untested. But we are confident it will work."

Well, that was the best I could hope for.

Quickly, I pulled the small strip of parchment and quill from my satchel, using a tree trunk as a table to write a short note as best I could to let Emrys know I had found Aegan and Lysia. Then I bent to allow the raven to perch on my forearm, and handed the note to him.

"Take the note to Emrys. Give my regards to Feyleen, Jasper, and Korvyn. Thank them for their kindness as well," I said. "And thank *you* for everything. I shall miss you, Goro."

I pulled my arm in toward my chest and Goro rested his head against my shoulder. I patted his back in a hug.

"I shall miss you too, my lady," he said when I lifted my arm again. "Fair thee well."

Goro flew off into the sunset, back toward the castle. I turned back to Aegan and Lysia.

"Oh, Emrys wanted me to give you a note," I said, suddenly remembering it.

At the mere mention of his name, I found myself fighting a strong compulsion to follow Goro back to the castle, to return to my husband. Emrys had warned me about the blood bond and told me I needed to fight it, but this was proving to be nearly as strong as any enchantment.

"Are you already feeling the pull back to Emrys, dear?" Lysia asked, eyeing me with suspicion as she observed my reaction.

"Yes," I admitted.

"I am afraid you'll be feeling that pull for quite some time. Such is the nature of blood bonds. But you mustn't let it influence you to return if you wish to make it safely through the Void."

But panic started to rise up in my chest despite her words. "No, I need to go back to him. I need to go back now."

As I began to turn, Lysia grabbed my arm. "The blood bond is strong, and you care for Emrys, I know. But his wish is for you to make it through the Void. He needs to do what he must, dear, and if you desire your freedom in the Outerlands, you must resist the compulsion to return."

Reluctantly, I nodded. She was right; I needed to stay strong.

"Let's go then," I said, croaking around the growing lump in my throat.

Aegan, Lysia, and I began our journey toward the Outerlands. With each step taking me closer to freedom.

But farther from my husband.

48

Emrys

MY BED FELT VERY EMPTY THAT NIGHT AND sleep was hard to come by. The sheets smelled of Rose so strongly, they all but drove me mad. The morning brought no relief. Instead, I felt like I was being torn apart. The physical feeling when a faerie was separated from their blood-bound spouse was not comparable to anything I knew. It was a whole different type of pain that I had not been prepared for.

As a human, Rose was likely fighting her compulsion to return. For the fae in the marriage, the suffering was a whole other level. When I first agreed to the marriage, I never quite knew the pain would be equally as bad as the feeling of having my unwilling soul shoved back in my body. Only this pain didn't seem to wane.

If the pain of loss was worse than this, well... I didn't know how the king survived after Maeve died. Armynd must have been in sheer agony for years following her death. A pain that could only lessen on its own with time as the blood bond slowly wore off.

I found Rose's blood vial and tucked it into my pocket. That seemed to help quell the effects a little. Though the ache was ever-present, just beneath the surface.

After getting apprehended by Rogyn and Pery, I had retired to my room as directed by the king. I *hated* not yet knowing whether my wife had made it to safety. Though if there was one thing I'd learned, it was that my wife proved capable of taking care of herself. Still, I prayed the gods watched over her. For a long while, I stared out the window, waiting for word from Goro. He did not arrive until dawn.

The raven perched on the windowsill, and I approached.

"Goro," I greeted. "Do you have a note for me?"

But Goro did not. I frowned as I checked his feet and beak and didn't see any parchment attached.

"Aegan and Lysia found Rose. She is safe," Goro said. He sounded breathless.

"That is good news." I sighed in relief. Now, she just needed to make it to the Void. And *through* it.

"But there is more. I am sorry, Lord Emrys. The king's guards intercepted me and took my note. I tried to get away but..." Goro hobbled to show me that his leg was injured, likely broken.

Anger flared, piercing through to my bones. The emotion was trailed closely by guilt.

"No, I am the one who's sorry. Goro, I put you in harm's way by making you carry messages behind the King's back. I should've known it would come to this one day."

No sooner had I said those words than I heard footsteps coming up the turret stairwell.

"Hide, Goro." I didn't want him coming to anymore injury by helping me. I placed him on the floor gently. He hopped on one foot toward the shadows beside my wardrobe.

Four guards burst through the door and I was surrounded. One of them was Rogyn, judging by the scarred brow.

"The king requests your presence," Rogyn said.

I was marched to the throne room like a man being led toward his execution. Perhaps that was true. Once there, the king vacated his throne and walked toward me. His face was a mask of pure disappointment.

"Did you really think you could sneak Rose out without my knowing?" the king said without further fanfare when I was forced to my knees before him.

He held the note that had been intended for me. Armynd read it out loud. *"I've found Aegan and Lysia. We are safe. Rose."* I gave my best impassive expression, refusing to react to the words. Though I felt the blood drain from my face nonetheless.

"She was scared after Ophelia and Orinthia were executed. She was frightened that what happened to them would happen to her," I said. That was not a lie.

The king shook his head. Clucked his tongue. "My, the hold she has over you. If she had been caught, she would've been immediately thrown in the dungeons. And do you want to know why?"

I said nothing. The king would tell me regardless.

Armynd made a gesture behind him. "Rhea, why don't you tell him what you found today?"

My frown deepened. With everything going on, I hadn't even noticed Rhea's presence.

Rhea's accusing glare locked on me. Her full lips twisted upward. "I found Talyn's body. The west tower guard too. The guard was stabbed in the throat and Talyn had been badly burned. Set ablaze by your *witch*."

Rhea's voice broke. She was a good actress when she wanted to be. I knew for a fact that she never gave a shit about Callum much less Talyn. She tolerated him at best.

"I didn't just find the bodies; I saw it happen right in front of me. I hid like a coward, but she was crazed in her murdering, with this wild look in her eyes. I was shocked, terrified she would do the same to me—or worse—after I embarrassed her as I did the night of the banquet." Rhea was so full of shit. I caught myself before I could roll my eyes.

But I was also caught off guard by the news. I could only assume Talyn had attacked Rose. He must have tried to prevent her from leaving, and she did what she had to. Gods, I should've been with her. She shouldn't have had to face Talyn and the guard alone. Fuck Rogyn and Pery for getting in my way.

"Emrys," Armynd said, "I will ask you a question now, and I compel you to answer it directly. Did you or did you not tamper with your witch's collar?"

I hung my head, already knowing I could not lie. Nor could I answer in a roundabout way anymore. "Highness, I—"

"YES OR NO!" he screamed.

My eyes squeezed shut. *Fuck.* It sat right in my throat, the lie. The *no.* But faeries discovered very early in life that the lie would simply never leave their tongue. No matter how hard they tried. "Yes," I mumbled. Hating what I had to confess.

"I knew it."

In the king's eyes, Rose was now guilty of the highest treason beyond shadow of a doubt. A witch who killed a faerie. On king's ground no less. One was a member of the king's court, and there was a witness. No matter how credible Rhea was. And me? I was the conspirator who helped her escape. Which meant I was also guilty of treason by association.

"What do you plan to do?" I asked, dread rising to my throat. The two guards at either side of me held me steady.

Armynd's brown eyes met mine and narrowed. "Your witch was right; I *did* push the shopkeeper in front of the Void pocket the night of the siege. I knew your witch had exchanged pleasantries with the shopkeeper—Rhea had witnessed as much—and figured that she was reckless enough to dive in its path, because she thinks herself a hero." The king snorted at that as though the idea were laughable.

Now I settled back on anger. "Why would you do that?"

"I wanted to see how the pocket responded to a witch directly in its path. I had been wanting to attempt as much for quite a while now, but opportunities rarely presented themselves, so I took the opportunity I was given."

"And what did your test prove?"

"Only what I had long suspected." The king did not elaborate further. He clasped his hands together and drifted off from the topic. Paced back and forth. "We'd heard rumors that there were more surviving witches colonized somewhere. I had the witches in our dungeons questioned, and they finally revealed something most interesting. It was a shame they were too weak at that point to be of any further use, and they were both executed. But now, I know another witch who could help our plans. Your wife."

My lips curled back from my teeth. "You leave her out of this."

"I'm afraid I cannot. She is needed."

"Needed for what?"

"That is not your concern."

"She is my *wife*. Of course, it's my concern," I barked.

The king shook his head slowly. "You are a fool to throw everything away for a witch, and now you have been branded a traitor as well. Is that really what you wanted?"

"I will do what I must to save Rose. No matter what that makes me."

"Then you have made your choice. Oh, Emrys. I had such high hopes for you, too." His tone emanated a genuine sorrow as he said, "Have I not been like a father to you?"

"You have," I admitted. "Once."

"Why do you insist on undermining me in every way. Why choose a *witch* over me?"

This was the most vulnerable I had ever seen the king. "I am sorry," I said. "But I made a vow to her. We are bound by blood. And you forced my hand, highness."

"And you have forced mine."

The king snapped his fingers again. The guards holding me down moved to drag me out of the room. Before I could shift to wolf form, a pair of cuffs were slapped around my wrists. They fucking *burned.* My skin instantly blistered beneath them. *Iron.*

I looked up in question and the king lifted a brow. "Did you think we only made cuffs to contain witch magic? Iron weakens faeries quite effectively, as you know. Also hurts like a bastard when pressed to a faerie's bare skin. Deep down, you are still the naïve child I saved, Emrys. And now, you will feel the full pain of losing your witch wife."

King Armynd leaned close. Sniffed. Then he reached inside my jacket and pulled out the vial of Rose's blood. His sense of smell could compete with any shifter. Without hesitation, he threw the vial to the ground. Smashed it under his foot.

The pain was instant, blinding. Far worse than the mere burning of the iron. "What have you done?" I groaned.

"You brought this on yourself." The king's lips curved into a smirk. He looked to the guards again, his tone thoroughly disgusted. "Now, take him away."

Then I was dragged from the room. Writhing in agony.

49

Rose

WE HAD BEEN TRAVELING FOR TWO DAYS already, and I missed Emrys.

How was it possible for me to miss him *so much?* And was it even right to miss him? I didn't know the answer to that, but I *did* know that I did not want him to die. However, that was his choice. His right. I could not intervene. Even if I could before, it was too late now.

Although every bone, every muscle, every fiber in my body was telling me to turn around and go back to him—the blood bond compulsion. It proved impossible to resist.

"Something is wrong." Dread crept through me, first as a trickle, then a full flood. A sense of doom skittered about like spiders in my belly, while my heart swelled with longing. "Emrys is in trouble. I must go back for him!"

"No, you cannot turn back," said Aegan. He directed their horse in front of mine, cutting off my path when I tried to turn.

"I think it's time to read her the note," said Lysia. She peered over her shoulder at Aegan.

"What note?" I asked.

"The one Emrys sent with you."

"Oh." I blinked. "Right."

"You didn't know what the note said, did you?"

"No. I didn't have a chance to read it."

"I'll tell you. My love?" she addressed Aegan, reaching out a hand to the side palm up. Aegan placed a paper in her palm, and she cleared her throat and began to read.

"Aegan and Lysia, I must ask that you please see my wife safely through the Void. No matter what she feels, do not let her return to the castle. It isn't safe, and I refuse to allow her risk her life. Take care of her as long as you can. I do not have the words to thank you both, but please know I will eternally be in your debt for this. With love, Emrys."

"I have to go back," I whispered. Tears pricked my eyes.

"No. Did you not hear what I just read?"

Aegan smiled this time. "Honor your husband's final wishes. Do not return. Carry on."

"But—"

"No buts." Lysia's eyes narrowed. "Do you wish for me to slap you and knock some sense into you? Because I will, child."

My chest heaved and I willed my pulse to slow. "No," I replied, finally.

I clicked for my horse to continue onward. I was near having a breakdown, but thank the goddess, the compulsion was starting to fade ever so slightly. I just needed to stay strong and keep breathing through it.

You can do this.

Aegan and Lysia shared a horse, leading the way in front of me. I followed close behind on the second horse they'd brought, just as Emrys had said.

We had traveled through most of the night, eager to put distance between us and the castle, and had only paused for a couple hours of sleep just before dawn. I was tired, but alive, and wished to stay that way.

It was now late morning. The trees had thinned out, and now we were traversing a clearing with just a few patches of trees here and there. According to Lysia, we would see no more woods until we entered the Enchanted

Forest. While I wasn't much looking forward to the Enchanted Forest or the Void, out here in the open, I felt exposed, as though we might be attacked from any side at any moment. It was only a matter of time before the king tracked my location and sent his guards after me.

We paused to eat and drink and give the horses a break. My horse was a cream-colored mare named Tippy, such a gentle creature, like Stardust was. Lysia handed me a biscuit and some water from their stallion's saddlebag, and I graciously accepted.

"You are both so wonderful," I gushed. "To be doing this for me. For being there for Emrys all those years, and for risking yourselves for us both."

Lysia's answering smile was tight and didn't quite reach her eyes. She gave my horse a pat on the rump, gentle, and leaned on a nearby tree—one of the few trees in the field, the trunk wide enough for Aegan to lean beside her.

A sudden noise cut through the temporary tranquility. A cawing came from overhead, and a large bird swooped down and landed near Aegan's feet. A hawk. I leaned forward with interest, as did Aegan and Lysia.

I frowned because if the note was from Emrys, surely he would've sent Goro back. Unless something happened to Goro. Or unless this note was not from Emrys.

Aegan reached down to perch the bird on his forearm, and he noticed a small pouch tied around its leg. Aegan opened the pouch and unrolled a little note, reading quickly before shoving the note into the folds of his cloak. I swore there was a slight hint of panic in his eyes as he read it. Or was that my imagination? Aegan walked over to Lysia, and they whispered to each other. I cleared my throat, feeling slighted.

"Who is it from?" I asked, wary.

"Oh, don't you worry," Aegan said, waving a dismissive hand. "Just something Lysia and I must discuss is all."

"What must you discuss?"

"Nothing you should concern yourself with," Aegan replied curtly.

"Really?" I couldn't keep the skepticism from seeping into my tone. "Are you going to send a message back?" I nodded to the hawk, still perched on Aegan's arm.

"No response necessary," he said.

He flung his arm upward to allow the bird to get a good boost for flight. The hawk darted past the trees and swooped through the sky as we mounted our horses again and carried on.

Despite the pit in my stomach telling me something was very wrong.

50

Emrys

A RAT SCURRIED OVER MY FOOT. I PAID IT NO mind, idly dragging my shackles across the bars with metallic clacks for lack of anything better to do. Boredom. Pain. Guilt. All of them eating away at my brain, my body. Before, I was a hollow shell. Now, I found I was brimming with emotions to the point of bursting. I wasn't sure which was worse.

Presently, I didn't even know what time it was. I thought a full night had passed. But with no access to the sun, it was anyone's guess.

Pain flared like a hot poker sticking me right in the heart. *Fuck.*

Fuck the pain. This shithole. The king. I needed Rose. I wanted my wife, and it was all I could think about. I could still taste her, smell her. Hear her voice, her rare laugh. See the crinkle in her brow when she frowned. And I was miserable without her.

I looked around me. Not that there was much to see. There was a separate prison for fae criminals, but the king had made it a point to lock me in the witches' dungeon. "Because of your witch wife," the guard had said before throwing me in and slamming the door shut in my face.

Thankfully, the initial shock of agony had lessened a little. I still ached, but I could tolerate it now. Somewhat.

Sometimes, the sudden jolts of pain to my heart momentarily stole my breath. I wasn't proud to say I nearly passed out more than once.

With blood bonds, the farther you strayed from your spouse, the more intense the pain became. I expected the agony to return soon with full force. Especially after Rose made it through the Void.

As if the mere thought of losing Rose wasn't agony enough in itself.

Now, there was a clatter. The dungeon door swung open. A sudden burst of light spilled forth that made me wince. I didn't bother to stand, figuring it was just one of the guards coming to toy with me.

"Emrys?"

My head snapped up at the voice. It was the sweetest sound. Also the most alarming and unexpected, considering the circumstances. "Rose?"

"It's me."

I scrambled to my feet. Ran to the bars and looked out. My jaw dropped because it *was* my wife. She wore her red cloak. Her green eyes locked with mine, blinking rapidly.

"What are you doing here? You should be long gone by now. How..." I looked around, listened for any other heartbeats. "How did you even get in here?"

"I am sorry," she said. Her voice trembled. "But they caught me." With shaking hands, she pushed back her hood. Her auburn hair sprang free, cascading about her shoulders. And then a second voice pierced the darkness. A far deeper, more menacing one.

"Yes, I caught your witch."

My skin prickled. *Armynd.* The king stepped forward and gripped my wife's shoulders with talon-like fingers.

"Take your hands off her," I snarled through my teeth.

His expression remained stoic as his hand curved around her neck from behind. He wanted me to see this, and

I wanted to tear his hands clean off his body. Leave bloody stumps cut off at the wrists.

"No," I shouted. Gripped the bars so hard my knuckles popped. "Let her go!"

"You brought this on yourself, boy. Now, I want you to watch," the king said cruelly.

His lips curved. Then he threw Rose to the ground right in front of my cell and straddled her. Wrapped his arms around her throat and squeezed as she thrashed and tried to get away. Soon her face was as red as her cloak. I dropped to my knees and screamed until my throat was raw. Rose had no weapon. She couldn't use her magic in here and the king was much stronger physically. She clawed at his hands, bucked beneath him. To no avail.

"Let her go!" I punched the cell bars. Again and again. My hand throbbed, knuckles bloody. I forced my shoulders against the bars as I tried to reach her. To save her. But I was shackled with iron, too far away.

Rose's eyes locked on mine as they bugged out of her head. The whites were red as veins burst, her lips turning blue.

Now I was all but sobbing. "I will *fucking kill you*, Armynd!" But I could do nothing. *Nothing.*

Rose stilled, the fight leaving her body. Her heart stopped, face still turned toward me. Now lifeless. I slunk against the bars, defeated.

"No," I whispered. My voice cracked. "No, no, *no.*"

I squeezed my eyes shut. When I opened them again, Rose and the king shimmered from view as though they'd been nothing more than a mirage. Or sprites. Vanished all at once.

"What the..." I looked around wildly, trying to compose myself. This had been a trick, a glamour. I sighed in relief and silently thanked the gods that Rose was alright. For now, at least.

I had known things could be bad in here. I even knew that there were glamours around the prison. But having never experienced it for myself, I had no idea how very real it would feel. Horrendous and *real.*

Nearby, the dungeon door clanged again. Opened. I hopped up and moved away from the bars, now tense.

This time, it was Rhea. She sauntered up toward my cell. Just when I thought things couldn't get worse. "Believe it or not," she cooed, "I do hate seeing you behind bars, Emrys. Well, the cuffs bring back good memories. But not the bars."

"You're another glamour," I accused. "Here to torment me."

"Afraid not," she said.

Now I was irritated; I would much prefer a fake Rhea over the real, insufferable thing before me. "In that case, I can think of no one I would rather see less. What do you want, Rhea? Because now is about the worst time possible."

"I can see that." Rhea nodded toward my bloodied knuckles. They were split from punching the bars. "Although I like having you as a captive audience."

"Spit it out. Whatever it is you're here for."

She licked her lips. Traced her finger down one of the bars. "I spoke with your witch before she fled. In fact, I saw her kill Talyn. Then the tower guard attacked… and I killed *him* before he could lay a hand on her. I *let* your witch leave."

"Bullshit."

She arched a brow. "Which part?"

"All of it. One thing I know about you is that you are far from altruistic, Rhea."

She scoffed. "Well, whether you believe it or not, it's the truth."

"Why would you help Rose?" I'd play along for a moment. Not like there was anything else to do.

"Perhaps because I want you to think better of me."

I tilted my head. "Or perhaps because there's something you want."

Her lips pulled to one side, a smirk. "You're right. I want many things, Emrys. I want my uncle to wake up. I want the war to be over. I want you to live." She leaned close, stroked the bar with her finger again. Her pupils dilated. "And I want you to kiss me. One last time."

I stiffened. "Never going to happen."

Her eyes followed the trail of her finger. Then she looked back to me, adopting a tone of innocence. But she had all the innocence of a snake hunting its thousandth meal. "I know exactly what my uncle plans to do with your witch. Kiss me... And I will tell you everything."

Another clanking noise interrupted the conversation and I was grateful for it. In fact, I might kiss whoever walked in the door next. Guard or not.

To my surprise, the prince entered. His expression was a mask of apprehension. He paused when he spotted his cousin. Obviously, he hadn't been expecting to cross paths with her in here.

"Rhea, I require privacy with the prisoner," Korvyn said.

I bristled at him calling me *prisoner* instead of *Emrys*. If this was any indication of how the conversation was about to go, I doubted I would much care for the outcome.

Rhea's eyes narrowed. "We weren't finished."

"Yes, you are."

I smirked. Interesting. This was the most assertive I'd seen the prince in recent history. And I quite loved seeing anyone put a muzzle on Rhea.

She put her hands on her hips defensively. "You do *not* tell me what to do."

Korvyn puffed out his chest, standing tall. "I do, actually. I am the prince, not you. I am the king's heir, and my authority is greater than yours. Now, leave."

Another huff. Rhea didn't like being dismissed. But at least she was smart enough to pick her battles. She left reluctantly, grumbling all the while. The dungeon door slammed shut behind her. *Good riddance.*

"Korvyn, what are you doing here?" I asked once Rhea was gone.

"I am not entirely sure, myself. I just knew I needed to see you."

"Hm." I frowned and changed the subject. "How is Jasper recovering?" Korvyn smiled tightly at the question.

"He is mending. He will make a full recovery. I'll see to it that he does."

"I'm glad of it."

The prince approached the bars. His gaze swept over my face. His brown eyes far warmer than his father's. "Do you really stand by your witch?"

"I stand by my wife, yes."

"She killed Callum and Talyn," Korvyn said. His glamour was well placed today, barely a hint of shine across his features. Perhaps he was finally getting better at it. "And the Void pockets... You saw how the flames went around her."

"She had nothing to do with the Void pockets. She was just as surprised by the flames. As for Callum, Rose didn't kill him. I did."

"What?" Korvyn's mouth gaped and froze that way for a moment, like a tableau.

"Callum attacked Rose. Enchanted her to hurt herself. He was a threat to my wife and I could not let that slide. So, when the wights attacked, I saw my opportunity and took it."

Korvyn swallowed hard and took a step back as though I were a crazed, rabid dog. "And Talyn?"

I sighed. "I wasn't there. I should've been, but I was not. I do know that Callum *hated* her, and Talyn blamed her for Callum's death. He cared for Callum like a brother. I have no doubt that he had tried to apprehend her or hurt her in some way. He forced her hand, I'm sure of it."

"She still committed high crimes, Emrys."

"I have too. None of us are without sin, Korvyn. We are all guilty. Every last one."

He chewed his lower lip thoughtfully. "I suppose that's true."

"The king means to have Rose killed as soon as he's used her for whatever purpose he's been keeping from me. I don't know if I could live with myself if anything happened to her. I cannot allow it."

Not only did I want to save Rose but for the first time in my entire life, I also found myself not wanting to die. And the reason was her. I wanted to stay alive for *her*. To help her, to be by her side. This was all new territory for me. I knew beyond a shadow of a doubt that I made a grave mistake in not leaving with her. And now, if she were to die because of me... no, I could not allow that to happen. But what was I to do from inside a cage?

The prince looked genuinely surprised by my admission. Like Rhea before him, his attention turned toward my bloodied knuckles.

"I'd heard that this prison showed occupants their greatest fears, though I'd never experienced it for myself. Did you see your greatest fear?"

"Yes," I said. Not wishing to relive the vision again.

"What was it?"

My voice was deep, cracking as I replied, "I watched Rose die. Strangled by your father."

The prince's nostrils flared. But he nodded as though he suspected that answer. "You really do care for her, don't you?"

"I love her, Korvyn." That was easier to admit than I had ever dreamed possible. I only wished I'd come to the realization sooner and not stubbornly clung to my need for self-destruction.

"Then you must go after her." When I looked up in astonishment, the prince smiled. "I am breaking you out, Emrys. My father has gone too far, and I fear his next steps. As you said, Rose will ultimately die if you do not go after her. I have turned a blind eye to the king's ways for too long. Not anymore."

I grasped the bars and dragged myself to my feet. "But you will get into trouble for this. The king will come to the conclusion it was you."

"He may punish me, but the king would not kill his only heir. I will be fine. Besides, I know what it feels like to be in love. Who am I to stand in the way of someone else's happiness?"

"You and Jasper," I said knowingly. The prince nodded, smile deepening. Did I grin like an idiot around Rose without realizing it? Perhaps. Although, I suspected I was usually too busy trying to be miserable instead.

"One day, Jasper and I will escape this place together. But for now, you must escape. You must save your witch. I will keep watch and ensure no one chases you. Not for a while." Korvyn slid a key into the cell's lock. Turned it with a click. A single click that whispered of sweet freedom.

"I do not know how to thank you."

"You don't need to." He tugged the cell door open. It gave with a groan of rusty hinges. Cautiously, I stepped outside my prison. I almost expected another cruel vision to flatten me like a rolling boulder. Thankfully, that didn't happen.

Before the prince could leave, I stopped him as I thought of something else. "Please take care of Goro for me. His foot is broken and needs mending."

"Done. I am fond of Goro, myself. He will be my loyal companion. He can even stay in my room if he'd like." The prince set to work on my cuffs with a different set of keys.

"How did you get these keys?" I asked.

"Goro is quite the pilferer when he wants to be, broken foot or not. As I said, I am quite fond of Goro. But Goro is also very fond of *you,* Emrys."

My cuffs popped free. I flexed my wrists. Gods, it felt good to get them off. My skin was raw and blistered where the iron had touched it, but I barely felt the pain anymore. "Please thank him for me."

"I will. Now, wait here. Leave in about five minutes. I will keep the guards distracted in the meantime."

"And how do you intend to keep the guards distracted?"

Korvyn lifted his chin. "When the crowned prince calls for help, all guards in the immediate area are obligated to abandon their posts and help. After that, however, you will need to figure out your own way. Gods speed, Emrys."

Without further delay, he disappeared out the main dungeon door, which he left ajar. I heard him greet the guards outside. Sounded like two of them; I could heart their heartbeats.

A couple minutes later, I heard his distraction—a blood curdling scream.

Well done, Korvyn. That scream would have been enough to convince *me* had I not already known our plan.

Once I was sure the guards had gone, I eased open the dungeon door. The damp air had rusted the hinges a bit. I cringed at the loud creaking.

Without looking back, I ran. My feet pounded slick stone. Damp earth. Unlike the rest of the castle, the dungeon floors were never finished.

I followed the tunnel up. Wound through corridor after corridor, keeping to the shadows and listening for anyone in the vicinity.

Near the entrance to the drawbridge, a noise grabbed my attention. The sound of several heartbeats. For a moment, I counted the thumping beats. Judging by the number of thumps I heard, I concluded that three fae lingered nearby. I pressed myself as tight against the wall as I could. Held my breath and flattened my back flat against cold stone. *Fuck,* I still ached. But I needed to ignore it. Breathe through the pain.

In the distance, I could still hear Korvyn's screams.

"What's happening?" I heard one of the drawbridge guards ask.

"Prince is screaming for help, demanding we go search the castle for something," the other guard answered. "I have never seen him like this."

I smirked. Thank you, Korvyn.

"We need to alert the king."

My smile fell. *Shit.* He'd see right through the charade and realize there was a diversion at play. Time was of the essence.

I clung to the shadows until the footsteps had passed me. Then I sneaked out of the castle and crossed the drawbridge into town, careful to stay out of sight. It was early morning. The sun just barely poked over the horizon and the town was still mostly asleep. I reached the main city gates and paused. Everything hinged on what I did next. I trusted my gut and prayed that the king's communication problems would be his downfall, as suspected.

The two guards just inside the city gates looked to me in surprise as I approached. "Emrys, where are you off too?"

I smiled nonchalantly. "I am searching for a witch." That much was true.

"King Armynd send you for another bounty?"

I did not respond to the question directly. If I had, I would've needed to lie. Something I still could not do. Instead, I replied, "I think it best I get an early start."

For a long, tense moment, I wasn't sure if my plan would succeed. The guards exchanged a look. But then, the guard on the left smiled back. "Bring us a good one," he said. He made a gesture overhead. Whistled. The gates clicked open.

I breathed a sigh of relief. It was fortunate the king often kept his plans so secret. The wall guards hadn't even known I'd been taken into custody or imprisoned. They probably didn't even know Rose had escaped. Armynd did not want to risk more unrest amongst his people right now.

I drew a deep breath and passed through the city gates undisturbed. Once safely behind the tree line and out of view, I shifted.

And then I sprinted as fast as I could.

I RAN WITHOUT BREAK FOR REST. REFUSED TO pause for food or water. Sharp pains nearly derailed my plans more than once. But my singular, driving need was to find Rose. I followed her scent that still lingered faintly on the air, along with Aegan and Lysia's.

I must get to my wife. I must get to her *now*.

But the woods felt so endless. Sythea felt so vast at that moment, as though Rose and I were worlds apart. At times, the pain of separation threatened to cripple me. I breathed through it, willing my body to move. To work as it had never worked before.

When I burst forth from the tree line into the large clearing that eventually led into the Enchanted Forest, I knew I was closing in. But still far from quickly enough.

ROSE RED

All I knew was that I needed to find my wife.
Before it was too late.

THE ENCHANTED FOREST

51

Rose

SOMETHING HAD CHANGED IN LYSIA AND Aegan since receiving the hawk's message. They kept exchanging looks on their horse in front of me, whispering back and forth as though plotting something that they were intentionally keeping me out of. As if the strong compulsion to return to the castle wasn't bad enough, now I had to worry about my guides scheming as well. I prayed I was just reading too much into their behavior.

I patted Tippy's head as the horse huffed beneath me. Then I frowned, realizing something about our surroundings was... unsettling. "Haven't we been past this patch of trees already? It looks familiar." In fact, I felt as though we had passed it multiple times.

Aegan brushed off my concern from up ahead. "You are tired, Rose. Many patches of trees look similar."

It wasn't lost on me that he didn't answer my question directly. I may have been tired—it was the afternoon now, and I was going on only two hours of sleep—but I knew *something* was definitely wrong.

"What are you doing? Why are you taking us in circles?" I stopped abruptly, and Aegan and Lysia doubled back toward me. Aegan looked to his wife, raising a brow. When she nodded solemnly, Aegan sighed, his shoulders slumping as though burdened with a great weight.

"I am afraid our journey must end here, Rose. We cannot take you through the Void," Aegan said.

Somehow, I had known this was coming. My freedom always did seem too good to be true. I just hadn't expected it to be Emrys's old friends who hindered my escape.

"It was the hawk." It was not a question. I rubbed my forehead against a sudden throbbing in my skull. "That was one of the king's guards, wasn't it? What was in that note?" When neither Aegan nor Lysia replied, I kept going, unable to stop now as the truth was plainly written on their faces. "The king told you to bring me back and we went in a circle because you were still trying to decide what to do with me. Or you were just trying to stall long enough for the king to arrive. Did you place some sort of confusion enchantment upon me? Because I am usually a far better navigator and should've realized we had been circling long ago." That would explain the sudden headache, as well, and neither of them denied it.

"What does it matter? We've made our decision, and you are going back to the king."

At once, Aegan gave a command to my horse in a foreign tongue. Tippy reared up on her hind legs, throwing me from her back.

I recovered quickly, tumbling and clamoring to my feet as Aegan and Lysia dismounted their horse. I drew my sword, prepared to fight. But no sooner had I pulled it from its sheath than Lysia raised a hand to stop me.

"Drop your sword," Lysia commanded.

My hand opened and the sword clattered to the ground. Of course, Lysia would possess enchantment powers, because life insisted on being as difficult as possible. Her powers were surprisingly as strong as Callum and Talyn's. Enchanter fae were supposed to be rarer than other forms of fae, yet I somehow seemed to be meeting all of them.

But I had powers of my own, and this enchantment said *nothing* about using magic.

"Teine," I whispered, and a fireball grew in my palm.

"Now, none of that, dear. Be still!" Lysia commanded.

My body stilled even as I tried to resist, fire extinguished.

Aegan stepped forward, circling around me. "My wife's power is most impressive, is it not?" His tone spoke of a great admiration for his wife, one that lit up his eyes. I might admire Lysia's power too if I wasn't currently caught in its frightening grip.

"Now, Rose, must we use another enchantment on you, or are you prepared to come quietly?" Aegan said.

"Emrys will hate you for this." But I bit my tongue, because Emrys might care about me, but he did not care enough to want to stay alive for my sake, either. Though he said he would at least wait until he received word of my safe passage before… doing what he needed to do. "How could you betray him like this?"

"Everyone has a price," Aegan said. "And ours is our lives. Lysia and I have every intention of keeping them."

"You believe the king will kill you if you don't hand me over?"

"We don't just believe that. We *know* it. It is treason, going against the king. We would hang."

Now it was Lysia who spoke. "Dear, we hated your kind after what they did to so many of ours. To Emrys especially. His whole family. You didn't see him as a boy, so scared and alone. The pain." I was surprised to see tears pooling in her violet eyes. "We don't hate you personally. You seem quite lovely and Emrys is fond of you. But you are still a witch, and we must protect ourselves. If the choice comes down to you or us, then we choose us."

"As I said, if we do not turn you in, we will be branded traitors and executed for high treason," Aegan said. "So, you see, we really do have no choice."

"There is always a choice," I spat.

"It is truly nothing personal," Lysia sighed, still holding me steady in her enchantment. She spoke with genuine remorse. "Please, you must understand that."

"You do know that the king intends to torture and murder me," I said. "Emrys risked everything to ensure I made it out of the castle safely. If the king had the foresight to send you a note to capture me, that means he has figured out everything. That means..." I swallowed hard as I realized the awful truth. "That means Emrys may already be dead at the king's hands, or imprisoned. What if we could save him together?"

"I am sorry, dear. But Emrys, as much as we love the boy, has made his choice. And now, *because* of his choices, our hand is being forced," Lysia said. "The king doesn't intend to kill you, at least not outright. He intends to *use* you."

"For what?" I asked.

"That is for you to find out. We do not question the king. We can't, if we wish to continue living."

I struggled against the enchantment, wriggling—or attempting to—but still could not budge. Lysia was so strong. I could only grunt, muscles feeling aflame. Lysia smiled in sympathy of my struggles. "Save your energy, dear. You may need it for whatever the king has in store for you."

"Please..." I tried again, but the words died on my lips.

"Now, Aegan will place you back on your horse," Lysia continued. "He will ride with you and you will remain still and silent for the entirety of the trip back to the castle."

But we never got the chance to mount the horses. A noise sounded behind us, branches and twigs snapping near a small tuft of trees, and then a low growl cut through the air. A wolf emerged, snarling, stamping its paws in the dirt.

Emrys. I was too stunned to even gasp in shock.

He transformed back into his regular form. His strong jaw was clenched, dark hair mussed, golden eyes fierce. His gaze locked with mine and for a brief moment, a distinct look of relief flooded his features, but it quickly faded to anger directed at his old friends.

"I know what you're doing," Emrys hissed, turning his attention to Aegan and Lysia. The horses huffed beside us, and I clenched my fists, still caught in the enchantment. "You will let Rose go *now*. Let *both of us* go."

Aegan's eyes widened at the challenge. "We will not leave without her, Emrys. We *will* turn her into the king. That is what we must do to avoid being charged with treason."

"Do not do this, Aegan," Emrys pleaded. He took a step forward. "You were my friends. Practically family."

"Yes, exactly. Lysia and I have cared about you since you were a boy, took you in when you had no family even before the king swooped in to steal you away to the castle. And this is how you repay us? You would really choose this witch you have known a few weeks over not only your own kind, but over *us,* who you've known for most of your life?"

"This is why I am begging you to rethink. Go home. Forget about Rose," Emrys said. His voice trembled a bit.

Aegan shook his head slowly. "No. We cannot. The king will execute us. You know how relentless he can be."

"You can flee with us. Join us in crossing through the Void. We will all leave together. We can find safety together. Please..." Emrys gestured to the path ahead. Now, I could see how tired he looked, how weary and disheveled. I wondered when was the last time he slept.

"You expect us to leave behind our inn, our lives, everything we have ever known, permanently? All for a witch? I think not."

Lysia had my sword now, freshly plucked from the ground. She pressed the tip to my throat, and Emrys growled. "It is her or us. Who do you choose? Once and for all?"

"I choose Rose."

This could not be easy for him, but his eyes were alight with anger again; Lysia holding the blade to my throat was his tipping point. I inhaled a sharp breath, feeling the pinch of cold steel against my tender flesh.

"You can't be serious," Aegan said, eyes darting back and forth between Emrys and his wife.

"I am very serious. You are the one who forced me to choose, and I chose my wife."

I felt my chest tighten, my heart beating faster at his words. Emrys was still too far away though, and when he tried to approach, Lysia pressed the blade harder to my throat. This time, it just barely broke the skin, and blood beaded up. "Come any closer and she dies right now. No waiting for the king," Lysia said.

"No!" Emrys shouted. "Hurt her and *you* die, Lysia."

Lysia reeled back, hurt and offended by Emrys's words. Her response was tinged with sorrow. "You can't possibly mean that."

"I do," Emrys replied, his tone pained yet resolute. "I mean it. Anyone who hurts my wife answers to me, and that includes you. Perhaps the king will accuse you of treason if you let her go. Maybe he'll come after you. But never forget I gave you the choice to flee with us. And if you lay a finger on Rose, so help me, I *will* kill you right where you stand."

"You dare threaten my wife?" It seemed that was *Aegan's* tipping point. He let out a growl that could rival Emrys's even at his most fearsome.

Without warning, Aegan produced his own knife, pushed Lysia aside... and stabbed me right in the middle of my abdomen.

The motion was so fast, I had no chance of stopping it, even if I'd been able to move. I crumpled to the ground, in agony, in shock, the enchantment broken. Blood pooled around my knees and I fell to the side, landing in the sticky puddle.

Emrys let out a roar, transformed, pounced.

And promptly tore out Aegan's throat, cutting so deep in a single bite that his old friend was all but beheaded.

Lysia screamed in horror, "No! Aegan!" Her glare turned to Emrys. "I will *kill* you!"

But Emrys was upon her before she could take another step, attacking viciously. My sword fell from her hand. There were shrill cries of pain and the wet tearing of flesh as Emrys shook her like a bleeding doll. She let out a final shriek, disturbing a nearby flock of birds who burst above the tree line as a giant, agitated cloud. Then she moved no more.

Once she had stilled completely, Emrys raised his snout and howled toward the sky, a howl of pure anguish, letting out all the hurt and betrayal he felt. He let out a final, trembling gasp and shifted back to normal form.

"You left me no choice." He addressed the bloodied bodies of Aegan and Lysia as though they could still hear him. He repeated the words again, his words barely a whisper. "You left me no choice."

He turned his attention to me, jogging the last few steps between us and dropping to his knees by my side, examining the damage.

"Gods, no," he whispered, his hand pressing to my wound. I winced at the pain caused by the pressure, felt the warmth of blood pooling around my abdomen. I knew I would die soon. The panic was apparent in Emrys's voice as he spoke to me. "I am going to fix this, Rose."

"H-how," I asked weakly, sweat gathering around my temples.

"We can make it if we ride hard."

"Emrys..." I wanted to tell him that it was too late for me, that we'd never make it—wherever *it* was. I wanted to tell him that I would forever be grateful that he returned for me, that I would never forget our time together. But I was too weak to say any of those words. My eyes slid shut.

"*No,* Rose!" Emrys cried. "Stay with me. You need to *fucking stay with me,* do you hear me?"

His hand cupped my face, urging me to stay awake, begging me to keep fighting, but I was powerless to respond, to do anything. My head was thick with dizziness, my limbs nothing but dead weights.

He gathered me in his arms, cradled me against his chest, my leaden limbs dangling as I was lifted. I felt my sword being sheathed, and then I was hoisted onto one of Aegan and Lysia's horses.

Emrys climbed on the horse behind me, the hard lines of his chest pressing against my back as his arms formed a cradle around me to grasp the reins. He flicked the reins and the horse jolted forward.

As we moved, I could hear Emrys repeating one phrase over and over just before I slid from consciousness.

"Gods, save her. *Please.* I cannot lose her now."

52

Emrys

I RODE HARD. AS HARD AS I COULD. THE LAND WAS beginning to change now. The former clearing gave way to sparse patches of evergreens, which soon began to fill in and thicken. The horse stumbled over a stray root or two. I had to shift my left arm to cradle Rose about the waist so she wouldn't fall off the horse, which meant I was holding the reins with one hand. Not ideal.

We approached the Enchanted Forest. So different than any other forest in Sythea. Here, the trees spoke to each other. Here, roots often took on the shapes of people. Of fae or witches that had fallen and been reclaimed by the earth. Or so the stories said; I'd never stepped foot in the place myself.

In front of me, Rose moaned.

"Stay with me, Red," I murmured.

She moaned again and stirred, but her eyes did not open. She was so pale, as white as a sheet. Her face pinched in unconscious pain and her skin was cold to the touch. Too cold.

The horse grew more skittish the closer we got to the forest. I clicked at it. "Easy boy," I said.

"Emrys," Rose muttered, though still her eyes did not open. Blood had gathered around her abdomen. It dripped down my leg, the side of the horse. Rose was fading fast, but I refused to lose her. No matter what it took.

"Hush, you'll be alright." I brushed my lips across her temple. "We are almost there."

The Enchanted Forest loomed ahead. Its impossibly large trees reared up like watchful sentinels standing in an endless row, guarding the land behind it.

The horse gave a nervous whinny beneath us. "Easy," I said.

I flicked the reins to keep the beast moving as we were swallowed by the forest. The air felt heavy around us. A strong wave of dizziness hit me like a launched cannonball. The trees whispered overhead.

"To whoever keeps watch over this forest, hear me now," I bellowed. "I require your healing pool. Reveal it to me!"

For a long moment, nothing happened. Though I swore the whispering of the trees grew louder overhead, as though they were discussing my request. I needed them to discuss really bloody fast. The horse huffed nervously. Up ahead, the foliage rustled and parted. The trees bent out of the way to clear a path. The forest was guiding me, and I did not hesitate in following.

Then, there it was. The pool, just as my mother had described it. It knew that Rose was in need and that I would do anything to save her. I had found it. No, that wasn't accurate; the pool had found *me*. I did not care about the price, either. I would've given anything to save Rose. I had already watched her die once when the dungeon showed me my greatest fear. The king strangled her right in front of me in my vision. But I steadfastly refused to watch her die in real life.

The waters of the pool beckoned, reflecting the light from the sun that shone through the parting in the trees overhead. At the opposite end of the small lake were three identical waterfalls falling from the small peaks there.

Sheer cliff faces dotted with trees and greenery and vines, all emptying into the pool below.

Quickly, I dismounted the horse. After tying its reins to a tree, I reached up for Rose. She had grown colder now, paler. Her body was limp as I lowered her to the ground and began stripping us both down to our lowest layers. She was slipping from life too fast.

I hissed when I spotted all the blood from Rose's open wound under her cloak. It was even worse than I'd thought. Viscera poked through the laceration. Frankly, it was a miracle she'd even held on this long. It proved how much of a fighter she was. How strong. Even now, she stubbornly clung to her last vestige of life. I was grateful for it; I just hoped it would be enough.

Cradling her in my arms once more, I carried her inside the water. Walked forward until we were both as submerged as we could get. Rose's breathing was shallow, nearly non-existent.

"Gods, help her. Help her now!" I demanded, tilting my head skyward. "I am here, and I am willing to give whatever is necessary." I paused. Waited. But Rose did not stir.

No. *No,* this had to work.

"Come on, Red," I whispered, holding her head. Willing her to live. "Open your eyes. Please, look at me."

There were several long, tense minutes of not knowing if it worked or if this had all been in vain. And then, finally those endless moments granted me mercy. I heard the most welcome sound of all.

A heartbeat. Rose's heartbeat, growing stronger. She stirred, her lips parting.

And her eyes opened.

53

Rose

I OPENED MY EYES TO SEE EMRYS'S HANDSOME face hovering above mine. My gaze skimmed his jaw, his lips, settling last on his gold eyes that brimmed with worry for me.

"Rose?" Emrys blinked down at me, cradling my head like it was a precious thing.

I grasped his hand, holding it firm to my face. "I'm alright." I reached out my other hand, tracing his cheekbone, his scar, assuring myself that he was real.

Relief flooded his features. "Thank the gods," he muttered.

He pulled me into a hug and I clung to him like a barnacle, burying my nose in the curve of his shoulder, holding tight. His body trembled; he'd been so *scared* for me, and the thought overwhelmed me with emotion. I must have been trembling, too, because he pulled back the next instant to look at me.

"I'm not hurting you, am I?"

I smiled. "No." Even if he was, the feeling of being in his arms once more would be worth it. "You came for me," I whispered.

"Of course, I did." His fingers squeezed mine. "Turns out, I couldn't let you leave without me."

I realized that Emrys wore only his breeches, not his shirt, his muscled, bare chest and scars on full display. I wore only the chemise that had been under my dress and cloak. Furthermore, we were both in a pool of water... Where were we, exactly?

That was when I remembered what else had happened, right after I'd been stabbed.

"You killed them," I said, thinking of the corpses of Aegan and Lysia, their throats torn out. "Your two long-time friends. You killed them for me without hesitating."

He nodded, swallowing hard. "Yes, I did."

"You loved them like family."

"Yes. I did once."

"Then why?"

"Why?" He said it in such a way that it was ridiculous for me to even ask. "Because I cannot bear to lose you. Because I was barely living when I met you. Hundreds of years of existence, and you are the only one to make me feel like I want to live a thousand more. And if given the choice between them or you again, I would choose you. Without question."

My heart grew heavy at his words, filling to the brim with joy. "Emrys..."

"I'm not finished," he gently admonished, brushing wet strands of hair behind my shoulder. His fingers created a trail of gooseflesh in their wake. "Do you want to know why I really pushed to marry you in the first place? Because my family in the Otherworld told me to bind the blood. They wanted me to marry. I think, even from the Otherworld, somehow, they knew... That you would be my salvation."

Overcome with emotion, I pulled his mouth to mine, tasting the salt of my tears as I kissed him with my whole heart. But the sounds of the strange world around us made me break the kiss quicker than I'd intended, and I took in our surroundings with a furrowed brow.

"Where are we?" I asked.

"A healing pool in the Enchanted Forest."

I lifted a brow in surprise. "We are in the Enchanted Forest?"

"Yes."

"And the pool healed me?"

"Yes."

"How? And how did you even know about it?"

"I don't know how, Red. But my mother used to tell me stories about it a lot. I figured it was worth trying. Anything that gave me a chance to save you was worth a try, and I'm glad it worked."

"Me too."

His eyes clouded over with a sudden sorrow. Maybe he was thinking about Aegan and Lysia. His old friends gone in seconds, by his own hand, no less. I ached for him.

I was also happy to be alive despite everything, though I soon realized I had blood in my hair, and I was eager to wash it out. I dipped my head back and allowed my hair to splay out in the water, the strands floating and churning on its surface like little red eels. I was *alive,* and I wanted to savor that feeling.

When I lifted my wet head back up, Emrys was right in front of me. Before I knew what was happening, his mouth was on my neck, his fingers between my legs, shoving aside the soaked, remaining bits of material to plunge them deep inside me. I couldn't help the moan that escaped my lips as he whispered in my ear.

"Do you know how I've been dreaming about this, Red? Dreaming about what I'd do to you once we were reunited and safe, and I had you alone again. I almost lost you, and *oh*, do I want you now."

"Emrys, we're in a healing pool. We should leave before we do this..."

"We cannot leave yet."

"Why not? I wouldn't want to disrespect—"

"I don't care," he interrupted. "Our time may be very short. I don't care where we are. I intend to have you one more time. Right now. If you'll have me."

Emrys's words—and the edge to his tone—made me narrow my eyes in suspicion. He spoke as though he knew something I did not, almost like he expected this to be our final moments together. But before I could ask what was wrong, Emrys's teeth scraped along my throat, shifting to the other side of my neck, and I was lost to the moment, all too eager to have him to myself.

I threw my head back to grant him easier access, my arms locked around his neck, my feet unable to touch the ground under the water. But his could, and he anchored me in place, lifting me higher above the water so that my breasts were exposed. He feasted upon them like a man dying of hunger, teasing my nipples until they peaked, pulling them between his lips.

"Emrys," I gasped. When he finally came up for air, I unwound one arm from his neck to reach down between us, to grab the hardened length of him in my hand—when had he even shed his breeches? "I want you."

Emrys let out an absolutely feral sound in the back of his throat, and then he was inside me without further fanfare, thrusting hard and deep. His arms held the weight of my body under my shoulder blades, and I leaned back on the lake's surface, weightless, each thrust sending my head bobbing out into the water. From this angle, when I opened my eyes, I saw blue sky and tree tops. And when I tilted my head back just a little, the world appeared above me at an angle.

"I could do this all day," Emrys grunted, his pace quickening, and I squeezed my eyes shut. "I could stay inside you forever and die a very happy fae."

My reply was a moan as his words sent shivers through me, his thrusts sending tingles of pleasures up my spine, gradually building toward that sweet, desperately needed release. Emrys and I clung to each other, crashing down together. He held me tight against his chest and groaned.

But our pleasure soon turned to horror as Emrys looked behind me and gasped, puncturing our bubble of bliss. Something big was swimming toward us in the water.

"Emrys," I yelled, shooting up to grasp his shoulders as he was still buried deep inside of me. "What is it?"

The look on Emrys's face changed in an instant. Something that was a much stronger swimmer than either of us was approaching fast. We needed to move to get out of this lake now. But before we had a chance to flee, something wrapped around my ankle. Tightened and pulled.

And then I was yanked back into the water.

"Rose!" Emrys cried as I was dragged into the depths. Just before I was submerged, I saw a large wave as tall as Emrys push him back, further separating us.

At once, my lungs filled with water. I could not breathe, the world dark around me, water filling my ears. But then I was hoisted from the water, once again breeching the surface. Somehow, I was suspended just above the pool, my arms rigid at my sides. Was this another fae enchantment?

Beside me, something materialized out of the water, something else I had never seen but only heard stories of as a child. A beautiful, deadly creature.

A water nymph.

The nymph had me under her spell. And not just any spell—a water spell. Because soon I realized exactly *how* I was floating. Water was wrapped around me, banded around my arms, solid as if it were steel. I was unable to move and, it seemed, unable to speak as well. But I could see the look of sheer horror in Emrys's eyes. He had been pushed to the shallows, where he stood now, ankle deep in water, somehow with his breeches back in place.

"Hurt her, nymph, and I will—"

"You'll do nothing," the nymph hissed.

She was striking, her blonde hair flowing past her curvy hips. Her skin was lightly scaled, shimmering and aqua in color, complementing her deep blue eyes, like the water of the pool itself. But the looks were deceiving, as water nymphs were notoriously treacherous. "If you move any closer, she dies. You will do what all who use my waters must do. I will give you the price you must pay for her healing, and you must accept the terms. Only then will you be allowed to leave, with or without your love."

Emrys nodded knowingly. He'd been expecting this. He'd known there would be a steep price for saving me and that he'd have to pay it before we could leave. That explained his urgency to make love to me once more, before the cost was demanded.

The nymph hissed in my ear; her breath sickly sweet. "It would be such a shame if I had to kill you," she said. "I smell great power on you."

I wanted to ask more. But even if I could, I doubted the nymph would ever give me a straight answer. The band of water around my middle tightened, squeezing air from my lungs.

"Speak to me, nymph," Emrys demanded.

"I once made men answer riddles as well, but there is no point. That is not the test. The real test... is what you offer for your sacrifice." Her tone grew serious again. "And now, I will give you the price you must pay for her."

"Name it," said Emrys, lifting his chin.

The nymph's lips curved almost cruelly—she enjoyed this part. "Your sacrifice will be your family. You will be barred from the Otherworld, never to see them again. And when you die, your soul shall die with your body."

Emrys paused, brows pinched together as he contemplated the nymph's words. I knew what his family meant to him; this was an impossible choice. The nymph spoke again.

"You must decide now. Choose to never see your family again, or choose to reverse the healing and let your lover die."

He ran his tongue over his teeth, stalling. He'd clearly meant to trade his life for mine, it didn't seem he'd been expecting this outcome. I could see how much the decision was wearing on him. His pained, golden eyes darted to me, his expression panicked, introspective. It wasn't fair to make him choose like this. "Is there nothing else I can offer as a sacrifice?"

"No. I decide what you give up, not you," the nymph said, tilting her head. "So, are you going to let your lover die... or will you accept my terms?"

Emrys squeezed his eyes shut, drew a deep breath. He opened them again and nodded resolutely. "Then I accept your terms," he said without further hesitation.

"Emrys, no!" I shouted.

Well, that is what I *wanted* to shout, though I still could not speak. And it was too late. The nymph accepted.

"Very well. The witch is yours. You may go." The nymph turned to me then, speaking low so only I could hear. "You are now free to go as well, with your life. But remember these words. Your power will soon be unleashed in a way that surprises even you. Do not fight it. Use it."

She released me from her thrall and disappeared back into the depths of the pool. I swam forward and rushed to Emrys, collapsing into his arms on the shore.

"You shouldn't have done that," I said, breathless, speaking against his chest. "Giving up your chance to be with your family... That is too great of a sacrifice, Emrys."

He backed away slightly so he could grab my face between his hands. "Hear me now. *Nothing* is too great of a sacrifice to save you. I made my choice, and I would make it again. We won't dwell on it."

I grasped his wrists and a tear trailed down my cheek, speechless at the depth of what he'd just given up for me. I raised on my toes to kiss him deep. When I pulled back, he leaned his forehead against mine. "I'm so sorry," I said.

"It's alright," he whispered. "My family has each other. They died together, and I know they carry on in the Otherworld together. I spent so long wanting to die, Rose. And now... Now, all I want to do is live a thousand lifetimes with you. But if all I am given is one lifetime, then I shall make the most of our time given."

He had just given up so much for me, and the sacrifice was still so fresh. There *was* no way to thank him properly for the magnitude of what he had just done.

"I don't want you resenting me for making you give up your family. Your friends."

"You did not *make* me do anything. I chose, and I could never resent you."

I breathed a sigh of relief. "Then what shall we do now?"

"Well, you know we can't stay in Sythea," he replied.

"Because the king can track us anywhere in Sythea through our marks." I nodded knowingly.

"In theory."

"I guess those are the best odds we could hope for. Unless I could break the magic in our tattoos to prevent the king from tracking us. Let me see."

Without waiting for his reply, I yanked his arm toward me and remove his now-wet bracer. The eyeball twitched and looked around, blinking, just as unsettling of a sight as before. I shuddered to think that I sported the same mark on the back of my own neck. Thankfully, I could never feel it aside from the initial branding, though I never forgot it was there.

Emrys spoke again. "The marks were forged by ancient faerie magic, not witch magic. As I said before, you cannot remove them. There is nothing you can do. Any magic you attempt to use on it may backfire."

As I examined his tattoo, I quickly realized that he was right. This was magic I could not touch, at least not with any spells I presently knew. With a sigh of defeat, I laced his bracer back into place.

"As I said, we have nowhere to go but away from Sythea." Emrys placed a gentle finger under my chin and tilted my head upward to meet his gaze. "We will be alright, Rose. Together, we *will* survive. I promise you."

"Don't make promises you cannot keep," I whispered.

"This one, I can. And I will." He dropped another light kiss upon my lips, his hand winding through my hair, skimming my jaw

When he pulled back, I let out a sigh. "So, now what do we do?"

Emrys looked to the land ahead, to the looming forest, his expression resolute. "Now, we complete the journey through the Enchanted Forest. Then we cross into the Void together, and finally see what's on the other side."

"Yes," I agreed, my voice trembling. "To the Void."

54

Rose

THE ENCHANTED FOREST MAY HAVE BEEN A part of Sythea, but it seemed a whole world of its own. The weather was changing in Sythea, making the switch to full Autumn. Leaves had started changing colors and falling, the air growing crisper and cooler. But in the Enchanted Forest, everything was still shockingly green, the weather warm as late spring.

Also, I had the uncanny feeling the trees were *alive,* watching Emrys and I from above and judging us. Even in the way the branches shook and leaves undulated without any wind present to disturb them.

Though I could hardly focus on the eeriness, still taken aback by all that had just transpired, shaken to my core that I had nearly died and feeling undeniable guilt that my husband had sacrificed so much for me.

Emrys's voice interrupted my thoughts. "I know what you're thinking, Red."

I sighed. What could I say that was remotely adequate toward someone who had just given up everything for me? "Emrys…"

"Don't." He halted abruptly, grasping my hand. "I already told you I wouldn't change a thing. I meant it."

"But what if you end up regretting your decision?"

"Are you serious?" He yanked my arm, pulling me against his chest. His free hand wound through my hair, thumb hooking under the back of my jaw, forcing my chin up to meet his gaze. "Look into my eyes," he commanded. "Do I *look* like I regret anything?"

For a moment, I held his gaze, transfixed by the intensity within it. I saw nothing reflecting back in his golden eyes but sincerity and warmth. Any sorrow he'd had in the moment of making those heart-wrenching decisions was gone. He had already moved past it, or was trying to. I sucked in a sharp breath, still feeling a pang in my stomach.

"But—"

"No buts. Not another word about it. Do you hear me?" His tone was soft, yet stern. He meant it, and I decided against arguing further. Instead, I nodded, and his mouth pulled up at the corner. He bent to press a chaste kiss to my forehead. "Now, let's carry on," he murmured after pulling back, letting go of me to lead the way once more.

As we moved, I nearly tripped over another strange, thick root. Many of them were distinctly person-shaped, where someone had died and been claimed by the forest. At least, according to Emrys, who seemed far more well-versed in the secrets of this forest than I was. The root bodies could've been fae or witch, for all I knew. On occasion, I swore I saw a couple of low fae buzz past in a flurry of motion. But it could've been anything else, like some undiscovered species of speedy butterfly. Who knew what other peculiar creatures roamed in here?

Emrys was quiet for a while as we walked. I knew he was thinking about his family, about Aegan and Lysia, no matter what he said to the contrary. Maybe he didn't regret the decision, but that did not mean he wouldn't still miss them. Though he'd said he did not want to speak about it anymore, and I honored his wish.

That is, until the whispering trees grew louder overhead. It was unsettling. The foliage was too thick to ride a horse through, which was good, because the forest had spooked our horse away some time ago. So, we were back to traveling on foot whether we wanted to be or not.

"Do you hear that?" I asked Emrys as we resumed walking, cautiously. It was a silly question; of course, he did.

He nodded. "It's the Enchanted Forest. The trees are known to conspire."

"I wonder what they're conspiring about."

"Not sure. I do know that we are closer to the main Void here than we've ever been. Stay alert and watch for pockets." He shot me a sidelong glance. "Oh, and do not touch anything, if you can help it. Vines, roots, mushrooms, any one of them can come to life if you're not careful."

"So, all the plant life is sentient?"

"Well, not all. But it's impossible to tell which ones *are*. Best be careful and not touch anything."

On cue, a thick, green vine slithered up the trunk of a tree right next to me, like a snake. "How did the forest become enchanted like this?" I asked.

Emrys shrugged. "Some say it has always been enchanted since its inception. Others claim the forest was simply caught up in the magic battle between witch and fae. The Void *does* border the eastern edge of it. Perhaps some magic seeps out from there as well. The forest isn't dangerous to the astute, but it is also not friend to human or fae. Rather a neutral yet mischievous place. So, we must keep our wits about us."

He did not have to tell me twice. This forest was so different from the White Forest, and part of me felt like a hunted rabbit wandering into a snare. I was about to ask Emrys how he knew so much of the forest, but the answer was obvious. His mother had been the one to tell him stories of the healing pool; she must've educated him on the forest as a whole.

After walking for ages—pausing only for fresh food and water that the forest seemed to have a merciful abundance of—our surroundings changed a little. The forest opened into another small clearing shaped like a bowl.

"Maybe we can stay here, just for a few hours of sleep," I suggested. "Rather than risk traveling through the Void at night while exhausted?"

But was it safe? When I said this out loud, I received an answer, and not from Emrys.

"You can rest. You will come to no harm," the trees hissed, the sound seeming to come from all around, above us, beside us. Emrys and I both looked up and spun around, startled. *"She has been saved by our waters, and we will keep her safe for now. But when the fae king approaches with his army, we will not risk burning for her. After tonight, you must keep moving."* Strangely, the trees spoke in the same voice as the nymph, as though the forest was interconnected. A gentle breeze ruffled my hair.

"Why?" I asked, and it was Emrys who answered this time.

"Because the forest healed you, I suppose the forest plans to also keep you alive while you're inside it."

In that case...

I turned my face back up toward the canopy overhead. "Thank you?" I couldn't help the upward inflection as I bellowed toward the tree tops, feeling utterly ridiculous. Then I looked back to Emrys, who shrugged.

"I believe the forest will stay true to its word and keep you safe." He blinked and shook his head. "Not a sentence you hear yourself say every day."

The light was quickly fading. I yawned, and Emrys smiled, reaching for my hand. "Shall we?"

"We shall."

He guided me down a soft embankment at the base of a wide tree trunk. He leaned back, drawing me close, our limbs tangled together and my head pillowed against his neck.

"*Talamh,*" I muttered sleepily.

A leaf overhead grew to blanket size and folded over us like a cocoon, shielding us from the elements. Emrys held me tight, and soon, we both fell asleep to the sound of whispering trees.

A HAND STROKED MY HAIR AT THE SAME TIME A voice spoke softly into my ear. "Wake up, Red."

I stretched my arms wide, hearing a joint pop. "What hour is it?" I asked groggily.

"Nearly dawn," Emrys replied. "We slept longer than I had intended. We should move."

I nodded and, reluctantly, disentangled myself from Emrys. He stood and bent to pull me to my feet with ease. As soon as I was upright, prepared to follow my husband, I felt two taps on my back. Yelping, I turned to see a branch extending out toward me, bearing what looked like two pieces of fruit. Maybe bright blue apples, the likes of which I'd never seen.

"*Eat,*" the trees whispered above, clearly offering us breakfast. Who knew a forest could have such hospitality?

I exchanged a look with Emrys. "I don't suppose we want to insult the forest by refusing," he said, reaching around me to pluck one of the pieces of fruit, and I plucked the other.

"Thank you," I said, hefting the apple in my palm.

The branch retreated back to its tree. Truth be told, my stomach was grumbling fiercely. I took a bite and my mouth burst with sweetness.

We continued onward, munching our strange fruit and trekking for several hours through increasingly thick brush. But Emrys and I refused to use our blades to slash at any branches in our way, afraid we might upset the forest. Besides, the forest never allowed the path to grow *too* thick for us to pass. Vines and branches swung out of the way to allow us through, even if the fit was tight at times, and we had to navigate our steps carefully.

The forest canopy above was a bit more open now, exposing blue sky. There was also a clearing ahead through the trees, visible now. We were officially nearing the forest's exit.

"We're almost there," Emrys said. I nodded with excitement and anxiousness.

We were so close now. I could all but taste freedom—if we could survive the Void first.

But then I stopped in my tracks, as did Emrys. There was a strange noise overhead, the distinct flapping of large wings rustling the canopy. It stood out because it was unlike any other noise we'd heard in the forest so far.

"Do you hear that?"

Even before the words had left my lips, I knew Emrys heard it too. He tilted his head upward and sniffed the air, and his eyes widened as though he recognized the scent.

"I smell them," Emrys confirmed. "The king's guards are here."

55

Rose

A LARGE, FLYING CREATURE DOVE AT MY HEAD. It squawked and clawed at the back of my skull, its talons tangling in my hair and tearing out chunks. I threw up my hands and yelled, hearing Emrys—now in wolf form—grunting against a similar attack nearby.

"Gaoth," I shouted, even as my arms flailed wildly. I pictured a massive surge of wind targeting the hawk and ripping him clean off of me.

The wind responded with a howl. It charged forth and hit the hawk with the speed and force of a galloping horse, throwing the bird across the clearing where it collided and sank to the ground. He landed beside the other hawk, who Emrys had thrown off of himself.

But these shifters were tough. The pair got back on their feet rather quickly, shaking their heads and flapping their wings. Side by side, they stood and promptly transformed into their faerie selves. Definitely two of the king's guards. Twins. They blocked our path now, the final obstacle between us and our exit.

"Rogyn and Pery," Emrys greeted them, shifting back to regular form, himself.

"The king knew you would be here," the one on the right said. I had no idea which was which. Their eyes both narrowed, heads tilting at the same time.

"We are his fastest guards in our hawk form," said the other.

"So, he sent us."

"And we are under orders to drag you back—"

"—or to kill you."

Emrys sighed. "Why must you two be such a bloody nuisance?"

"We serve the king, and our king needs Rose," the one on the left said.

"Can we at least talk about this?" Emrys asked.

In response, they took two menacing steps forward in unison.

"Guess not," muttered Emrys.

My skin prickled, chest laboring under shallow breaths as my pulse increased, preparing to fight.

"Do not come any closer," I warned, holding up my hands and producing a small fireball. Beside me, Emrys bared his teeth and snarled, preparing to shift back to wolf form and attack.

The guards exchanged a murderous look and nodded. Their heads slowly turned back toward Emrys and me in unison and then, they charged with matching battle cries.

But the forest responded in a way I had not expected.

Two vines shot out from two trees, one from the left side of the small clearing and the other from the right. They hooked each of the shifter twins around their ankles and dragged them back toward the base of two opposing trunks, kicking and screaming. Once they were flush against the trunks, more and more vines shot out, covering them, wrapping around them until they were no longer visible, becoming one with the forest. Soon, they were nothing more than two person-shaped roots, forever trapped twenty feet away from each other.

I looked to Emrys, speechless, and his expression reflected back every bit of shock I felt. "Did... you see that?" I asked, rather pointlessly.

"Rogyn and Pery turned into two tree statues by the forest? Yes, I caught the show. It was quite hard to miss."

"That means the forest is still protecting us."

"It would seem so." He paused for a moment, scratching his chin. "The forest accepted my sacrifice and granted you your life. I suppose it will continue to protect that life as long as you are within its boundaries. For that, I am grateful." He tipped his head upward and shouted up at the trees. "Do you hear that? You have my undying gratitude."

I did not wish to question the forest's generosity, either. But the trees heard us and responded.

"That is the last we will help. You are on your own once you exit our forest."

The forest went quiet then. The trees no longer whispered, vines no longer snaked up trees, and not a single creature stirred. It was as though the magic of the forest had gone dormant, and now we were just standing in an ordinary patch of woods.

Together, Emrys and I moved past the root-covered bodies of Rogyn and Pery, and I could not help feeling sorrow for them. They were, after all, only doing their jobs, and now they were little more than tree food. But they had made us choose; it was them or us, and we needed to keep moving.

Now, we emerged from the forest and up ahead was the most welcome—yet unwelcome—sight. Currently, it was our route to freedom, yet also our route to a potentially swift ending. We had arrived in front of the Void, which reared up across one last clearing. I stared up at the giant wall of mist in front of us, the beckoning yet foreboding barrier separating us from the Outerlands.

"You had said that Aegan and Lysia could guarantee safe passage through the Void. How were they planning to do that? Did they know of a certain path through the Void?"

Emrys shrugged and shook his head. "They never shared all the details, but fae do not lie, and they were confident they knew a way through. Still, I should've never trusted you with them to begin with."

"You couldn't have known. They were your friends." I drew a deep breath as I continued to look ahead. "But that still means the path we forge right now will be our own, and one misstep could mean certain doom."

"It could," Emrys agreed.

"But if we stay on this side, we will be hunted. The king will find you. He'll find both of us. He will never stop, especially now that four members of his court have been slain either by our own hand or while in our pursuit."

Emrys touched the bracer on his arm, the one that concealed the eye tattoo. "That is also true. There is rumor that the king's eye can only watch on his own land. That the world beyond Sythea exceeds the boundaries of the magic. If we manage to cross into the Outerlands, we should be safe. We will know if the eyes stop moving. That means the magic is dormant."

"Which means our only path ahead is a path forward. Through that." I pointed ahead, jerking my finger as though accusing the Void of murder—which, I was certain, it had murdered plenty.

"Yes."

"Do you know why they called it the Void?" I didn't wait for him to answer, launching straight into an explanation. "My father once told me it was because the mist was a place of horrors void of happiness, void of light, void of hope. A place of true despair and sorrow. A place of death. And standing here, in front of this foggy barrier, I don't know that my father's words were far from the truth."

I looked up at the cloud as though it was our executioner—or our gallows. But I could not think that way. The Void was, at best, an unknown variable. Staying here, marked as we were by the king, with bounties likely the highest he had ever set... *that* would be ensuring our swift demises. In the Void we at least might have stood a chance.

But as I took a step forward, I felt a sharp tug on my wrist. I was spun around, my face grabbed between two large hands, and then I was being kissed until I felt dizzy. I responded in kind, wrapping my arms around Emrys's neck, drawing him closer to me, breathing him in. And I knew the very thing that was on both our minds: should this be the end of the road for us, at least we were approaching that end together.

Emrys leaned his forehead against mine and sighed, his hands trailing down to grasp my hips, giving one last, firm squeeze before releasing me.

I blinked, eyelashes fluttering as my eyes opened. Emrys stared down at me, sporting that crooked grin I had grown to know so well. Even with my eyes closed, I could map out every line of it.

"I believe I'm ready now," he said, and I smiled back up at him, summoning my courage.

"As am I."

Emrys took my hand. We stepped forward toward the mist.

Together, we entered the Void.

56

Rose

IF I'D THOUGHT THE ENCHANTED FOREST WAS A strange place, the Void was even more so. The sky was dark. Swirling mist gathered into thick bands overhead, almost as though it was about to storm despite it having been clear and sunny just outside the Void. And now, there was another problem.

"I cannot shift into wolf form," Emrys muttered beside me. I watched him try again and again, his features scrunching up with the effort, but to no avail.

I wondered if my magic worked, and we did need some light in this dim place, so it was worth a try.

"Sorcha," I murmured as a test, and at once, my fingertips sparked, providing enough light to guide us. Apparently, *my* magic worked fine.

Though part of me was sorry it did.

The light exposed bones littered all over the ground. Hundreds of them. It could sometimes be difficult to tell fae remains from human bones, because their pointed ears were made of cartilage just like humans, and those decayed long before bones did. But if you looked closely enough, fae bones possessed a certain sheen to them that human bones did not. In addition, some of these fae had wings, which was a distinct feature to tell them apart from humans. Piles of ash also flanked the bones, as though many of the remains had been charred, set aflame. Only my wildest nightmares could begin to imagine what did such a thing, and I shuddered at the possibilities.

Even worse, wights wandered nearby, too, shuffling aimlessly... until they saw my light. Their glazed eyes snapped to glare at Emrys and I in unison.

And we were immediately surrounded. Caught in the beams of those horrible, bottomless eyes as their bony jaws grinded and snapped in our direction.

They stared at us with those horrible, bottomless eyes, clacking their teeth in our direction, circling us like sharks. The stench of death wafted forth, combined with stale earth and burned flesh.

"Emrys," I whispered, instinctively nudging closer to him.

These wights would kill us. I had my sword, my magic, and Emrys his heightened senses, speed, and dagger, but we were vastly outnumbered. Emrys swung his fists again and again, punching wight after wight right in the face and knocking them down like a bow hunter shooting ducks. But they never stayed down. We would be overpowered in minutes. Maybe seconds.

But I could not allow it. We had come too far for this to be the end.

I thought about the nymph's words; she had said my power would surprise me. In many ways, it already had, considering my quick mastery of wind. But I had a feeling I'd only just begun to scratch the surface. And now my power churned through me, threatening to burst free as my emotions reached an all-time high. I did not fight it. Rather, I leaned into it just as the nymph said. I peered down at my arms and found my entire body glowing.

"Red..." Emrys's voice was apprehensive, and he took a single step back at the sight of my glowing skin.

He could not step far, because more wights closed in quickly, reaching toward us with their knobby fingers. They snapped and growled, their moans speaking to a pure, driving hunger for flesh. The time to act was now.

"Get down!" I managed to yell.

Just as he hit the ground, fire burst from every pore, my body emitting a burning, blinding light. Emrys gasped in surprise as my magic let loose, making the darkness of the Void seem like pure daylight, wiping out all the wights around us in one quick wave of flame. The smell of sizzling flesh and piercing wight shrieks was overwhelming.

When the fire dissipated, every wight within view was dust. At once depleted, I collapsed on the ground. Emrys crawled over to kneel beside me.

"Are you alright?" he asked. His face hovered over me, alight with concern.

"Just tired. That is more magic than I've ever used at once."

His thumb stroked my temple, fingertips resting behind my ear. "You are remarkable, Rose. Where did that come from?"

"My grandfather, I think. When he died, I felt some of his magic move into me. That is how I picked up the new wind power and I think it might have magnified my existing powers as well." It was the only explanation, and it still terrified me, if I was being honest.

Slowly, I sat up. With Emrys's help, I climbed back to my feet.

"Can you walk?" he asked. "Because I believe it prudent that we keep moving."

"I agree. Although I find it hard to imagine anything worse than wights."

"Don't say that, Red. The Void might see it as a challenge."

As if on cue, Emrys hunched over, his hands clapping over his ears. He groaned in pain.

'What is it?" I asked, still wobbling on my feet.

"I don't know. Something loud. You can't hear it?"

"No," I said, perking my ears but unable to pick up on whatever it was that he heard.

Maybe it was only something his sensitive fae hearing could detect that my dull human ears could not. But finally, Emrys removed his hands from his ears and stood up straight, looking all around.

"Well, that was fun." His tone dripped sarcasm and his left ear dripped a thin line of blood.

Before I could ask if he was alright, the ground started to rumble, and a mighty roar sounded. Now *that,* I heard.

Emrys's gaze flicked back to mine. "I blame you for taunting this place with your challenges," he murmured. "This way!"

Emrys grasped my hand and dragged me to the right, where a black, craggy rock jutted from the ground, just enough to block us from view of whatever approached. Though likely not for long. While my strength may have been slowly coming back, I was far from strong enough to use more magic. Certainly not to the level I just had.

The ground rumbled more intensely and the air heated around us to an almost intolerable level, as though we sat inside a quickly heating stove. The skin of my face felt like it might blister. Emrys and I huddled together behind the rock, pressing our backs to its flat, craggy surface. Another roar sounded, closer now. Much too close. The same roar I'd heard before in the Void pocket, though far off in the distance. Emrys and I both peeked over the rock together.

And gasped in unison.

"Is that a... *dragon?*" My mouth gaped. I had certainly never expected to utter those words within my lifetime.

"Yes?" He couldn't seem to help the upward inflection, appearing every bit as baffled as I felt.

The dragon was massive, at least ten yards long, its skin scaley and deep crimson in color, like dried blood. It bared its teeth, with each pointed tooth looking as long as my arm. It flapped leathery wings, and I couldn't even fathom a guess at the wingspan. It huffed and stomped its clawed feet, its eyes fierce yellow in color. From its flaring nostrils came puffs of smoke. This was a fire-breather. Now, all the charred bones made sense... and the flames that had shot out of the Void pockets during the castle siege. They were from a dragon.

"I thought they went extinct thousands of years ago," I said.

"Seems not. Because that's a dragon. And it is most certainly breathing."

The dragon edged closer to our hiding place with loud *thunks* that shook the ground and loosed little pebbles from our boulder. Soon, it would easily be able to peek over that boulder, spot us, and make us sizzle right where we sat.

Emrys peered over the rock again, then without warning, he crouched and hurled his dagger at the dragon, on a perfect collision course with the beast's eye. But midair, the dragon breathed fire, and Emrys's dagger met the flames. It melted, falling to the ground as nothing more than a rain of molten metal. It was clear blades would not work, and I was still too weak to summon more magic, meaning we were utterly stuck.

And the beast was even closer to our hiding place now.

"Go Rose, get out of here. I will distract it," Emrys said, resolute, but I grabbed his arm.

"No, you are mortal now. You can *die.*"

"I can think of no better way to die than giving you a chance to live. You deserve that."

"So do you! Would you quit being so irritatingly sacrificial?"

"No," he replied, most stubbornly. "I am not letting this *thing* get you."

I threw my hands up. "Fine, then you want to die here? Well, I've killed too. My hands have blood on them, and I shall die beside you. As your fellow murderer... And wife."

"No, Rose. You have to get through the Void. I can never make amends for my sins. But you can. You must *live*."

Emrys kissed my forehead, so tenderly. And then he jumped up without further delay, without giving me another chance to stop him.

And ran straight towards the beast.

57

Rose

"YOU PROMISED ME, EMRYS," I SHOUTED AFTER him. "You promised me we would survive together and fae are not supposed to lie!"

But he did not turn, did not acknowledge my words. Instead, he ran right toward the dragon, who roared a warning at him. A hot tear streamed down my cheek as I watched this unfold in sheer horror.

I could not let this happen. I *would not.*

I cried out as the dragon knocked Emrys clean off his feet with one well-timed swipe of its tail. The dragon hunched over Emrys, ready to breathe its fire upon him, to incinerate him so he was no more than ashes and charred bones like all the other fae remains here.

That was when a thought occurred to me.

All the remains are fae.

Suddenly, everything clicked into place. The king's questions, Aegan and Lysia "knowing" a way through the Void, Emrys not being able to shift... Now, it all made perfect sense.

Steeling my courage, I sprang to my feet and ran from my hiding place, screaming.

"Rose, no!" Emrys's voice was hoarse. But I skidded to a stop in front of his prone body, waving my arms up at the dragon and refusing to back down.

"I am not fae, I'm a witch," I yelled up at it, not certain it could understand me but praying it did. "You do not kill witches in here, only fae. And you're attacking Emrys, not me. But what you don't know is that Emrys is *with* me. So, you will protect both of us, because—"

The beast growled, a menacing, spine-chilling sound. Red heat glowed behind its bared teeth, gray smoke streaming out through the spaces between its massive canines. But I held my ground despite every muscle in my body tensing and telling me to flee.

"Hear me, I said you will protect both of us. Because I, a witch, *command it.*" The beast flared its nostrils and cocked its head slightly, its pupils pinning as though contemplating my words. "Now, heel, beast. Swallow your fire."

I knew Emrys could hear my heart beating like a drum in my chest; I wondered if the dragon could hear it, too.

The dragon looked at me curiously, and much to my surprise, it sat back on its haunches. It continued to stare with a tilted head, waiting for me to make a move.

Licking my lips, I edged closer and drew a deep, calming breath.

"What are you doing, Red?" Emrys hissed from the ground.

I didn't reply, my gaze locked on the beast's. It blinked slowly and let out a puff of heated breath that came out as white steam. Its eyes were a muted orange, its pupils elongated, vertical slits that were slightly rounded at the edges.

I held out my hand and inched closer still until I was within arm's reach, testing the dragon's reaction. When he did not flinch, I gingerly placed my palm upon the side of its snout, finding its skin dry and scaly. It jerked a little under my touch, but then seemed to relax, letting out another quick huff of steam through its nostrils this time. It blinked again like an exhausted person fighting against heavy eyelids.

Emrys looked between me and the beast incredulously, seeming unable to comprehend what was happening. It was surreal for me as well. We'd thought dragons had died out long ago, and yet here I was standing in front of one, in the flesh, with my hand upon it while hidden inside a dark Void separating Sythea from the Outerlands. Life certainly had a way of surprising us all.

The dragon groaned, and it was then that I realized it was in pain of some kind. It was not just blinking; it was *wincing*. It repositioned itself to lay flat on its belly, stretching his hind legs out behind him. Even while lying down, the dragon was as tall as at least two of me standing feet on shoulders.

"Stay still," I whispered, circling around the dragon's side to inspect. Sure enough, an arrow protruded from one of its haunches.

"The king's arrow," Emrys said in recognition. He slowly climbed to his feet but hung back. "He must have hit the dragon during the castle siege."

I nodded, remembering the king firing into the Void pocket and making something shriek from within when the arrow hit its mark.

The dragon.

"I will help you," I told the beast.

The arrow could not stay in the dragon's flesh or it would continue to fester. Without delay, I pulled the arrow free. The beast roared and its mouth puffed large smoke circles.

"It is alright," I said, examining the wound. It still bled a little, the edges red and puckered, coated in a thin layer of another shiny substance. It looked quite sore. "When I can, I will bring you a salve to soothe this. I promise."

I walked back around to the dragon's front, looking into its eyes as I spoke. His nostrils flared out again as he continued to watch me. "We seem to have a lot in common, you and I," I said, feeling a strange urge to further connect with the beast. "You have fire and so do I. See?" To demonstrate, I summoned a spark on my fingertips with a mumbled, *"Teine."* It was the tiniest of fireballs since that was all I had the energy for.

"Do not encourage its fire. My eyebrows are already singed enough," Emrys joked.

But the beast blinked in surprise at my fire, reeling back a little. A noise rumbled deep in its belly and I realized... it was *laughing?* I didn't even know that dragons were capable of humor. It peeled back its lips to flash a toothy grin—each tooth indeed as long as my arm and slick with saliva—and I smiled back. I kept my voice calm and even as I spoke again.

"Will you ensure our path is cleared of any more wights, and will you allow us to pass without further incident?" I asked. "If you do, I promise I will bring you back some salve when I can to help your wound heal faster. And show you more of my fire."

The dragon blinked several more times, then nodded slowly. With a pained groan, like an old man stretching his aching joints, it stood and turned its back to us, walking a few paces before taking off in flight. The wind created by its wings made my hair flutter wildly, and soon the dragon was gone from view, entirely swallowed by the mist of the Void.

Emrys stood beside me, bemused, with eyes trained on the misty sky where the dragon had disappeared. "Well, that was something." His head swiveled to look at me. "I think you just made friends with a dragon, Red."

I shrugged, just as bewildered by the encounter.

Together, we moved through the Void, towards the other side. Any remaining wights gave us a wide berth, and we did not stop until daylight became visible once more. I could feel the sunshine upon my face, a most welcome warmth.

Emrys and I left the Void—injured, but still breathing—and crossed the border into the Outerlands for the first time.

THE OUTERLANDS

58

Rose

WE WANDERED FOR A WHILE IN THE Outerlands, marveling at the sights. It was actually quite peaceful, not at all the wasteland I had expected to encounter. Although honestly, I had never been quite sure what to expect. I'd never thought that far ahead because part of me was convinced I would never set foot here.

In front of us was another forest, gently sloping hills, trickling streams. Some of the trees were yellowed or barren, some still green, and all was mostly quiet save for a lone bird chirping here or there. The occasional chirp provided the only indications of life; I didn't even spot any ants, spiders, or bees. Peculiar.

At first, Emrys was quiet, but then he stopped abruptly and removed his bracer. "Just as I suspected," he said as he held his arm out toward me. I leaned over to inspect. The eye tattoo on his wrist was still. Dormant, just as he'd predicted.

"So, the king cannot track us anymore?" I asked, hopeful. Instinctively, I touched the tattoo on the back of my own neck.

"That's right. We're free, Red." He shook his head as though disbelieving his own words. "We're *free*."

"We're free." I repeated the words on a whisper, and suddenly, I could not control my emotions. I found myself crying tears of joy, tears of sadness, tears of uncertainty.

Emrys and I had escaped. We had successfully fled Sythea. Together. My heart brimmed with joy, feeling close to bursting.

Emrys pulled me into his arms and kissed me thoroughly. Somehow, a moment of simple joy and comfort took a swift turn and I found myself wanting him, *needing* him right now. I did not care what in the forest might be watching. My hand slid down between us, cupping the hardened length of him. Emrys broke the kiss and looked down at me in surprise.

"Are you trying to kill me?" he rasped.

"Quite the opposite," I replied coyly, my grip tightening ever so.

A growl sounded low in the back of his throat, his nostrils flaring as he looked down at me. I needed this. Our last attempt had been interrupted by the nymph. And now, after all we had been through, and now that we were safely through the Void, we *both* needed this release. Though Emrys was holding back.

Not for long, if I could help it.

Purposely, I reached up to gently caress the shell of my husband's ear. His response was immediate.

"You know full well by now what that does to me. Do not start something you don't intend to finish," he warned, voice husky.

"Oh, I intend to finish."

"Thank fuck," he said. "Because I couldn't stop now even if I wanted to."

On my next breath, I found myself shoved, my back pressed against a tree. Emrys's knee wedged between my legs, forcing them apart. I pushed against his knee, moaning at the sweet friction it created. His mouth left my lips in favor of my neck, nipping and teasing with his teeth, pushing my cloak down my shoulders. His hands slid over my breasts, peaking my nipples through the material of my dress.

He lifted his head, his voice rough as he spoke a single command, gold eyes narrowed and pupils dilated with desire. "Turn around, Red. Right now. Brace your hands on the tree."

I did as I was told, turning and bracing my hands on the tree, wondering exactly what Emrys had in store for me. Without further fanfare, my skirts were lifted. Emrys must've shed his breeches in seconds because he sank into me from behind, deep, hard, each thrust forcing my palms to scrape against the rough bark. It seemed neither one of us had the patience for anything but the main event, and I was fine with that. I did not care that my palms would likely be torn open after this. Did not care that we were in the middle of an open forest in an unexplored world. Right now, it was just me and Emrys. Nothing else mattered.

His large hand curved around my throat from behind, applying gentle pressure. The fingers of his other hand dug into my hip. He moved faster still, each thrust hitting new spots inside me. Part of me felt like he was trying to split me in half and it hurt... but it hurt *so good.* This angle provided a whole new experience, and Emrys grunted behind me.

I did not want to stop. I let out a strangled cry, hands gripping the tree trunk like I was trying to squeeze water out of it.

"Come on, Red," he said through clenched teeth.

He reached around in front of me, his fingers finding that sweet spot between my legs, and his thrusts deepened as he stroked me in the most amazing way. It didn't take long. I was gone, gone, riding a wave of pleasure and behind me, I could tell Emrys was close, too.

Grunting, he pulled out of me all at once, but he was not done with me yet. He pulled me upright by the upper arms, spun me, and lifted my legs about his waist. Then he sunk into me, pushing my back against the tree this time. Like with my hands, the pain didn't bother me. In fact, I felt myself swiftly building towards another climax. Emrys's gold eyes flashed wolf amber, his growl feral. And when he bent to sink his teeth into the tender curve where my shoulder met my neck, I was pushed over the edge just as Emrys cried out his own release.

His arms wound around me as he eased me to my feet, my legs wobbly. Suddenly overcome, my knees buckled and I sank down to the forest floor, dragging Emrys with me.

Spent, I reached down to pull my dress back into place, and Emrys's teeth nipped lazily at my jaw as I did so. He cradled me between his knees as we both caught our breath. But when he laced his fingers through mine, he frowned and lifted my hand, exposing small cuts all over my left palm. I couldn't see it, but I could feel that my back had suffered its own share of scratches, as well.

"Perhaps I got a little carried away," he said with an edge of remorse to his voice.

"No. It's alright, I liked it."

The corner of his mouth pulled into a smirk. He lifted my palm to his lips and gently kissed each little cut. "I hate seeing you hurt, Red."

He lowered my hand and dragged his lips across my neck where his teeth undoubtedly left their indent. His tongue teased the flesh there, and I shivered.

"But I do love seeing my mark on you. Letting the world know you're mine," he purred, barely a whisper.

Strangely, I didn't mind; I *wanted* the world to know I was his, too. We belonged to each other. That much was abundantly clear now, and I wished to never be parted from him again.

"Must we move again?" I said after a while, and Emrys chuckled behind me.

"I'm afraid so. I'd much rather stay here and ravish you a dozen more times, but we are still in unexplored land. We need to keep moving."

I groaned, but he was right. Moving slowly, he stood and bent to offer me his hand, which I accepted, and he pulled me to my feet in one fluid motion.

"Do you think anyone lives on this side?" I asked.

"I'm not sure. It seems unlikely many made it through the Void in one piece."

"Although, the Void did seem to be targeting you, not me," I pointed out. "I noticed that all the bones were fae, and so were the wights. There were no witch remains inside the Void, at least none that I could see. That's what made me take a gamble with the dragon. If he was only targeting fae, I thought maybe he would not harm me."

"You nearly made my heart stop, jumping in front of the beast like that."

"I did what I had to," I replied. "Besides, you threw yourself in front of the dragon first."

"Fair point." His eyes narrowed then, head tilting to the side as he looked around and drew a deep, centering breath. "I need to try something."

I frowned, watching him. He stood still, feet shoulder width apart, his face a mask of pure concentration. After a moment, he released his clenched muscles and shook his head. "Just as I thought. I couldn't shift when we encountered the Void pocket back in the forest on the way to the castle. I couldn't shift while inside the main Void. And now, I cannot shift after having crossed through the main Void into the Outerlands."

"That actually makes sense." I nibbled my lower lip in thought. "Emrys, I don't think the Void was created due to a clash of magic, but solely by witches *for* witches. To protect them and target the fae. To give them a safe space to retreat to. That would also explain why I can use my magic in the

Void but you cannot. It is an area protected from fae magic, not witch magic. I think the king knew the same. He had tortured the truth out of Ophelia and Orinthia before he had them killed, the truth about how the Void came to be and its true purpose. I had a feeling that they had known more than they'd let on."

Emrys nodded. "Aegan and Lysia must have known it, too."

"The fact that you still cannot shift on this side tells me some of those protections are still in place in the Outerlands as well."

Emrys paused for a minute, letting those words sink in. "If that's true, then maybe we are not alone on this side. Maybe some of your kind—"

"Who goes there?" a voice demanded as though on cue.

Emrys and I whirled around to spot a very real living human, looking at us in curiosity and clutching a weapon. She meant to use it, too. Her hands drew back a wooden bow, lining up a shot. But when she examined my human features more closely, she lowered her weapon with eyes wide in shock.

"Another witch?" she said in question. "We'd thought most if not all were gone from the other side."

"We," I said. "There are more of you?"

She smiled wide. "Well, of course!"

The woman—witch—wore a flowy, midnight blue cloak that was so dark it was nearly black. Her neck and wrists were decorated with various baubles and charms that clinked when she moved. Suns, moons, stars, pentacles. She had a small, round face, her features close together, her nose sharp. Her hair was a light brown, unbrushed and skirting her waist.

I noted she had not introduced herself yet, though I was honestly so happy to be seeing one of my own kind alive and not in chains that I could cry.

The woman looked to Emrys with distrust, though he kept silent, his astute, golden eyes assessing the situation. "Why are you traveling with a faerie?" she asked, not taking her eyes off him even as she addressed me.

Frowning, I stepped between Emrys and the witch. "This isn't just any fae. This is my husband."

Her gaze snapped to mine, confounded. "Your *husband?*"

"Yes."

She placed a hand upon her hip, the other hand still tightly clutching her bow. "And why would you do such a horrendous thing as marry a fae?"

"His family endured great suffering at the hands of our kind. He has every reason to hate us, but he does not. He married me to keep me safe from his own king," I explained.

Her mouth twitched. "You think him noble?"

"I do."

"Well," she scoffed, "we will have to be the judge of this ourselves."

"You mean to bring us back to your camp?"

She nodded. "Mm-hm. The faerie's powers will be useless here and he is vastly outnumbered, so he poses little threat at the moment." Emrys did his best not to look offended by that, and the woman made an impatient gesture. "So, come. Follow me, and I will present you both to the coven."

Coven. Again, the word almost made me cry while also making me near giddy with excitement.

She set a brisk pace towards a thicker patch of forest where I assumed their coven was located, and I looked around in wonder, holding Emrys's hand all the while. It was partially to make a statement, and partially because I was trembling so badly, I felt as though I may fall down.

I spoke to the other witch as we walked. "So, the Void was created to allow witches safe passage through to the

Outerlands?" I asked, trying to make sure I had the story straight.

"That is correct," said the witch, her eyes trained on the path ahead.

"And the dragon?"

The witch laughed. "Oh, that's Rhegus. Remarkable, isn't he? The last of his kind and a wonderful guardian."

"He is something special." I paused as we entered the thicker patch of woods, careful to watch my step. Emrys had to let go of my hand to walk behind me as the path narrowed. "I don't believe I caught your name?"

"I don't believe I gave it," she said simply. She hesitated for a long while before giving me an answer. "I am Sera."

"I'm Rose," I replied. "Rose Doyle."

The witch paused in her walking mid-stride and turned to face me, eyes widening. "You're a Doyle?"

My brows furrowed at her reaction, unable to figure out if it was a good or a bad thing. "Yes, I am. Did you know anyone in my family? Did they pass through here?"

"Yours is a very powerful line. Some might even say *infamous*," she said, though I had the uncanny feeling that there was more to the story. She leaned forward and squinted at the necklace around my neck then, noticing it for the first time. Her hand darted out to lift the pendant, turning it over in her fingers. "Where did you get this?"

I looked down and felt a pang. "A witch named Ophelia gave it to me."

Her eyes widened further. "Ophelia? Was she with Orinthia?"

"Yes," I replied with surprise. "I met them both."

"Where did you see them?"

"I..." I trailed off, my voice breaking. "I saw them in the fae dungeons. I am sorry to say that... they were both executed."

"No." Sera's eyes began to well up, her hand going to her mouth. I knew what she was feeling all too well. "They were my sisters. I should have gone with them."

"I am so sorry." Not knowing what else to do, I removed the necklace and placed it into Sera's palm, closing her hand in my own. "It belonged to someone you loved, so you should have it."

"Thank you." She sniffled, her expression dissolving into a frown. "This necklace has touched dark magic."

My mouth gaped a little, thinking back to how I had used it in a locating spell. When I didn't respond, Sera looked to the necklace again in her palm and her eyes darkened.

"I believe we have crossed paths for a reason, sister. It seems you are willing to do what it takes to win this war, and we need more of that around here."

I did not know what that meant, nor how to respond. Behind me on the narrow path, Emrys stood so close I could feel his body heat against my back.

Sera continued. "Ophelia and Orinthia were executed by the fae," she said, and her accusing glare darted over my shoulder to Emrys, who had been staying wisely silent this entire time.

His hand curved around my hip possessively, like he feared where this conversation was headed. So did I.

"Not by Emrys," I replied quickly. "He tried to help them. We were planning on breaking them out together, but the king got to them first."

"Why couldn't he have gotten them out sooner?"

"It is complicated. And difficult to sneak out of castle grounds undetected."

Sera huffed, clearly looking to lay blame. "Still, it was his kind that killed them."

She jerked her finger in Emrys's general direction. The next instant, I felt Emrys's lips near my ear. "Do not escalate this, Red," he warned. "Not on my behalf."

But I did not acknowledge his words. Of course, I would come to my husband's defense. "Maybe, but as I said, it was a witch who did terrible things to his family when he was a mere child—a Doyle, my own flesh and blood. Neither side is blameless. I understand that you are grieving, Sera, and I am very sorry for your loss. But we cannot lay blame on a single individual for the sins of their entire kind's past."

She disregarded everything I said in favor of asking another question. "Did Ophelia and Orinthia suffer?"

My breath hitched in my chest. "They were hanged. I believe it was quick," I lied.

Sera must have seen through my lie, because she let out a sob of anguish, her hand clamping over her mouth once more.

"You were the coven leader they spoke of," I said. "Ophelia told me, 'Keep your faith, sister. Time is the prize.' That was you, wasn't it?"

Sera nodded, a quick jerk of her head. "This was my fault. I was supposed to go with them, but I had to stay to help ward off the blight." A tear slipped from the corner of her eye.

"What blight?" I asked.

She sniffled, hastily wiping the tear from her cheek as she replied. "There is a blight slowly taking over the Outerlands. It's been killing all the plants, making the wildlife sick. We don't know where the blight is coming from, but no amount of magic aimed at it can stop it, only slow it a little at best. We sent Ophelia and Orinthia back to Sythea to try to determine if the source of the magic was somehow faerie, and also to observe how things looked in the mainland overall, if the fae were relenting. But it seems my sisters were captured, never to return. We sent out some

Void pockets to look for them as well, but could not find them." She shot a dark look in Emrys's direction. "And now we know why."

That explained the increase in Void pockets; they were looking for Ophelia and Orinthia. Maybe they had sensed another witch in the process—me—and assumed I was in danger with my fae companion. The Void pockets were only trying to help a fellow witch. Which meant they also must have been responsible for the castle siege. I was about to ask, but Sera looked so devastated, it stayed lodged on the tip of my tongue.

"Obviously, nothing we did made any difference," Sera lamented, hand over heart as though she felt a physical ache inside her chest. "And now, they are dead. Oh, my sisters."

"I am so sorry." I reached out to touch her arm, to offer what little comfort I could, but she flinched back. Sera's eyes flicked to Emrys again, and my stomach twisted at the amount of hatred in her eyes. My hand retreated away from Sera, reaching back for Emrys instead. He didn't hesitate to lace his fingers through mine, letting me know he was there, right behind me.

"Come," Sera finally said after swiping away the last of her tears. She turned her back on us to lead again. "We are not too far now."

As we moved, I could see what Sera meant about the blight. We passed two dead rabbits, a dead squirrel with its black tongue sticking out, even a deer, all in various stages of decomposition with no outward signs of trauma. They were not attacked; they had just *died.* Additionally, the deeper we got into the Outerlands, the more I saw grass and plants that were dried up and yellowed in places, many of the trees shedding leaves that hadn't even turned brown, but black. It was unsettling.

I thought about the curse in the grimoire, the one that withered crops and killed livestock. Was it possible a witch—a dark witch—had been responsible for such a blight? But the kind of magic it would take to bring a blight to an entire land as opposed to just one household... it would be magic beyond my comprehension. Though the Void had been created by similar magic; it was not impossible. But why would a witch do this to their own people?

A thick patch of pines rose up before us. Thankfully, those were still green. The path widened again such that Emrys and I could walk side by side once more. He exchanged a questioning glance with me, and I could only shrug.

Up ahead, Sera remained quiet, leading without speaking and never slowing her pace. Overhead, charms and talisman tinkled in the breeze from low branches. Multiple tree trunks bore carvings of symbols—I recognized some of them as symbols to ward off evil, a sure sign that witches roamed nearby. My heart pounded. Emrys heard it and squeezed my hand.

After another half hour's walk through the throng of trees, the forest opened to a wide clearing. At the far side of the clearing were the distinct shapes of a village, and yet again my jaw dropped. It was much more extensive than I had imagined, slightly reminiscent of the castle village in mainland Sythea, though not nearly as big or bustling. But there were a couple little booths that were akin to markets, a small square, and rows of wooden huts that served as homes, with thatched roofs.

There must have been dozens of surviving witches, maybe even a hundred. More than I ever dreamed possible, all just at the other side of the Void. All this time, my family and I had a safe haven to go to without even realizing it. Maybe if we had known and fled here, my parents and my grandmother would still be alive. The thought was like a swift punch to the stomach.

By the time we reached the thick of the village, dusk was swiftly approaching. The village began to light up with flickering torches all around, casting shadows against the setting sun that painted the sky with bright colors.

Sera took us on a quick tour. She showed us the gardens and vegetable patches behind the shack houses. Some of the crops were withered, but enough still grew to provide for the village. That would likely not be the case for long as the blight spread, and their stores might not be enough to last through winter, either.

Beside the crops were the animal pens. They seemed rather sparse, containing just two cows, three horses, five chickens, and one bleating sheep. Surely, that couldn't have been *all* the animals they possessed. Unless the blight had already taken out that many.

Sera did not say much, merely pointing things out as she led us toward the bonfire and ritual location. There was a large circle of dirt filled with little stones, ash, and charred wood. Beside it, a large circle made of carefully placed stones.

And beside *that*... I gasped at a noose hanging from the thick limb of a massive, craggy tree. It swung gently in the breeze as though waving at those below. I wondered how many had hung there. And *who* had hung.

My head spun as other witches gathered around of all ages, shapes, sizes, and colors, all staring at us curiously. They murmured to each other, their eyes never leaving Emrys and me. Two intruders, and one of them faerie. Some of them even looked a little frightened. I did not feel any warmth or welcome coming from them. Rather, they stared at me with cold distrust, their expressions identical in their judgment.

"Now, I am afraid there is some business we must attend to," Sera said once the brief tour was complete.

"And what is that?" I asked.

She pointed her chin at Emrys. "The fae."

Emrys and I exchanged a look. "What about him? I told you he is my husband."

"Child, it does not matter who he is to you; he still *is* what he *is*, and we have a rule here in the Outerlands. In fact, it is one of our *only* rules."

"And that is?" My mouth dried as I awaited Sera's reply.

What came out of her mouth next made my heart sink to my toes. She licked her lips and looked pointedly at Emrys as she spoke.

"That any faerie who enters here must face trial."

59

Emrys

ROSE'S EXPRESSION GREW PANICKED AS I WAS seized for custody by two large male witches. I did not fight them. Deep down, I had known this was coming. I could tell that Sera didn't trust me. Could feel the hate rolling off of her in waves. I understood the feeling all too well. That consuming, driving need for vengeance.

Iron shackles were slapped around my wrists the same way I had once slapped them around Rose's wrists. The same way I'd shackled *so many* witch bounties. Rose jumped in front of me, waving her hands. Her voice shook.

"He is my husband," she said. "Surely you can make an exception for that."

"We make exceptions for no fae," Sera replied.

The witch's eyes narrowed. I recognized someone who'd already made up their mind when I saw one. She would not budge.

"Even the *fae king* made an exception for me. When I showed up to the castle married to Emrys, he could've had me hanged on the spot. Instead, he welcomed me."

Sera lifted a brow. "And how *welcome* did you *actually* feel?"

"That doesn't matter. The point is that he never put me in a dungeon or on trial."

"Only because one of his own decided to make you his little pet." Her gaze darted to mine quickly. Like a snake flicking its tongue.

Rose scoffed. "I am not Emrys's pet. I am his wife."

She was right about that. And Sera was really starting to piss me off with her assumptions.

"Is that what you keep telling herself?"

I didn't care for the witch's smug look, either. As though she considered herself above Rose for never having been "tricked" by a fae.

"It's true." Rose put her hands on her hips. Held her ground. "He loves me. He gave up everything for me. And I love him."

Her emerald eyes met mine. My throat constricted.

"Well, we are not fae, nor do we make any exceptions for them," Sera repeated. "How do you think we managed to survive all these years? We set up the Void to protect us, but on several rare occasions, a faerie or two has managed to sneak through, the ones Rhegus and the wights couldn't take care of."

"And what became of them?" Rose asked. Though judging by her tone, she already knew the answer. As did I.

The two witches at either side of me tightened their grip needlessly. I wasn't planning to fight. Not right then, anyway.

Sera replied, "We put them on trial to determine they were pure of heart. The ones who were not pure of heart were executed by the next rising of the moon."

Rose's face paled further. "And how many of them passed the trial and were released?"

"None," Sera replied evenly, and now Rose gasped out loud.

"Emrys is *good.*" She practically shrieked the words. "Can you not trust the word of a fellow witch?"

"The word of a witch is compromised when she has been bedded by a fae. How do we know you weren't enchanted by him?"

"He's a shifter. He does not possess enchantment powers, and his magic is nullified in the Outerlands. Surely if I were under an enchantment, it would have worn off now." Rose's face reddened. She was fighting so hard for me and I loved her all the more for it. But I already knew that this was a fight we would never win. Any attempts on Rose's part would just get her into deep shit, too. I was already firmly planted in shit; she didn't need to be stuck in the pile beside me.

"Rose," I whispered. I knew she heard me; that heartbeat always gave her away.

"Well, we cannot be too safe when it comes to the sneaky and manipulative fae," Sera continued. "And we will not break tradition now. His trial will occur by the midnight high moon."

"No!" Rose shouted as the witches pinned her arms to her sides to keep her from running to me. As they dragged me away. "Emrys!"

I wanted to tell her everything was going to be alright. But I knew nothing of the sort. Instead, I held her gaze. I mouthed the words, "I love you." And I went willingly with the witches.

"Let *go* of me!" I heard Rose shouting. Her voice soon faded.

The witches gripping me tight steered me through the village, deeper into the woods. They dragged me into a small, secluded building.

Their dungeons.

I said nothing as the witches opened the door. Nothing as they yanked me inside. Nothing as they shoved me into a damp, empty cell.

E.J. REKAB

And I continued to hold my tongue as they slammed the door and left me alone in the darkness.

60

Rose

"WHERE ARE THEY TAKING HIM?" I demanded. Sera's hand was on my arm, holding me back. I tried to wrench free, but she held tighter—the woman was strong.

"To our jailhouse. The accommodations aren't that bad for prisoners. Certainly, better than the accommodations witches are given in the fae dungeons," Sera said. "And I suggest you calm yourself, or we will be forced to calm you by our own methods."

My body trembled with rage, with fear, with uncertainty. I had been so excited to find some of my own people, only to realize they were just as bloodthirsty as the fae. I could barely stand the thought, my disappointment nearly palpable.

"Please, just let my husband go," I begged. "All we want is to continue on our way and live in peace."

"Peace?" Sera shook her head in disbelief and stifled a mirthless chuckle under her hand. "Sister, we gave up any hope for peace long ago. It is kill or be killed. This is how we survive. As for your *husband,*" she said the word with distaste, "if he proves to be pure of heart, he will be released. So, you have nothing to worry about, unless your fae has something to hide."

I said nothing in reply. I was quite certain Emrys had many secrets he would prefer this community of witches never learned about.

Sera sighed. "Sister, I worry about you. Consorting with the faeries as you are. I fear you have been tainted."

"Tainted?" Now it was my turn to sigh. "I spent the better part of my life running from the fae. I lost my mother, father, and grandmother to them. I was taunted often while in their castle. I saw others suffer great cruelty at their hands. Believe me, I know perfectly well what the fae are capable of, and I will never forget it, either. But I also know that not *all* fae are bad. Just like us, there is both good and bad amongst them."

"You dare compare witches to fae?" Sera's face pulled into an expression of disgust. "At least we give them trials. That's a bigger courtesy than any faerie has ever afforded a witch."

"She is right. All fae deserve death. Remember what they did to your family." My head snapped up at the familiar whispering in my mind.

But... I wasn't in the castle near the grimoire anymore. I had thought I was beyond its influence for now. Unless...

"Do you have a grimoire here?" I blurted, and Sera looked to me in surprise.

"You hear it calling to you?"

Should I admit to such a thing? Although, I had little choice; Sera likely recognized the signs of a grimoire calling to a fellow witch, meaning I could not hide it. "I do."

"Come and find me," the voice said, this one raspier than the last.

"What is the grimoire telling you?" Sera asked, brow raised.

"It's telling me that I need to find it."

Sera's lips curved into a slight smile. "Then, the grimoire beckons you wisely. They do not call to every witch, you know. Only those with the most power."

Lucky me, I thought.

"I think you ought to see it. Perhaps it will get you thinking more clearly." She turned away and beckoned me forth. "Come."

I felt the eyes of other witches upon me, judging me just as harshly as the fae had. Hugging my middle to self-soothe, I followed Sera. Emrys still had his trial before any decisions were made, and I would find a way to stop all this. But for now, I had no choice but to do as Sera asked.

She led me through camp, past other witches who stared at me curiously. "She married a faerie?" I heard them whispering to each other, and I felt my ears grow hot.

At the far edge of the witches' encampment sat a small hut with a woven grass roof. Sera led me through the door. Inside, the room was tiny, nothing more than a single window, four wooden chairs, and a little table which housed the grimoire. It called to me louder now, and I was afraid, yet I was drawn to it like a bee to a flower. My voice shook as I spoke.

"You just leave it here out in the open? Don't you fear it will be taken?"

"Taken?" She laughed it off. "No. But the grimoire calls to you. Touch it."

Before I could protest, she grasped my hand and placed it on the leatherbound book, and at once, my hand tingled, from my fingers up to my shoulder. I yanked my hand back.

"You feel its power," she observed.

My eyes were drawn to the cover. I recognized it because I had seen it once, long ago. It felt instantly familiar, yet foreign, like I recognized the energy it gave off even at a distance. Even buried beneath the dirt.

This was my family's grimoire. The one that was lost.

"How did this get here?" I asked.

"It was recovered from the ruins of Astyrtown."

"It once belonged to my family."

"That isn't surprising." Sera nodded as though she had expected as much. "The Doyle line is very strong."

And very corrupt, it seemed.

Unable to resist, I opened the book. There were sleeping spells, memory extraction spells, nightmare spells...

Its writing and illustrations were very similar to the grimoire in the castle. Also, there were pages torn out, and I wondered if one of the torn-out pages was an immortality spell like the one my grandfather used.

There were also spells to reanimate the dead, and I instantly thought of the wights. This all but confirmed that the Void had been created by witch magic—the dark arts, no less.

"What do you think?" Sera asked.

I did not reply, transfixed.

"Should you get any ideas," she continued, "this grimoire is heavily protected by magic. So, your fae husband could not steal nor use it, nor could you steal it. No one can; this book cannot leave this room. I only brought you here to test the grimoire's influence on you, to see if you can hear it. And you can. Of course, you can."

But did I want to?

I remembered how adamant my grandmother had been about never touching the grimoire.

No, I did not want to be corrupted. I did not want to give myself to dark power, to blood magic.

"Kill them all," the voice in my head hissed, and I slammed the book shut.

This had been a mistake. I wanted nothing to do with the grimoire, no matter if it belonged to my family or not. Sera was studying my expression, eyebrows knitted together.

"I need some air," I said.

Abruptly, I left the hut and walked outside, hugging my middle and shivering.

Hearing the grimoire calling me back all the while.

61

Emrys

IT WAS MY SECOND TIME BEING CRAMMED INSIDE a dungeon within a few days. Couldn't say I was a fan.

The night was strangely silent. In Sythea, you would typically hear the chirping of crickets. The gentle hooting of owls. A shout or two from the village, the drunken stragglers who made their way home well after everyone else. The silence here quite reminded me of the Void. Perhaps it was the so-called blight at work, taking even the nighttime creatures and leaving them for dead.

There came a clatter. The door to the dungeons opened and moonlight spilled into my cell. Two witches stepped inside. It was the same two who had dragged me in here earlier.

"Time for your trial, fae," one of them said. Couldn't even look me in the eye. Though the other one glared at me enough for the both of them.

I could only nod as they unlocked my cell and grabbed me. I didn't struggle as they marched me back through their village. As they dragged me toward the ritual area clad in iron shackles, not caring a lick if I stumbled in the process.

A bonfire was already going. Flames raged high, dancing in the moonlight. Adjacent to the fire, dozens of witches had gathered. They formed a perfect circle beneath the moon's glow.

The witches were all cloaked, faces obscured by hoods. They chanted and swayed together. Buzzed like a hive. The circle parted as I approached, providing a wide enough opening for the guards to shove me into the middle and push me to my knees. Then the circle closed again, swallowing me whole. I could just make out Rose's form between some of the other witches' shoulders. I sighed in relief; at least she was alright. But she looked so frightened for me. I tried to offer her a small smile of reassurance.

"It's alright," I mouthed. In all likelihood, I was fucked. But if Rose was alright, I was too. That was all that mattered.

The witches stopped chanting and began to hum low as Sera stepped into the circle and flipped back her hood. Her eyes locked on mine. Reflected back the moonlight. Her voice boomed almost as loud as King Armynd's when she spoke.

"Emrys of the High Fae, you stand trial now for your crimes. During this trial, we need to determine that you are pure of heart. If your heart is found to be pure, you may go free. If not, however, you will hang with the rising of the next moon."

I nodded slowly, accepting my fate one way or another. Surrounded as I was, there was no stopping this anymore than one could stop the sun from rising. I waited with bated breath as Sera stepped forward and placed her hand upon my forehead. The witches began to chant louder and sway again as Sera herself mumbled some words. She closed her eyes to concentrate.

And with her concentration... came rolling waves of pain.

It started from my head, emanated through my skull. It felt like she was digging with a hot poker through my brain. Plucking memories one by one as a hook would a fish from a pond.

I could not help but let out a startled cry as memory after memory was torn from me, and I felt a distinct ripping sensation. As the tearing sensation intensified, I almost feared my spine was about to be yanked out through my skull.

I could see the memories as she dislodged them from the far corners of my mind. I saw myself as a child being cursed, bare feet slipping in the blood of my family. I saw myself meeting Aegan and Lysia and the king. I saw myself agreeing to be a part of the king's employ, and then... *shit.* I saw myself hunting down bounties. Watching witch after witch hang. Finally, I saw myself meeting Rose in the woods for the first time. Slapping shackles around her wrists. My hand curved around her throat... And then...

And then it was over.

I let out a grunt as Sera released me. Her eyes flew open and she cradled her hand against her chest as though I had burned her.

"This fae is *not* pure of heart," she bellowed. "He was a bounty hunter for the high king himself! He served on the king's court! I saw it right there in his memories. You should have seen how many of our kind he shackled and dragged to the king for torture and execution. And he did it for nothing more than his own personal gain."

The witches in the circle now hissed like serpents toward me. Pulled their lips back from their teeth. One threw a large rock, bashing me square in the face. Warm blood trickled from the open gash it made. I cursed, spit. But took it. Rose screamed my name. More witches hefted stones in their palms and their eyes spoke of vengeance, of bloodlust. Directed at me.

Before they could launch their projectiles, Sera held up a hand.

"Stop!" she shouted. Immediately, everyone fell silent. Sera paced the circle slowly. Caught the gaze of each individual she passed in turn. This witch had the clear authority here. "You know how this goes. Drop your stones for now. You all will have your justice." She turned her attention back to me. Her mouth curved as she said the words I had been dreading. Yet expecting.

Well, fuck.

"This faerie will hang by the rising of tomorrow's moon."

62

Rose

*T*HE FAERIE WILL HANG BY THE RISING OF *tomorrow's moon.*

Those were, quite possibly, the worst words I had ever heard. It was nighttime now, and Emrys's execution would be tomorrow night, which meant my husband had one day left to live. Unless I could find a way to stop it.

"No," I gasped, desperate to reach Emrys.

He was already being dragged away again through a part in the opposite side of the circle. I tried to shove through the crowd to get to him, throwing my elbows into the sides of the cloaked witches hissing at him, only to be shoved back with force.

"Emrys!" I shouted, but my cries were swallowed by the angry crowd.

I would not let this stand. I would *not* just sit here and let them drag my husband away to his execution, no matter the consequences.

"Teine," I shouted.

A fireball grew in my hand, taking on the shape of a raven. I would burn these witches. I would burn them *all* to get to Emrys, to get him safely out of here. But I never got the chance as I felt warm breath next to my ear.

"Sleep, sister," were the last words I heard before I passed out cold.

ROSE RED

I BLINKED AWAKE, MY SURROUNDINGS SLOWLY coming into focus. I was... lying on a bed? The material was rough, stuffed with grass, much like mine was back in the cabin. But this was not my cabin, so where was I? My memory was foggy.

I stared overhead at a thatched roof. I was in a cottage—one of the witch's homes. Then it all came rushing back in an instant, and my pulse began to speed, chest shaking with each breath as I remembered what brought me here.

Emrys.

He was in danger; he had been sentenced to death. Oh, stars, what if it was already too late?

My gaze darted out the window and I sighed in relief. It appeared to still be close to noon judging by the high position of the sun. Unless I had been sleeping for longer than a day and already missed the execution. I had no idea how long a sleeping spell would last, which must have been what made me slip from consciousness so readily. It was clearly a spell lifted from the grimoire, which was, at best, unpredictable.

Panicked, I sat up straight in bed, head darting around wildly.

"The faerie has not hanged yet. It is only midday," Sera confirmed as she walked toward the bed, bringing me a wooden bowl.

Had she been here this whole time? It took me a moment to realize the bowl was filled with hot broth. I accepted it, unsure what else I could do at this point. Throw it in her face? What good would that do? Though I did not lift the bowl to my lips, just letting it sit on my lap instead.

Sera sat beside me on the bed. "I am glad you're awake, because there is so much I need to ask you," she said. "Child, how did you survive all that time out there, and how did you stray so far?"

"There is too much to tell in one sitting," I said. My voice wavered, suddenly fighting back tears, which I did my best to blink back. I inhaled a deep, calming breath before speaking again. "Did you cast a spell on me?"

"A sleeping spell," Sera replied. Of course, it was her who cast the spell. "Just to calm you. You were breaking down and created a fireball that could have injured someone. Your magic certainly lives up to the Doyle reputation."

Sera, obviously, consulted the grimoire far more frequently than I had imagined, which made her a master of the dark arts. I shuddered at the thought. That did not sit well with me at all, because I'd always thought my kind to be above that. But then, it was one of my kind who also put a horrible curse on Emrys as a child—my own flesh and blood, no less.

"I do hope you are seeing reason now," Sera continued. "We need you as part of the resistance, sister. You are powerful, and you are important to our cause."

"What cause? What resistance?" I set the bowl of broth onto a small wooden table beside the bed and leaned forward with interest.

"We have been testing our control over the Void," she explained. "Namely, expanding the Void into pockets that can appear anywhere throughout Sythea, pockets we can send our wights through, our dragon through, and even walk through ourselves to lay siege. Pretty soon, the Void pockets will work past any faerie magic and protections, and we will be able to walk directly through the Void into hundreds of pockets that can open into any part of Sythea.

We can siege to our heart's content. Take back everything that is ours, everything that was taken from us."

"When you attacked the castle with those Void pockets, that was all you conducting a test." It wasn't a question, because I already knew the answer. I just wanted Sera to confirm my suspicions aloud.

"We knew it was the center of the fae community and decided to see if we could slip past its defenses. We were successful, and now that we know it is possible, we are moving forward with our plans. All the fae will perish so that we can take back what they so brutally stripped from us. Tell me, sister, are you on our side?"

So, the witches were plotting to expand the Void and release its many terrors and creatures upon the fae, and they wanted my help.

I thought about the innocent fae children in the castle town, and people like Emrys, and Korvyn, Feyleen, Goro. Despite being human, even Jasper would likely get caught in the crossfire. The witches were speaking of full-on slaughter without discrimination, meaning they would be cutting down good people along with the bad.

"You know what we could really use to turn the tides in our favor? A grimoire," I said, wanting to test how far Sera was willing to go, how afraid I should be.

"Of course. That is the plan." I tried to suppress the shudder that coursed through me as Sera nodded in excitement, her eyes lighting up. "Did you know the Void was created with grimoire magic?"

I did now. "Are you afraid of giving yourself over to the dark arts?"

"Not if it means defeating the fae," she replied quickly.

"What if I told you that I know another grimoire still exists, aside from the one you have here? With even more spells?"

"You have one in your possession?"

"I do not. But I believe I know where one is being kept. And I will help you all get it. Surely, two grimoires are more powerful than one." The lie rolled off my tongue; I was doing what I must to endear Sera to me, to convince her that I was on her side.

I refused to participate in mass slaughter, no matter which side it came from, and I knew that I would have to find a way to stop this war at all costs. Because there would likely be nothing left of Sythea. And if it took betraying my own kind to stop this madness, then that was what I had to do.

Sera's smile turned wicked. "Yes, we can always use more power." The smile melted into a skeptical expression. "But given that you married a corrupt faerie, why would you help us willingly?"

"I wish to have revenge, also," I said evenly, trying not to let my tone betray anything. "You were right. It turns out I *was* under a faerie enchantment. It took being around my own kind for a while and being put under that sleeping spell to wake up with a clear head. I know now that I married Emrys against my will; it was all for his personal gain. Why else would I marry the bounty hunter who threatened to turn me over for torture and execution?"

"In his memories, I saw him shackling and choking you, the brute." Sera placed her hand atop mine and squeezed like a friend might, though I knew she was not my friend. No matter how she pretended, all she wished to do was use me, and it took an effort to not recoil. "I am very glad you are safe and free, and very glad a witch as powerful as you is joining our cause. We need you." I tried not to flinch.

"Thank you for saving me. You pulled me out from under his evil grasp and I will forever be in your debt."

"It is what we witches do for each other. It is how we protect our own kind." She sighed deeply. "We are preparing for war, Rose. With the blight encroaching more and more, we will soon run out of resources here. But the coven and I will spread the Void throughout Sythea. And we will not rest until every scum of a fae is dead."

I simply nodded and bit my lip despite her words making me physically ill. Deciding to change tactics and begin enacting what little plan I had so far, I put on a show of wincing in pain.

"Are you injured, sister?" Sera asked.

"Yes, I was injured earlier coming through the Enchanted Forest and Void." I gestured toward my shoulder, concealed by my cloak. "Nothing a good salve can't fix."

"Well, we have plenty of salves. I will bring you what you need."

Sera left briefly and returned a couple minutes later with a small bottle of dark-colored salve. "Would you like me to apply it for you?" she asked, holding up the bottle.

"No, thank you so much. I can apply myself, if I could just have a moment of privacy?"

"I will step outside for a moment while you apply then. And please, drink the broth," she said, gesturing to the bowl on the table beside the bed. "It is bone broth, very nourishing."

Once she stepped out and pulled the door shut behind her, I snuck the bottle of salve into the folds of my cloak. The salve was not for me, of course, but for something else that needed it. I had a plan... involving a dragon.

When Sera knocked again, I stood up slowly. "May I please just speak to Em—the fae, once more before his execution?"

Her brow arched. "Why would you wish to see your captor again?"

"I simply... need closure. I must find out why he did what he did, and tell him what I *really* think of him and his horrid kind."

Sera examined my expression and for a long, tense moment, I had no idea how she was going to respond. But mercifully, she nodded. "That can be arranged. I do not blame you for wanting to get your last word after what he did to you."

I forced a shaky smile upon my lips. "Thank you."

"Come, child. The sleeping spell should have worn enough for you to walk."

I followed her out the door, through the village, deeper into the woods towards what I could only assume was the prison where Emrys was being held. I was surprised to see it was little more than a windowless cabin, though I could only assume the interior contained cages with magic-reinforced bars.

Sera unlocked the outer door and moved to walk inside with me, but I stopped her.

"Please, can I have a moment alone with him?" I asked. "There are some things that transpired that... I am embarrassed for others to hear, things that happen between a husband and wife that I... need to confront him about. Alone. I will not be long, I promise. Keep watch at the door if you must."

Thank the goddess, Sera was quick to comply, and I only hoped I could come up with a plan in the meantime.

"Of course, sister," she replied. "Take the time you need. I will be waiting just outside for you. And do not worry, the fae cannot harm you. Not only are his powers nullified in the Outerlands, but he is also weakened by the iron bars of his cage."

Ironically, the fae was not the one I was worried would hurt me. Not anymore.

I walked through the door and Sera closed it behind me. It was dark inside, as there were no windows, similar to the dungeons at the castle. The only light came from the slight opening under the main door.

"Sorcha," I whispered, my palm sparking.

With my hand light guiding me, it did not take long to spot Emrys at the far end of the room. He stood inside a small cage, staring at me through the bars. The cage was tall enough for him to stand—barely—but not wide enough for him to lie down without curling his long legs up. He did not seem surprised to see me; he had probably smelled me before I even entered, and his eyes were beams trained on mine now. As I approached, my heart felt like it might leap from my chest at the sight of him, and the state he was in.

"I am so sorry. I wish I could've come sooner, but they had me under a sleeping spell. I had to convince them I was under a fae enchantment before to get them to agree to let me visit you at all."

Emrys shook his head. "You've nothing to apologize for."

"Yes, I do. These are my people."

"Hush," he gently admonished, and I held my tongue to let him speak. "Know this. Even if I should hang come nightfall, I would do so with no regrets. At least I will die having had the privilege of loving you. And I shall die happy."

A tear escaped my eye and trailed down my cheek. "You cannot talk as though we've already lost this fight."

He lifted a brow, his scar dancing. "Haven't we?"

"No. I refuse to accept that." I grasped Emrys's hand through the bars. "I hate seeing you in this cage," I murmured.

He pulled back. "I don't. I was responsible for the incarceration and deaths of so many of your kind. The coven was right in their judgment."

"No, they are not. I can guarantee there is not a soul among them—other than the children—without blood on their own hands. And they plan to slaughter the remaining fae indiscriminately. They cannot act this way and pass judgment on you. It is hypocritical."

"Well, it's no matter. I will hang in a few hours. The sun is already getting lower outside, and dusk is swiftly approaching."

"No," I replied, my voice breaking. "I love you. Stars, *I love you,* and I refuse to watch you hang." It was not the first time I'd said the words out loud, but it was the first time I said them directly to Emrys.

Emrys's nostrils flared at my admission, mouth curving into a sad smile despite the situation. "I love *you,* Red. Too bloody much to let you throw everything away for me. I can see in your eyes that you are about to do something very stupid on my behalf. Don't."

"That is not your choice." My gaze shifted. "These bars are iron. They may burn and weaken a faerie, but witches are unaffected by it. I will break you out."

"Then you will be a traitor to your kind. You will never be welcomed back. They will *hunt* you."

"You mean the same way you are now a traitor to *your* kind after what you did for me?" I shook my head. "We will simply both be in the same boat. But that's alright. We can survive together, can't we?"

"Perhaps, but—"

"But what?"

"I cannot let you—"

"You are not *letting* me do anything." I was already directing my attention at the bars. "Step back. These bars are iron, but I also sense a certain power coming forth from them. They are likely guarded by a little witch magic as well. But given that I am a witch, I should still be able to do this…"

"Do what?"

Rather than explain further, I showed him. *"Teine,"* I muttered, and my hands warmed as I touched the bars.

The magic on the bars protested, stinging my flesh, but I refused to let go until I had melted enough of the metal to break the spell and strip it away. I held on, grunting against the pain pricking my hands as the bar melted under my grip. When the metal was pliable enough, I bent the bar downward, then did the same thing to the next one, providing a wide enough opening for Emrys to slip through. We needed to move fast; Sera would be coming in at any moment to see what was taking so long

Holding his breath and making himself as flat as possible, Emrys squeezed through the opening between the bars, still cuffed.

This part was trickier; I would have to be extra careful to not burn his skin. He must have realized what I was thinking, because he said, "Do what you must, Red."

I nodded. Emrys held his hands as wide apart as he could, stretching the chain as far as it would go. I pinched the middle link between my fingers, attempting to focus all the heat there. Emrys hissed as the metal around his wrists heated, too. But I was almost done. The link in the middle of the cuffs glowed red.

"Try pulling them apart?" I said.

He did as I asked and the cuffs snapped apart. Emrys had blistering around his wrists, but not as bad as I had imagined. Emrys, hands now free, reached for me, but a loud bang made us both jump.

"Are you alright in there, sister?" Sera's voice called.

"Yes," I shouted back. "I am almost done!"

We desperately needed to move, but Emrys caught my arm. "Are you very sure you wish to do this?"

"Yes."

"Before it's too late, I could tell them you are still under my thrall and I forced you to melt the cage bars. But once we leave here, I do not think they will ever welcome you back."

"Then so be it. All I know is that this has to stop. We need to find a way to bring peace, Emrys. No matter what. Neither side will be satisfied until both our species are wiped out."

"Alright. But before we can stop any wars, there is still the matter of making it out of this jail alive."

But I had a plan for that too. *"Gaoth,"* I muttered.

A gust of wind burst through the prison like a stampeding bull, blowing a hole right in the far wall, big enough for Emrys and I to climb through. I could see forest outside—our path to freedom.

"Now, we run," I said. "Straight to the Void."

THE DEADLANDS

63

Rose

"TRAITOR!" SERA SCREAMED AFTER US AS we burst forth into the forest. "Help!" she bellowed, calling for the others.

She had been waiting for me in the front of the prison, but the building was very small, and she'd be upon us in no time. We could not slow, could not look back. One misstep could spell our doom.

We had a long run ahead of us, and I didn't know if we would make it all the way to the Void going full speed, meaning we would have to outmaneuver the other witches somehow.

I heard Sera toss a curse after us, hex after hex lifted from the grimoire, I was certain.

"Talamh," I shouted just as Emrys and I passed through a narrow path between the trees. I envisioned my intent, and at once, the branches of the surrounding trees grew across the path, blocking it completely. That would only buy us a few extra minutes at best.

We were quicker than Sera, maybe, but she had others with her now, and their combined power was likely far greater than my own. Sera wasn't the only one who dabbled in the dark arts, and the possibilities were endless, which meant we would have to get creative. We would have to hide.

I knew my limbs couldn't take me much farther running full speed. Emrys had more endurance as a fae than

I did as a human, and he gripped my hand tight to keep me in pace with him, but I knew I couldn't keep this up forever. In fact, I was already slowing us down.

When we reached the edge of the patch of forest, I skidded to a stop.

"What are you doing?" Emrys hissed. "They're right behind us!"

"Trust me," I said, breathless from running and barely able to speak.

If we burst out into this clearing now, the witches would spot us before we crossed to the other side. Meaning, we had to throw them off our scent.

So, I would have to enact my plan now.

Thinking quickly, I lied down on the forest floor and gestured for Emrys to do the same; he trusted me enough by now to do so without question.

"Talamh," I muttered.

And when the grass began to grow up over us, he did not protest or panic. The foliage hugged us, dragging us down into the earth. Soil gathered around us, leaving us just enough room to breathe. Unlike Rogyn and Pery, the earth would release us—it was just shielding us, not burying us for good.

And we were just in time. Above, I could hear the muffled voices of the witches, undoubtedly wondering which way we had gone. There was pressure against my chest; someone must have been standing right on top of me. I could hear Sera and at least two others.

"These witches betrayed you. Kill them all. You are powerful enough now to do it."

The voice in my head was back. And I could see myself shooting up from the dirt, sending fire and earth after each witch and laughing as they died slowly.

I ignored the voice inside my head in favor of attempting to listen to whatever was occurring at the surface. I was hardly able to distinguish their words, but I think it was something like, "I don't see them. They must've run back farther into the forest. Let's go!"

Then their footsteps thundered away, the pressure on my chest released.

Quickly, I reversed the spell, and the earth began to receded back, pulling away the grass, the foliage, clearing the soil until I could breathe fresh air again. Emrys and I emerged from the ground, pausing only for a moment to catch our breath before we continued onward. We only paused once or twice, and finally, finally, the giant wall of mist reared up in front of us.

Without hesitating this time, we entered the Void once more, not slowing even as we tripped over skulls and stones, the mist cool upon my skin. Wights moaned nearby, but they did not approach. As before, they continued to give Emrys and I a wide berth, as long as we stayed close together. And I knew Rhegus couldn't be far. I never figured out how big this Void was, exactly. It always seemed to stretch on forever in either direction. Yet the ground beneath us was still warm, the rocks around the area freshly charred. A dragon was nearby.

"Rhegus," I called, hoping that the use of his name would endear him further to me. "Come out!"

It didn't take him long to respond. The ground shook, and then there was a roar as Rhegus answered the call. A trail of smoke billowed around him as he moved.

"Just stay still," I whispered to Emrys. "Remember, he likes me, but he does not much care for you."

"I am very much aware, thank you," Emrys muttered in reply.

Rhegus emerged through the mist and paused directly in front of us, sniffing the air. He rose to full height and bowed out his long neck, like a person puffing out their chest to look intimidating, while his massive claws tapped the ground. He growled a little in Emrys's direction, baring his teeth.

"No, leave him be," I warned. "Emrys is my husband, remember? He will come to no harm, just as we will not harm you. In fact, I have come to help you."

The dragon tilted its head, regarding me with interest now. Its nostrils flared, pupils widening in his orange eyes.

"Please, let me see your wound." I took hesitant steps forward, and Rhegus did not flinch, instead continuing to stare at me curiously. He huffed smoke.

"Careful, Red," Emrys hissed.

I nodded as I walked around to examine the dragon's injured haunch. The arrow wound still looked sore, puckered and red. "I have something to help you," I said.

I grabbed the bottle of salve Sera had given me, still tucked in my cloak pocket, careful to keep my movements smooth to avoid spooking Rhegus. Next, I poured some of the oily salve—which smelled like a pungent, strange combination of ash and honey—into my palm before gently rubbing it into Rhegus's wound. He flinched and recoiled at first, a growl gurgling deep in his chest.

"Please, hold still," I said, and thankfully, the dragon cooperated long enough for me to fully coat the wound.

I could tell that the salve immediately seemed to help, and he calmed quickly. Once I was finished, Rhegus let out a sigh; whatever Sera had given me, it was good stuff.

"How does that feel? Better?" I asked, hopeful.

The dragon nodded. His head curved around to look at me over his shoulder, watching my every move. I stepped forward to gently touch his snout as I had before, and the creature accepted my touch, leaning into it.

"Rhegus, do you think you can take Emrys and I away from the Void? We are in danger." I had promised the dragon help, but we needed help in return.

Rhegus blinked twice, large head cocked to one side. After a long while, he nodded once, tipping his scaly head down. Without being asked, he lowered his body fully to the ground, allowing us to climb aboard. I briefly wondered who had ridden him before, as this seemed to be something he was used to.

"Red?" said Emrys.

"Yes?"

"You mean to tell me you really plan for us to traverse the Balmor Sea on the back of a dragon?" Emrys looked to the beast skeptically.

I raised a brow. "Unless you have a better idea?"

"Fresh out, I'm afraid." He sighed loudly, shaking his head in disbelief.

The dragon splayed his front left leg out such that it created a gentler slope to climb up. Using his scales for leverage, I climbed on first, with Emrys right behind me. I tried to think of it like mounting the back of a massive, scaly horse with wings and fire breath, although the thought was not much of a comfort.

Thankfully, Rhegus had bony ridges protruding from his back with enough room for Emrys and I to slide between, nestled in like a saddle. I was able to grip the top of the ridge to hold on and prevent myself from sliding off while in flight. Hopefully.

Once we were settled, I leaned forward. "Fly, Rhegus," I said. "Take us to the Astyr Mountains."

"I have a feeling I am about to loathe this part," Emrys muttered from behind me. His arm slid about my waist, securing my back tight to his front, his other hand grasping the top of Rhegus's backbone.

Before Emrys had a chance to say anything else, Rhegus took off, nearly darting straight off the ground with mighty flaps of his wings, and Emrys and I held on tight. He flew up, up, up, until he punctured the top of the misty

Void—exposing blue sky—and we were looking down at it from above.

It was incredible to see how vast the horrific fog truly was, how treacherous it seemed, writhing this way and that stories below us. It almost looked alive from this angle, as though it might reach out with misty fingers and drag us back down at any moment.

But soon, it was behind us as we flew toward southern Sythea and our path toward the Balmor Sea.

LATER, RHEGUS EASED US DOWN ON A PEAK OF THE highest part of the Astyr mountains. The view was quite fetching, and I had certainly never seen Sythea from this angle. Far below, I could see forest scattered all about.

There was snow atop the highest peaks, which Rhegus seemed to love. He scooted his snout into it, emerging with white dust on his nostrils, which he huffed off. I laughed as Emrys and I sat on a rock nearby and drank water from his pouch, made from melted snow. It was quite an easy process; Emrys would pack snow into his pouch, and I'd heat it with my magic, just enough for it to melt.

By now, however, I was shivering, even with Emrys's arm around me, offering me his heat. And I knew we could not linger up here for too long. For many reasons.

When Rhegus was rested enough, we climbed back on and carried on.

Later, when I spotted the ruins of Astyrtown—in the south just off the coast of the Balmor Sea—I knew we must stop once more. I patted Rhegus to let him know to descend again.

"Bring us down here, boy."

Rhegus nodded beneath me and landed in the ruins of Astyrtown.

As Emrys and I dismounted, I looked around and shivered, but this time it was not from being cold. Astyrtown was where I had once lived so long ago, where I'd spent my childhood before we'd relocated to the White Woods for safety. Right where we stood was once the main, bustling strip of the human and witch town, once crowded with just as many people as the fae castle town. People smiling and happy and *together*. Now, it was nothing but rubble and ruin.

Emrys walked up beside me, examining my expression. "Are you alright, Red?"

I sniffed. "Yes. And no."

"You are from here. From Astyrtown."

"I grew up here. And that, right over there," I pointed across the way, at the ruins of a little shop, "was my father's shop. He was a master swordsmith. A master smith of anything metal, really."

I'll bet if I were to sift through the rubble, I could still even find some of his creations right now. But I did not have the heart to do so, afraid of what feelings that might stir up.

"Your father sounds like mine," Emrys said. "A true working creature. Whereas your father was a master of metal, mine was a master of leather. He had a tannery once, long ago."

"In East Sythea, where he made his sheath?"

"Yes."

I smiled, then turned to point behind Emrys. "We used to live just around the corner. Not even a twenty-minute walk from here."

"Do you wish to visit that too?" Emrys asked.

Behind us, Rhegus sniffed the rubble like a dog looking for a bone. Around here, there were plenty of bones for him to pick from. Everywhere, near my feet, wedged under rock and rubble, were human remains—noma and witch alike—some of whom I was sure I once knew as a child. Long ago before we moved to the woods. I was terrified to find out who, and I did not dare look any closer.

"No." The simple word nearly choked me, and my head shook rapidly, my hair swishing about my shoulders. I cleared my throat, barely able to speak. "Seeing the rubble of my childhood home wouldn't do me any good. I would much prefer to picture it always the way I remembered it as a child. I couldn't bear to see it in shambles."

Emrys nodded. "Well then, after we get some food, we should really be going. We mustn't linger anywhere in Sythea long, where the king can track us. We will only be safe once we cross the sea."

My gaze darted toward the coast. It would not be a far walk from here. I could picture it now, could smell the salt air and hear the ominous sounds of the very tall and angry tides the sea was notorious for, the cold waves that slapped the rocky shore relentlessly, slowly carving out new patterns in the rock face.

"Thank the goddess we have Rhegus to get us across the sea. I cannot imagine we'd survive long on a ship," I said.

The coast of Sythea was also littered with shipwrecks because the Balmor Sea was treacherous. Even the most weathered of sailors struggled to navigate the waters without facing ruin and death. The worst, most dangerous stretches were between East Sythea and the Outerlands, which was why no one attempted to navigate their way around the Void via the sea; it would be a lost cause.

The sea was slightly calmer on the west side, the side separating West Sythea from the Deadlands. But even that was still dangerous to someone who didn't know what they were doing. In fact, my father used to have friends who were merchants, who traveled up the coast of West Sythea. He'd lost quite a few of them to the sea, ones who never returned home. I wondered just how many ships the sea had swallowed, how many wrecks lain in the depths of the cold, dark water which had become their tomb, and I shuddered.

Behind us, Rhegus scooted aside a rock and bent down to chomp on something. Maybe some rats or field mice left to run amuck amongst the ruins. Emrys and I left him to it for a while we searched for food of our own. But the dragon had it covered; he stomped over and dropped the bloodied carcass of a rabbit near my feet. I peered down at it and Emrys whistled beside me.

"Well, looks like you might get your rabbit, after all," he said.

It took another hour to clean the rabbit, cook it over a fire, then eat. After, it was time to leave again.

"Come, here," I said, waving my hand. Rhegus traipsed back over to us, appearing rested enough to complete our journey. "Are you ready to go, Gus?"

Emrys cleared his throat. "Red."

"Yes?"

"Did you just call him *Gus?*"

"Yes."

"You cannot call a dragon *Gus.*"

"And why not? You get to call me *Red,*" I pointed out. "Can't a dragon have a nickname, too?"

Emrys jerked a hand, palm open, toward said dragon, gesturing to all of him. "He's a fire breather. The name *Gus* does not exactly strike fear in the hearts of one's enemies."

"Oh, but Gus doesn't mind. Do you boy?"

I turned my attention to Rhegus and patted his head. Gus sniffed me, letting out a little purr. Though he paused to pointedly bare his teeth at Emrys, who grumbled and held up his hands in surrender.

"Now, Gus," I said. "Take us to the Deadlands."

64

Rose

THE FLIGHT ACROSS THE BALMOR SEA WAS surprisingly smooth, unlike the white-capped waves of the angry waters below. I was exceedingly glad to be on Rhegus's back rather than attempt to navigate the treacherous sea, which bested even the most seasoned sailors.

Rhegus flew at a steady clip, and Emrys and I held on tight. We flew so high I could nearly reach out and touch the clouds. A flock of birds flapped nearby, looking to us in confusion.

A moment later, I felt Emrys's arms wrap around my waist, his lips at my ear.

"Just wait until we land. Send Rhegus off to hunt. You and I still have..." his mouth brushed my neck, "unfinished business."

"I seem to remember us both finishing."

"My business with you is never finished, Red."

"You are insatiable," I murmured as his teeth grazed my ear. "We will have to scout the lands first, once Rhegus brings us down." I shivered when his lips found their way to my neck.

"You," he whispered, "are no fun at all."

Gus turned sharply then, throwing us both a little off balance and Emrys cursed, breaking the spell of the moment.

We arrived over the Deadlands much quicker than I had imagined we would. Thank goodness dragons had so much stamina.

Emrys and I scanned the land below for a good place to bring us down, but it seemed as though the landscape was pretty much nothing but flat rock—no green as far as the eye could see—so anywhere made for a decent landing.

With a gentle tap on the back of Rhegus's head, he began to descend, swooping until we reached the ground. The landing was a bit bumpy, jostling me forward, but we had arrived in one piece. Rhegus lowered his large body to the ground and allowed us to dismount. Then, we were climbing off of the dragon and setting foot upon the Deadlands for the very first time.

There had been a lot of firsts over the last few weeks.

All around us were relatively flat yet craggy bits of bedrock that the elements had carved and whittled into horizontal crags of stones throughout the years. Even now, the fierce, biting winds made my hair flap wildly about my face. The winds were bitter, and my cheeks reddened. This place was desolate, and there appeared to be no sign of life around us, no persons nor animals. My stomach began to churn as I wondered exactly how we were going to survive here.

I walked up toward Rhegus's snout, his wide nostrils flaring with each breath as I spoke gently to him. "Go, hunt in the water. Return when you are done."

Rhegus nodded, rose to his feet, and flapped his wings, landing within sight in the shallows of the coast, searching for prey of any kind. I hoped Rhegus could find enough fish to sate him, though if dragons were anything like I'd read, they were master hunters, much like hawks. They could pick out fish from a mile away, dive, and catch them with their claws before the fish even knew what hit them.

Emrys and I turned our attention back toward the interior of the landscape.

"Shall we?" Emrys asked, nodding ahead.

"I suppose we came this far."

"But watch your step, Red." Emrys's brows crinkled in the middle as he looked ahead.

He was right; navigating this barren land proved even harder than it looked, because the terrain was uneven, with gaps that were several inches—sometimes several feet—wide in some places between each carved rock. Just enough to get a foot caught if not careful. In some places, the gaps were even wide enough for a whole person to fall into. Since the ground was relatively flat, the fall wouldn't be far, but it seems like getting stuck would not be beyond the realm of possibility.

The bedrock sloped upward ahead of us.

"You know," Emrys said. "I don't know much about the Deadlands. But there has *got* to be more than just rock. Hasn't there?"

The rocks jutted out in the upward slope, the edges sloping downward around each side, forming a sort of mound in the middle. Emrys and I descended down one side, turned, and...

"How about a cave?" I said, looking to the opening in the bedrock in front of us.

"Would you look at that." Emrys shook his head in disbelief.

"What do you think is in there?"

"I have no idea, but there is only one way to find out. My Lady?" He raised his brows and extended a hand toward me, palm up.

"My Lord," I replied with a grin, placing my hand into his to allow him to assist me over the jagged rocks at the mouth of the cave. We both knew I didn't need the help, but I had grown to realize that it was still alright to accept help every once in a while, regardless.

Once we'd cleared the rocks of the cave mouth, Emrys began to lead the way, carefully navigating the dark space in front of him. His senses *were* sharper than mine, so he was better equipped for mapping out unexplored territory than I.

The cave was narrow at first, winding off to the right. The walls got even narrower to where Emrys struggled to wriggle through, and he had to duck to keep from banging his head on the low ceiling. But then the cave opened into a wide room, with moisture dripping down the limestone formations overhead. The cave was all white rock, and I heard the drippings hit the floor of the cave and echo.

We had to step carefully, as the rocks were slippery. But it was good to know that there was water here, drinkable water that wasn't salty ocean water. We might manage to survive here for a time, after all. Next, we would have to figure out food if we were to stay. But we also had Rhegus, so maybe it wouldn't be as big of a worry as I feared.

"Sorcha," I whispered, sparking fire from the ends of my fingertips. I held the fire up, giving me a better chance to survey our surroundings.

There were tunnels branching off from the main room of the cave, at least three that wound in different directions. For all I knew, this cave could go on for miles—likely did. It could take months to fully explore the whole system. But maybe we would never get the chance.

The finer hairs on my neck stood up with the uncanny feeling that we were being watched. That we were not alone.

"Emrys," I whispered, extinguishing the fire on my fingertips and reaching for my sword instead, unsheathing it from my back.

His muscles tensed as he looked around. "I heard something," he said.

He shifted into wolf form, crouching down onto all fours and allowing his limbs to lengthen and bend, baring his teeth and ready to pounce on anything that meant us harm. I held my sword at the ready, clutched in sweaty hands.

From the corner of my eye, I spotted shadows darting from left to right, splashing across the moistened cave floor, scuffing loose rocks. A short, stout creature appeared, his face covered in dirt. Beside me, Emrys frowned, a strange look for a wolf. His fur rippled.

"Trolls," I muttered in surprise.

The trolls had left Sythea decades ago, tired of being caught between the human and fae war. No one knew exactly where they went, and some thought they had died out. Others believed they landed in the Deadlands, but no one bothered to come here to check because it was the *Deadlands*, and *nothing* was supposed to be able to live here. Not even trolls.

But it seemed the trolls proved them all wrong.

They were everywhere now, emerging from small hiding spaces tucked away in the cave walls, some high and some low. They whispered about us in a foreign language, staring at us and stroking their beards thoughtfully.

"Trolls are friendly, right?" I whispered to Emrys, who had now shifted back to his regular, two-legged form.

"I don't believe they will attack unprovoked," Emrys replied.

"And how certain are you of that?"

"Quite certain." He paused, bit his lip, and amended his words. "Somewhat certain."

"That response doesn't fill me with confidence, Emrys," I whispered harshly.

"Well, I haven't encountered many trolls in my lifetime," he fired back. "So, perhaps we should avoid provoking them?"

Something shuffled from the farthest branching tunnel then, something far larger than mere cave trolls. Footsteps echoed from within, and I braced myself, preparing to draw my sword. Beside me, Emrys growled instinctively.

Two figures emerged from the tunnel, standing tall inside the cavernous room. There were two people amongst the trolls. I could not tell if they were fae or human, not with them still cloaked in shadow. I slowly unsheathed my sword, gripping it tight. Emrys stuck close by my side, lips curling back from his teeth and canines starting to elongate.

"Identify yourself," a voice said, floating toward us. My heart nearly stopped, because that voice was so familiar.

One of the shadowy figures stepped forward and I gasped. As once, I felt the strong urge to pass out, legs wobbling and head growing fuzzy as shock jolted through my body. I knew that figure. I knew that face. That voice.

I grasped Emrys's arm to steady myself as I said the word.

"Mother?"

65

Rose

SHE HELD OUT HER ARMS AS THOUGH TO embrace me, but I stepped back.

"This is a trick. My mother is dead," I said, shaking my head.

Emrys stayed close to my side, his gaze darting back and forth between me and whoever this person claiming to be my mother was. I'd seen shifting spells in the grimoire. Not animal shifting like fae, but spells that allowed a witch to take on the visage of another person. This had to be a trick, a dark witch using blood magic, because my mother was *dead.* I had seen the evidence with my own eyes.

But you never did find any bodies, I reminded myself.

"Rose, it's really me," she replied.

It very much *sounded* like my mother, but deceivers could be very convincing when they wished to be. Her clothes were tattered, worn. Her hair dirty. But those eyes...

"Then prove it." My voice shook as I spoke. "What was the last thing you said to me before you left and never came back?"

She blinked in surprise. "Promise me you will stay and look after your grandmother, my Rosey."

I inhaled sharply, wanting this to be true so badly. But still... "And what was the song we always used to sing around the campfire?"

She smiled. "Are you really going to make me sing it?"

I nodded, but she only managed to get out the first line of the first verse when my resolve crumbled and tears began to fall. "Are you a sprite, Mother?"

"You are welcome to come here and find out." She opened her arms.

Unable to stop myself, I ran toward her, slipping on a wet rock and practically falling into her arms. She caught me, and we collided in an embrace. She was real, solid and warm.

"Oh, my Rosey," she cried, and I wept freely, tears of joy and relief mixed together.

"You're alive," I said, incredulous. "I thought you were dead."

"I survived."

"And Papa?" I swiped my tears away and looked up at her, hopeful.

My mother sat on a large rock jutting out from the cave wall, suddenly seeming exhausted. She propped her head on her hand, elbow resting atop her knee. "Your father died the very day we were ambushed. We fought back and... he ended up being killed right in front of me. I was captured."

I inhaled sharply. "By the king's bounty hunters?"

"Yes."

On instinct, I crept closer to stand beside my mother, reaching out to lift her hair—the same red shade as mine. She eyed me with curiosity, but did not stop me. Sure enough, at the nape of her neck, my mother sported an eye tattoo identical to Emrys's and mine. Also like ours, it was unmoving now, its magic ineffective outside of Sythea.

"I have one too," I whispered as I dropped her hair. "The eye mark; you have it too."

Mother swiveled her head to face me, and I walked back in front of her. "Then you were taken too?"

"Yes." My gaze flicked to Emrys, who shifted rather uncomfortably. That was going to be rather difficult to explain, so I wouldn't yet. "There is something else. I found a grimoire."

"You did?"

"Two, actually. The first one inside the castle, being protected by a noma, a bard named Jasper. The fae can't do anything with it, not really, because it is witch magic. But the witches can do whatever they want. And... they have their own grimoire, too."

"I know," Mother said, rubbing her eyes. "That grimoire used to belong to us. To our family. I should have brought it with us when Keera and I fled, to keep it out of their hands, but we barely escaped. We had no time to retrieve it."

"Yes. There are some frightening spells in there."

"You read it?" She stood up quickly, practically hopping from the rock like my admission startled her.

"Yes. I glimpsed at both of them."

"Oh, Rose. You should never have even opened it. Either one." I also left out the part about consulting the book for a locating spell. My mother would certainly fear for me if she knew I used a spell from the dark book.

"I know that now. But I also know why you wouldn't want the other witches to have it; I felt the same way."

My mother nodded solemnly. "Sera is walking a very dangerous path and dragging all the other witches with her." Something else caught her gaze then, a glint of metal. Her brows lifted. "Is that..."

"Papa's sword. Yes."

She held out her hands palm up, and I gently laid the sword upon them so she could examine it closer. She smiled wistfully as her fingers ran across the blade, the hilt. "You've taken such great care of it."

"I've tried." Her attention was still trained on the sword, but mine had shifted. A troubling thought. "Why didn't you come back for me?"

My mother's head snapped up at that, gaze meeting mine. "I wanted to. Every day I wanted to, my girl. But it was too dangerous; I was a fugitive who could have led the fae right to you and your grandmother, and I couldn't risk that."

I sucked in a sharp breath at the mention of Gran. My mother had no idea of her fate, either. And now, I would have to be the bearer of that terrible news.

"Gran is dead. She was under a fae enchantment and she died trying to protect me."

"Oh, Rose." Mother's voice was strangled with emotion. "I am so sorry for all you have been through."

"She never came back."

Her brow raised. "How do you mean?"

"She said she would visit me as a sprite. Why didn't she?"

"Not all sprites come back. It's rare that they do. Perhaps your grandmother knew you were strong enough without her, that you did not need her guidance."

"Did Papa ever visit you as a sprite?"

"No." Her shoulders slumped. "Though I wish he had."

"Forgive me for intruding," another voice said.

The other human who had been in the cave with my mother stepped forward. She had eyes that were rounded like an owl, yet distinctly kind, her features soft. She was several inches taller than my mother and me, with warm brown skin and dark, curly hair that fell to mid-back. She appeared to be roughly the same age as my mother.

"Rose, I feel like I already know you. Your mother spoke of you so much," she said.

I tried to smile but found myself frowning, instead. Sensing my unspoken question, my mother supplied the missing information. "I was captured by the fae, but I escaped before we even made it to the castle. It was Keera who helped me. She was part of another coven who had been living in the woods. She saw me in fae custody and used some rather impressive magic to help free me."

Keera stepped forward, grasped my mother's hand, and kissed the back of it.

"And I would help my Lilly a thousand times more," she said with pure adoration in her tone.

Oh. At once I understood that they were lovers, and quite frankly... I wasn't sure how to feel about that. It had been two years since my father had died, and I found myself wondering how long it took my mother to move on. Because right now in the wake of realizing my mother was alive and confirming my father was dead, it felt like I had just lost him all over again.

"As your mother said, I was with my coven hiding in the White Woods. We had heard rumors about the Void, that it was safe for witches to cross through," said Keera. "Our coven—what was left of us—saw your mother with the fae, shackled. We intervened, overpowered them, and we all crossed through the Void together, to the Outerlands."

"But then," Mother continued, "we realized what the witches were planning. Total slaughter. And as much as I hate the fae for what they've done, I... I just could not get behind their plan. So, Keera and I fled together to the Deadlands. The rest of the coven agreed with the other witches, so we could not trust anyone else to flee with us. It was just us two."

"How did you navigate the Balmor Sea? Isn't it very treacherous?" I asked.

"Keera knew of a fae who would help witches in need, at his own peril. He helped us acquire a boat and navigate here, at great risk to himself. Nearly capsized twice, fell overboard more than once. But we made it. Keera's water magic helped a lot."

"And now you're here. With the trolls," I finished for her.

"Yes. The cave trolls are a good, hard-working, peaceful species who keep to themselves. It's the rock trolls you have to watch out for, as they are far bigger with a rather poor temperament. Though they generally stay at the far end of the Deadlands. It's exceedingly rare that we encounter any."

"There are bigger trolls, too?" I asked incredulously.

"You have much to learn," Mother replied with a chuckle. "Oh, my precious Rose, it is so good to see you. To hear your voice again."

She drew me into another hug and pressed a kiss to the side of my head, the mother's touch I had been missing for so long. Gran had done a great deal to fill the void left by my parents' absence, but she was only one person, and their loss weighted me down every day. I could only thank my lucky stars that at least one of my parents had been returned to me.

This whole time, I realized that Emrys had just been standing there, listening. I gestured for him to join us, reaching my hand out toward him.

"Mother, this is my husband, Emrys."

Her eyes widened. "You married a fae?" Now it was her turn to sound incredulous. But it was the reaction we had grown accustomed to from all sides.

"I, too, have much to tell." I squeezed Emrys's hand, and he squeezed back. "But Emrys is—"

"Good. I know."

I raised a brow in question. "How do you know that? I should think you'd believe all fae to be evil."

"Because I know my daughter would not have married anyone evil. And because I know in my heart that not all the fae are bad, that we just need to learn to understand each other and stop killing first and asking questions later. Only then can we have true peace."

"I agree. And we want to help bring peace, as well. But first, I need to know... How are we to survive here? How have *you* managed to survive here all this time? Where do you get food? Do you fish in the sea?"

My mother shook her head. "No, the sea is much too treacherous for fishing. You have to go too far out to catch anything good, and the waves would just tear any small vessel we'd create to pieces."

"If you cannot fish for food, then how have you managed to survive here all this time?" I asked, thoroughly confused.

The Deadlands were supposed to be *dead.* Nothing was supposed to be able to live here, so they likely could not grow crops, nor could they keep livestock. Emrys and I came here out of desperation, needing a chance to regroup. We weren't sure what we would encounter, but it certainly wasn't this.

But then again, everything I thought I knew had already been turned on its head.

"Well," Keera replied, "we survive the way the trolls do. Let me show you something."

Mother smiled. "Watch Keera. This is a very fun discovery."

Keera paused for a moment, then let out a high-pitched whistle. Suddenly there was tittering about the cave, wet slithering sounds as worms the size of my forearm came crawling out of hiding, agitated by the pitch of the whistle. They began to light up, an iridescent blue glow that illuminated the cave, twinkling all around us. Keera snatched one of the huge, glowing worms from the cave wall, and it wriggled in her hand.

I looked to Emrys, his incredulous expression lit by the blue glow. His jaw slackened as Keera approached with the worm in hand.

"We survive off of these glow worms," Keera explained, holding the writhing creature up. "The way the trolls do, too."

I wrinkled my nose, trying not to show my distaste. I understood the drive to do what you must to survive, and had eaten my share of less than desirable things. But never worms. Not yet. Mother couldn't help but notice my reaction, and she laughed.

"Oh, Rose. We cook the worms over a fire and they're really not so bad, just a little tough once cooked. The flavor is bland. But they provide sustenance and keep us strong, keep us living."

"Supper!" one of the trolls cried, snatching it out of Keera's hand and taking a bite out of the side of the worm, not even bothering to kill it first much less cook it.

Strings of goo dripped down the troll's mouth. My teeth clenched and I tried hard not to blanche. The troll munched happily, sitting on a rock, and called to one of its friends in its own language, who came over to share the meal.

"The trolls are not as particular about cooking their food," Keera said as the glow worms began to dim around us until the cave was once again dark, slithering back into the hiding places they came from.

"Well, I don't think you'll have to survive that way for much longer."

"And why is that?"

Emrys and I exchanged a knowing look. "Gus. I mean, Rhegus," I replied. "He's out hunting in the ocean right now. It might have been too treacherous for humans to fish, but it isn't too treacherous for a dragon."

"Oh, how I would love some fish after all these months of worms."

"How did you and the trolls come to understand each other?" I asked, listening to the two eating trolls speaking in their own language. I recognized none of the words.

"Languages may differ, but body language is universal," Mother said. "Over time, we came to understand each other well enough, even picked up a few words in each other's language."

To demonstrate, Mother said some words to the trolls eating on the rock. They sounded like gibberish to me, but the trolls must have understood whatever she said, because they started slapping their knees with their palms and holding their bellies as they rumbled with laughter.

"What did you tell them?" I asked, eyebrows knitted together in confusion.

"Oh, just that they eat like barnyard animals. The trolls find insults quite humorous."

Just then, a flapping of wings arose outside, and the trolls jumped up, working themselves into a frenzy. Their voices raised an octave as they spoke to each other. It did not matter that I didn't speak their language, it was pretty easy to tell when something was anxious.

"Dragon!" one shouted, and the little creatures ran toward the cave mouth to see.

"That would be Rhegus," I replied, and my mother grinned.

"I would very much like to see him," Keera said.

With Emrys by my side, we followed the trolls to the cave mouth. Rhegus was curled up into a ball, munching happily on a very large fish—he'd found some just as I suspected, and I also suspected it would be quite easy to train him to bring *us* back some. At this point, only the head of the fish and some bones were left. The trolls had gathered around him, pointing, but Rhegus ignored them, too busy savoring the last of his meal.

"He really is a fascinating creature," Mother said. "I nearly died when I first saw him in the Void. I had no idea dragons still existed."

"Me neither," I said.

"He took us all by surprise," Keera said. She stepped forward and touched Rhegus's side, giving him a familiar pat. "I didn't know he would let anyone ride him, though. He seems to respond to you very well, Rose."

"Why do you think that is?" I asked. "I did heal a wound of his, so perhaps that endeared me to him."

Mother shrugged. "Dragons are complex creatures who bond with riders for specific reasons. But above all, dragons are drawn to two things: power and kindness. You showed him kindness by healing him. And your power, Rose... well, it speaks for himself."

"I did show him my flames, as well. He seemed impressed."

"Of course, he was." She laughed.

"And it's a good thing he trusted me, because he will be very important for our cause," I said. "We will need him. We will all need to work together to stop the war that's coming. No matter what it takes."

"Together, we will," Mother said. It was a promise.

It was a relief to know that we were all on the same page, that we were prepared to fight. There was still much I had not told my mother yet: my great grandfather, my new power, the immortality curse. But there was plenty of time to catch up now.

As Keera and my mother went back inside the cave with the trolls, I found myself wandering out on the rocks past Rhegus, staring out toward the ocean with my arms crossed over my chest.

A moment later, I felt Emrys's tall form press against my back, his arms circling my waist. He spoke right into my ear.

"You know, I am very glad that there is life here, and that you mother is alive. But on the downside, it is going to be *very* hard for us to find alone time. Without traumatizing a few trolls in the process, that is."

I couldn't help but laugh at that, and Emrys chuckled too, pressing a kiss to the side of my head. I leaned back against him, but he must have noticed the crease in my brow, because he stepped in front of me to examine my expression fully.

"What's wrong?" he asked.

How did he always manage to be so observant of my moods? But then, I was observant of his as well. Whether it was the blood bond or not, we were connected.

"Ever since I touched the grimoire, I've been hearing these whisperings in my head telling me to take a grimoire for myself. That I need to use blood magic from the grimoire and give in to the dark arts. Absorbing my grandfather's magic only seemed to amplify that voice, and it frightens me. I am terrified of becoming like my grandfather. Especially with my new, heightened powers I still don't fully understand."

Emrys frowned and grasped my hands, peering down at me. "That is ridiculous, Red. You could *never* be like him."

"How can you be so sure? I didn't have much of a problem killing even *before* I absorbed my grandfather's powers. But I was not *obsessed* with vengeance then. I killed out of pure desire for survival, to be left alone, and I took no real pleasure in it. But now..." I sighed. "Emrys, when the witches convicted you and took you away to hang, I envisioned myself killing each and every one of them and *enjoying* every second. Maybe I shouldn't have Rhegus in my possession. He might be dangerous in my hands. What if I go too far?"

"You are nothing like your grandfather," Emrys repeated. "Or Sera, for that matter. Besides, you have your mother back now. She would never let you go too far. I can tell."

"And what if she cannot stop me?"

A glimmer of a smile twitched upon Emrys's lips. "If you stay in the light, I will be content to bask in it with you. Should you ever give in to darkness... I shall walk through the bastard right by your side. Wherever you go, that is where I wish to be, Red. Always."

He bent to kiss me, and I wound my arms around his neck. I felt all his emotions warming me from the inside out, locking my heart steadfast in its grip. A heart that I willingly gave.

When we broke apart, I stared out toward the coast, dreaming of a future without war.

A future we would bring about together.

ACKNOWLEDGEMENTS

It's rather difficult to express the appropriate amount of gratitude when there are so many who have helped me so much along the way, but I'll try.

First of all, thank you to my wonderful friends and family. To all those folks who make me laugh, listen to my rants, and make life a little brighter every day, you are very much appreciated. Especially those around me who have been helping me through the rough patches in life. I couldn't do this without you.

Secondly, thank you to BookTok and all those who blew me away with their support of this little fantasy story just based on a few twenty second videos. ROSE RED was my very first attempt at new adult epic fantasy romance, and let me tell you, y'all know exactly how to quell those "will this be good enough" jitters.

To all those who showed up to comment, like, share, and to those who were kind enough to buy, to read, or to review: you give me all the motivation I need to keep yanking these vivid hallucinations out of my tired brain and organizing them on paper for the world to read. Thank you.

To all my early readers who provided invaluable feedback in shaping ROSE RED into what it is today: Birdie Teop, Ashlee, Gaynor, Courtney, Sophia, Nancy, Kayla, Emily, Helen, Amy, Grace, Amber, and Angel. Thank you for helping me to see the stuff that... well, wasn't quite working (and helping me gain confidence in the things that *were* working). The end result is much stronger for it.

And last, but most certainly not least... to my mama. Mom, I don't have the words to express my thanks for all you have done for me throughout my lifetime. You are the kindest, most caring, most selfless, bravest, and strongest person I have ever known. You are my rock, my travel buddy, my confidante, my biggest fan, the first person I report every book sale and five-star review to, the first person I call for life advice. My best friend. You will be in my heart always and forever, and I know you will be with me no matter where I go.

"Don't cry because it's over, smile because it happened."

OTHER BOOKS BY EJ REKAB

THE REAPER TRILOGY

A town not even the Dead can escape. A teen who dreams of freedom. Can Abbie save her loved ones before Everhaven claims their souls forever?

"Rekab has crafted a truly unique paranormal thrill ride... A brilliant debut, and a promising start to the Everhaven Trilogy!" - E.E. Holmes, best-selling author of the Gateway Trilogy and Gateway Trackers series

HAWNT

Being dead is a real drag...

"HAWNT blends elements of paranormal romance and horror with memorable characters and a fast-paced build to the dramatic climax for a fun, gripping page-turner with wry humor, twists, and chills galore." - Cameron Gillespie, IndieReader

APOCALYPSE, UPLOADING

In the game of Apocalypse, their survival is humanity's last hope...

"An absolute MUST read!!" - Reviewer

THE GHOST JUNKIES

An escape like no other. Can Mel discover the truth of her abilities before the ghosts claim her as their own?

SPARK OF THE PROPHET

Demons wreaking havoc on Earth.
A secret council run by mysterious angels.
A warrior whose dreams could save the world.

NEWSLETTER SIGN-UP

Want bonus content, book news, event announcements, and access to perks before anyone else?
Sign up for Elizabeth J. Rekab's newsletter to receive all the goodies. Straight to your inbox, guaranteed.